THE

favor

MEGAN HART

THE
favor

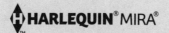

Recycling programs
for this product may
not exist in your area.

ISBN-13: 978-0-7783-1440-0

THE FAVOR

Copyright © 2013 by Megan Hart

For questions and comments about the quality of this book, please contact us at
CustomerService@Harlequin.com.

Printed in U.S.A.

First printing: July 2013
10 9 8 7 6 5 4 3 2 1

This book is dedicated to my grandmother, Eileen Garner,
who taught me how to cook a turkey.

I love you and miss you, Gramma.

ONE

HOME ISN'T ALWAYS THE PLACE YOU GO BECAUSE they have to take you in.

Sometimes, Janelle Decker thought as she crested the hill and took that final slope toward the town she hadn't seen in nearly twenty years, home was the place you couldn't escape no matter how far or fast you ran. Her battered Volkswagen Rabbit pickup, which had seen better days, but so far, thank God, not many worse, drifted to a stop at the traffic light. She didn't remember the fast-food restaurant to her right or, just a bit farther, the pair of hotels on the hill to her left, but she remembered the small white building beside them. Decker's Chapel, one of the tiniest churches in the country.

"Look, Bennett. Over there." Janelle craned her neck to stare into the backseat, where her son was bent over his new toy, the iPad her mother had bought him for his birthday. In seconds the light would turn green, and it had somehow become imperative she show him this sight. "Bennett. Hey. Hello!"

The boy looked up through a shock of red-blond bangs that fell over bright green eyes. His dad's eyes, though Connor's gaze had never, in Janelle's recollection, been as bright and clear and curious as her son's. Bennett looked out the window to where she pointed.

"See that little church?"

"Yeah."

Janelle eased her foot off the brake and pressed the cranky clutch, hoping for the sake of the half dozen cars lined up behind her that the truck wouldn't stall. "One of my great-great-grand-relatives built that church."

"Really? Cool." Bennett sounded underwhelmed. "Are we almost there?"

"Another five minutes, buddy. That's all." On impulse, instead of continuing on along the incongruously named Million Dollar Highway into town toward her grandmother's house, the end point of this seemingly endless trip, Janelle put on her left turn signal.

If there'd been traffic heading toward her she might not have bothered, but the only traffic on the road was heading into town, not away from it. That seemed somehow meaningful, but she didn't let herself dwell on that. Instead, she turned into the gravel-gritty drive that serviced the two hotels as well as the chapel. She parked and stared through the windshield.

Her arms ache from where he grabbed her, the bruises still so fresh they've barely darkened, though they will. She'll wear them for weeks. Her hands on the wheel, gripping so tight her fingers hurt from it. Foot on the gas, foot on the clutch, the Rabbit truck bucks and sputters as she guides it to the side of the road. The parking lot of this tiny church is empty, thank God. There's nobody to see her press her face against her hands, nobody to watch her break apart.

Nobody to watch her leaving.

"I thought we were going to Nan's house."

"In a few minutes."

Bennett, her get-along-guy, her complacent child, let out a long, stuttering sigh of irritation. Janelle didn't blame him. They'd been driving for hours with no more than a quick pit stop. Before that, other than the week they'd spent at her mom's, they'd been on the road for what felt like forever.

"I want to go into this church, okay? Really fast." Janelle looked into the rearview mirror. "Want to come in with me? Let me rephrase that. Come in with me."

Her son looked a lot like his absent father, and that she understood. Genetics and all that. But sometimes the kid acted just like his dad, too, and that always floored her, since she and Connor O'Hara had been finished before he even knew the night the condom broke hadn't turned out to be, as he'd so valiantly and foolishly promised her, "okay."

"It'll be cool," she told Bennett. "Really. And if it's not, you can add it to the list of things I've done to permanently scar you."

This earned a small smile. "Okay. But I have to pee real bad."

"Hold it just a little longer. Can you?"

"I guess so." Bennett made a face that said he wasn't convinced.

She'd never actually been inside the chapel. Built of white clapboard with a miniature bell tower and a single door in the front with a wooden ramp leading up to it, the chapel really was tiny. It had been built in the 1800s; she remembered that much.

Janelle got out of the truck, snagging her keys from the ignition, but not bothering to actually lock the vehicle. They were in St. Marys, after all. Secluded, isolated, ninety-nine percent Catholic of the "attend Mass daily" variety. And they were going inside for just a minute or two, the way she'd promised.

She couldn't tell if her heart raced because of daring to leave her vehicle unlocked with all her worldly belongings inside, or for a slew of other reasons that had been plaguing her for the past few months, since she'd made the decision to come back.

The chapel was unheated. Bennett danced from foot to foot, having, of course, forgone his brand-new, heavy winter coat. Janelle herself blew a plume of frost on her fingers and rubbed her hands together to warm them as she walked slowly around the wooden kneelers, an altar and a votive display at the back, no candles burning. She thought about dropping a dollar in the slot and lighting one, if only for the brief flare of warmth it would offer, but she hadn't brought her purse inside and her pockets were lamentably empty.

"Do people get married here?"

"I don't know. I guess they could." Janelle looked at the map on the wall and the framed documents telling the Decker's Chapel history.

"Would you?"

She laughed. "Um…no."

"How come? If you think it's so cool and all that." Bennett ran a finger along one of the half-size kneelers and gave her an innocent look that didn't fool her for a second, because she'd seen it in her own reflection more than once.

Janelle rolled her eyes. "C'mon. Let's go. I'm freezing."

Back in the car, buckled up tight, she once again looked at her son in the rearview mirror. He'd already bent over his iPad again, thumbing the screen in some complicated game, his headphones firmly settled in the tangles of his too-long hair. This was her boy. Her life for the past twelve years. She hadn't messed him up too badly so far.

But there was still time.

"Whoa, look at the size of that Pepsi cap!" Bennett sounded way more excited about that landmark than he had about the chapel. He added a chortle that cracked her up. As if the kid had never seen a giant Pepsi cap on the side of a building before. Come to think of it, he never had.

It took a few more than five minutes to get to Nan's house. There was a lot more traffic than Janelle remembered, for one thing, and some of the roads had changed. The Diamond, as the locals called it, ran in one direction only, and though she knew she had to get off on the first street, somehow she ended up going all the way around the circle of traffic again before she could.

"Big Ben," she murmured as they passed the town's snow-covered Nativity scene, still holding pride of place in the square, though it was already the day after New Year's. "Parliament."

Bennett, familiar with the joke, though not the movie she was quoting, didn't even look up. Janelle concentrated on getting off the Diamond and onto one of the side streets. G.C. Murphy's, location of many a summer afternoon's dawdling, was long gone. Janelle felt a sudden pang of nostalgia for Lee Press On Nails and Dep hair gel. Her car bump-bumped over the railroad tracks as she headed up Lafayette Street, pausing at the intersection to point out the elk heads, antlers alight with bulbs, adorning the building on the corner.

"This place has a lot of weird things," Bennett said matter-of-factly. "Maybe they're in your app, Mom. We should check them off."

He meant the application on her phone that listed the odd and offbeat attractions littering the American countryside. Biggest balls of twine, and mystery spots, that sort of thing. They'd spent a good portion of their trip from California to Pennsylvania taking back roads to catch a glimpse of some forgotten storybook forest or an abandoned "Fountain of Youth" that turned out to be an algae-infested and crumbling well alive with frogs. In the past couple days, though, busy with the holidays at her mom's house and then the final portion of this journey, they hadn't even checked to see what weird delights might await.

They'd already passed a dozen landmarks that had always marked off the distance between her mom's and this town like hash marks on a ruler. The Mount Nittany Inn, with its spectacular view. The child's sneaker-shaped scooter attached for no good reason to a high fence, which she could remember looking for during every trip to visit Nan. Janelle had thought about rallying Bennett to scream out "Weed!" as they passed through the tiny town of Weedville, the way she and her dad always had, but knew he wouldn't understand the joke—nor did she want to explain to him the old comedy skit about a pair of stoners incapable of keeping their stash a secret when visited by the cops.

Now she spotted another landmark Bennett wouldn't really "get"—the Virgin Mary statue in the corner lot they were passing. Common enough in a town named for her, not so much in any place they'd lived. Janelle slowed a little as she passed to give the praying Virgin a silent nod.

Janelle hadn't been inside a church for years, but she still wore the Blessed Virgin medallion she'd had since she was eighteen. It lay against the hollow of her throat, warmed by her flesh. She wore it constantly; it had become as much a part of her as the small but genuine diamond in her nose and the shooting star tattoo on the inside of her left wrist. She never took the necklace off unless she was getting dressed up to go somewhere fancy, and replaced it with her single strand of good pearls—and it had been a damn long time since she'd done that. She never thought much about it, in fact, unless she forgot to put it back on, and wasn't that the way of things?

You didn't notice them until they weren't where you expected them to be.

She traced the medallion with her fingertips, so familiar by touch, though honestly, if you'd asked her to identify it in a photo, she'd probably be unable. Mary's features had become worn from the thousands of such touches over the years. The metal had tarnished. Janelle had replaced the chain twice that she could recall. It hardly looked like the same necklace that had been given to her so long ago.

Past Deprator's Beverage, down one more street, one more turn. Her heart beat a little faster at the sight of the familiar green shingled house. She pulled into Nan's driveway and let the truck idle for a minute or so before turning off the ignition.

Don't be a stranger, Janelle. This will always be your home.

I know, Nan. I know.

Come back soon, Janelle. It's been so long since I've seen you.

I'll come soon, Nan. I promise.

She'd had the heat going on the highest setting, but now the frigid air was finding its insidious way through the cracks and crevices. She told herself that's why she shivered, why the hairs on the back of her neck rose, why her nipples pebbled beneath her multiple layers of clothes. She got out of the truck, one hand on the roof, one foot propped on the running board. Her sudden chill had little to do with the actual weather.

"We're here," Janelle said. "We're home."

TWO

Then

THERE'S A GIRL WITH RED HAIR IN THE BACK-
yard of the house next door, and she's blowing soap bubbles
from a big plastic dish. She dips the wand in the liquid and
holds it to her puckered lips, then laughs as the bubbles stream
out, one after the other, like beads on a string. Like pearls,
Gabe thinks. Like his mom's pearls, the ones in the drawer
in the back bedroom, in the box his dad doesn't think Gabe
knows about.

The girl with red hair glances up, sees him looking and
frowns. Gabe stands on one of the cinder blocks that keep
his yard from falling into hers. If he steps down he'll be on
her grass, so he stays where he is. His yard is higher, which is
good because he thinks she's taller than him, and that would
be annoying.

"Hi," she says. "You're Gabe Tierney. My dad says you have
twin baby brothers."

He does. Michael and Andrew. Gabe doesn't question how or why this girl's dad would know that. Everyone knows about the Tierney boys. His bare toes curl over the edge of the cinder block, but he doesn't step down.

The girl stands, her fist dripping with suds. "I have bubbles, look."

"I have bubbles in a big jug. Had," Gabe mutters. "I spilled 'em."

It had been an accident, but he might as well have done it on purpose since he got in so much trouble for it. The soap had soaked into the rug in the front room, making a squishy patch he'd been unable to clean up no matter how much water he used. Mikey walked through it, then onto the linoleum floor in the kitchen, where he skidded and slipped, hitting his head on the table. Then Dad came through, yelling, and he slipped, too. Went down on his butt. It would've been funny, kind of like something on TV, except Dad didn't laugh about it. He hadn't spanked Gabe, but it might've been better if he had. He'd not only taken away the rest of the bubbles, but he'd sent Gabe to his room for a whole day. No lunch, no supper. Gabe's belly had hurt from being empty.

"I'm Janelle." She holds up the wand. "Do you want to blow some bubbles? You can use mine."

Gabe does want to blow bubbles, but he stays put. "My dad says I'm not supposed to leave the yard."

Janelle puts her fists on her hips. Her lower lip sticks out in what Gabe's mama used to call a pouty. "Gaby's putting a pouty on," that's what she used to say. Before.

Janelle shakes her head. "What are you, a baby?"

He's not anything close to a baby. Heat floods him, not from the summer sun beating down but from someplace deep inside. It comes from the same place that gets hot whenever he overhears someone talking about "those Tierney boys."

Which is a lot. Without another thought, Gabe jumps down from the cinder block and into Mrs. Decker's yard.

"Be careful. Your dad might yell." Janelle looks toward Gabe's house, which is taller than Mrs. Decker's. Made of brick instead of painted wood. Gabe's house has three stories and he's pretty sure the third floor is haunted.

"He's not home. He's at work." Mrs. Moser wouldn't yell if she came out from inside the house and found him in the yard next door. She'd be happy to see him playing with a friend. She'd be happy for him to stay out of the house, out from under her feet like she said, though it is the twins who are always crawling around under her feet. Not Gabe.

"Oh." Janelle grins and holds out the bubble wand again. "So come and blow bubbles! It's really fun."

"Bubbles are for babies," Gabe tells her, knowing it will wipe the smile off her face.

That's what Dad says. *Wipe the smile off your face.* But it's never like wiping your face with a cloth or a napkin or the back of your hand. Smiles always melt like Popsicles in the sun. Drip, drip, drip.

Janelle does stop smiling. That line appears between her eyebrows again. She puts one hand on her hip, the other still holding out the wand. "I'm not a baby, and I like bubbles! But if you're too much of a baby to come into my Nan's yard…"

"I'm not a baby!"

"Nope," Janelle says with a grin that melts something inside him that's nothing like a smile, "you're a jerk."

Gabe Tierney was still a jerk. He knew it. Cultivated it, as a matter of fact, because it was easier that way. People gave you a wide berth if you were an asshole. They left you alone. Well, most people did. Some women didn't. For them, a sneer was as good as a smile, maybe better. For them a kiss from a fist was better than nothing, but Gabe would never hit a woman, not even if she hit him first, and he'd had plenty of slaps to prove it. He'd deserved most of them, though if you asked him, any woman who went after a man who told her right up front he wasn't ever going to be her boyfriend probably shouldn't get bent out of shape when that turned out to be true.

There were lights on in the Deckers' second-floor bedroom, which meant he could see right in. There hadn't been a light on upstairs in months, maybe even over a year. Mrs. Decker never went upstairs anymore, and though she sometimes had visitors, she didn't have overnight company. Gabe moved closer to his window, hands on the sill. His breath fogged the glass, but he didn't wipe it clean. He just waited patiently for it to clear.

Earlier he'd seen the woman inside, moving back and forth, emptying boxes and arranging the furniture. Her hair was darker now than it had been in childhood, but still red. He bet she still had freckles across her nose, and that twisted sense of humor. Other things would've changed over time, they always did, but surely that would be the same.

Janelle Decker had come back.

The door to that other bedroom opened, and there she was again. In the dark, behind the shield of his curtain, Gabe watched, waiting to see if she'd look over. She didn't. She straightened and slid an elastic band off her wrist, then used it to fasten her hair on top of her head. She stretched, rolling her neck and shoulders with a wince.

Gabe had once sworn he'd get the hell out of this place and never look back, but Janelle had been the one to actually do it. At least until now. What was she doing back here? Easy enough to guess—Mrs. Decker was getting older and more frail. She'd fallen not too long ago, and Gabe supposed she needed caretaking. That explained the boxes and stuff in the upstairs bedroom, instead of only a suitcase or two.

"So," she says. "That's it? It's over?"

"Nothing's over. For something to be over, it has to start."

"I did it for you!" she cries. "You asked me for a favor, and I did it!"

Then she's leaving and his hands are on her. Too hard. He doesn't know how to tell her he doesn't want her to go, and he can't make himself ask her to stay.

And after that, everything fell apart.

THREE

IN WHAT BENNETT CALLED THE OLDEN DAYS, this big room, separated into four sections by a T-shaped half wall, had belonged to four of her uncles. The smaller bedroom across the hall had housed Janelle's dad, the oldest of the five brothers, until he moved out and the next oldest took his place. Ricky, Marty, Bobby, Joey and John, the Decker brothers. Her dad had often joked that if the others had learned to play instruments the way he'd taken to the guitar, they could've had a band to rival the Oakridge Boys or maybe the Osmonds. All five had shared the bathroom off the hallway, and Janelle shuddered to think of what that must've been like—the stink alone must've been enough to kill a couple of elephants. And it wasn't a big bathroom, she thought as she settled one more box of toiletries on the floor. It would be a hardship sharing it with one medium-size boy, much less an army of brothers.

Of the five brothers, four remained in contact, though none of them had stayed in St. Marys. John and his wife, Lisa, lived three hours away in Aliquippa, their three kids and spouses and grandkids close by. Bobby and Donna lived an hour and a half away in Milesburg, their four kids and their families scattered across the country. Marty and Kathy in Dubois, close to Joey and his wife, Deb, but that was still about an hour away. Marty and Kathy's daughter, Betsy, lived with her family twenty minutes away in Kersey, but her brother, Bill, was unmarried and traveled the world as a journalist. Joey and Deb had one son, Peter, who lived at home in their basement and, to be honest, sort of creeped Janelle out and always had.

Janelle's dad, on the other hand, had pretty much fallen off the face of the earth a few decades ago, and it was good riddance as far as she was concerned.

"We were wondering if you'd be able to come and stay with Mom," Joey had said without preamble three months ago when he'd called her. "She had a fall recently, and she's been diagnosed with a brain tumor. Inoperable."

Janelle had barely had time to ask him how he and his family were before he'd leveled her with that bit of news. In retrospect, she appreciated the bluntness, but at the time it had sucked the wind from her lungs.

I promise I'll come back soon, Nan.

It had been almost twenty years.

"The doctor says she could have anywhere from a few months to a few years," Joey had said. "She wasn't showing any symptoms. They only found out because she hit her head, and they did an MRI. She says she's going to be eighty-four years old and doesn't want chemo or any sort of treatment like that. But she needs someone with her, Janelle. We thought... you might be able to. Whether it's a few months or a few years, she doesn't have a lot of time left. Even if you can't come to stay, you should at least come to visit."

She'd never appreciated a guilt trip, especially not from an uncle she hadn't spoken to since she was a teenager, but as it turned out, Joey wasn't just asking her to come and take care of Nan in her last years. He, along with his brothers, were making her an offer she couldn't refuse.

Janelle would have medical power of attorney, with limited power of attorney granting her access to Nan's checking and savings accounts for the purposes of maintaining her grand-mother's lifestyle. There had been a lot of legal paperwork stating that she would be responsible for maintaining the house until Nan passed away. After that, Janelle would be in charge of selling it and splitting the income among Nan's sons. Janelle would keep her dad's share of the proceeds for herself.

Her uncles were buying her and making no real pretense otherwise. She respected that as much as Joey's initial blunt-ness in telling her about Nan's failing health. But Janelle could be blunt, too.

"Why me? You live close by. Betsy and Peter do, too, right? None of you can check in on her?"

"She needs someone there full-time," Joey had said. "She won't accept a nurse—we tried that. She won't go into a home—we suggested that, too. And we all have houses and lives and families, Janelle. We can't pick up and move in with her."

Janelle could've protested that she couldn't, either, but the fact was, it made sense. She wanted out of California. St. Marys was a four-hour drive away from her mom and step-father, Randall, and also her brother, Kenny, and his family. That was far better than a six-hour flight. And really, what else did she have in California but debts she couldn't seem to get out from under no matter what she did? In for a penny, in for a pound was one of Nan's favorite sayings. Janelle had listed her house and its upside-down mortgage with a rental management company, sold most of her stuff and packed up the rest. Here she was.

First things first. She'd unloaded most of her boxes from the truck. She should make the bed. Then create some order in the bathroom so she could convince her son to take a shower tonight before he went to bed. Bennett might not think he needed to face his first day in a new school with clean hair and clothes, but his mother did.

Before she could do any of that, a quavery voice came from the bottom of the stairs. "Janelle? Will you and Benny be ready for supper soon?"

Janelle went to the head of the steeply pitched staircase. "Yeah, Nan, I'll be down in a couple minutes."

"I have leftovers from New Year's dinner. I'm making turkey soup with spaetzle."

Janelle's stomach rumbled, and she immediately headed down the stairs. "Nan. You shouldn't be cooking anything. Let me get that."

Her grandmother gripped the newel post with gnarled fingers. She'd always been short but pillowy. It hurt Janelle's heart to see how frail she'd become. When Janelle impulsively bent to hug her, she could feel every one of the bones in Nan's spine. She didn't want to grip too hard, but found it almost impossible to let go.

Nan tutted and waved her hands. "It's already made. I just need to warm up the rolls...."

"Nan, I'll get it."

For half a second, her grandmother's shoulders slumped. Then, feisty as ever despite the weight she'd lost and the cancer nibbling away at her, she shook her head. "No, no. You go upstairs and work on putting your room together. The soup's heating up, and I have the rolls all ready. You go. Go!"

Janelle had spent her entire life heeding Nan's instructions. Even when she'd ignored Nan's advice, even when she'd deliberately disobeyed her, Janelle had always at least made a show of listening. Old habits didn't simply die hard, they rose like the undead and kept walking. Now she backed up the steep stairs, catching her heel on every one and keeping her eye on Nan, who took her time, centering herself with a hand on the newel post again before she was steady enough to move across the living room's polished wooden floor.

As she turned and went up the stairs, Janelle heard Nan singing, the tune familiar though she couldn't place it until she got into her room and recognized it as a particularly filthy pop song by an up-and-coming rapper. Laughing, she slotted the bed rails into the head- and footboards, then wrestled the box spring and mattress onto it. The bed itself she pushed kitty-corner under one of the dormers.

Then she looked out the window, hung with beige lace curtains, ugly and useless at blocking the light. Or the view. She could see right through them and into the second-floor bedroom of the house next door.

As she'd been able to do back then.

Just one minute. One nostalgic minute. That's all she meant to take. The alley between the houses was so narrow that she could easily lean out her window and shake hands with someone doing the same on the other side. Close enough to string a tin-can telephone—and with the memory of that, she stood on her tiptoes to run her fingers along the top of the window frame. The piece of string was still there, stapled into the plaster, the end frayed where it had been cut years ago.

Hello. Hello. Vienna calling.

"Mom?"

Janelle turned, easing onto her heels, and wiped her dusty fingertips on her jeans. This room would take more work than setting up the furniture and making her bed. "Yeah, buddy."

"I'm hungry. Is it time to eat yet?"

"Yeah. Nan made us soup. Let's take a break. How's your room coming along?"

Bennett shrugged. "It's okay."

Which could mean anything, from he'd completely unpacked or hadn't slit the tape on a single box. Janelle poked her head in his doorway and found the room in a state someplace in between. Books and clothes covered his bed, but the small combo television and DVD player, hooked up to his game system, had been set up on top of his dresser the way it had been in California. Priorities, clearly.

"Bennett, c'mon. Get this stuff cleaned up and put away."

"I'm getting to it."

"No comics or video games until this room is clean," Janelle said. "I mean it. And it's early to bed tonight. School tomorrow."

Downstairs, the good smell of homemade soup was overshadowed by the acrid odor of smoke. A baking sheet of crescent rolls rested on the stove, the tops golden-brown, the bottoms burned black. Nan had opened both windows over the sink as well as the door leading to the enclosed porch, but the smell lingered. She was in the family room, setting a handful of spoons on the table.

She turned a little when Janelle came in. "Where's Benny?"

"I'm here, Nan." Bennett ducked around Janelle. "Something stinks."

"Bennett," she warned.

Nan laughed. "Oh, I burned those rolls all right. Lost track of time. Should've kept my eye on 'em, but oh, well. We can just tear the tops off, right, Benny? Janelle, grab that bowl of mashed potatoes and bring it in here."

"My mom burns them all the time," Bennett said as he sidled around the table to sit in the chair closest to the wall.

"Sometimes so bad we can't even eat them. She catches the toaster on fire, too. And once she burned popcorn—"

"Bennett! Just because something's true doesn't mean we have to tell the whole world." Janelle set the ceramic bowl of mashed potatoes in the middle of the table next to the platter of cold sliced filling. Nan made the best filling and mashed potatoes in the whole world. Nan made the best everything.

"Like this," Nan said to Bennett when he put a spoonful of potatoes on the edge of his plate. She scooped some into her bowl, where the potatoes dissolved around the leftover turkey, corn and spaetzle to make the thin broth into something thick and creamy and delicious. "That's how you do it. But first, let's say grace."

Bless us, Oh Lord, and these thy gifts, which we are about to receive from thy bounty, through Christ our Lord. Amen.

Janelle hadn't said that or any prayer in years, but the words rose as easily to her lips as they once had. Bennett, brows raised, looked at her, and a sudden pang struck her. The blessing and the after-holiday turkey soup with mashed potatoes mixed into it had been a staple of her childhood visits to Nan's house. But just like the prayers she'd never taught him, when had she ever made a turkey, much less kept the leftovers to make soup? Never. The traditions of Janelle's childhood had split and splintered after her dad disappeared for good, and after leaving St. Marys that last time she'd carried forward only the ones from her mom's side of the family.

"It's good." She plopped a hefty portion of potatoes into her own soup and stirred it into a thick stew, not reaching for the salt or pepper because Nan would have already seasoned it to perfection. Janelle blew on it and took a bite before it was cool enough, suddenly eager for the familiar flavors. She burned her tongue and didn't care.

"It's good," Nan agreed. "Eat up, Benny. I have ice cream for dessert."

Nan always had ice cream for dessert. Vanilla and chocolate and strawberry. Always in a bowl, never in a cone because you could fit more in a bowl. The bowls were the same. The spoons. The laughter was the same, too, Janelle thought as Nan listened to Bennett's silly jokes and told a few of her own.

Nan was different, but Janelle supposed she was, too. That's what happened with the passing of time. People got older. They got sick. They died.

But not yet, Janelle thought. *Please, God. Not just yet.*

FOUR

Then

THOSE MOTHERLESS TIERNEY BOYS. THAT'S what people always called them, with a mixture of pity and fond disapproval. When they show up in mismatched clothes, their hair a mess, chocolate milk on their upper lips. When they miss school altogether. Or church. Blaming the fact they don't have a mom is an excuse, it makes people feel better, that's what Gabe figures. If people can point at them, they don't have to pay attention to themselves.

Andy and Mikey don't remember Mom, not even from pictures, because their dad threw them all away. There used to be a big photo of her and Dad on the wall in the living room, but one day Gabe came downstairs and found only a bare spot where it had hung, the paint a little lighter than the rest. The frame was in the garbage, but the picture was gone. Gabe did have a picture of her holding him when he was a baby. He had it tucked away in his drawer, way at the back, but his dad didn't know about that one. If he did, he'd probably throw it away, too.

Gabe remembers his mom, the way she smelled and the feeling of her hair on his face when she bent to pick him up, but that was from a long, long time ago. Sometimes he thinks he might just have imagined all of it. If it wasn't for Gabe's picture he could believe he came out from under a cabbage leaf, just like Mrs. Moser says.

Mrs. Moser gives them cookies while they're doing their homework. The twins hardly have anything to do because they're only in kindergarten, but Gabe's in the fourth grade and he's got so much schoolwork he can hardly get through it some nights. Right now he's struggling with some social studies maps he's supposed to color, but all the crayons are broken or worn down to nubs. Dad said he'd bring home another box, but he's not home from work yet. Maybe he won't be home until it's too late, when Gabe will be asleep. And this is due tomorrow.

"Finish up your work so you can watch some cartoons while I finish dinner." Mrs. Moser talks in a thick German accent. She's kind of fat and has grayish hair, and her arms are flabby, but she makes great cookies. If she was around all the time, Gabe thinks, nobody would ever have any reason to look at them with pity, because they'd always be clean and their clothes would match.

But Mrs. Moser comes in to do for his dad only a couple days a week. Sometimes she doesn't show up for weeks in a row, because she has a bad back and has to take a break. Or because his dad hollers about something she didn't do right, like buying the wrong kind of shampoo or getting the lunch meat sliced too thin. Ralph Tierney likes things the way he likes them, that's what he always says.

Gabe knows for sure his dad doesn't like *him*. When he

looks at Gabe, his face wrinkles up as if he smelled something bad. He loves the twins, though. They sit on his lap while he reads them books. They get away with everything Gabe never could. They cry and stamp their feet and throw tantrums to get their way, and Gabe's not even allowed to say a word. If they hit him, he can't hit them back. If they take his stuff and break it, he's not allowed to complain. If he does, there's a good chance Dad will blame him for whatever happened, anyway, so he says nothing. But if he can get in a punch when nobody's looking...

"Gabriel. Are you finished with your work?"

Gabe shows Mrs. Moser the unfinished map. "I need crayons."

"What happened to yours?"

Andy broke them all up and mixed the pieces together, then put them in the oven to melt into a "supercrayon." Gabe shrugs, the truth not worth saying. Mrs. Moser clucks her tongue.

"You should be more careful with your things, Gabriel. Your father—" she says it like *fazza* "—he works hard."

Gabe feels his entire face wrinkle like a raisin. "I need them for school! It's not my fault Andy broke them! I'm tired of everyone blaming me for stuff that's not my fault! I hate it!"

Crash goes the chair. *Bang* goes the table when he slams it. *Slap* go the papers when he shoves them to the floor. Mikey looks all goggle-eyed, his upper lip pink from the punch Mrs. Moser let him have with his snack, because milk gives him a bellyache. Andy looks scared.

Gabe is a dragon, he's a bear, he's a dinosaur. His fingers hook into claws. He roars and stamps, and it feels good, letting all this out. Making noise. It feels good to watch his brothers cry and squirm away from him. It even feels good to run away from Mrs. Moser, because she's too old and fat to catch him.

He's still running around the table when Dad shows up in the doorway. Gabe runs right into him. Dad's solid, like a mountain. Gabe hits and bounces off, lands on his butt so hard tears fill his eyes from the pain.

"Jesus, Mary and Joseph! What's going on in here?"

Andy and Mikey start up with the wailing while Gabe struggles to get to his feet. Mrs. Moser tries to explain, but Dad reaches down to grab the front of Gabe's shirt and haul him upright. Dad smells like sweat and dirt and cigarettes. He shakes Gabe, hard.

"What the hell do you think you're doing?"

"I was just playing."

"Playing like an idiot. Jesus Christ." Dad wipes his face with one big hand. His eyebrows are big and bushy. His breath stinks like the peppermint candies he's always sucking. He shifts one now from side to side, clicking it against his teeth.

When Dad lets him go, Gabe stumbles. His butt still hurts, bad. His back, too. It will hurt for almost a week, and when he twists to look in the mirror later, a huge bunch of bruises will have blossomed there.

"I don't understand you, Gabe. I swear to God, I don't." Dad shakes his head. "Go to your room."

"He hasn't finished his homework," Mrs. Moser says.

Dad looks at her. "Well. That's his own damn fault, isn't it? Go to your room. Where's my goddamned dinner?"

Gabe goes to his room. He's not tired, but he gets into bed, anyway. There's nothing else to do. His teacher will be mad if he doesn't do his work, but he can't make himself care. He can't finish the project without crayons, so what difference does it make?

He sleeps, finally. Wakes a little when Mrs. Moser brings the little boys up and oversees them getting into their pajamas, brushing their teeth, tucking them into their matching twin beds in the room across the hall from Gabe's. He keeps his eyes shut tight, his face to the wall, so she doesn't know he's awake. He drifts back to sleep amid the whistling snores of his brothers, who both have colds.

He wakes again when the stairs creak, and once more keeps his eyes shut tight, his face turned to the wall. Maybe tonight those footsteps will move past his doorway and not come inside. Maybe not.

The floor also creaks. It makes music. It's like the school chorus Gabe didn't try out for, but had to participate in, anyway, for the Christmas show. Every voice blends together to make a whole song. Each step on this creaking, squeaking floor has a different voice, but most every night it sings the same song.

Tonight the footsteps don't stop across the hall. They keep moving toward Gabe's bed. His eyes squinch tighter, tighter, his fists clutching at the sheets. He doesn't dare move or breathe or shift or so much as let his eyelids twitch.

A big hand brushes over his hair. Gabe braces himself, but the hand retreats. The floor creaks, the song changes. When at last he dares to open his eyes and look to make sure the bogeyman has indeed retreated, he sees something on the dresser that wasn't there before. He has to sit up in bed to make sure. The light in the room is dim, so he also has to touch it. But when he does, he takes the offering into bed with him, lifting the lid and breathing in the best smell in the whole world, over and over.

A box of brand-new crayons.

Gabe thought of those crayons, that fresh and brand-new box of crayons, when he saw what the old man had left him on the kitchen table. He poked it with a fingertip, his lip slightly curled. Couple packs of cigarettes, his brand.

"What's this for?" he asked from the living room doorway.

The old man didn't even look up from the TV. "Had Andy bring 'em home for you. What, you don't want 'em?"

It wasn't that Gabe didn't want the cigarettes. Smokes weren't cheap, and if his father wanted to gift him with a couple packs, he wasn't going to complain. But the old man's gifts never came without a price, and Gabe wanted to know what it would be before he accepted.

"What do you want?" he asked evenly.

His dad still didn't look at him, another sign he was working up to something. "Nothing. Why do I always have to want something?"

"Because you always do." Gabe came into the room to look him over. "Shit, old man. You stink. Why don't you take a shower once in a while?"

"Why don't you shut your pie hole," the old man muttered, shifting in his recliner. The flickering light of the television reflected in his eyes for another few seconds before he finally looked at his son. "I need you to take me to the doctor tomorrow."

Gabe didn't say anything for a long minute, during which his father shifted uncomfortably.

"What time?"

"I have an appointment at four."

"Jesus." Gabe sighed and rubbed at his eyes. "You couldn't have asked me this a week ago? A couple of days, even? How long have you known about it?"

"Language," the old man reprimanded. "I knew you'd say no, that's why."

Gabe rubbed his tongue against the back of his teeth until it ached. "I didn't say no. What's the appointment for?"

His father gave him a shifty glance. "It's private. I just need to go. Can you take me or not?"

"I have two jobs going on tomorrow. I can maybe juggle the second one, yeah. But you know, you have to ask me this stuff ahead of time so I can make it work. I can't just be at your beck and call." Gabe paused, eyeing him. "You sick?"

"No."

"So what's wrong with you, then?"

"I got piles, okay?" The old man scowled. "Hurting something fierce. Is that what you want to hear? Fine, I'll tell you!"

Gabe laughed. "If you got off your ass once in a while, maybe you wouldn't have that problem."

His dad raised a trembling finger, his lower lip pooched out. "You can just shut your mouth. Disrespectful son of a bitch."

It was an old insult, one that no longer stung. Gabe shrugged. "I'll take you. Thanks for the cigarettes."

He pocketed both packs and went out back to smoke. Light spilled from the Decker house next door, golden and somehow warm even in the frigid January chill. From this angle he couldn't see inside, but shadows moved in the square of light from the kitchen window. Janelle, he imagined. Washing the dishes, maybe. Standing at the sink, looking out into the snow-covered backyard.

The light upstairs went on, sharing his gaze. From here he couldn't see inside any more than he could into the kitchen, but more shadows shifted up there. He imagined her pacing. Unpacking a box, making the bed.

Dancing.

"When I dance," she says, "I feel like I can do anything."

A shudder rippled along his spine that had nothing to do with the cold outside. Gabe drew again on the cigarette, but it made him cough unexpectedly, burning his throat and the inside of his nose with smoke and frigid air. Above him, a figure appeared in the window. Staring down at him? Maybe, if only at the cherry tip of his cigarette. Surely she couldn't see the rest of him, tucked away in the shadows. Still, he dropped the butt into the coffee can of sand on the porch railing and stepped back from the edge, making sure there was no way she could even glimpse him.

The swing of lights in the street alerted him to Andy's return. His brother laughed as he got out of the car that had brought him home, and he was still laughing when Gabe met up with him inside the house. Andy waved a fistful of lottery tickets in Gabe's face.

"Got the winner this time, I know it." He pinned them up on the corkboard next to the fridge, where they kept the calendar and his work schedule and messages from Michael.

There were a few there now. He called every other day on the house phone to talk to their dad, though he couldn't be bothered to visit more than a few times a year. Somehow, the only person this seemed to bother was Gabe.

"What would you do with that money if you did win, anyway?" Gabe asked.

Andy looked thoughtful, then shrugged. "Take you and Dad and Michael on a trip. He went on that cruise, remember? He said it was fun. Maybe I'd buy some new video games."

"What if you won really big?" Gabe looked over the tickets. His brother spent hours analyzing the numbers, certain he could figure out the next big hit. "Wouldn't you want to get out of here? Wouldn't you want to leave?"

Andy had been rummaging in the fridge, but now turned. "Where would I go?"

"Nowhere," Gabe said with a shake of his head. "Never mind."

FIVE

JANELLE HAD NEVER WEPT WHEN BENNETT started school, not even kindergarten. And Bennett hadn't been one for tears, not even as a baby. Today, with his breath puffing out in the frigid northwestern Pennsylvania mountain air, his cheeks red and lips already chapping, he looked as if he might break down, and that was enough to send Janelle's heart surging into her throat.

"I'll be okay, Mom."

"Sure. It's going to be a great school for you." She nodded firmly. "I know it won't be like the academy, but it'll be great."

"Don't cry," Bennett warned.

She'd always driven him to and from school. Montrose Academy had limited bus service, and Bennett's after-school activities would've meant she needed to pick him up, anyway. Music lessons, sports and art classes, in addition to what the academy provided. No dance lessons; he'd never been interested in that. She'd spent hours ferrying him from one class to the next. Thousands of dollars, all to make sure he had every possible opportunity.

"And you get to ride the bus," she told him. "That'll be fun."

His expression told her he didn't believe her. The bus appeared at the end of the street and stopped at the intersection. For a moment it looked as if it would continue without turning onto Dippold Street. The first day of her senior year of high school, Janelle had had to run for the bus. She'd lost a ballet flat, had to go back. Everyone had been laughing at her when she got on the bus, red-faced and panting, the carefully tousled hairdo she'd spent an hour fixing a mess.

This time she'd called the school four times to make sure of the stop location so they'd be at the right place on this first day, but her heart still pounded uncomfortably until the bus made the lumbering turn and headed toward them. It screeched to a stop on the opposite side of the street with that distinctive braking noise. The lights flashed and the red sign flipped out to prevent the nonexistent traffic from passing. Bennett headed for the bus without a backward glance.

"Wait!" Janelle cried. "Do you have your…lunch money? Your gym clothes?"

She should've driven him to school, just this first day. Walked him to the office, made sure he had everything he needed. Switching from private to public school was a difficult enough transition without a cross-country move, including a climate change on top of it.

Bennett didn't even look back. Janelle stared at the faces peering at her from the bus windows, and kept herself from running across the street after him. The bus driver waved. She waved back. The bus drove off.

That was it, then.

Her teeth were chattering and her fingers numb. The house

would be warm, but before going inside she took the time to look up and down the street. Not much had changed.

Those Tierney boys, Janelle thought, turning to look at the big redbrick house next to Nan's. It sat higher on the hill than hers. An intricately constructed railroad-tie wall had replaced the cinder blocks that used to keep the yards distinct. The same concrete walk led to the back porch door. It had once been lined with flowers, but now butted directly against the wooden ties.

And… Oh. Andy. He stood on the front porch, bundled in a bulky red coat, the fur-edged hood hanging down his back. He waved at her.

"Hi!"

Janelle tucked her hands into her pockets and quelled her chattering teeth long enough to cross to the edge of the Tierneys' yard. The new winter boots her mom had given her for Christmas were too big, too heavy. In California, Janelle lived most of the time in flip-flops or sandals. Slow and unwieldy, she felt like she was walking on the moon, without the bonus of being able to leap and float.

"Hi, Andy." Janelle waved.

He'd gotten older, of course, the way they all had. Yet she knew that face. The slope of his chin, his nose, the hollows of his eyes and cheeks. The silver glinting in his dark hair came from age, but the thicker stripe of white along the part hadn't. That was from the bullet.

"You know me?" Andy rocked back and forth on his heels. In contrast to his heavy winter clothes, he wore bedroom slippers on bare feet. His ankles stuck out a few inches below the bottom of his flannel pajama pants.

"Yes. Do you remember me?"

Andy's brow furrowed. "No."

His lack of memory didn't surprise her, but her disappointment did. Thick as thieves, that's what they'd been once upon a time. Janelle and all three of those Tierney boys. She didn't let even a toe prod the frosty grass of his yard.

"Janelle Decker. We—"

"Mrs. Decker lives next door." Andy jerked a thumb at Nan's house. "She makes the best cinnamon buns. But she hasn't made them for a while."

Nan did make the best cinnamon buns, that was true. Janelle smiled. "Yep. We used to go to school together?"

She let the statement lilt at the end, though it wasn't a question. They'd done a lot more than go to school together, but their adventures had been of the sort you didn't just quote casually on a January morning after half a lifetime. Andy cocked his head.

"I'm sorry. I don't remember you."

"That's okay. It was a really long time ago. I'm Mrs. Decker's granddaughter," Janelle said, wondering if that would spur any sort of recognition.

No light appeared in Andrew's eyes. No miraculous recovery. She ought to have known better, but was still disappointed.

Andy's hand crept up to stroke along the white strip. His expression clouded. "I don't... There are lots of things..."

"It's okay, Andy. Really. You don't have to remember." Impulsively, she hopped over the invisible boundary between grass and cement and up the small hill to the porch. Her boots gave her plenty of traction so she didn't slip. She put one on the bottom step and held out her hand. "Nice to meet you. Again."

Andy took her hand gently. His fingers didn't curl all the way around hers; his grip was well-intentioned but weak. "Meetcha. What are you doing next door?"

"I'm going to be staying with her."

"For a visit?"

Janelle paused, then shook her head. "No. For a while."

"You're going to take care of her because she's sick." Andy nodded as though it all made sense, as if he'd just put together the pieces of a puzzle and could see that the picture matched the one on the box. "She has cancer in her brain."

Janelle swallowed. "Yes. She does."

"Will she die soon?" Andy said this so matter-of-factly, so calmly, that all Janelle could do was gape. He gave her that look again. "I almost died once. Did you know that?"

Her mouth was dry, but she managed to say, "Yes. I did."

Andy's mouth tipped on one side. He'd once had a brilliant smile, just like both his brothers—wide and bright and infectious. When Andrew Tierney grinned, he did it with his entire face. Or had, until things had gone bad. Now only one-half really moved.

"But you're here now. You'll take care of her."

Janelle nodded. Her shivering had stopped with the uprush of emotion heating her from inside. Her cheeks felt flushed, her armpits sweaty.

"Good. I was worried about her. We used to play cards all the time, but not since she went to the hospital. I haven't gone over since she got back, because Gabe says she probably doesn't want to be bothered. I would help her, you know. But this—" he knocked a fist against the side of his head "—makes me stupid. I'm stupid now."

Janelle wasn't sure what to say. Nan had never mentioned playing cards with Andy. She hadn't said a word about any of the Tierney boys in years, not since she'd called to tell her about the accident. Janelle suddenly felt dumb. Of course, Nan wouldn't say anything about them to her, but that wouldn't mean she didn't see or talk to them. Or, apparently, play cards with them. They were her neighbors, after all, and in a town the size of St. Marys you didn't ignore your neighbors un-

less you had some reason to feud. Nan would have no reason
for anger.

And Janelle didn't, either, did she? Everything that had
happened was long past, and the man in front of her had paid
a far greater price for it than Janelle ever had. There'd be no
sense in holding any grudges, and it was obvious Andy wasn't
capable of it, anyway.

His brother, on the other hand, obviously was. Gabe glared,
first from the window, then the front door. His gaze skidded
over her, then went to his brother.

"Get inside here, Andy. You're going to freeze your balls
off."

Andy let out a guffaw of laughter and charmingly ducked
his head. It was hard to tell if he was blushing beneath the
wind-chilled red of his cheeks, but Janelle thought he was.
He shook his head.

"Gabe!"

"Get inside. Your breakfast is waiting. Jesus." Gabe stepped
aside so Andy could go in.

He did, but looked over his shoulder at Janelle. "This is my
brother Gabe. Do you remember him, too?"

"She remembers me. Get inside." Gabe waited until Andy
had moved past him, then closed the door a little too hard.
He stared at Janelle. He wasn't dressed for the weather, but if
the cold bit at his bared arms or feet, he didn't show it.

Gabe also had silver in his hair, at the temples and dark
stubble at the scruff of his neck. Maybe a glint or two in his
bushy brows and most certainly in the tuft of hair curling up
from the V-neck of his white T-shirt. Time had been good
to him, and Janelle wasn't surprised. Gabe Tierney had a face
that could make angels weep and devils dance.

He crossed his arms over his chest and stared at her. Daring her, but to do what?

"Hi, Gabe."

"You're moved in."

Janelle glanced toward Nan's house. She supposed she should start calling it home. She looked back at him. "Yep. Me and my son. Bennett. He just turned twelve."

Gabe didn't crack even half a grin. "It's been a long time."

She knew that well enough. "Seems like it hasn't been so long. Not much has changed."

Gabe put a hand behind him to twist the knob of the front door without turning. It stuck, so he pushed it with his foot, hard enough to force it open. He shook his head once, twice, slowly. "Nothing ever does."

Then he went inside.

Janelle let out a breath that frosted in front of her face. As kids they'd held their fingers to their lips and exhaled, pretending to smoke. As teenagers, they'd actually lit up. Now she let the air in front of her face fog her vision for a second or two before she took her foot off the front step.

"Nice to see you, too." More frost hung the words in the air, frozen. If she reached out, maybe she might've been able to knock them to the ground like something solid, but instead Janelle slipped down the icy hill toward the back door of Nan's house.

On the enclosed porch, she stamped snow from her boots and slipped them off, dancing a little in the cold that seemed strangely deeper now that she'd come inside. Unzipping her coat, she went into the family room to find Nan at the table. There was no formal dining room in the house, just this overlarge space where they all gathered to eat every meal and watch TV or talk. Oh, and play cards, she thought. That was where they did that, too.

Nan had an array of bottles set out in front of her, carefully lined up on a small plastic tray, with the labels facing her. She also had a piece of lined notebook paper filled with looping, familiar handwriting. She pointed to one of the lines. "What's this say? I don't have my glasses on."

"Let me see." Janelle craned her neck to look at the paper, which listed different medications for high blood pressure, anemia, pain management. "This says you need to take your Ferradix in the morning with food."

Janelle read a few of the other instructions, most stating the dosage for each pill or liquid, the time of day it needed to be taken, with food or without. It was complicated, the paper creased and the ink smudged in places. She'd have to see if she could rewrite it, maybe even type it up on her laptop and print it out in bigger letters so Nan could see it more easily. She watched Nan fumble with one of the pill bottles, the childproof cap giving her trouble. The bottle slipped, and her grandmother hissed in pain or irritation.

"Nan, let me get that for you."

It was the wrong thing to say. Nan looked up at her with both eyebrows raised. "I can do it."

"I'm going to make myself some breakfast. Can I get you something?" Janelle backed off, careful to tread the line between being solicitous and overbearing. It was a line she often missed with her son, but for the moment Nan seemed happy enough to accept the offer.

"English muffin with some peanut butter, honey, thank you. I made coffee. You can bring me a cup of that, too." Nan sighed and looked at the bottles. One of them had a small cup tipped over the lid, like a shot glass, and she poured a dose of brown liquid into it and tossed it back with a grimace. "Oh, that's nasty."

The coffee turned out to be pitch-black and full of grounds. Janelle had yet to unpack her own sleek coffeemaker that not only ground the beans but also had different temperature settings and a milk frother, but seeing this mess she resolved to make finding it a priority. Nobody who liked coffee could drink that swill, and Janelle didn't just *like* coffee, she considered it its own necessary food group. When she lifted the plastic top to peek inside at the filter, she found the basket overflowing with sodden grounds that looked as though they hadn't been dumped in weeks. Digging a cautious finger into the mess, she unearthed a patch of mold.

"Nan," she said in the doorway, careful to keep her voice neutral. "When's the last time you made coffee?"

Nan looked up from a bottle she was trying to open. "Oh. I don't drink it much, when it's just me. Making a whole pot seems like such a waste. But now that you're here, honey, you'll drink it, won't you? You like coffee."

Janelle did indeed, but the stuff in the kitchen looked like a harbinger of the zombie apocalypse or something. A couple swigs and she'd become Patient Zero. Still, Nan had her pride.

"Something happened to it. I need to make a fresh pot, okay? It will be a few minutes. Unless you'd rather have tea?"

Nan looked thoughtful. "I wouldn't mind a nice cup of Earl Grey, honey. Sure. But if you want coffee…"

"I'm fine." She'd have to be, at least until she cleaned the coffeemaker or unpacked her own.

Janelle filled a teakettle and found the tea in the corner cupboard where it had always been kept, on the shelf above the candy jar. The candy inside, sour balls in multiple colors, had melted and stuck together into an inedible mess. Janelle put the jar in the sink and filled it with hot water, hoping to dissolve the candy enough to wash it. Behind the jar she found a couple bags of unopened candy, the same sour balls and starlight mints, along with an ancient package of gummy spearmint leaves. It was the candy she remembered from her childhood, and from the look of the packages might've been purchased that long ago.

"Nan…" Janelle, candy in one hand, went to the doorway. At the table, her grandmother had put her face in her hands. Candy forgotten, Janelle rushed to her. "Nan! Are you okay?"

She looked up, her forehead creased and her mouth thin. She looked unfocused for a second, then pinned Janelle with her gaze. Her eyes had once been the color of a summer sky fluffed with clouds, but they'd gone a duller, dimmer blue. Washed out, Janelle thought. Everything about Nan had faded.

Janelle took her hand and chafed it gently, mindful of the arthritis. "What's wrong?"

"Oh, I just got a little headache. My pressure might be up a bit too high, that's all. I b'lieve I'd better lie down for a while." She drew in a shuddering breath, but found a smile and patted Janelle's hands. "It's time for my nap, anyway."

"Nan, it's, like, eight-thirty in the morning."

Her laugh, at least, hadn't faded. "When you're as old as I am, honey, your sleep gets all messed up. I was up at four this morning."

At four this morning, Janelle had been tossing and turning, in the midst of a series of weird dreams in which she tried desperately to send text messages, but was unable to read them. She remembered peeking at the clock around that time. Maybe a noise from downstairs had woken her. Knowing Nan had been up and about without anyone else awake made her frown.

"You don't want to eat your muffin first? How about your tea?"

Nan shook her head. "If I drink it now I'll just have to pee, and I don't want to have to worry about getting to the bathroom on time. I don't always make it."

Something twisted inside Janelle at Nan's casual admission,

but she didn't let it show. "How about I help you to your bedroom and let you sleep, then."

"I don't need you to help me," Nan said. "I'm fine."

"Of course you are."

Still, Janelle pushed back her chair and held Nan's arm to help her up from the table. The chair legs caught on the thick orange shag Janelle remembered from her childhood. She'd get one of those plastic mats from the office supply store, Janelle thought as her grandmother grunted but finally shoved the chair back far enough to get up. Or better yet, replace the old carpet with something more up-to-date and salable.

"I'm fine," Nan said in a steely voice.

Against her better judgment, Janelle let go of her arm. When her grandmother sounded like that it was better to do what she said. Janelle stepped out of the way so Nan could get around the table, her slippers shuffling on the carpet, then on the linoleum. She walked slowly, bent, but she seemed steady enough. From the kitchen, the kettle whistled, and Janelle followed Nan to take it off the heat.

"You'll have plenty of time to get yourself situated." Nan paused in the hallway, one hand on the basement door frame for support as she turned. "And honey, I'm so glad you're here. So glad. You've been gone such a long time."

I promise to visit soon, Nan. I promise.

But she never had. The years of phone calls, cards, letters, all the same. Reminding her she had a place here in Nan's house, that she was always welcome. No matter how far she'd run—dancing as a chorus girl in Las Vegas or selling newlyweds their first town houses in California—Janelle had never been able to leave this place and that year behind. And yet she'd allowed herself to be kept away by what had happened.

"I'm glad, too, Nan."

It was almost even true.

SIX

FIRST THINGS FIRST. THAT WAS THE WAY TO GO about any set of tasks. One at a time, prioritize, get the work finished.

Or sit in the middle of the complete chaos that was your bedroom, with open packing boxes all over the place, and look at your old yearbook while you listened to records on a player that hadn't seen the light of day since…well, since she'd left Nan's house, probably.

Janelle had found the player and the milk crate of records tucked into one of the dormers. They'd belonged to her dad, though she'd made them her own during her year here. Lots of classic rock, punk like the Sex Pistols, some New Wave stuff including Siouxsie and the Banshees. He'd also had an entire shoe box of random 45s he'd bought from some discount store. None of the songs had ever hit the radio, at least not that Janelle had heard, but she'd listened to a few of them over and over back in the day.

"Don't Get Fooled By The Pander Man," by Brinkley &

Parker. The black record with its orange label spun on the turntable as she flipped the pages of the yearbook she'd found in a box of books she thought she'd left in storage.

Oh, God. Her hair. Her natural color had darkened to a deep auburn over the years from the strawberry-red she'd hated as a kid, and she wore it just past her shoulders with a few layers around her face. Most of the time she pulled it back in a ponytail, low maintenance, wash-and-go. That's who she'd become. Someone's mom.

In this picture, she'd not only dyed it black but also cut it asymmetrically so that one side was shoulder length and the other cropped at chin level. She vividly remembered the mornings she'd spent with a curling iron, the barrel the girth of her pinky, and an industrial-size bottle of hair gel. All those hours she'd spent on her hair, her makeup, her clothes...

It seemed so ridiculous now.

The song ended and Janelle got up to take the needle off the record. She winced at the creak in her joints. If looking at the old photos hadn't made her feel ancient, that crackity-crack of her neck sure did. She'd been at this since Bennett left for school, with only a few short breaks to check on Nan. He'd been home for about an hour, and from his room came the sound of much more modern music, some rap song she'd let him buy, but only the clean version. Ninety percent of the song was bleeps.

"Hey. I'm going to get a snack. You want something?"

Bennett looked up from his bed, where he was leafing through a stack of comics. The rest of his room looked as if a tornado had blasted through it. She opened her mouth to scold, but stopped herself. *Pot*, she thought, *have you met kettle?*

"Okay."

"I'm going to check on Nan first. Why don't you wash

your hands. With soap," Janelle added as Bennett hopped off the bed. He rolled his eyes, but didn't argue.

Downstairs, Nan dozed on the couch in front of the TV. It was showing a religious program—at least there was a nun painting in watercolors, but she wasn't talking about Jesus, so it was hard to tell. Janelle didn't wake her grandmother. They'd have dinner in a couple hours, and by then Nan would probably be up.

"How about cookies and milk, buddy? I'll make dinner in a little bit." Janelle found the ceramic cookie jar tucked back in a corner by the paper towel holder. Nan always kept cookies there, a constant like the tides. Or political scandals.

The jar's handle was a squirrel missing its tail. The paint had worn off its fur. Nostalgia swept Janelle again as she lifted the lid. How many times had she helped herself to cookies from this jar? Too many to count.

Inside were the homemade chocolate chip cookies she was hoping for. "Mmm. These are gonna be so good. Grab some glasses, bud. Get us some milk."

"Should I take it to the table?" Bennett held up the two glasses he'd filled.

She thought of Nan, still napping. "No, let's just eat them in here."

Bennett looked around the small kitchen. "Standing up? What?"

Janelle laughed. "Um, yeah. Are your legs too weak to hold you, or what?"

"You always tell me not to hover around dropping crumbs," he protested. "You always tell me to sit down at the table like a human being, not a cow at a feed trough."

This was true, but Bennett's prickly reaction was unusual. Janelle offered him a cookie. She wasn't sure she could deal with a breakdown at the moment. Everything felt too close to the surface—the move, this house, the past rising up to bite her like a snake. Nan on the couch, so still and silent Janelle thought she ought to have checked to make sure she was breathing. If Bennett, who hardly ever gave in to an emotional display, started up, Janelle wouldn't be able to help him through it. She'd dissolve right along with him, and probably worse.

"Cookie," she said firmly, and handed him one. "Milk. It's good, Bennett, just try it."

The look of horror he gave her after he bit into the cookie he'd dunked in the milk seemed like a joke—until he bent, choking and spitting, over the sink. "Mom!"

"Oh, Bennett, c'mon. What?" The cookie she snagged was a little burned, but rock-hard. The milk would fix it.

Unless, of course, the milk was sour. Janelle spit her own mouthful into the sink, then ran the water to rinse her mouth. She looked at her laughing son. "You think that's funny, huh?"

Bennett shook his head, but grinned. "Gross."

Janelle checked the date on the milk. Sighed. It was expired by two weeks. "Was this open when you took it out?"

"Yes. But I didn't do that to it!"

She laughed, loving him so much it hurt. "I know you didn't."

The carton was almost full, even taking into account the two glasses Bennett had filled. Which meant the milk had been opened but barely touched. Joey had told her that up until her fall, Nan had still been able to get around on her own. In the three months it took for Janelle to tie up her business in California and get out here, she'd assumed someone had been checking on Nan at least weekly—though seeing her now, it should've been daily. Janelle opened a pantry cupboard, studying the contents. Canned soups, dry cereal, plastic bins of pasta. The fridge was also crammed with plastic containers, but the first few she pulled out were expired, too. Clearly, she needed to take a good inventory.

"What are you doing?" Nan sounded hoarse, but her eyes were bright. "Oh, are you hungry? I can make some sandwiches...."

"Nan. No. That's okay, I'll make dinner in a little while." If there was anything to make dinner with. "When's the last time anyone brought you some groceries?"

"Oh." Nan shuffled forward, paused with a fingertip to her lips, thinking. "That would be Deb and Joey. They came for New Year's dinner. Donna and Bobby, too, along with the kids. And Joey a few days before that to bring me the turkey and my pills from the pharmacy."

Janelle made a mental count. "So...a week or so? Did they bring you stuff for New Year's, and other groceries, too?"

"They took me out to dinner." Nan tugged at the fridge door, which at first didn't want to give until she grunted and pulled harder. "I didn't eat all of it—I brought some home with me. Where is it... Oh, there."

She turned with a foil-wrapped container in her hands. "I had some spaghetti and garlic bread. I could heat that up for my supper, honey. You don't have to make me anything."

"Nan, you can't eat that. If you want spaghetti, I can make some."

She frowned. "It's such a waste...."

Janelle took the foil package from her and peeked inside. "No, look. This is no good. You'd get sick eating it. And your milk was spoiled. I think I need to go to the grocery store. Like, tonight. Now."

Nan looked briefly confused. "Okay, let me get my coat."

"You can stay here." Janelle tossed the leftovers in the can under the sink, now full, and pulled it out. Tying the bag shut, she bent to replace it with a trash bag from the normal spot.

She looked beneath the sink, expecting to see bottles of dish detergent and other soaps, trash bags, a package of sponges. Nothing. "Shi—oot."

"What? Mice? I had them come and put traps."

Mice? "Good Lord, Nan, you have mice?"

"Well, no," Nan said. "But I might get them someday, right?"

No argument there. Janelle checked for traps, just in case. She didn't need one snapping on her fingers. The space beneath the sink didn't have any. She took a deep breath.

First things first.

"Okay. I'm going to run to the store for some things, and tomorrow we'll go through the house and make a list of everything we need, maybe take a trip out to the store together. How's that sound?"

"Oh, yes, sure." Nan nodded. "I can make a list."

"But for now—" God, she hated talking to her grandma like she was a toddler "—I need you to just go back to the couch and relax. Bennett…"

She didn't want to leave Nan alone, but leaving her with Bennett didn't make Janelle feel much better. She'd only started feeling comfortable having him stay by himself, no longer than an hour or so. He'd been complaining about it for months.

"You have your cell phone. You call me if you need anything, okay? Go upstairs and clean your room. Don't open the door for anyone. Nan, don't *you* go upstairs, okay?"

Bennett apparently wasn't going to wait around for her to change his mind. He took off at once.

Nan frowned, already shuffling back toward the living room. "Good heavens, Janelle. I haven't been upstairs in months. Why would I go upstairs?"

Because Janelle wouldn't be home and there to stop her, that was why. Because bad luck, especially of the falling-down-the-stairs-breaking-your-neck sort, didn't just happen. It was almost always the result of bad choices.

Janelle grabbed her coat and keys and got in the truck, starting off without waiting for it to warm up. A block away, she let out a breath. Then another. Two deep, sobbing breaths that lifted a weight from her so devious it had disguised itself as maturity. Now she recognized it as relief, and it made her so giddy she almost ran a stop sign when her foot slammed the gas.

Three days, that's all it had been.

Oh, God. How was she going to get through the rest of the week, much less a longer time than that?

California had never seemed so golden. So warm. So far away.

She parked along the curb in front of Pfaff's, the small market closest to Nan's house. She first checked her phone for the text or voice mail she just knew would've come in during the ten-minute trip. More relief swept her when she saw nothing. She dialed her uncle's number. Deb answered.

Trying not to sound accusatory, Janelle explained the situation. Her aunt sighed. "She throws it away."

"What?"

"The food," Deb said. "Sometimes she throws it away, because she wants us to think she ate it. Or because she thinks mice have gotten into it. But sometimes she gets rid of the new stuff and keeps old food.... I don't know what her rationale is, hon. She's old and not well. And she doesn't want us to worry about her, so if she hasn't been eating—and you know she doesn't eat right—then she tries to make sure we don't find out. There were mice last winter, but Joey took care of them. I haven't seen any signs since."

Janelle pressed the pad of her thumb between her eyebrows.

"Okay. Well…I'm here at the market, picking up a few things for dinner tonight. I'll take her shopping tomorrow. Is there anything else I need to know?"

"You can use the debit card. There shouldn't be any problems."

Janelle loaded a basket with eggs, bread, milk, butter, flour and pancake syrup. Also a bag of frozen hash browns. They could have breakfast for dinner.

"You must be Mrs. Decker's granddaughter," the cashier said as she tucked Janelle's purchases into a pair of plastic bags.

Too late, Janelle thought of the reusable tote bags she'd brought with her from California. She'd have to dig them out. "Yes. I'm Janelle. Could I have paper, please?"

The cashier looked surprised, but pulled a couple of paper bags from under the counter and started transferring the items. "I'm Terri Gilmore. Your grandma and my mom are in card club together. She told us all about how you were coming to do for her."

Janelle smiled. "Yep."

"And you have a son? Right?"

"Yes. He's twelve." Janelle took the bags. "Sixth grade."

"You lived with her, didn't you? When you were in high school." The woman's smile seemed a little wider now, but also a little less friendly. Kind of predatory, actually.

Janelle paused. "Yes. I did."

"Next door to those Tierney boys."

"They still live there." Janelle kept her voice steady despite the stepped-up thump of her heart. "Well, not Michael, but…"

Terri nodded. "Of course not. But Andrew, God love him. And his brother, of course. And old Mr. Tierney, though I hear he's not well. Not at all."

"Oh. I don't know. I haven't seen him." Janelle hefted the

bags and backed away. "Nice meeting you. I'll tell Nan I met you."

"Gabriel Tierney," Terri called after her, the words as effective as a hand clutching the back of Janelle's coat to stop her.

Janelle half turned. "What about him?"

"He was in your grade, wasn't he?"

"Yes. He was." They'd shared some classes. They'd ridden the bus together, though he'd sat in the back and she'd always preferred the middle. He'd always had cigarettes. Sometimes other stuff, harder stuff.

Terri shook her head, eyes wide, smile gone. "Shame about what happened, wasn't it? Such a shame."

The woman stared at her expectantly, as if Janelle was going to come back over and start to dish. Janelle shifted the bags again. She didn't know if she should nod or shrug or what.

"Were you still here when it happened?"

Janelle had to clear her throat to answer. "Um…no. I was gone by then."

"Oh." Terri looked disappointed, then brightened slightly. "You know what happened, though, right?"

"Yes." She knew.

"Such a shame. Such a sad, sad shame. To shoot your own brother like that." Terri clucked and shook her head. "You give your grandma my best."

"I will." Janelle escaped.

At home she sat in the driveway for a minute or two longer than necessary. The little pickup had just heated enough to be tolerable, and she was unwilling to leave it for the cold. The family room lights in Nan's house were on, but the Tierneys' house next door was dark.

What had happened. Such a shame. Terri's words echoed in

Janelle's head as she gripped the steering wheel and pressed her forehead against it.

Where you still here when it happened?

No, Janelle had said. But that was a lie.

SEVEN

GABE NEEDED A BEER AND BED, IN THAT ORDER. He'd scheduled several early appointments tomorrow, nothing strenuous or complicated, but 6:00 a.m. seemed to come earlier and earlier the older he got, even when he wasn't out too late the night before. He'd have gone to bed an hour ago, but the old man had been wheezing and shouting at the TV, and showed no signs of wanting to turn it off and go to bed himself. Besides, Andy wasn't home yet, and even though his brother didn't need Gabe to wait up for him, he never felt right hitting the sack until the front porch lights were out and the doors locked.

Andy had called to tell him he was going to the movies with a couple of the girls he worked with, and that was fine with Gabe, because he could count on Tara to bring Andy home. She was a good kid. He'd worked with her dad at the Sylvania plant before starting the handyman business. It was the other two or three she hung around with that Gabe wasn't too sure about. Giggly, giddy girls just out of high school, no college in their futures. They wore their skirts a little too short and their lipstick a little too red. They were the sort of girls Gabe would like in a few years when they started hitting the bars, but seeing them fawn and coo over his brother left a bad taste in his mouth.

Not because he didn't think his brother should get laid now and again, so long as he was careful about it. Michael liked to lecture Andy on abstinence and chastity, but Gabe had made sure to hammer into their brother's sad, broken brain the necessity of using a rubber, no matter if the girl told him she was on the pill or what. Gabe didn't like how the girls treated Andy, as if he were stupid. They took advantage of his generosity, that's what Gabe thought, and though he'd tried to explain to his brother that he didn't always need to pick up the check, especially for girls who could easily afford their own popcorn, Andy didn't listen.

As if on cue, the phone rang. Gabe checked the number—it was Michael. He'd have let it go to the answering machine, but the old man picked it up. The low murmur of conversation began from the living room.

Gabe cracked the top off a beer and sipped at it, savoring the cool sting. A cigarette would go best with the drink, but he didn't smoke in the house, not with the old man's oxygen tank ready to blow them all up with the flick of a spark. Besides, Gabe liked to smoke. He just didn't like to eat and drink smoke, or sleep with it on his pillow or wake up with it. So for now, he drank slowly at the kitchen table and read from a battered paperback copy of *The Books of Blood*. He'd lost track of how many times he'd read it, but he'd had it since he was a teenager, back before the days of the internet where you could find anything you wanted with a well-typed search. Back then he'd had to special-order it from the bookstore at the mall in Dubois and wait weeks for it to arrive.

Janelle Decker had turned him on to Clive Barker's books.
Gabe had seen that *Hellraiser* movie, but she was the one who
told him it had been based on a novella, and that there were
other stories, too. She'd brought a box of paperbacks with her
from home when she moved into her grandma's house. Lots
of horror, lots of historical romance, a few classics. He wondered if she still read the same kinds of books.

He wondered if she still loved to dance.

The light in the hall came on, and moments later the old
man shuffled out in his bare feet, his hair corkscrewed into
spikes. Without a word he dragged his oxygen tank toward
the fridge and dug around inside, found a coconut cream pie
Andy had brought home from work and plopped it on the
table. He brought out two plates and two forks. He took his
seat with a heavy sigh and sat there for a moment with his head
hanging before he looked up, his expression strangely defiant.

"It's hell getting old, you know that?"

Gabe wasn't yet forty, but his joints creaked and his hair
was starting to silver. When he looked in the mirror he had
to suck in his gut a little more than he used to. He could only
imagine what it was like for his father, who'd been an old man
already by the time he was Gabe's age, and had done nothing
but become ancient since.

"So die," Gabe said. "Save yourself any more trouble, and
us, too."

The old man snorted and dug his fork into the pie. He
licked the tines and pointed it toward Gabe. "Maybe you
should fill your mouth with pie. You won't feel the need to
talk so nasty."

"I don't like coconut cream."

The old man grinned. "I know."

"So who's the second plate for, then?"

"For your brother, dummy." The old man pointed the fork

at him again. "He'll be home soon, won't he? Andy likes coconut cream. He'll sit here and eat a piece with me. Keep me
comp'ny."

"What do you need company for?"

The old man paused with the fork halfway to his mouth.
"Why not?"

When Gabe was younger, his father had spent time with
his buddies in a bar or at hunting camp. Sometimes he went
to play poker at Al Hedge's house, though Al had died about
ten years ago and nobody had taken up the game after him.
And sometimes, when Gabe was much, much younger, his
dad had left them overnight and gone to who-knew-where,
but it must've been someplace nice because he always spruced
himself up a lot before he went. Other than that, his dad had
never been what Gabe might've considered the sociable sort,
and time hadn't improved that.

Gabe shrugged. "I just figured you liked sitting in front of
the TV by yourself all day long. Why else would you do it?"

The old man said nothing for a few minutes while he dec-
imated his pie. When he'd finished a hefty slice, he dropped
the fork onto the plate with a clatter and pushed back from
the table. "What do you know about me, anyway?"

The truth was, Gabe knew more about his father than he
ever wanted to. More than he ever should have. "I know
you spend all your time on your ass in that recliner, cultivat-
ing your piles. If you want company, why don't you go out
somewhere?"

"Where would I go?"

"Wherever you want. Go visit some of your buddies, go to
the VFW. Hell, go to church."

The old man hadn't been to church in so long Gabe couldn't
remember the last time. Maybe when Michael had been con-

secrated. Of course, that was the last time Gabe had been in a church himself.

"Church." The old man snorted, then coughed. The cough turned into a choke, which became a wheeze.

Gabe watched impassively, wondering if he'd need to jump across the table in a minute to resuscitate him. Wondering, if push came to shove, if he'd bother. The old man's choking tapered off, and he gave Gabe a glare.

"Wipe that smile off your face."

"Didn't know I was smiling," Gabe said. "Sorry."

His father wiped his mouth with a paper napkin from the basket in the middle of the table. His hands were shaking. When he looked at Gabe, his eyes were red-rimmed and watering.

"You think I hate you, but I don't."

Gabe got up to pour his unfinished beer into the sink. "I'm going out for a smoke."

"But *you* hate *me*."

Without looking at him, Gabe pushed open the back door and stepped onto the porch. A light swung into the alley from a vehicle in the Deckers' driveway. A few minutes later he heard the crunch of boots on the ice and salt. Janelle, arms full of brown paper grocery bags, made her careful and slightly unsteady way down the alley toward the back door. Her movements lit the motion-activated spotlight at the back of the house.

He watched her struggle for a minute before she looked up to see him standing there. "Hey."

"Hi," Janelle said quietly. She shifted both bags to one arm so she could open the door with the other. "You're going to freeze."

"Hot-blooded," Gabe said without thinking, forgetting for a minute she was the one who'd first called him that.

She laughed, and it was just how he remembered it. Full-on, no holding back. She shook her head a little and pulled open the screen door, one foot on the bottom step. She looked back at him from just inside the back porch.

"Good night."

She didn't wait for him to answer. And Gabe, hot-blooded though he might be, was suddenly aware of the cold. He went back inside the kitchen, expecting to find his father gone to bed, or if not that, back in his usual spot in front of the TV.

The old man hadn't moved from the table. He hadn't eaten more pie, and hadn't bothered to put it back in the fridge or take his plate to the sink. Neither was a surprise.

"I don't hate you," the old man repeated in a low, rough voice that didn't sound like his own at all. "You always thought I did. But I never did. Maybe one day you'll stop hating me?"

It was a question, but Gabe had no answer.

"I'm going to bed." He didn't point out all the hundreds of ways over the years Ralph Tierney had expressed his feelings for his sons.

Hate or love, either way, it was too late for whatever it had been to become anything else.

EIGHT

NAN HAD HAD A FEW BAD DAYS, BUT SHE WAS having a good one now. By the time Bennett went off to school, she had already baked a pan of cinnamon rolls from scratch and done half a book of number puzzles. She sat at the kitchen table in her favorite fuzzy blue housecoat, her hair covered by a matching bandanna tied at a jaunty angle.

"Helen will be over later to do my rollers for me." White icing clung to the corners of Nan's mouth. "We have card club tomorrow, you know."

Card club consisted of ten or so women Nan had known since grammar school. She'd confided to Janelle that it had been months since she'd hosted her turn or even attended a meeting, but with Janelle here it made everything so much easier. And if it made Nan happy, that's what counted, Janelle thought as she slid into her seat with a cinnamon roll in her hand.

Delicious didn't do the roll justice. Gorgeous. Awesome.

Amazing. "Awesomazing," Janelle murmured, licking sweet icing from her fingers. "Nan, you're such a good cook."

"I should teach you how to make them before I go."

"To card club?" Janelle asked.

Stupid.

Nan didn't answer, just smiled and tapped her book with her pen, peering over the top of her reading glasses when Janelle licked her fingers clean. "Your daddy used to do that same thing. Lick his fingers instead of using a napkin. Didn't matter how many times I told him."

Janelle paused, then grabbed a napkin from the holder on the table. The question came out before she could stop it. "Do you...miss him?"

Nan took off her glasses and set them carefully on the table, then rubbed the small red marks they'd left on the sides of her nose. She tapped her pen on the puzzle book again. "He was my oldest boy, Janelle. Of course I miss your dad."

"Do you ever hear from him?"

"No." Nan frowned. "And maybe it's better that way. When someone breaks your heart over and over again, sometimes it's better to just let them go."

Janelle had let her dad go a long time ago for that very reason. Until now she hadn't ever thought about how it must've made Nan feel to have lost touch with her son. Until she was a mom herself, Janelle wasn't sure she'd have understood. She couldn't imagine letting Bennett go, not like that. She reached across the table to squeeze Nan's hand.

"How about something to drink?"

"Nothing for me, honey," Nan said, her eyes bright, but without so much as a sniffle. "I'm going to finish my puzzle."

Ice-cold milk would be perfect with the cinnamon roll. Even better than the coffee Janelle hadn't made yet because she was still looking for her coffeemaker. She pulled the carton from the refrigerator and poured a glass, noticing too late that the one she'd pulled from the back of the cupboard was etched and striped with dirt. So was the next she pulled out. She held it to the light, twisting it.

Filthy.

Bennett was in charge of loading and unloading the dishwasher here, the way he'd been in California, and for a brief, irritated moment, Janelle wondered if he'd been too lazy to make sure the dishes were clean, or if he'd been too inattentive to notice. Or a twelve-year-old's winning combination of both.

She checked the dishes in the cupboard quickly. The ones closer to the top of the stack, ones they'd been using regularly, seemed clean enough, but some beneath were crusted with bits of dried-on food. Just a few here and there, but enough to make her stomach turn. The flatware in the drawer was much the same. Some of the pieces looked fine, but there were a lot of dirty spoons, and forks with bits of food clinging to the tines.

Everything would need to be rewashed. She loaded dishes in the dishwasher. Added the soap. Turned the dial—because wow, was this machine old. An hour later she checked it and found it full of wet dishes that were still pretty dirty.

"Nan? Is there something wrong with your dishwasher?"

Her grandmother shuffled into the kitchen doorway. "I don't think so."

Janelle checked the dial settings, thinking she must have chosen some Light or Delicate option. Nope, she'd turned the dial to Normal Wash. She opened the dishwasher. Closed it again. "I think it's broken. When's the last time you used it?"

"Oh…" Nan looked apologetic. "I just wash the dishes by hand."

"But you had people over for New Year's dinner!" That

meant not only dishes, but pots and pans and serving platters and extra silverware. "Nan, you didn't wash everything by hand, did you?"

"No, no. Everyone helped do most of it." She nodded firmly. "And when they left, I just did the rest."

"Oh. Nan." Janelle sighed and opened the dishwasher again. "I think you're going to need a new one."

"They're expensive." Nan sounded worried.

"You don't need to worry about that." Though of course, she would. And it would require some discussion with her uncles, since this was an expense that fell under improving the house, and Janelle was only approved to handle the daily household needs.

"Maybe we can just get it fixed," Nan offered hopefully.

Before they could say anything else, the back door opened. Nan didn't seem surprised, but Janelle was still in the California mind-set—nobody left their doors unlocked, and anyone who came in uninvited and unannounced might as well have a target painted on their chest.

It was Andy. Today he wore a striped, long-sleeved T-shirt and jeans, his feet in socks, not slippers. He'd probably kicked his shoes off on the back porch. He looked totally put-together, and if you ignored the thick white stripe in his slicked-back hair, hardly different than he had as a teen. He gave her that grin.

"Janelle! Hi!" He remembered her name this time, at least.

"Hi, Andy." She gave him a cautious smile. "What are you doing here?"

"Oh, he came over to play cards with me. Get me warmed up for the club." Nan gestured. "Come on in, honey. Janelle, bring those cinnamon rolls in here to the table."

"Your Nan makes them the best," Andy confided. "I missed 'em."

"You could've come over anytime, honey, you know that," Nan said.

He hesitated, looking a little guilty. "Gabe said not to bother you. I sent flowers, though, when you were in the hospital. Did you get them?"

"They were lovely. And you're never a bother. Sit down, honey. Sit."

"Andy, do you come over to play cards a lot?" They'd spent hours, back in the day, playing poker for M&M's or pennies. Andy had had an amazing poker face. They'd played other games, too. Bullshit had been a favorite. Blackjack. She smiled, remembering.

"Sure, whenever I can. When Dad's napping and Gabe's at work, and if I don't have to work." He opened the corner cabinet and pulled out the worn box filled with multiple decks of cards that had been around since Janelle's childhood. "You wanna play?"

"No, thanks. I need to figure out what to do with the dishwasher." She eyed him. "Where do you work?"

He named the town's bigger grocery store. "I work in the stockroom. Or I help bring the carts in. They don't really like me to bag the groceries because of my bum hand. I drop too many jars."

She'd assumed he couldn't work. Somehow knowing he had a job made Janelle feel better. *Like you have the right to feel good about anything that happened,* she thought. "Oh, that's good."

Andy's laugh had always been as sweet as his smile. "It's okay. Gabe says I should try for something else, maybe. But I like what I do."

"Something else?"

Andy dealt out the cards, solicitously moving the pile close enough to Nan so she didn't have to stretch for it. "Yeah. Like school or something. Maybe. But it's okay. Mikey went to college. I don't need to go."

Janelle leaned in the doorway. If she was thirty-eight, Andrew would be thirty-four, or close to it. "Gabe thinks you should go to school now?"

Andrew shrugged. "He thought I should go before. But now, I don't know. I can't drive because of the seizures. Can't remember stuff. School seems like a waste of time."

Janelle kept her voice neutral. Gabe had always talked about leaving St. Marys. Becoming something.

"I'm getting out of here," he says as the smoke curls out of his mouth. "Never coming back."

She's feeling lazy and hazy and has no idea what she's going to do when school's over, when she has to enter the real world. "What do you want to do with your life?"

"Just get out of here." He's dead serious. "Get away."

"Did he go to college? Gabe, I mean."

"Nope. He worked at the plant."

Nan sorted her cards. "Their daddy retired from there, but Gabe wasn't there for very long, was he? He started his own business a while ago. He's a handyman, isn't he, Andy? How long's he been doing that?"

"Nope. Since..." Andrew frowned. "Since... I'm sorry, I don't remember lots of stuff. It sucks sometimes."

A handyman. That made sense. He'd always been good at fixing things. Breaking them, too.

"It's okay. You and Nan play the game. I'm going to figure out what to do with this dishwasher." Which first meant unloading it and washing the dishes by hand.

All of them.

There was actually a kind of contentment in it. Filling half the double sink with hot water and soap, setting up the drain rack. Taking the stuff from the dishwasher, biggest to smallest, and making sure each piece was cleaned and rinsed. Scrubbing at the dried-on dirt. It was the pleasure of a job done carefully and well, but there was something more to it, as well.

"C'mon, Janelle. Let's go!" Andy pokes his head in the back door, grinning. "Gabe says he won't wait anymore."

They're supposed to go out to the cabin in the woods to shoot guns. Snow day. Nan's at work, and Janelle has chores.

"I have to finish the dishes first."

Gabe wouldn't put a foot inside this house, but Andy doesn't hesitate. "I'll help. It'll go faster that way."

And it does, even with the suds going all over the place, especially when Mikey's sent inside to see what's taking them so long. They pull him into the suds fight and the three of them make a mess and clean it up while they laugh and Gabe waits, stewing in the truck. He's so mad he won't talk to any of them until they get to the cabin.

She was nearly finished when Andy came into the kitchen. Without a word, he went to the drying rack and started putting things away, being sure to wipe the wet ones with a towel he pulled from the drawer. Janelle handed him a few forks she'd just rinsed, watching as he held everything carefully against his body so he didn't drop it.

"How was the game?"

"Good. She won." He grinned. "She's napping on the couch."

Andy's phone rang from his pocket. He didn't reach for it, though it chirped at him several times. At Janelle's curious look he said, "It's my brother."

"Won't he worry if you don't answer it?"

Andy looked exactly the way Bennett did when she asked him if a teacher wouldn't scold him for not turning in his homework. "I left a note on the counter. It's not like I ran off without telling him."

A moment later, the phone rang again. Andy dried his hands

and pulled the cell from his pocket, flipping it open. "Gabe, I told you, I'm over at Mrs. Decker's. Playing cards. Yeah. Well, yeah. Tomorrow at three, Candace said she'd give me a ride. Yes, I took them. No." Andy sighed. "Fine, all right! I'll get to it, I told you! Fine. Hey. Hey, Gabe?"

But apparently Gabe had already disconnected, because Andy shoved the phone back into his pocket. "I was going to ask him if he could come and take a look at the dishwasher."

"Oh, that's okay."

"No, really." Andy sounded eager, which also reminded her of Bennett and how he could be when he wanted something for some reason he didn't feel like he could be up-front with her about. "He fixes all kinds of stuff. He's supergood with his hands."

She laughed at that, though she had no suspicions Andy was talking in innuendo. "Oh, I'll bet he is."

"He can fix a lot of things," Andy said wistfully. His gaze went unfocused for a few seconds as he stared past her with such intent Janelle turned to see what he was looking at. Then his gaze snapped back to her face. "Not everything, though."

"Nobody can fix everything, Andy."

"Too bad, huh?" he said.

"Yeah," she said. "Too bad."

NINE

Then

"EVENTUALLY, I'M GOING TO GET A GENERATOR out here. Propane tank. Maybe some solar panels—I read in *Popular Mechanics* how it's the wave of the future. Self-sufficient houses." Gabe flips the light switch up and down. Nothing happens, of course, since the wires in the walls, which still aren't covered with drywall, don't connect to anything.

Janelle shivers. Her breath puffs out in front of her in a silver plume. "I can't believe you built all this yourself. How long have you been working on it?"

"A long time. Years. My dad used to take me hunting with some buddies, but they stopped going when I was about twelve. And I missed it. So…" He shrugs, pretending it doesn't mean very much. Anyone else would've made him feel stupid about all this, but Janelle never does.

"Is that a loft?" She's already put her foot on the ladder and is halfway up before Gabe can think to warn her off. Janelle peeks over the edge of the railing, then twists to look down at him. Her giggle sends heat all through him, welcome in the unheated room.

"Nice," she says. "Porn-o-rama."

It's just a collection of old skin mags and a beat-up mattress with a sleeping bag. A camping lantern. He's slept out here only a few times. Eventually, he'll make the loft into a full second floor, maybe with a couple bedrooms.

"Do you bring other girls out here?" She disappears over the edge of the loft.

He can hear her shuffling around up there, and goes to the ladder. "No."

Janelle peers over the edge. "No? Really?"

"Really."

She dangles her feet. He could grab her ankle if he wanted, she's that close, but Gabe only climbs the ladder halfway.

"How come?" Janelle sounds serious, not smug.

He wonders if she'd have been jealous if he'd said yes. Sometimes a few buddies, sometimes his brothers. But no other girls. "There isn't any girl I'd want to bring out here."

"Seems like a great place for a party," she says. "I can think of loads of girls who'd like to come out here with you."

"I don't have parties."

"I know you don't, Gabe." Janelle rolls her eyes. "But if you did, you could have them here. Who owns the land?"

It's a practical question, and he shouldn't be surprised she asked it. She's a practical kind of girl. "My dad. He started this place. It was really just a storage shed where he kept some hunting supplies. He always said he was going to turn it into a real camp, but he didn't. So I did."

"What does he think?"

Gabe climbs the rest of the ladder to sit next to her with his feet hanging over the edge. Below them is the square room without dividers, a space blocked out for a kitchen. He's planned on a small camp stove, a propane-powered fridge. There may never be indoor plumbing—that's beyond what he thinks he can do—but there is an outhouse in the back and he's done some research into composting toilets. The work's been haphazard, piecemeal, and cobbled together from scrap lumber and scrounged materials. It's garbage, most of it, but he's done his best and it's not too shabby a job.

"He doesn't know."

She twists toward him. "What do you mean, he doesn't know?"

Gabe shrugs. "There's a lot the old man doesn't know."

"He doesn't come out here anymore?"

"Not really. If he does, he's never said anything. And he would, if he knew about it." Gabe's sure about that.

Janelle pulls up her feet and scoots backward. She stands, her hands on the railing, to look over it. From this angle, she looks so tall, but he knows she's not. She'd fit just under his chin, if he ever hugged her.

She takes a few steps back to the mattress and sits. She flicks through one of the ancient magazines and pushes it aside. "I'm cold. You're always so warm. Hot-blooded, Gabe. That's you. Come here."

The sleeping bag's not really big enough for two, but they manage to squeeze into it, anyway. Janelle pulls the flap up over their faces like a tent. Other girls smell like perfume. Janelle smells of cigarette smoke and hair spray and fresh air.

"Why'd you bring me here?" She turns on her side, her butt against his groin, and takes his arm to put around her.

It's easy to answer her when he doesn't have to see her face. "Because...I thought you'd get it. You'd understand."

She doesn't say anything for a long time, so long Gabe starts to doze. If this was another girl, she'd expect him to kiss her now. With another girl he wouldn't be able to sleep like this. His heat has warmed the air inside the sleeping bag, enough that a trickle of sweat tickles down his spine. She's linked their fingers and put his hand flat against her belly, inside her coat, under her shirt.

"Understand what?" She sounds as sleepy as he is, and somehow this also makes it easy to answer.

"How it feels to need a place that's only yours, so you never have to..."

Janelle takes a snuffling breath. "Never have to what?"

"Rely on anyone for anything. You know what it's like to want a place of your own so that when everyone else leaves, you still have a place to go."

She's quiet for another long few minutes, so long he starts dreaming. When she shifts and rolls toward him, her head does fit right under his chin. His arms go around her. Her knee nudges between his. They fit together like puzzle pieces.

He's wide-awake now, embarrassed to be wrong. His heart pounds. He tries to push away from her, but the sleeping bag's too small, and Janelle's got her arms around him, too tight.

He's said too much.

Janelle doesn't tell him he's right.

But she doesn't tell him he's wrong.

TEN

AT THE KNOCK ON THE DOOR, THE OLD MAN shouted, "Tell them we don't want any!"

Gabe, who'd been reading on the couch, ignored him. At this time of evening it wouldn't be a salesman or a Jehovah's Witness, but that didn't mean whoever was on the other side would be any more welcome. He answered it, anyway, surprised to find Janelle.

She wore a heavy coat, a knit cap squashed down over her hair, a long striped scarf wound around her throat. She smiled brightly. "Hey."

Gabe didn't open the door wide enough to let her in, and he didn't glance over his shoulder to look at the old man, who shouted out, "Who's there? Who is it?"

"Hey, Mr. Tierney," Janelle called, peeking around Gabe. "It's Janelle Decker from next door."

"Jesus, don't keep her standing in the cold. Let her in."

Gabe didn't move to do that. He stepped outside and pulled the door shut behind him. "What's up? Andy's not here."

"What makes you think I'm here for him?"

"Because he's been over there a lot since you moved in." Gabe's breath became smoke, and he wished it was from a cigarette. "Just figured you'd want to talk to him. But he's at work until ten."

"I know. I came to talk to you." She bounced on the soles of her feet, still grinning. "You're not going to let me come in?"

She'd never, in all the times he could remember, ever come in the front door. Always through the bedroom window. Once or twice through the back. Never through the front, and tonight wasn't going to be the first time.

He hadn't said a word, but her smile faded. "Umm...okay, well...I just came over because Andy said you could fix our dishwasher."

"What's wrong with it?"

"I don't know. It doesn't wash the dishes. I guess if I knew more than that, I could fix it myself, huh?" She eyed him. "I could call a service center. I just thought I'd ask you instead."

"Save yourself some money."

Janelle's smile tipped a little wider. "No. I'll pay you. It's not that, Gabe."

He didn't ask her what else it was, but she told him, anyway.

"It's good to see you again. I thought maybe..." She trailed off, sounding uncertain in a way he could never remember her being.

He didn't want to hear any more. "Yeah. I'll come. Let me grab my tools. Now?"

"Sure. Or another time, if you want, that's fine. I mean, sooner rather than later, obviously." She bounced again, rubbing her mittened hands together and blowing out a steamy breath. "God. So cold."

"I guess it would be, when you're used to California."

Janelle paused, tilting her head just a little. "You know about that?"

He'd said too much. "I'll be over in a few minutes."

He shut the door in her face. The old man looked at him expectantly. "Was that the Decker girl? What did she want? Why'd you make her stay outside? Ashamed of your old man, that's what you are."

Ashamed wasn't the right word. Gabe ignored him and got his tools from their place in the kitchen closet. He thought about going out the back door without a word, but the old man would wonder, and it would be worse when he came back.

"I'm going next door to the Deckers' to see if I can fix the dishwasher."

"Oh, she crooks her finger and you go running?"

"Dad, please. Shut up," Gabe said. "You don't have any idea what you're talking about, okay?"

The old man laughed heartily and pointed. "Maybe if I had a set of titties you'd be more interested in fixing things around this shit hole."

Gabe's jaw went tight, but he knew better than to rise to the old man's jabs. Ralph Tierney wanted to be discontent and grouchy, and he'd always find a way to do it. Gabe lifted his tools in farewell instead, and left his father alone.

Next door, he entered a world of warmth and the good smells of something baking, and laughter. A boy, Janelle's kid, slapped down an Uno card on the table and tossed back his head, his hair too long. He crowed with glee as Mrs. Decker, sitting across from him, fanned out her cards and shook her head.

They both looked up when he came in the door. Mrs. Decker appeared surprised, the kid only curious. Janelle poked her head around the kitchen doorway.

"Hey!"

"Gabe Tierney," Nan said. "What on earth?"

"I asked him to come over and fix the dishwasher," Janelle explained. "Come on in. Bennett, this is Mr. Tierney."

"Gabe. Mr. Tierney's my old man."

"You're Andy's brother," Bennett said. "He said you were good at fixing stuff."

"I guess we'll find out." Gabe lifted the tools, uncomfortable under Mrs. Decker's scrutiny.

She gave him a steady, solid look that made him feel like that seventeen-year-old punk again, the one defiling her granddaughter. He'd lived next door to Maureen Decker his entire life. She'd never been unkind to him, but she'd never been overly sweet to him, either, the way some adults had been while he was growing up. If "those Tierney boys" had ever curled Mrs. Decker's lip or moved her to pity, she hadn't shown it. She'd given him Popsicles and chased him out of her apple tree and put candy in his trick-or-treat bag. She'd hollered at him more than once, when she thought he needed it. She'd treated him like she treated all the other neighborhood kids, and Gabe had never forgotten that.

Janelle showed him the dishwasher. "It's ancient. I'm not sure you can do anything for it, really."

"I'll take a look." Gabe got on one knee and hunted for a screwdriver to open up the bottom panel. It came away easily enough, and what was inside wasn't anything he'd never seen before. If anything, these older models were easier to fix because they didn't rely on all the electronic bells and whistles the new ones did.

He was aware of Janelle watching him. Too aware. Her heavy winter clothes had been hiding a pair of black leggings and an oversize T-shirt cut at the neck so it hung off one shoulder. She wore thick, bunched socks and stood with one hip against the counter and her foot propped against the inside of her calf. It was strange seeing her as a redhead, even though that was how he'd always thought of her even when she'd been dying her hair black.

"Do you think you can fix it?"

"Yes. It'll need a couple new parts, but you can get them at the hardware store. I'll write a list."

Janelle sighed. "Will they be expensive?"

Gabe looked up at her. From the living room came a burst of laughter that gave him pause before he answered. "Cheaper than a new dishwasher."

"Yeah. Of course." She laughed. "And better than washing all the dishes by hand, I guess."

They didn't have a dishwasher, working or broken, at the Tierney house. The old man had probably never washed a dish in his life. He'd firmly believed chores like that belonged to women and children...even grown children who still lived at home.

She was still watching him, her gaze a tickle on the back of his neck. Gabe carefully replaced the screws on the front panel and got to his feet. "Do you have some paper and a pen? I'll write down what you need."

"Yeah, sure. In the drawer." She leaned past him to reach it. She smelled good.

Gabe backed up a step. She noticed, of course. She was sharp like that. She pulled open the drawer, the contents rattling, and sighed.

"Huh, not here. I'll have to get some from upstairs. Be right back." She looked into his eyes when she moved past him, holding his gaze for several long seconds.

She'd been gone for only a minute when Bennett came into the kitchen. "Hi."

"Hey." Gabe looked up from the tool bag he was putting back in order. "Bennett, right?"

The kid nodded and brushed his hair out of his eyes. "I came to get a drink."

Gabe got out of the way, shoving his bag with a foot so it slid across the linoleum. The kid took a glass from the cupboard, then opened the fridge to pull out a gallon of milk. "You want some?"

"Uh...no, thanks."

"You want a soda? Or my mom has a few beers in there." The kid gave him that same curious head tilt his mother had.

Gabe shook his head. "No, thanks."

Bennett sipped some milk and licked at the mustache it left behind. "Did you fix it?"

"Not yet."

"But you will," the kid said.

"I hope so. If I can get the right parts. It's pretty old," Gabe said. "But...I'll do what I can."

The kid beamed. "Good. Loading and unloading it is my chore, but if it's broken, guess what my chore is."

"Taking out the trash?"

"That, too," Bennett said. "But also washing the dishes. It freaking sucks."

A smile tugged at the corners of Gabe's mouth, though he did his best to keep it straight. "Hey, language."

Bennett looked surprised. "You think *freaking*'s a bad word?"

He didn't, exactly, and it wasn't even his place to have said anything to begin with. It had just slipped out automatically. To his horror, it was the sort of thing his old man would've said. Gabe grimaced.

Bennett frowned. "Don't tell my mom, okay? She'll be mad."

In high school, Janelle had had a vast and colorful vocabulary. It had included a lot of creative curses that went well beyond the normal four-letter words. *Freaking* wouldn't even have registered on her radar.

"You knew my mom when she was little, huh?"

It was weird the way he'd echoed Gabe's thoughts from just a few moments ago, and Gabe stuttered a little bit on his answer. "Um, yeah. I did."

Bennett nodded. "Nan said you did. She said you've lived next to her since you were born. How long is that?"

"A long time."

"So you knew my mom when she lived here, with Nan?"

Gabe looked at the ceiling again, wondering if he could just write down the parts he needed at home and give them to Andy to bring over. Hell, he could just go to the hardware store himself and buy them. He didn't want to stand here talking to Janelle's son about knowing her, but the kid was clearly waiting for an answer.

"Yeah, I knew her."

"You went to school together?"

"Yeah."

"Same grade?"

"Yes," Gabe said, irritated now. "Jesus, kid. What's with the interrogation?"

Bennett frowned for a second. "Sorry. My mom says the only way to ever find anything out is if you ask questions. I just wanted to know what she was like when she was younger."

"So why don't you ask her?"

Bennett shrugged. "Duh, you think the stories she tells me are the ones I'd think were more interesting to hear? Or just the sorts of things a parent tells a kid."

"What kinds of things would you want to hear?" Gabe nudged his tool bag with a toe, getting ready to pick it up and make his exit.

THE *favor*   81

"You know, the good stuff. Maybe you don't know any good stuff."

Gabe looked at the kid seriously. "If I did, you think I'd tell you?"

"Maybe." Bennett shrugged again. "Andy knew my mom in high school, too—she says he did. But he doesn't remember her at all. So I figured you must remember. Especially if you were good friends."

"Did she...tell you that?" Gabe bent for the tool bag, hefting its weight so the contents jingled. "She talked about me?"

"Nope. Not really. But you knew each other. You lived next door. Went to school together." The kid gave Gabe another of those curious head tilts; it made his hair fall in front of his face until he shook it out. "She talks a lot about her other friends. Mom says the friends you make in school are the ones you remember best, and if you're lucky they stay with you."

"Sometimes if you're unlucky," Gabe muttered.

"The kids here are dickweeds."

Gabe shouldn't have laughed; the kid was clearly serious. But he looked so much like his mother. It reminded Gabe of too much that had happened, and he couldn't do anything but stare. Bennett's smile, so much like Janelle's, slid off his face.

"I've moved four times since I was born. Including this time, that's five times." Bennett ticked them off on his fingers. "We moved when I was a baby, two times. I don't remember it. Then when I was in first grade. Third grade. Now here. I had friends in my old school, but I haven't made any here yet."

"You will."

Bennett scowled. "I liked California better, but Mom says Pennsylvania's nicer in the summer. And no earthquakes."

The kid paused expectantly, waiting for Gabe to answer. Again, he had nothing to say. The kid was chatty. Weren't kids supposed to be shyer than that? Most kids around here gave Gabe a wide berth.

"Bennett! I thought you were bringing me something to drink!" Mrs. Decker called from the other room. "Did you fall in the sink and go down the drain?"

"Just a minute, Nan." Bennett filled a second glass with milk and put the jug back in the fridge. "Sure you don't want anything, Mr. Tierney?"

"Call me Gabe."

Bennett shrugged. "Okay, Gabe."

That's when Janelle finally came back into the kitchen, carrying a legal pad and a pen. Gabe saw what had taken her so long upstairs—she'd pulled her hair on top of her head into a soft bun that he knew from past experience looked casual and messy on purpose, but had really taken effort. She'd swiped on some gloss, maybe powder or something on her nose and cheeks to fade her freckles a little. Nothing major, nothing he was supposed to notice she'd done…but he did.

"Sorry it took so long. I have a lot of stuff still shoved in boxes." Janelle smiled as she held out the paper and pen. "Here."

In order to take it, Gabe had to set down the tools again. He did so quickly, ignoring the kid still standing there with the two glasses of milk, along with his mother and her makeup and her familiar smile. Gabe wrote the list, three items, scrawling the last so fast it was illegible.

"Your handwriting hasn't changed much," she noted.

"It says it's a hose," Gabe snapped. "Just look closer."

Bennett took that as a cue to leave. Janelle looked at Gabe with her mouth slightly parted as though she meant to speak, but didn't. After a second, her brow furrowed and her mouth thinned. She was pissed.

"Sorry," she said. "I'll get these things tomorrow. Maybe you can..."

"I'll be busy tomorrow." Gabe lifted the tool bag and moved past her into the living room, where Mrs. Decker was busy passing out cards.

Janelle followed him onto the back porch and beyond, catching him just outside the back door. "Gabe, wait."

He didn't turn at first, then did, slowly. "I have to go."

"Just let me know when you can do it. I can pick up these things tomorrow and you can let me know. Okay?" She gave him a half-watt smile.

"I have a lot of jobs scheduled."

"You can come anytime. I'll be here...."

"I'll be working. Or sleeping." Gabe shifted the weight of the tool bag to his other hand. "Look, maybe you should call a service center. I'm not a dishwasher repairman. You should get a professional."

"And here I thought you *were* a professional. What with your own business and all." Janelle's voice dipped the way it always had when she was doing her best to get her way. He hadn't known back then when he was a stupid kid what she'd been up to, but a couple decades of experience with women had taught Gabe a lot.

He didn't stop or turn again, but that didn't keep Janelle from calling after him even as he hopped over the retaining wall and climbed the steps to his own back porch.

"I said I'd pay you, Gabe. It's not like I'm asking you to do me a *favor.*"

There it was at last, the accusation he'd been waiting for, and could he blame her for sounding so pissed off about it?

"I only did it because you wanted me to," she says. "Because you asked. I did it because you asked me to, Gabe! How can you blame me for that, when you asked me to do it?"

"Gabe!"

"Hire someone else," was all he said as he went inside his own house. "You'll be better off."

ELEVEN

THEY'D MADE IT THROUGH THE FIRST COUPLE weeks of the new school and new routines. Bennett was testing out of some of his classes but woefully behind in others. Apparently the academy had been great with providing plenty of alternative and arts education, but not so helpful when it came to standardized tests. Sure, her kid could identify a Van Gogh, a Dali and a Warhol, but he couldn't figure out a word problem.

Nan had been in good spirits and perky, for the most part, but she insisted on doing so much for herself that Janelle felt run more ragged than if her grandma simply stayed on the couch and allowed herself to be waited on. If she wasn't trying to cook something, setting off the smoke alarm, she was up at all hours of the night trying to run the washing machine or watching television with the volume set too loud. She'd lived alone too long, was Nan's explanation, and she was used to doing for herself. At least as long as she could, anyway.

It would take some time to fully settle in. Janelle had expected that. She hadn't imagined how exhausting it would be just trying to get into a routine that worked for all of them.

Tonight, Bennett's own weariness showed in the faint circles below his eyes and the way he picked at his dinner. She'd ordered pizza, along with hot wings and garlic sticks and a two-liter bottle of soda. Friday night had always been pizza night at Nan's house.

"How was school?"

He shrugged, silent.

It wasn't an answer, but Janelle was too tired to push. She folded her slice in half to keep all the good grease from dripping out. "Nan, is anyone coming over?"

Nan had taken only a bread stick to start. She looked faintly surprised. "Who'd come over?"

"Betsy and the kids? Uncle Joey and Aunt Deb?" Janelle licked orange grease from the heel of her hand and gave a little moan of appreciation. Pizza in California was just not the same. On the other hand, she was pretty sure she wasn't going to find any decent sushi in St. Marys.

"Why would they come over?"

"To visit?" Everyone had always gone to Nan's house on Friday nights to play cards, eat pizza. Later, to watch rented movies on the VCR. The kids would play while the adults talked and drank beer. When Janelle was older, Friday night had still been pizza night, only the Tierney boys had usually come over for cards and late-night TV.

"Oh, honey, they're all busy."

"Too busy to visit you?" Janelle frowned.

Nan shrugged. "They have families of their own. It's really too far to drive in just for the evening."

Of course, Janelle had known that, but she'd forgotten what that really meant. St. Marys was at least an hour's drive from

Dubois, more on snowy, icy roads. But Betsy lived in Kersey. That wasn't so far.

Nan picked apart the bread stick with shaky hands and put the pieces on her plate. She dabbed some marinara sauce next to them, but didn't eat anything. She took a slice of pizza and began dissecting it the same way.

Janelle watched this carefully. She'd had a friend in high school who'd practiced the same sort of deception to hide an eating disorder. "Nan, if you don't want pizza, I can make you something else."

Nan frowned. "Don't be silly. I love pizza."

"Not enough to eat it," Janelle pointed out.

Bennett, God love him, rallied and reached for another slice. "It's good, Nan. This is the best pizza I ever ate."

Both women looked at him. Bennett, unselfconscious, bit into the slice and tore the cheese from it in a huge, gloppy string that splashed sauce all over his shirt. He chewed, making snuffling sounds Janelle reprimanded with a look.

"Nan, let me make you some toast or something. I could heat up some soup. I have chicken noodle or tomato."

Her grandmother shook her head, then covered her eyes with her hand, leaving her trembling mouth to show she fought tears. "I don't want anything, honey, I just need to go to bed."

Janelle's stomach tightened. "Don't you feel good?"

Stupid question—the woman was eighty-three years old, suffering from high blood pressure, anemia and a brain tumor. Chances were she never felt good. Nan shrugged without taking her hand away from her eyes.

Janelle got up and put a hand on her shoulder. "Let me help you to bed. I can bring you something in a little while, if you want. Bennett, finish up and then clear the table."

Nan didn't protest when Janelle hooked a hand under her

elbow to help her up, proof of how bad she really felt. Janelle guided her grandma through the kitchen and to the hall, though Nan paused at the bathroom.

"I need to go."

"Okay. I can help you."

Nan made a noise, but didn't argue, just let Janelle help her to the toilet. Janelle lifted her nightgown, helped her pull down her incontinence pants. The toilet had been fitted with a high seat and bars, but Nan was still a little unsteady as she sat.

There was no good way to do this, no way to make it anything but awkward. Janelle had changed her son's diapers and nursed him through a variety of childhood stomach bugs, but that was completely different than standing in the bathroom doorway as her beloved grandmother groaned with cramps. Nan gripped the railing and turned her face.

"I'm sorry."

"Don't be sorry." Janelle forced herself not to cover her mouth and nose with her hand, but after only a few seconds, she had to step outside the bathroom. She closed her eyes and put her face to the door frame, but only for a second because Bennett spoke up from the kitchen.

"Mama?"

Janelle donned a smile, turning toward him. "Yeah, buddy."

"Can I go play my game?"

"Is your homework finished?"

"It's Friday," Bennett began, then sighed. "After I'm done?"

"If you do it now," she pointed out, "you won't have to worry about it for the rest of the weekend."

The toilet flushed, and Janelle peeked inside the bathroom. Nan was still looking away from her, frail shoulders slumped. "I have to help Nan now. Go do what I asked you to do, please. And we'll watch a movie or something after I get her to bed."

In the bathroom, Janelle stood for a moment, uncertain

of how to help. Nan looked at her, and though her face was wan, there was a bit of a twinkle in her eyes. She gestured at the built-in wall cabinet.

"Baby wipes are in there, honey. We can use those." The twinkle faded as her mouth turned down. "I'm sorry to even ask you…"

Janelle opened the cupboard, found the wipes. Shook her head. "Shh, Nan. Don't."

Nan gripped her arm as she moved to help clean her up. "Thank you, Janelle. For coming here."

Janelle looked into her grandmother's eyes. "I'm happy to do it. Let's get you into bed."

It still took much longer to get Nan ready for bed than Janelle had anticipated. First the meds, a plethora of pills from a small plastic case with sections for each day of the week, entirely different from the ones she took in the daytime. Then she had to brush her teeth, which she could still do on her own, but took twice as long as seemed normal. She had to put on her face lotion, not for wrinkles, she said, but to keep her skin from being too dry. Also a simple task that took so much time Janelle found herself itching to take over and just do it for her, rather than watching. She didn't.

At last, Nan was in a soft flannel gown and tucked into the double bed that had been her wedding furniture, propped on her pillows, the lamp on and giving her enough light to read by. She held the thick hardcover in shaking hands for a moment before she sighed and let it sink onto the blankets covering her belly. She needed a lap desk, Janelle thought, but a pillow would have to do. She folded one in half and propped the book against it.

Nan smiled. "Oh, that's so much better, honey. Thank you. I'm only going to read for a while, then go to sleep. What are you and Benny going to do?"

"Watch a movie or something." There was laundry waiting, the kitchen to clean. But Nan didn't need to know that. "I'm pretty tired, too. I'll probably turn in early myself."

The sound of breaking glass woke Janelle some hours later, after she'd finally managed to fall asleep. Eyes wide and heart pounding, she bolted from bed, out the bedroom door and halfway across the hall before she even really knew she was awake. She went automatically to Bennett's room, finding his door cracked a little and a faint light from inside. He'd never needed a night-light in California, but had found one here and had been using it. Janelle hadn't said anything about it and was grateful for it now as she pushed his door open just enough to see that he was sleeping soundly, mouth open, one arm flung above his head.

She'd been dreaming about Gabe and his brothers, of that night in the woods when everything went wrong, and her skin felt clammy, her pajama shirt damp with sweat that still trickled down her back. When she licked her upper lip, it tasted of nightmares, so she swiped at it with her sleeve. She paused at the head of the stairs, imagining herself tumbling down them headfirst to end up broken at the bottom.

She might've convinced herself she'd dreamed the sound of glass breaking, if not for the hint of light at the bottom of the stairs. She raced down them as fast as she could without making her imagined fall come true. The light was coming from the kitchen. Not bright enough to be from the overhead light. Something smaller. The fridge, she discovered when she went into the kitchen and found Nan at the sink, holding her hand under the water. Glass littered the floor, along with a puddle of spilled juice still spreading as it gurgled from the container lying there.

"What happened?"

Nan half turned, the front of her nightgown soaked through with juice. "I was thirsty. Got up. Danged glass was slippery."

"Let me see." Ignoring Nan's frown, Janelle turned on the overhead light and took her grandmother's hand gently. "You cut yourself."

The wound didn't look deep, but it was still bleeding. Janelle glanced at the mess on the floor, the juice and glass, then again at the cut. She wrapped it in a clean dish towel. "Stay right here. Don't move."

She shut the fridge door, then tossed another tea towel over the mess on the floor to sop up the juice as she found the broom and dustpan. The glass had broken neatly enough into two sections that didn't appear to have shattered too badly, though she knew from experience that her bare feet would find any pieces she didn't sweep up. The floor would be sticky until she could mop it, but for now the mess had been contained.

She moved back to Nan, who stood patiently at the sink. "Let's get this taken care of."

First, she washed the cut gently, careful not to press too hard. Nan winced, anyway. Janelle spread a thin layer of antibiotic ointment, then wrapped it in gauze bandages. She helped Nan back to her bed and beneath the blankets.

"What were you doing?" Janelle tried not to sound accusatory or angry.

"I was thirsty," Nan said with a frown.

"You should've called for me. I'd have brought you something."

"I'm not crippled," Nan protested. "Besides, you were sleeping. I didn't want to wake you."

"It's what I'm here for, Nan."

Her grandmother frowned again, shifting under the blankets. "I didn't want to wake Benny."

Janelle sighed. A monitor, that's what she needed. Like

the one she'd used for Bennett as a baby. "You can't... You could've really hurt yourself. That's all. I'm supposed to take care of you. From now on, if you need to get up in the middle of the night, just call for me, okay? I'll help you."

Janelle bent to kiss her cheek. So many times as a child, Nan had bent over her this way, and Janelle found herself echoing what her grandma had always said, what Janelle had always said to Bennett since he was a baby. "Good night, sleep tight, and may the angels watch over you until morning."

"They will," Nan said.

Upstairs in her own bed, sleep didn't return so easily. Where were her angels? Janelle turned on her side, looking at the window. She didn't have any, she thought. She didn't deserve any.

She thought of the dream she'd been having, of that night in the woods. Of what had happened after. Terri Gilmore had asked her if she was still in town when Gabe shot Andy in the head, and she'd said no, feeling it was a lie. The truth was she'd already gone, but what she'd done had set everything in motion.

She might as well have pulled the trigger herself.

TWELVE

Then

"LOOK. I HAVE THE STRING AND THE CANS. IT'LL work, it'll be fun. C'mon, Gabe." Janelle shows him the paper grocery bag with all the stuff in it.

Gabe is so tired he only wants to sleep, but Mrs. Moser shoved him out of bed this morning and won't let him back in the house until lunch. The twins are playing out back in the sandbox, all their trucks and cars rusted. Their buckets are broken, too. They always ask him to come build racing tracks and castles with them, but he doesn't feel like it today.

So he's stuck with this girl and her stupid ideas for a stupid tin can telephone. Gabe refuses to admit he thinks it would be pretty cool, if it works. He looks into the bag. Chicken-and-stars soup. They never have chicken and stars, only chicken noodle. He bets stars taste better.

"You go up to your room and I'll go up to mine, and you throw the can across to me," Janelle says.

"We'll get in trouble."

"Who's gonna know?" she says with her hands on her hips.

"Anyone who looks up there, dummy."

Janelle rolls her eyes. "Who's gonna look up? It's a skinny string, and there are already wires from the 'lectric pole up there."

"Great, so we can get electrocuted?" Gabe yawns without putting a hand over his mouth. He's so tired his stomach hurts. So tired he wants to die.

Janelle yawns a second after him, because yawns are the same as colds. Contagious. "We won't. But if you don't want to do it, fine."

She crumples up the top of the bag and makes like she's going to go into her house. She doesn't get very far before Gabe's telling her to wait. She turns, smiling, and he feels like a jerk because she played him.

"I can't go in the house," he tells her. "Mrs. Moser is cleaning and she said I have to stay out here."

Janelle frowns. "Huh?"

Gabe gestures at his house. "She says we can't come in until it's time for lunch."

"What if you have to go to the bathroom?"

Gabe points to the hedgerow at the back of his yard.

"What if it's number two?" Janelle makes a face. "Gross!"

If Mrs. Moser knew Gabe and his brothers all happily peed outside behind the hedge, he's sure she'd not only insist they come inside to use the toilet, she'd also make them scrub their hands in bleach or something, and he has no idea what sort of cleaning she'd do to the bushes. She already thinks Gabe and his brothers run "too wild."

"I know," Janelle says with a snap of her fingers, before Gabe can come up with a supergross description of where they poop when they're not allowed in the house. "Get your brothers to ask for a snack, and while she's distracted, you sneak in the front door and go upstairs."

She's good, this girl. Sneaky. Gabe can't stop himself from grinning back at her.

"Why do you want to do this so bad?"

"Why don't you?" She asks with that tilt of her head she usually has when looking at him. As if she can never quite figure him out. "It'll be fun."

Fun? Gabe doesn't know about that. Janelle visits her grandma only once in a while, and even if she is pretty cool for a girl, they'll get to use the tin can telephone only a few times. If it even works.

"You don't have anything better to do," she points out. "Later, my Nan says we can hook up the sprinkler if you want, but not until after lunch. Can you ride your bike to the park?"

Gabe shakes his head. "I'm grounded."

"You're grounded all the time. You must get into trouble a lot."

He does and he doesn't. But Gabe doesn't want to tell Janelle about how his dad gets. Her dad's young and fun. He drives a motorcycle and wears a leather jacket. She'd never understand.

Gabe takes the cans and the string, studying how to put them together. "We need a nail and a hammer."

"I bet Nan has some in the shed."

The shed, set back on the Deckers' property, looks like a little house. Inside it's dark and hot, smelling of gasoline from the lawn mower. Tools, deflated basketballs and old sleds line the walls. Built into one side is a set of bunk beds, as if this was once a clubhouse. It's full of spiders, and they get out in a hurry.

Gabe punches a hole in each can, and Janelle threads the string. Then she calls the boys over. They come at once. Mikey and Andy like Janelle.

She explains the idea to them, how they're to go to the back
door and ask Mrs. Moser for Popsicles. If she won't give them
Popsicles, they need to ask for cold drinks with ice. And then,
Gabe's sneaking in the front door while his brothers distract
Mrs. Moser at the back.

He climbs the stairs quickly, holding the cans and string
close to him so he doesn't drop them or get anything tangled
up. In his room he opens the window, to see Janelle at hers.
She opens it and leans out so far he thinks she might fall.

"Look, Gabe. We could almost touch hands." Janelle
stretches farther. "Look how close we are."

"You better be careful."

She laughs and wriggles out the window a little more. "You
don't even have to throw the can! Just pass it to me."

Gabe leans out the window. If he falls, he won't just break,
he'll splatter. He stretches to pass her the can, his belly pressing the windowsill. It takes hardly any time at all for them to
stretch the string tight.

Gabe can't sit here all day fooling around with it. It's almost
time for lunch, and he has to sneak down the stairs to go outside before Mrs. Moser calls for him. He closes the window
and the curtains.

He's at the top of the stairs when he gets caught. He didn't
know his dad was home from work that morning, so when
the old man's voice slithers out from the shadows of his dark
bedroom, Gabe's caught like a mouse snatched up by a snake.

"Come in here."

Gabe's feet don't want to obey, but he makes himself go
in, anyway. He's no longer tired from being woken up last
night and then being unable to fall back to sleep. Now he's
wide, wide awake.

Dad's in bed, but not in his pajamas. His curtains are shut
tight, the blind drawn. He's propped on his pillows, on top of

the blankets. The small light clipped to his headboard is on, but the rest of the room is dark. In front of him is a box full of pictures and letters.

"You're supposed to be outside."

"I know," Gabe says. "I came in because—"

His father waves a hand at him. "Shut up. I don't care. Come over here, closer."

Gabe does, thinking he could scream if he has to. Last night and all the nights before that, there wasn't anyone to hear him, so all he had was the ability to fight. Some night, he thinks, he's going to be too tired to do that anymore. But today Mrs. Moser is downstairs, and surely, if he screams, if he runs, she'll hear him. She'll help him…won't she?

The old man doesn't touch him. He just looks at him. Hard, and for a very long time. No smile, nothing that looks like anything nice. He stares until Gabe starts to sweat.

"She's the one who wanted kids, you know that? She wanted 'em, I didn't. I said, 'Marlena, why do we gotta go and mess up a good thing?' We had money, we could go out to dinner whenever we wanted. Nice car. I could buy her as many pretty dresses as she wanted. But no, she wanted kids, she said. So she got 'em. And then what? She found out they were as much a pain in the ass as I'd told her."

Gabe says nothing. It's nothing new; he's heard this story before. Or ones like it. The details change sometimes, but the stories are almost all the same.

"*You* made her sick. You know that?"

Gabe nods, hoping that if he agrees the old man will let him get out of here.

"She got sick, and now she's gone." His dad heaves a heavy sigh that turns into a choking cough.

He's crying. Gabe looks away. He's seen his father cry before, that's nothing new. Grown-ups aren't supposed to cry, he thinks. He won't when he's a grown-up. He won't now, no matter what.

"This is your fault, you remember that. You just remember it, Gabriel." Gabe's dad looks up at him with red eyes, his nose snotty. "And you better understand something else, too. If it's not you, it will be one of them."

Gabe jumps as if someone punched a fist through his chest and grabbed his heart. His stomach is a stone that hits the floor. He can't breathe or speak; he can't even move.

"So you just remember *that*," the old man says. "Now you get out of here before I take it into my head to give you the belting you deserve."

Gabe does as his father says, making it only halfway down the stairs before his stomach heaves up and out of his throat, and he has to run for the bathroom to lose his breakfast. Mrs. Moser finds him there, crouched over the toilet. She doesn't scold him. She wets a cloth and puts it on the back of his neck, and despite his every intention, Gabe can't stop himself from crying.

It won't be him. It won't be him. It won't be him.

THIRTEEN

AT FOURTEEN, JANELLE STILL WORE HER HAIR
in a ponytail and slept with her collection of stuffed toys.

At fifteen, she pierced her nose and dyed her hair black; she
bit her fingernails but painted them black, too. She pierced
her ears multiple times and wore a safety pin in one.

At sixteen, she painted her eyes with thick, dark eyeliner
and mascara, but left the rest of her face pale. She sneaked
out with older boys to drive to Harrisburg and Lancaster to
see bands she didn't even really like. Sometimes she let those
boys kiss her.

At seventeen, she smokes pot she buys from the farm boys
looking to get some extra cash to fix up their muscle cars
or buy steers to show at the Farm Show; she doesn't ask and
doesn't care. She steals liquor from her stepfather's cabinet and
tattoos a small star on the webbing of her right hand between
her thumb and forefinger. It takes her mother four months to
notice, though Randall figures out about the vodka and bour-
bon a lot sooner than that. At seventeen, Janelle doesn't have a

boyfriend she secretly hopes to marry, one who gives her his class ring or his letterman's jacket. She has a lot of boyfriends, but though everyone including her parents thinks she's sleeping with all of them, Janelle's still a virgin.

Janelle's mother tells her she has two choices—reform school or rehab. It's Nan who steps up to offer the third choice, to come and live with her. It sure isn't something Janelle's mom would've come up with on her own, and she's not happy about the idea. How on earth will Nan make sure Janelle behaves herself, when her own mother can't?

Maybe Nan understands that the booze and drugs, the makeup and clothes, are only things Janelle *does*. They aren't who she *is*. Maybe raising five boys makes Nan feel she can handle one wayward teenage girl.

Whatever it is, that's how Janelle finds herself unpacking her bags in Nan's upstairs bedroom the August before her senior year of high school. The last time she stayed here, two of her uncles were still in this room. She shared the small one across the hall with her dad, who was "taking a break" from the "grind of working" in order to focus on his music. The closet in that room is still full of his things. Boxes from his apartment, packed up and never opened. His leather jacket. A pair of boots. Nan said Janelle could have the small room if she wanted it, but Janelle doesn't want to be that close to all her dad's stuff.

The counselor at school told Janelle's mom it was normal for her to act out after her mom's remarriage. After the birth of her brother. After this. After that. The counselor and her mom both needed reasons and excuses. Janelle misses her dad, but she's not, as her stepdad says, trying to *be* her dad. It's ballsy of Randall to have an opinion about her at all, but Janelle understands that he needs reasons and excuses, too.

The truth is, it's all about power. Get a boy on his knees,

begging for just a touch, a taste, a stroking hand, and that's gaining power. Take a drink, smoke a joint, let your head get swimmy and the world go spinny—that's about giving it up. Give and take, high and low, up and down. Janelle hasn't decided yet which she likes best. Maybe there is no best. Maybe the world is one long and constant rise and fall.

Now she's here in Nan's house, sweating in the summer heat. Her shirt sticks to her skin. Sweat tangles her hair. When she runs her tongue along her upper lip, she tastes salt. She can smell herself, the tangy scent of her perfume and body odor, the lingering tinge of smoke from her clothes. Her mom confiscated all the cigarettes before Janelle left. She ran her hands inside the linings of Janelle's suitcases, in her pockets, searching for pot or pills. She found the stash easily enough; Janelle hadn't hidden it very well. She let her find it so her mom could go away satisfied she'd done everything she could. There'd always be more weed. It's all about power, and by giving her mom the illusion of it, Janelle keeps most of it for herself.

Opening the window might let in some cool air, but someone's painted the sill shut. It will take a screwdriver to pry it up. Muttering a curse, Janelle grips the painted wood. Her black nail polish is chipping, and she doesn't remember if she packed the bottle.

When her dad was working, he saw her once every few months for a weekend or a couple days. A week or so in the summer. Sometimes she came and spent a few weeks with Nan while her dad traveled. Janelle has many fond childhood memories of her time spent in St. Marys, but none of those visits have prepared her for what it's like to actually live here. One small movie theater. No mall. Still, even a town nestled so deep in the mountains it was like its own world had to be better than rehab or reform school.

And…hello. The brick house next door. That's where those

Tierney boys live. Gabriel is her age, and the twins, Andrew and Michael, four years younger. She used to hang out with Gabe sometimes when they were little kids, but she hasn't seen him in years.

Now she does.

A movement behind the curtains in the room directly across from hers alerts her, but with the light on in her room, it's hard to see. Janelle reaches for the lamp, turns it off. Blinking, she steps to one side to tug the curtain just enough for her to peer out.

Gabe Tierney went and growed himself up, Janelle thinks. He has the long, lean build of a swimmer, but his body is liberally sprinkled with hair. Something catches in her throat at the sight of his arms, abs and pecs as he turns from the dresser, where he must be searching for something to put on. She's been with boys before, but Gabe...he's a man.

Something strangled and low comes from her throat when he drops the towel. He's not facing her, but the back view is as nice as the front had been. More hair furs his thighs and a small dark patch at the base of his spine. She'd have thought a hairy butt would be gross, but all at once everything about him is so masculine she can't imagine how she ever thought smooth chests and bodies were attractive.

She can't handle the sight of his bare front, she knows she can't, but even though heat floods her, Janelle doesn't look away as Gabe pulls a pair of white briefs from his drawer. Turning with them in one fist, he's fully exposed. Everything. Every part of him is as perfect as the next, and she can't stand it. She's been with boys before, she's taken them in her fist and a few times even in her mouth. She's let them touch her, though their fumblings have never come close to making her feel as good as her own hand does. It's all about power.

And Gabe Tierney has it.

★ ★ ★

"No more," Janelle said aloud, twitching the curtains closed, though the temptation to keep watching was like a real physical force.

All of that had been a long time ago. They'd been kids, stupid, playing with things they didn't understand. She wasn't that girl anymore.

Downstairs, she found Nan dozing on the couch while Bennett sat at the table with his homework. The TV was showing a movie on mute, but when she crossed to turn it off, Nan jerked and woke. She clawed weakly at the air for a second before focusing.

"Oh, Janelle. Leave that on, I'm watching it."

"You fell asleep." Janelle grabbed the big-button remote and brought it over. "Can I get you something?"

Nan took the device in both hands. "I want to watch that horse movie."

Janelle had no idea what movie that might be, but didn't argue. "Bennett, how's the homework coming along?"

He shrugged. That wasn't a good sign. Looking over his shoulder, Janelle saw a page of haphazardly printed math problems with scribbled, indecipherable answers.

"Think you might want to redo some of those," she said mildly, but the sigh Bennett gave prompted one of her own. "Bennett. C'mon, buddy. We've talked about this. If I can't read your work, how can you expect your teacher to bother? If you don't put your best face forward—"

"I know, I know. How can I expect the world to take me seriously. I know." Bennett frowned. "Well, what if I only have one face, Mom? Huh?"

She reached to ruffle his long hair, but he ducked from her touch and she withdrew. "Nobody has only one face."

"Maybe I do."

"If you do," she countered, "it needs a scrubbing."

She meant it as a joke, but Bennett didn't take it that way. Instead, her sweet boy scowled, brows knitting and mouth turning down. A picture of his father. He turned away from her and hunched over his book again, the pencil with its worn eraser and teeth marks clutched so tight in his fist the knuckles turned white.

"Bennett."

"Forget it, Mom." He slapped the pencil onto the table, then slammed the book closed with a thump so loud Janelle jumped. Before she could say anything else, Bennett gathered his things and pushed past her into the kitchen. His feet thumped on the stairs moments later.

From her spot on the couch, Nan chuckled. "He's going to do his best to devil you, Janelle."

Janelle sat on the end of the couch near Nan's slippered feet. "He's a smart kid, he just doesn't apply himself. I mean, I know he gets the material, he's just… He just wants to rush through it to get to his video games and stuff. He doesn't take his time. He's not careful."

Nan laughed again. "Sounds like someone else I know."

Janelle's mouth quirked. "Hey. I was a good student."

"When you wanted to be." Nan gently shook a finger. "But there was no keeping you in that chair to do your homework, not if you didn't want to be there."

Janelle had another flashback, briefer this time. Sitting on her bed, knees drawn up to cradle the book in her hands, ostensibly studying, but instead watching Gabe Tierney walk naked from the shower.

"…if he's really having trouble," Nan said.

"Sorry, what?"

"I said, if you think he needs help with his math classes,

you should get Andrew to help him." Nan looked concerned. "Do you feel okay? You look a little flushed."

"I'm fine."

Nan patted her hand. "Your hands are like ice, honey. But your cheeks are all pink. Are you sure you're not coming down with something?"

Janelle squeezed Nan's fingers gently. "I'm okay. Are you warm enough? I can turn up the heat."

Nan shook her head. "No, no."

"Nan," Janelle said, "you know you don't need to worry about the oil bill, right? If you're cold, I should turn up the heat."

Stubbornly, Nan shook her head again. "I'm fine. I can just put on a sweater or get under the blanket. Bring me that afghan."

Janelle did, tucking the green-yellow-orange-and-brown-striped monstrosity around Nan's hips. "Did you make this?"

"Of course I did! I made it for your dad's high school graduation. Lordy, that was a long time ago." Nan plucked at the yarn, peering closely. "My goodness, how ugly."

Janelle laughed, then again, a little louder. She leaned to hug her grandmother. "Oh, Nan. I love you."

She smiled. "I love you, too, honey. And don't you worry about Benny. He's just having growing pains."

"I know." Janelle sighed and tugged the bottom of the afghan over her to warm her feet, tucked on the couch next to Nan's. "It'll all work out."

"Ask Andrew to help him, if he's struggling," Nan advised again.

"Andrew. From next door? Andy Tierney?" Nan nodded. Janelle laughed again, but saw Nan was serious. "But he's…"

"Oh, some things about him aren't right, that's for sure. The brain injury, you know." Nan leaned forward a little bit, to whisper, though there was nobody there to hear them. "And of course, he was always a little strange, anyway."

Of the three Tierney boys, Andy wasn't the one Janelle would've said was strange. Mikey had been a little weird. Gabe, just surly. Andy'd been goofy...well, mostly, at least until the end, when he'd changed. He had been smart in school, though. "How do you know he's good at math?"

"He plays those Sudoku puzzles." Nan waved an airy hand. "Also, he used to help me figure my coupons."

"Coupons...?"

"You know. All those coupon deals, buy three get one free, that sort of thing. Back when I was into that." Nan shrugged. "It got to be too much, but there were weeks I saved so much money, Janelle, I can't even tell you."

"And Andy helped you with that."

"You ask him," Nan said. "He'd be happy to help Benny with his homework, I'm sure of it."

FOURTEEN

ANDY MIGHT'VE BEEN HAPPY TO BE ASKED, BUT his brother was definitely not. By the way Gabe glared, you'd have thought she was asking him to donate an organ, not spend a few hours a week tutoring. Janelle glared back.

"I'll pay him, if that's what you're worried about."

"She'll pay me," Andy repeated, delighted as Bennett would've been about being offered a new video game or a trip to an amusement park. "Forty dollars a week, Gabe!"

"If that's not enough, if you think he deserves more…" Janelle shrugged. "I checked into the going rate for tutors through the school, and they get less than that."

"Oh, let 'im do it. What do you care about it, anyway?" This came from Mr. Tierney in his recliner, feet up, in the corner. "Always trying to act like you run the place."

Gabe didn't even glance at his father, but his mouth thinned. He crossed his arms over his chest. He didn't look at Andy, either. He stared unrelentingly and unblinkingly at Janelle. "He doesn't need the money."

"Everyone needs money." Mr. Tierney snorted into a hand-kerchief and folded it in half, then did it again. "You'd think so, too, if you didn't have enough."

"Who says I ever have enough?" Again, Gabe didn't look at his dad when he spoke, but at least he stopped staring at Janelle. "Between all that beer you're always drinking and Andy's lottery ticket habit—"

Andy did a brief, shuffling dance. "I'm going to win the lottery! I am! It's just a matter of finding the right numbers, the right numbers."

"You know why they call it the lottery, right? Because it's by chance. You can't predict it." Gabe shook his head and kept his gaze away from her.

Janelle understood why. He'd been in her face and belliger-ent since she walked through the door, but now he was embar-rassed. Ashamed, even. She might've reached out a comforting hand or even tried to give him a sympathetic look, but Gabe was having none of it. She shifted half a step forward and he took two back.

"I'm going to win," Andy repeated.

Awkward silence, broken only by the television's ranting and Mr. Tierney's honking nose. Janelle tried again, this time focusing on Andy. Giving Gabe space.

"Andy, if Gabe thinks you shouldn't help Bennett, maybe it's best if I get someone else." She kept her eyes on Andy's, ignoring the white streak in his hair and the way he shifted from foot to foot. "It's really okay."

"No, it's not!" His hands came together, fluttering, until the fingers linked and clutched. He made an obvious effort at holding them still. "I can do it, Gabe. I really can."

"Too much stress upsets you, Andy. C'mon. You know that. If you agree to do this, you can't just give up on the kid after a session or two. You'd have to stick with it until the end of the school year, or until he doesn't need you anymore. And you couldn't blow it off because you wanted to stay home and play your games."

Gabe sounded exasperated, and now Janelle understood. It must be exhausting dealing with his brother. Just because Andy could feed and dress himself, could get around—could tutor math, for God's sake—that didn't mean he wasn't disabled, Janelle realized. She was learning for herself how hard it could be to care for people who couldn't quite manage on their own but insisted on it, anyway. It was like having a child you'd never given birth to.

"I won't. I won't." Andy gave Janelle a pleading glance.

Oh, those eyes. Those blue Tierney eyes. They'd always been able to break her down, and this time was no different. "Honey, if Gabe says no..."

The endearment slipped out, made things worse, but Janelle lifted her chin and gave Gabe a head-on stare, daring him to say anything. He didn't, of course. How could he?

"Listen, you little shit. Let him do the damn tutoring, let the kid earn a few bucks. It's nothing off you. And you—" Mr. Tierney pointed a bent finger at Andy "—better buck up and stop that whining. Get your act together. You do this thing, like Gabe said, I don't wanna hear you whining about how you gotta go help that kid instead of farting around on that computer."

"I won't, Dad. I promise."

Gabe sighed and rubbed a hand over his eyes before scrubbing it back through his dark hair. The motion showed off the silver strands, and when he pulled his hand away, strain showed in his eyes, so much like Andy's in color but so different in the way they looked at her.

"Fine," he said. "Whatever, what the hell do I care?"

Janelle wondered that, herself.

"But you go there." Gabe stabbed a finger in the direction of Nan's house. "That kid doesn't come over here. You hear me, Andy? You go there, or meet him at the library, or whatever. He doesn't come here. Ever."

Andy nodded. "I got it. Jesus."

"Watch the mouth," Mr. Tierney said.

"Sorry, Dad."

Without another word or even a glance at her, Gabe stalked out of the room. The silence he left behind was louder than the TV. Mr. Tierney didn't seem to notice, and Andy definitely didn't.

"When do you want me to start?"

Janelle smiled at his enthusiasm and once again held herself back from ruffling his hair. "Tomorrow, why don't you come over around four-thirty? Bennett can show you what he's doing, and we can figure out how often you'll need to help him."

"I can come every day."

"I'm sure you won't need to do that, Andy." At the flash of disappointment on his face, Janelle added, "But I know my grandma loves having you over. So don't be a stranger, okay?"

Mr. Tierney's thick and rattling laugh turned both their heads. It changed into a cough, his shoulders shaking and his face turning the color of his red flannel shirt. He covered his mouth with the hanky, then spit into it. Then again.

"What's so funny?" Andy asked.

Mr. Tierney had blue eyes just like his sons, but his were rheumy, the whites yellowed. He showed his teeth, straight and too white to be natural. "You. You can't help being a stranger, can ya? Cuz that's what you are. Strange. Always have been, huh?"

Andy didn't look offended, but Janelle was on his behalf. "You come over whenever you want, Andy."

She reached to squeeze his arm, meaning to be reassuring, but she must've surprised him, because at the touch, Andy jerked his arm from her grasp. He whirled, eyes wide. It passed in a moment, nothing more than an automatic reaction, but Janelle stood with her mouth open and her arm outstretched. She pulled it back in a second, embarrassed and not sure if it was for him or for himself. Andy blinked, then grinned.

"Sorry," he told her matter-of-factly. "I'm a little crazy sometimes."

The grin had broken her heart, just a little. His statement finished the job. Janelle said a strangled goodbye around the lump in her throat, and let herself out the front door.

Andy stalks the halls without looking from side to side, gaze straight forward but seeing nothing. If you're in his way, he elbows past. If you step in front of him to catch his attention, you end up shoved against a locker.

"Hey!" Janelle says, pissed off. "Andy, what the hell?"

He turns, slow, slow, his face pale, blue eyes somehow dark. He looks at her without emotion. He says nothing.

Whatever Janelle meant to ask him is lost in the depths of that gaze, and she watches him walk away, feeling as if a goose is dancing on her grave.

Outside, the frigid air turned to smoke in front of her face, and the tears became glass on her cheeks. She paused on the bottom step of the Tierneys' front porch for a moment to swipe her eyes clear. The path was slippery enough without trying to navigate it with blurred vision. Snow crunched under her boots on the sidewalk as she headed for Nan's back door.

"I'm just looking out for him, you know. For both of them." Gabe's voice stopped her with her hand on the door handle.

Janelle turned. Gabe leaned against the back porch railing of his house, gazing over the shrubs that still looked new to her. The cherry tip of his cigarette winked at her. She'd given up smoking when she found out she was pregnant with Bennett, and had never taken it up again, but the old craving rose in her with a sudden fierceness.

"I understand."

"No," Gabe said. She couldn't see much of his face, but that hint of sardonic laughter was familiar enough. "You don't."

She wasn't going to stand out here in the cold and argue with him, but she didn't want him to have the last word, either. "So, try me. Tell me what your problem is, Gabe. Because you're right. I don't get it. I don't understand how it feels to be responsible for someone's welfare and well-being, what a burden it can be."

She drew a shuddering breath. "I sure as hell can't possibly know how it is to feel like everyone relies on you. I certainly don't have any clue what it's like to have guilt weigh you down so much that you'll do just about anything to make yourself feel better. Oh...wait. Yes. I can."

He laughed again. The cigarette went dark. He became nothing but shadow.

"Big difference," he said. "You had a choice."

Then he went inside his house and left her standing in the freezing dark.

FIFTEEN

ANY MOTHER OF A TWELVE-YEAR-OLD BOY HAD to also be an archaeologist. Sorting through the detritus in Bennett's backpack, layer by layer, Janelle could've written a dissertation on the social life of a sixth-grader. Along with the half-filled water bottles, candy wrappers and worn-to-the-nub pencils, there were also the crumpled, forlorn and ubiquitous pieces of paper.

She was looking for a permission slip for the field trip, which absolutely had to be turned in tomorrow or Bennett would have to stay behind in the principal's office. She found the needed form and set it aside. She also found a lot of other things.

With Nan napping, Janelle didn't want to holler for him, but neither did she want to haul everything up to his room. She settled for calling him from the bottom of the stairs. When he appeared at the top, she held aloft a rainbow of papers. "Come here."

Reluctantly, he did.

"What's all this stuff?"

Bennett shrugged. "I don't know. Stuff. Junk."

Janelle pulled out an insurance form, one for reduced lunches, another with instructions on how to deposit lunch money in his account so he didn't have to carry cash every day. She'd been killing herself trying to make sure she had small bills for him to take, and now she found out she could've just written one big check to last a few months.

"Some of this stuff isn't junk." She plucked at a creased paper covered in what looked like melted chocolate from a granola bar or something. "Some of this is important. From now on, please make sure you take everything out of your backpack when you get home and sort through it."

"Okay." Bennett had a foot on the stairs, easing upward, but he wasn't going to get away so easy.

"Hold it." Janelle shuffled through the papers again and pulled out a test emblazoned with a scarlet F. It had a space for her to sign. "Were you supposed to show this to me?"

His shrug was maddening.

"This says I was supposed to sign it and you had to return it. Obviously, you didn't." She dug farther and pulled out a note from his teacher expressing concern about Bennett's performance in math, and requesting a meeting. Janelle held it up, hating the way his eyes shifted from hers, how his feet shuffled. Connor had looked at her that way once or twice, and that had been enough.

"You can sign it now."

She'd known he was struggling with math, but not the extent. Andy had come over only a couple times to work with him. "Is Andy helping you at all?"

Another shrug.

Janelle sighed. "Is your homework finished?"

"Yeah."

"Math? Everything?"

Bennett paused. "Yeah."

That didn't convince her. She dug again and pulled out a reading log with spaces for books read, how many minutes spent and if a comprehension test had been completed. Half the log was blank but for red pen marks. Janelle's stomach tightened, anger making her grit her teeth. Math was one thing, but Bennett had never struggled with English or Social Studies.

"What is going on with you? You're supposed to be reading, and you're not? What?"

"I already read the books she has on her list. She won't let me skip them."

"So finish the tests on them, get the credit if you already read them. You have to do the work, Bennett." Janelle pinched the bridge of her nose against a headache. "No games."

"What? No!"

She nodded. "No games or anything else until you're caught up on your work. And you bring it to me. I'll check it."

Bennett sighed from someplace deep inside, turned around and went up the stairs. He didn't stomp or slam his door, but it was easy to see how put-upon he felt. Janelle hung her head for a moment, one hand on the newel post, trying to gather the strength not to be annoyed by what she knew was typical kid behavior. God knew she'd given her mother more hard times than Bennett, so far, had ever given her. She didn't know how her mom had managed.

"I almost didn't," her mom reminded her on the phone a few minutes later when Janelle called her. "I was at my wit's end with you."

"Rehab or reform school. I remember." Janelle laughed quietly. She'd taken her phone out to the back porch so she could be close if Nan called out. Spring was on its way, but it wasn't unheard of for March to have blizzards as bad as any in December, and though she was comfortable in a sweatshirt, the sky told her it shouldn't be a surprise when the temps dropped again. The air smelled good, though. Fresh. She breathed deep.

"But you went to Nan's instead. I was lucky."

"No," Janelle said. "*I* was lucky."

Her mother chuckled. "Looking back, I think I made so many mistakes with you because I was so determined to make you perfect."

"Really?" Janelle had never heard her say that before. "What made you think you had to?"

"Oh...so all the people who looked down their noses at me for having you without marrying your dad might be put in their place, I guess. I mean, sure I got knocked up out of wedlock, but look at my beautiful, smart, talented and well-behaved child. See what a good mother I am? It was a plan, anyway."

"You're a great mother," Janelle said.

"And you are beautiful, smart and talented," her mother replied. "The well-behaved part...not so much."

Janelle had spent some time feeling bad about what she'd put her mom through, but she snorted softly now. "I could've been worse. A lot worse."

"I know that now. But at the time, you seemed so out of control. You always were more your own person than Kenny ever was. You paved your own path. I shouldn't have tried so hard to make you fit into a mold, Janelle. I should've been more proud of you back then, for some of the things you did. For being unique."

"For not fitting in?"

It was her mom's turn to snort. "So you dyed your hair and wore weird outfits. So you pierced yourself and wrote rebellious essays. They were great essays. I guess I just didn't know how to deal with you. I thought I'd have a daughter more like

me, you know. Into pastels and teddy bears and stuff. But really,
I should've known better. I mean, I did know what your dad
was like."

By the time Janelle had found out she was pregnant, she'd
lost track of Connor. It had never been more than a fling,
him an exchange student from Ireland determined to sleep his
way through as many women as would have him. His smile,
that accent, those eyes—they'd given her a perfect reason to
go to bed with him for a few months, and an even better reason never to tell him he'd fathered a child. Janelle knew too
well what it had been like growing up with a charming des-
perado as a dad. She'd determined she'd never put her kid
through that.

"I look at Bennett and I see Connor. It's all over his face."

"You used to look so much like your dad it was scary."

"He has Connor's expressions. His sense of humor, sometimes. And it doesn't seem fair," Janelle said after another second or so in which she struggled to find the right words to
express what had always been a mishmash of emotions, "that
he should have anything from his dad, when I'm the one who's
raised him. I'm the one who's tried to teach him right from
wrong, and been with him when he was sick, and helped him
learn to read and tie his shoes.... I'm the only one who's here.
There's just...me."

"There's not 'just' you. You're a great mom. I'm so proud of
you, Janelle. Don't be so hard on yourself. I know how tough
it is to raise a kid alone—you remember I didn't marry Randall until you were in fourth grade. Before that it was you and
me. Sometimes your dad, sure. But mostly, it was us."

It wasn't the same. Janelle was a girl, raised by her mom.
She'd had a dad, even if his appearances in her life were haphazard and spontaneous. She'd had Nan, too.

"Don't you think a boy needs a father?"

Her mom laughed, not unkindly. "This from the girl who said marriage was the best way to ruin a relationship?"

Janelle smiled. "I've never been married, what do I know?"

Her mom made a thoughtful noise. "Well…sure. I guess it's better for a boy to have a dad. Or two parents—it's always better for kids to have two parents. But that's not always possible. Are you asking me if I think you should get married just to give Bennett a dad? If I thought that, I'd have told you to marry Ryan what's-his-name."

"You didn't like Ryan," Janelle reminded her.

"No, but you did."

"Obviously not enough," Janelle said with a roll of her eyes at the absurdity of marrying Ryan. "Since I broke up with him."

"You'll find someone, and when you do, you'll make that decision. And you'll do it because you want to marry him, and also because he'll be a great addition to your son's life. I know you, Janelle. You're not one of these women who need a man so much they'll jeopardize their kid just to have one. You might've been a trial as a child, and a pain in the ass as a teenager," her mom said, "but you're a wonderful woman and a great mother. Don't you forget that."

"I'll try."

"Gotta run," she added. "I need to get this last load of laundry in the wash before Randall gets home. We're going out to dinner and the movies tonight."

Thirty years married, and they still went on dates. Janelle and her stepfather hadn't always seen eye to eye, that was true, but he'd always been good to her mom. He was great with Bennett. In adulthood, Janelle had learned to appreciate Randall a little more, as he'd learned to judge her a little less.

With the phone call disconnected, Janelle tucked her cell in her pocket and stood, now chilled. Inside, she found Nan up and about at the kitchen sink, filling the kettle. "Nan, I'll do that."

Her grandma turned, water sloshing in the kettle. "I wanted some tea."

"I'd like some tea, too. How about a snack? I can put out something to eat, how's that?"

She wasn't terribly hungry. They'd eaten dinner just an hour ago, but Nan had picked at it and pushed most of it away. She'd need to eat something with her next round of meds. Without waiting for an answer, as Nan finished filling the kettle and put it on the stove to heat, Janelle pulled out the bowl of cut fruit she'd made earlier that day. She added a plastic container of cubed cheese and some baby carrots, along with a bottle of ranch dressing. Everything went on the table. The dishwasher still wasn't fixed. She'd had a service guy out, spent a hundred bucks for him to replace the parts she already knew needed replacing because of Gabe's list, and that hadn't solved the problem. Until she could figure out how to fix it or buy a new one, they were eating off paper plates and washing by hand.

Nan shuffled into the living room and paused, leaning on a dining table chair. She looked tired, though she'd been napping since shortly after dinner. She drew in a long breath and let it out slowly before looking at Janelle. "Can you get my pills, honey?"

The tray with its selection of bottles was in its place in the corner cupboard, and Janelle put it on the table in front of the chair. Nan hadn't taken a seat yet. "Sit, Nan. I'll get the water."

The kettle whistled. Janelle got it and filled a teapot she took from the cupboard. She added a tea ball filled with loose tea she'd picked up from the store. She'd brought the teapot and tea ball with her from California. She and Ryan, a long time ago, had taken a culinary course that had taught the proper way to make a pot of tea, according to the Brits.

Letting it steep, she covered the pot with a knitted cozy and settled it onto a tray she'd found tucked away in Nan's closet. She added a pair of mugs, thinking about her pretty teacups still packed away upstairs in boxes shoved beneath the eaves. She'd have to get them out. She also added a few packets of artificial sweetener and a small container of milk.

It looked great, all of it, but she nearly dropped the tray when she took it into the living room and found Nan slumped forward in her chair. With a low cry Janelle put the tray on the table, sloshing tea onto the cozy. She put a hand on her grandmother's shoulder, not quite shaking her. Nan looked up, her gaze unfocused only for a second before it turned sharp.

"Good Lord, girl! What are you doing?"

"Nan, are you okay?"

"I'm fine," Nan snapped. "I was just a little sleepy. I got tired waiting for you to bring the tea, that's all. I didn't feel like getting up."

Janelle's heart was beating too fast. She sank into a chair and put her trembling hands in front of her, flat on the table. "You scared me."

Nan's eyes twinkled and her lips twitched. "I see."

"Not funny." Janelle shook a finger. "I thought you were taking your pills."

"Oh. Yes. I was." Nan looked at the tray and bottles. "I did. I think I did. Oh, I'm not sure."

Janelle paused, trying to figure out how to tell, but couldn't. Taking more medication than the dose would definitely cause trouble, but missing a dose…honestly, she thought, as she poured tea for both of them, would it matter? Really? "Careful. It's hot."

"It's bitter." Nan eyed the tea ball. "Where'd you get that?"

"I brought it with me. You use it instead of a tea bag. So you can use loose tea."

"Do you know, my mother used to make her own mint tea. She'd grow the mint right out in her yard, bring it in the house. Sometimes she'd just add it fresh to hot water, sometimes she'd hang it up to dry. Oh, it smelled so nice." Nan took a deep breath as though she could smell it right then. "She'd have liked that thing. That whatchamacallit."

"Tea ball."

"Yes, she'd have liked it." Nan put a hand over her eyes and began to cry.

Alarmed, Janelle reached for her. "Nan, what's wrong?"

It took a few minutes for her to calm down, but when she did, she waved away Janelle's concern. "I'm an old woman, that's all."

"Does something hurt? What can I get you?" Janelle warmed her hands on the mug to keep them from shaking. She could never remember seeing Nan cry.

"I just missed my mother. That's all. I thought about the tea and I remembered her, and I just…missed her so much. She died in 1957. She was younger than I am now." Nan shivered and dabbed at her eyes with a paper napkin, then blew her nose with it.

Janelle knew a lot about her mother's family. Her maternal grandparents had kept a large family tree painting in their rec room, poster-size, with spaces for new additions to the family. With every birth, they'd added the names to the tree. Janelle's mom had taken it when they passed away, and hung it in her basement bar, though it hadn't been updated since Bennett's birth.

Of her dad's family, Janelle knew very little. Of course, Nan had a mother, but until this moment Janelle couldn't recall anyone ever talking about her. If her dad had ever spoken of his grandmother, it hadn't left an impression.

"Tell me about her," Janelle said. "I'd like to know."

Nan wiped at her face again and sipped some tea. She gave Janelle a shaky but genuine smile. "What do you want to know, honey?"

Janelle took a drink of her own tea. "Everything you can think of."

Nan talked for half an hour before the tea was finished and her voice gave out. She told Janelle stories of her life as a child, growing up right there in St. Marys. Of her brothers and sisters. Her aunts and uncles. She spoke in warm and glowing terms of her mother, but didn't weep for her again.

"Do you have pictures?"

"I've so many. Some are in albums. Some in boxes. So many pictures, so many years," Nan said. "We can look at them. If you're sure you want to."

Janelle squeezed Nan's hand. "Of course I do. I want to know about my family. I feel like there's so much I don't know. I guess I want to…I don't know. Feel like I'm a part of it."

"Oh, honey," Nan said, squeezing in return. "No matter where you were, or how long you were gone, you've always been a part of it. Don't you know that?"

Janelle was silent for a moment. "I'm sorry, Nan."

"For what?"

"For never coming back until now."

Nan squeezed her fingers again. "You had your reasons."

"No." Janelle shook her head. "You were there for me when I needed someone. You let me come and live here with you, you put up with me. You saved me, Nan. And I just up and left. Never came back, not even to visit. You asked me to, and I just never did."

"That's sometimes what children do, honey." Nan sighed. "They grow up and go away. You had to find your own path, Janelle. You think I didn't always know that about you? You had so much of your daddy in you that way—"

"No!" Janelle cried, and pushed away from the table. "No, don't say that. I'm not like my dad. I'm nothing like him."

The silence after her outburst was too loud.

"I b'lieve I'll have a little more tea," Nan said mildly, and held out her cup for Janelle to fill.

SIXTEEN

WATCHING ANDY AND BENNETT TOGETHER AT the table, Janelle felt a stab of something wistful. Andy was in his thirties, but still acted much younger. He reminded her of how he'd been as a teen, before everything had changed. He was...happy.

"See, you need to carry this over." Andy scribbled something on Bennett's paper. "Your teacher wants to see your work, so you have to show it. Like this."

Andy was so good with her son. The times Janelle had tried to help Bennett with his math, she'd struggled along with him. He'd been cranky. She'd lost her patience. Now she just stayed out of the way, making dinner in the kitchen while Nan napped or read or watched TV.

From the kitchen doorway she said, "You staying for dinner? I'm making chicken potpie."

Andy looked pleased, then concerned. "I dunno. I should make sure my dad's got something for his dinner. And if Gabe comes home and I'm not there and I haven't told him where I'm going to be…he gets mad."

"Your dad could come. Gabe, too. I made plenty." Too much, actually, having misjudged the recipe and doubled it by accident.

Andy laughed. "Oh. My dad won't come over here."

"My food's not good enough for him," sniffed Nan from her place on the couch.

Andy looked embarrassed. "He always used to eat whatever you sent over, Mrs. Decker. I remember that."

"Back in the days when I cooked." Nan twisted to look around the pillows she used to prop herself up. "But he got mad one day about the bushes in the back, never took anything I sent over again."

Andy looked even more uncomfortable. "He's…grumpy."

His fingers curled around the pencil, but not all the way. He had to force them. He did that now, not meeting Janelle's gaze.

"Don't worry about it, Andy. If you want to stay, you can. If you need to get home for your dad, that's okay, too." Janelle didn't want him feeling bad about it. She already knew Mr. Tierney was a curmudgeon. "You can call Gabe, tell him you're staying. See if he wants to come over."

"Okay. I'll text him. He probably won't," Andy cautioned.

"Oh, ho ho, I bet he will," Nan said, but then went quiet when Janelle gave her a look.

"Hey, Andy," Bennett said, as he watched Andy struggle with the cell phone. "What happened to your head, anyway?"

Andy's fingers crept slowly to his forehead, then along the white part in his hair, probing gently. "I got shot."

"Ouch," Bennett said. "Did it hurt?"

Andy took his hand away and shrugged. "I don't remember."

"I bet it did."

"Bennett," Janelle murmured. "Maybe Andy doesn't want to talk about it."

From the couch came the low mutter of Nan's snoring. Andy glanced toward her with a smile, then gave Janelle a slightly bigger one. "It's okay. I don't mind."

To Bennett, he said, "We were fooling around with guns, and there was an accident. My brother shot me."

Bennett frowned. "Why were you fooling around with guns?"

Andy looked at a loss for couple seconds and turned to Janelle for help. She shifted her weight from her good foot to her bad, then back again, trying to think of an answer. "People around here like to hunt, Bennett. So lots of guys, and girls, too, have guns."

"Guns aren't toys," Bennett said firmly.

Score one for her parenting skills. "Yes, that's right."

The obvious statement that Andy and his brothers had been reckless and foolish, and that their behavior had led to Andy's injury, remained unspoken. At least by her. Andy, however, leaned forward to make sure Bennett looked him in the face.

"Guns aren't unsafe, Benny. People are."

"Guns don't kill people, people kill people?" Janelle said.

"Well, that's true," Andy replied.

Janelle frowned. "It's also true that they're not toys."

"I know that." Andy shrugged, then looked at her. "You know what's more dangerous? Not knowing how to handle a gun at all. That's how accidents happen."

To Bennett he said, "My brother could teach you how to handle a gun. You want to learn?"

The boy lit up, already turning to her with hope all over his face. So much for her maternal lessons sinking in and making a mark. Janelle shook her head and noted his disappointment.

"I'm sure you can both think of a very good reason why I wouldn't trust Gabe with a gun around my son."

Andy laughed and shook his head in turn. "He's probably the best person in the whole world to teach Bennett how to be safe with a gun, Janelle."

"How do you figure that?"

"Because," Andy said, now serious, "he already shot one person by accident. He'll never do that again."

SEVENTEEN

Then

MIKEY'S USELESS WITH A HAMMER, BUT ANDY'S
pretty good about pounding nails in straight and also about
taking directions. Mike always wants to have a plan, a written
diagram or something; he's nervous about the way things fit
together and whether it's safe. Andy doesn't care about that.
He just likes using the tools.

Even though he's using his brothers for labor, this is still
Gabe's place. No question about it. Andy and Mike don't
come out here without him, and not just because they can't
drive and he has a car. They could lay claim to the patch of
ground as much as he does, even the cabin, since they've put
in a share of the work. But they don't.

This is Gabe's place.

"You're going to kill yourself." Mikey points toward the
loft, where Andy has climbed to add on to the flooring. "It's
not even attached right!"

Looking up, Gabe watches his brother grin, teasing his twin on purpose as he balances on a two-by-four that will eventually form the support for a new section of floor, expanding the loft. Andy holds out his arms, stands on one foot, pretends to teeter while Mikey shouts. Gabe laughs, though of course, the truth is that if Andy fell off the beam, he'd definitely break something, and it's a long, bumpy ride back to town.

"Don't be an asshole," Gabe says. "Finish that up. We need to get back before the old man does."

That sobers Andy right up, his smile disappearing. He frowns and eases back onto the loft flooring. He hefts the hammer in his hand, then looks down to the main floor, where Gabe and Mike have been cutting lengths of wood. A few minutes later he climbs down the rickety ladder and tosses the hammer into the toolbox.

"Let's go."

"We don't have to just yet..." They have a good couple of hours even if the old man doesn't stop off someplace after work, which he probably will. Gabe shouldn't have said anything. He'd wanted his brother to stop fooling around, not get freaked out.

"Let's go," Andy says again.

Gabe turns back to the board he was sawing. "We have time."

"I have homework and stuff. Mikey, too. C'mon. Let's go, Gabe."

Andy is dancing, eyes glittery with anxiety, and Gabe knows there's no way he'll get any more work out of his brother like this. Out of either of them, because what one feels, the other ends up feeling, too. Not like in that story, what was it...*The Corsican Brothers*. Gabe saw the Cheech and Chong version, hilarious as hell. Those twins felt the physical pain of each other, but it's not like that with his brothers.

More like they feed off one another, get each other revved up or calmed down.

Gabe looks around the cabin, thinking about everything it could be and all the things it wasn't. It was a mistake to bring them out here. His brothers make things complicated; they always do. All he wanted was to finish framing out the next section of the loft. He'd left them plenty of time, and now it wouldn't get done.

"Come *on*." Andy's freaking out, which in turn made Mikey start to dance as if he's going to wet his pants.

As it turns out, it doesn't much matter, because the old man is already home by the time they get there, and has been there long enough to get himself worked into a real snit. He's opened the fridge and tossed out everything inside into a huge, sloppy mess on the kitchen floor. He opened all the cupboards and left them ajar. He dumped the trash can on its side. He sits smoking in the middle of it all, with his feet on the kitchen table and acting as if he doesn't have a care in the world, when they come into the house.

"Nice of you to stop by," their dad says in that deceptively calm voice he uses just before he lets his temper fly. He draws in a long drag from the cigarette and flicks ash, not caring where it lands. "Bunch of little shits. I thought I told you to have dinner ready for me early tonight, 'cause I'm going out."

Mikey's the one who starts pacing and apologizing. He's the peacemaker. Andy says nothing, just goes to the closet to get a garbage bag and start picking up the trash. Gabe stares at the mess while anger uncoils in his gut.

"Why'd you do this?" He gestures at the chaos. "You could've made yourself a sandwich or something. It wasn't a big deal. Why'd you have to go and trash the place just because you didn't get your Hamburger Helper on time?"

The old man's up and on his feet before Gabe can do more

than take a step or two back. His fists are twisted tight in the front of Gabe's shirt. His breath is terrible, not just from smoke or beer, but the stink of teeth left to rot. Gabe turns his face, not caring if his father thinks it's because he's afraid.

He's not scared of his father. He could pound the old man into a pulp if he wanted to, and the time is coming when that might happen. But it wouldn't change him. Gabe once watched his dad go head-to-head with a guy twice his size who beat the shit out of him because the old man just kept swinging and wouldn't stay down until he was knocked unconscious. When he came to, the first words out of his mouth had been cursing the other guy. Fighting his dad won't make anything better, so Gabe just waits until the old man let him go.

"Sorry, Dad. Sorry," Mikey says over and over as he gets on the floor to help Andy clean up the ruined and wasted food.

Andy says nothing, just works as fast as he can. The old man kicks at a plastic container of leftover meat loaf so that it goes rolling, spilling the contents. He shoots Gabe a glare.

"What are you looking at?"

"Nothing." Gabe doesn't move, though his fingers curl into fists. Just because he isn't going to punch the old man right in the mouth doesn't mean he doesn't want to.

"I'm going out," their father says, "and this shit hole better be in tip-top shape when I get back, or you'll be sorry."

They're already sorry, that's for sure. But he can make them sorrier and probably will no matter what happens with the cleanup. Gabe stays where he is until the old man pushes past him. He waits until the front door slams before he moves, and then he kicks at the kitchen chair, which skids across the floor.

"Don't," Mikey says. "Just help us."

"It could be worse," Andy says in a low voice. "He could've

pissed all over it. It could've been our pillows, like that one time."

It could be worse. It can always be worse, and all three of them knew how bad it could really be. It doesn't make Gabe feel any better about this mess, about his brothers on their hands and knees scraping up splattered pork-n-beans and spilled milk because their dad had a stick up his ass about his dinner being late.

The mess is too much. Gabe can't deal with it. He wants to punch a wall. He wants to kick something harder than he kicked the chair. He wants to break something, and the closest thing is a glass jar, which he hefts in his hand and smashes onto the table without thinking.

"Gabe, cut it out! Stop it!" Mikey shoves him back a step. "You're just making it worse!"

Andy says nothing, his eyes shadowed. He stuffs the trash bag steadily. He barely looks up when his brothers shout, though when Gabe's fist rises he does stop what he's doing to stand.

Gabe doesn't want to hit Mikey, not really, and not because it would end up two against one. He doesn't want to hit him because he's not mad at him. At either of them. And yet he is...for a million reasons so twisted and complicated he'll never untangle them. Instead of hitting Mikey, Gabe stalks upstairs to turn his music up loud, leaving them to the mess.

Night's fallen. It's dark in his room. He turns the stereo up way past what the old man allows, but screw it, he's out, and the louder the music is, the less Gabe has to think about anything. He just wants to block out everything but the pounding beat of drums, the scream of guitars, the wail of vocals.

The window across from his lights up.

He shouldn't look, he shouldn't watch her; it's creepy and makes him a perv. But he can't help himself when Janelle starts to dance. She moves to the beat of a song he can't hear, but it must be a lot like the one he's listening to because her body moves in time to his music.

She wears an oversize T-shirt that hits her midthigh, a flash of baby-blue panties beneath it. She grinds her hips and puts her arms above her head. She wiggles and shimmies. She runs her hands up and down her body as she tosses her head.

He's mesmerized and hypnotized. He's paralyzed. His mouth hangs open as he stares, knowing he should stop, hoping she can't see him. Maybe hoping she can.

Janelle dances closer to the window, shaking her ass back and forth as if it's her damn job. It's a sexy dance and yet there's something about it that makes him think she's being silly, too. Having fun. Like it would be different if she had an audience, if she knew he was standing there with his pants getting tight in the crotch and that dull throb starting in his balls.

When she blows a kiss, Gabe steps back. She doesn't look through the window, doesn't acknowledge him, but...she had to see him. Right? She did, didn't she?

The thought's enough to send him back, all the way across the room and then down the stairs. Outside, where he pulls out a cigarette he stole from the old man's drawer, and lights it with shaking hands. His brothers are still cleaning the kitchen, both of them working together like the team they've always been. Gabe the outsider, his heart pounding and palms sweating, his dick still half-hard.

That's when the back door at the Decker place opens and Janelle skips out. She has jeans on, at least, and she acts so surprised to see him that Gabe knows she's putting it on. She leans against the door frame, looking him over.

"Hey," she says. "What's up?"

"Nothing."

She smiles the way she always has, but somehow it sits dif-

ferently on her face now that she's older. She could always
tease him into doing anything—bubbles, a tin-can telephone,
sneaking Popsicles behind Mrs. Moser's back. How could he
ever have thought that would change? If anything, it's worse,
because now she's grown a decent set of boobs and her ass is
so fine...so damn fine.

Janelle tips her chin at him. "Smoking's bad for you."

Gabe says nothing, not even when she hops and skips across
the narrow alley onto his porch, where she holds out a hand
for a cigarette. He doesn't have an extra on him and can't find
a way to make his mouth work to say so. He offers his instead.

She takes it like an expert, eyes squinting shut against the
smoke for a second before she hands it back to him. He can't
smoke it now. Her mouth was on it. He'll taste her. It's enough
to make his hands shake again.

"You wanna hear a joke?" Her eyebrows go up.

"Uh...sure."

Janelle grins. "Okay, so this guy goes to the doctor, right?
And he says 'Doc, I got this problem. One day I wake up,
I'm a teepee. The next day I wake up, I'm a wigwam. Teepee, wigwam, teepee, wigwam...it's crazy. What do I do?' So
the doctor says 'No problem, I can tell you what's wrong.'"

Gabe waits, but she just grins. "What's the punch line?"

Janelle laughs, leaning closer. She smells good, something
flowery that makes his skin flush hot. "'No problem,' the doc
says. 'You're just two tents!'"

She bursts into a gale of hilarity funnier than the joke.
Watching her laugh, her head tipping back, the way her throat
works...Gabe starts laughing, too. They laugh together, harder
and harder, until she's wiping tears and he thinks he might
puke from the pressure in his gut.

The back door opens. Andy's there, his hair standing on
end with sweat, his eyes wide. Mikey behind him.

"What the hell?" Andy says, but Gabe finds no words, only laughter, and it feels so good he doesn't want to stop.

"Andy, Andy, Andy," Janelle says, drawing him out onto the porch, knuckling his head fondly. "What's happening, brother? Want to hear a joke?"

Somehow, she gets Andy laughing, too, though the next joke she tells is just raunchy enough to make Mikey frown. The four of them stand on the back porch, giggling and sharing the cigarettes Andy goes inside to pinch from the old man's drawer. They stand there for an hour or more, until Mrs. Decker flicks the back porch light and Janelle has to go inside.

"She makes everything seem like not such a big deal," Andy says when they face the last bit of mess inside. "Doesn't she?"

Gabe doesn't reply, just gets out a broom and dustpan and starts sweeping. It's a question that doesn't need an answer, as if somehow admitting it aloud would change it or make him have to own up to something he doesn't want to. It's true, though, he thinks as they work together to put the kitchen back into shape.

Janelle always makes everything seem as if it will be okay.

EIGHTEEN

JANELLE HAD DROPPED A STITCH SOMEWHERE along the way. Probably more than one. Consequently, her afghan was lopsided and narrowing with every row.

"By the time I'm done, it will be a scarf."

Nan laughed, pushing a tissue against her mouth to shield a cough. It took her a few minutes to recover, and her eyes were watery by the time she did. She wiped her mouth and crumpled the tissue before tucking it into the plastic shopping bag she hung from her walker and used for trash.

"Rip it out and start over," she said.

Janelle sighed. "But I've been working on it for, like, two days. That's two days lost."

"Not lost," Nan said. "Just think of it as practice."

"Practice," Janelle said doubtfully, and held up the mass of yarn she was trying to make into something pretty.

"You can't get anything right if you don't practice." Nan coughed again, then gestured. "Let me see that."

In minutes she'd plucked out the last few rows. Her knitting needles clacked slowly, but carefully. Janelle could remember a time when her grandmother could finish an entire baby blanket over the course of a few nights' TV watching. She'd knitted them for friends, family, children in the hospital. Skeins and skeins of yarn in every color. Janelle had often done her homework to the sound of those needles clackity-clacking. It was painful to watch how difficult it was now for Nan to knit.

Nan held up the blanket. "See? There."

Janelle took the needles and yarn. "Thanks, Nan."

"You just need to take your time. Pay attention. That's all." Nan coughed again and lay back against the couch. Her cheeks were too pink, her eyes too bright. She didn't have a fever; Janelle had checked for that. And it was better than her looking wan and lethargic. Still, she didn't look like herself.

"Bennett! Let's go, you're going to miss the bus!"

Backpack slung over his shoulder, Bennett pushed past her, heading for the back door. "Bye."

"Where's your hat?" Janelle asked.

He shrugged. "I don't know. I think I lost it."

"Oh, Bennett." Janelle sighed and looked him over, noting a bruise on his chin. "What happened to your face? And how do you keep losing your hats?"

"Don't know."

Janelle considered calling him on the sullen tone, but then looked at the clock. "Go to school."

She watched until he'd left the room, then studied the tangle of yarn in her hands. "Maybe I'd be better off knitting him a bunch of hats."

"He doesn't lose them, you know."

Janelle looked at her grandmother. "What do you mean?"

Nan laughed. "He hides them. Because he doesn't want to wear them. The other children probably don't wear hats."

"Yeah, and they're probably more used to the cold," Janelle said. "But that makes sense. I'll talk to him about it."

"Your daddy always refused to wear a hat. He'd just throw them down, right in front of me, when he was small. Stomp his feet. Oh, he was stubborn. When he got older, he'd just say to me, 'Mom, I'm not wearing a hat, and you can't make me.' And you know what? I couldn't."

Janelle had no trouble imagining her dad as a rebel. "Did he give you lots of trouble, Nan?"

"Oh, yes. He was the first one, you know. I made all my mistakes with him." Nan shook her head. "But by the time the youngest came along, well, I guess I'd had enough practice."

"I feel bad, sometimes…."

Nan looked up, though Janelle had stopped herself. "About Benny? Being your only? Or about him not having a daddy?"

There was no point in pretending to be offended. In California it had never seemed to matter there was only a mother. Here it was different. "Yes. That. Both."

Nan waved a hand. "So get him a brother or a sister."

"The no-daddy thing sort of makes that hard, Nan."

Her grandma snorted softly. "You found one the first time, didn't you? You really think you couldn't go out and find another one, if you tried a little?"

From anyone else in the world, that would've sounded like an insult. From Nan it just sounded like good advice. Janelle shrugged. "Not sure I'm interested."

"In another baby? Or a man?"

"Both." Janelle focused narrowly on the afghan, making sure to count her stitches. Taking her time. She looked up to see Nan giving her a serious look. "What?"

"Just because you make a mistake once doesn't mean you shouldn't try again, Janelle. I mean, look at your mother. She moved on, didn't she?"

Janelle let her blanket project settle into her lap. "You think my mom made a mistake with my dad?"

"Oh, I don't mean you, honey. But…I think she made a mistake in loving him so hard. She should've given up on him long before she did. Hand me another tissue, honey." Nan wiped her mouth with the one Janelle passed her, then grimaced as she spit into it. She screwed up the tissue and put it in her trash bag.

Janelle watched in silence at first, not sure what to think. "But…he's your son."

"I know that. And I already told you what sort of boy he'd been, didn't I? You think I didn't know what kind of man he grew into? Maybe I should've remarried after Dick died. Maybe it was because your dad missed his father, I don't know. Or sometimes, some people just have trouble their whole lives." Nan shook her head. "That Gabe Tierney, for example."

Uneasily, Janelle glanced out the window, though of course, she could only glimpse the Tierneys' house and no sign of Gabe himself. "Oh, Nan. C'mon."

"He shot his own brother in the head, for goodness' sakes. And that business with his mother. And his father, that old grump…." Nan sighed. "I'm just saying that Gabe Tierney's had trouble his whole life, and probably always will."

"That's not a nice thing to say."

"Well," Nan said stubbornly, "it's true. And his brothers, nice as can be. Father Michael's a priest—you can't get much nicer than that. And Andrew, that poor boy. Well, he's had to make a life out of something terrible, and it's a struggle, but he makes it."

"You don't give Gabe enough credit."

Nan smiled. "Ahhh. So you do like him."

Janelle couldn't deny that, but wouldn't admit it. "Why didn't you ever get married again?"

"Oh…" Nan thought about it for a few seconds. "Because I loved your grandpa too much, I guess. Dick was my high school sweetheart, you know."

"I can't imagine that. Marrying the person you dated in high school."

"Can't you?" Nan asked, a little too sagely for Janelle's taste. "Anyway, that's what most of us did in those days, you know. And all the boys were going off to war. If you wanted to get married, well. You found yourself a man and you married him quick, in case he didn't come back home."

"How long did you date before you got married?"

Nan made a thoughtful sound. "Let's see. Well, I knew him my whole life, of course. But we started going as a couple when I was seventeen. The beginning of my senior year. And we dated, on and off. We didn't go steady until closer to graduation. It was different back then, you know. Dating meant just that, and even going steady didn't mean more than hand-holding or maybe a little bit of kissing now and then. Not if you were good."

"So how did he ask you to marry him? Did you know right away you wanted to?" The idea of loving someone enough to want to spend the rest of her life with him seemed so foreign. Unreachable. Unrealistic. Janelle knew it happened. She just couldn't imagined what it would be like if it happened to her.

"Well. He'd made me angry by making eyes at Angela Reynolds one time at the school dance, so I told him I didn't want to see him anymore. Oh, my, was I angry." Nan chuckled softly, a little sadly. "I told him if he didn't have eyes for only me, then I didn't want anything to do with him."

"Good for you."

"I was spitting nails," Nan added. "But a week or so passed, and he found out he was going to be leaving soon for the Navy. He came to my house and asked my father for permission to marry me. I was listening from the front stairs. I was sure my dad would say no...he liked to tease that way. But he must've known it was important, because all he said was, 'Dicky, if you want her, you're going to have to prove to her you're worth it.'"

Janelle's grandfather had died long before she was born, when her own father was only eighteen. She'd heard lots of stories about Grandpa Dick, but never this one. "So then he asked you, and you said yes?"

Nan laughed. "Oh, no. He gave me a ring. The tiniest, sweetest diamond you ever saw. I knew he couldn't afford much, but that wasn't what mattered. Some girls didn't get a diamond at all, you know. But I did. I knew then he wouldn't be making eyes at any other girl. But he gave me the ring and I told him I'd have to think about it."

"Nan! You didn't."

She laughed again, her eyes bright. "I did. So he told me he understood, but that he surely hoped I'd give him an answer before he had to ship out, because it would be nice to know that when he went away, he'd have me to come back to."

It was one of the most romantic stories Janelle had ever heard. "Wow."

"So, just before he was due to leave for training, he asked me to the pictures. And I put the ring on, but I turned it around so the diamond was on the inside of my hand, you know. And I had him sit to my left. Then, when he took my hand..." Nan's eyes grew bright with tears. "He took my hand and felt that I was wearing the ring. And that's how he knew I was saying yes."

Janelle swiped at tears. "That's a great story, Nan."

"He was a wonderful man. The love of my life."

"And that's why you never got married again?"

Nan sighed. "Well…at first. But of course, after a bit I did think I might want to meet someone else. Maybe get married. But the trouble was, when my boys were young I didn't want to meet anyone, and by the time I felt ready to, I guess I was just too used to being by myself. The only men who asked me out were widowers with kids of their own, and I was done raising children, especially someone else's. They all just wanted someone to do for them. Cook, clean, what have you. So I never met the right man, I suppose. Maybe there was only that one for me, God rest him."

"I think I'm just going to be alone for the rest of my life." Janelle's words were a surprise, though once they came out they felt right. "I don't think I want to deal with anyone else, you know? And I didn't even have a great love. Maybe I'm too selfish."

"You're not selfish, honey. No selfish person would've given up everything she had to come here and take care of me. Don't you say that about yourself."

Janelle didn't point out that coming to take care of Nan had been accompanied by a promise of financial reward. That she'd had nothing to stay in California for but the weather. That coming home was as beneficial for Janelle and her son as it was for Nan.

"I know how they got you to come here," Nan added before she could reply. "I told Joey, I said, she's going to get her share of the house. She's going to have a paycheck, just like if we hired a nurse. But you could've said no. You always could've."

"I wanted to come back, Nan." Janelle's throat closed. "I'm glad to be here, with you."

Nan shook her head. "So don't you go writing yourself off, you hear? You'll find someone, if you want to. And Janelle, I'm sure you want to."

Janelle laughed, though it came out sounding a little strangled. "Why does everyone assume a single woman must be in need of a man? Is it so strange to think I might just be happy how I am?"

"At the very least, you should find a...what do they call it? A friend with benefits?"

Shocked, Janelle guffawed. "Nan!"

She laughed. "See? I'm not so behind the times."

Instinctively, Janelle thought of Gabe, and her face flushed hot. More than hot. Inferno. He wasn't really a friend, but she remembered all too well the sorts of benefits they'd shared. And that had been as horny but stupid teenagers. She couldn't even imagine what it would be like to go to bed with him now that she actually knew what he was doing.

Nan sighed and closed her eyes briefly. "Oh, my, I think I'll take a little nap."

Janelle didn't bother asking if Nan wanted to move to her bed. She waited a few minutes for her grandmother's breathing to slow, then set her knitting aside to pick up her book. She'd put dinner in the Crock-Pot this morning and couldn't be running the vacuum or anything like that while Nan slept. Nan's naps were Janelle's reading time...just like when Bennett was a baby, she realized.

As a single mom living far away from her family, Janelle hadn't had anyone to rely on when her son was born. She'd been able to manage her schedule by working part-time from home and taking Bennett with her when she had to go into the office. She'd traded listings with other agents and found a decent babysitter for the times she had to do showings. She could vividly remember walking through a newly constructed condo with a newlywed couple and having to go into the bathroom to change her sodden breast pads because the neighbor's cat had meowed and her milk let down. Bennett's nap times had been precious, both because they were so fragile, so easily interrupted, but also because they were the only time Janelle had taken for herself.

Today, she'd read no more than a couple pages when her cell phone hummed in her pocket, and she went into the living room to answer it. Janelle had spoken with the school counselor many times on the telephone during her preparation for the move, though she'd never met her in person. "Mrs. Adams?"

"Ms. Decker." There was a pause. Silence. A sigh. "I'm sorry to bother you, but…you're going to need to come in and get Bennett."

"Is he sick? What's wrong?" Heart pounding, Janelle sank onto the couch, far less comfortable than the one in the family room.

"No. He's not sick. He's…" Another sigh, then Mrs. Adams's voice turned brisk. "Bennett got in a tussle with some other boys, and he needs a change of clothes. Because it's so close to the end of the day, I think it's best if you just come get him. We can evaluate the situation and make a decision then."

Janelle blinked. "I don't understand."

"They gave him a swirly."

"A swirly…" Janelle shook her head. "Some boys at school dunked my son's head in the toilet and flushed it?"

"Yes. There's been some trouble with Bennett and these boys before."

"Why is this the first I've heard of it?"

Mrs. Adams was quiet for a few seconds too long. "I think you'd better come get him, Ms. Decker."

"I'll be there in twenty minutes." Janelle disconnected without waiting for an answer.

Nan still dozed on the family room couch, and though Janelle debated waking her, she settled for scrawling a note and putting it on the dining table where Nan would be sure to see it. She got to the school in fifteen minutes and signed in, heading straight for the counselor's office. She spotted Bennett, hair wet, face red, shirt soaked, at once.

"Hey, buddy." She squeezed his shoulder, but he pulled away. "What happened?"

"Ms. Decker." Mrs. Adams held out her hand. "Let's talk about this in my office."

Janelle had spent her share of time in the counselor's office. And the principal's. She'd never been called in on her son's behalf, though. Bennett had always been a good kid.

"Bennett, why don't you tell your mom about what happened?"

"We were just fooling around," he said at once. "It got out of hand. I know we shouldn't have been doing it. I'm sorry."

Janelle looked at Mrs. Adams, who remained impassive. "Is Bennett in trouble? I mean, he's the one who got swirlied. Are the other boys being reprimanded?"

"Yes. They'll have detention. Bennett's being sent home today, but so far he hasn't been assigned detention."

"So far?"

"We're investigating what exactly went on today in the boys' lav," Mrs. Adams said. "When we know more, we'll take action."

"Is my son in trouble?" Janelle looked at Bennett, who studied the floor.

Mrs. Adams hesitated. "We have some concerns about his progress in some of the classwork."

"I got him a tutor. Is there something else?" Janelle twisted her fingers together in her lap. "Bennett? You want to tell me what's going on?"

"We were just fooling around," he repeated.

"That's what the other boys said, too."

"Mrs. Adams," Janelle said coldly, "I'm getting the feeling you think my son's not telling the truth."

The counselor didn't answer.

Janelle stood. "Come on, Bennett."

"Ms. Decker—"

"I'm taking my son home. If you have any further concerns, please feel free to call me." Janelle gestured at Bennett, who didn't move fast enough to suit her. "Let's go. Now."

In the car, he said nothing while Janelle counted to ten, then twenty, then another ten while she figured out what to say. "What's going on?" was all she could finally come up with.

"Nothing."

She thought of the missing hats, the dirt and scrapes. "Are you being bullied?"

"No!"

"You can tell me." She had to swallow hard to get the lump out of her throat. "If they're bullying you, Bennett, I'll talk to the school—"

"No," he insisted. "Mom, don't. It's fine. We were just fooling around, I told you. It's fine."

She said no more into she'd pulled into the driveway and turned off the ignition, but made no move to get out of the truck. "If something is going on, you know you can talk to me about it, don't you?"

He shrugged and got out of the vehicle. Janelle followed him to the back door, pausing to toe off her shoes, but her head went up at the sound of Bennett's startled cry.

"Mom!"

Heart dropping into her stomach, Janelle ran into the family room to find a chair overturned, Nan and Bennett nowhere to be found. They were both in the kitchen, Nan standing over a flaming pan on the stove. She backed away, eyes wide, as Janelle pushed past her to shove the pan off the burner. She twisted the knob to turn off the gas, but the flames didn't disappear. Oil sloshed as she grabbed the pan and turned to dump it in the sink. Nan cried out, but Janelle couldn't focus on her—she had to find the baking soda. Minutes later she'd dumped an entire box on the mess in the sink, dousing the flames.

The kitchen reeked, and everything was very, very quiet.

"Oh," Nan said. "I've made a mess."

There was the briefest second when Janelle imagined herself turning around and walking out the door. Getting in her truck. Driving away.

She didn't.

"Bennett. Upstairs. Take a shower. Change your clothes. Put your dirty clothes in the basket and put it in the hall. Do your homework, and no games." Bennett ducked away without protest, while Nan gave Janelle a trembling smile. To Nan, she said, "I've told you before, you need to let me handle the cooking."

"You weren't here," Nan accused. "I woke up and you weren't here."

"I left you a note."

Nan hesitated, shoulders hunched. She looked shrunken, diminished. "I didn't read it. I didn't...remember, honey. That you were supposed to be here. I woke up and was hungry for some fried potatoes. I didn't remember you and Bennett."

Janelle could think of no answer to that but words she didn't believe. "It's going to be fine. Everything's okay."

NINETEEN

JANELLE WAS MAKING A LIST.

Normally, she wasn't the list-making sort. That had never meant she was unorganized—she'd needed to be on top of her game in the real estate business—just that she'd never been the kind who gained satisfaction from checking things off on a to-do list.

This house, though, needed a list. And how. Not just the usual sort, cataloging the amenities—the built-ins, the original woodwork, the hardwood floors that could be gorgeous if refinished. But also a list of the upgrades and repairs that the house would need before it could go on the market.

She didn't want to make the list. Every item she wrote in her notebook was one more reminder that things were changing—had to change. No choice about it. She could refuse to get working on any of them, but it wouldn't make a difference.

The problem was not just the number of problems she found as she went around the house, checking light switches and outlets and fixtures, but the cost of it all. Everything came down to money, in the end. As Mr. Tierney had said, it always came down to money when there wasn't enough of it.

She peeked in on Nan, napping in her bed, before dialing Joey at work. He cut her off before she could do more than begin to describe the bulk of the work she thought needed to be done. He didn't mean to be rude, she was sure, but still the brusqueness irritated her.

"How much do you think it'll be? For the hot water heater and the dishwasher?"

"I haven't really done any pricing yet. I'm just trying to get things organized, put in priority." She paused. "It would be much nicer if we had a working dishwasher sooner rather than later. Same with the hot water heater. Right now I can get through one shower and one load of laundry—"

"The washer's new," he said. "We bought it for her just last year."

The inside of Janelle's cheek was already sore, but she bit it, anyway. "There's nothing wrong with the washer. It's the hot water heater. And about the rest...the big ticket items should be taken care of first. Someone might want to buy a house with outdated light fixtures or lovely wooden floors hidden under old and ugly carpet, but they're not going to make a good offer on one without updated appliances."

"What's the matter with the carpet?"

Oops. Land mine. "It's out of style and worn, that's all. I pulled up a corner to see what sort of subflooring was under there, and—"

"It's hardwood. When I was a kid, it was hardwood, but we paid for Mom to put in carpet for Christmas one year. We all chipped in."

Janelle had never known the house without the burnt-orange shag carpet, so that Christmas must've been a long time ago. "We might want to consider ripping it out...."

"I don't think so. No, I don't think anyone will agree to that. If someone wants to buy the house, let them rip it out."

Janelle wasn't going to push it. She'd seen people cling to dumber things for longer, and for stupider reasons than sentimentality. "Okay. That's fine. We can reevaluate it after... when the time comes."

"And the rest of it?" he asked after a pause. "Those other things. The problems with the wiring, redoing the back porch steps...how much can we get away with leaving as-is?"

"I guess that depends on the buyer. And the market. All the things on the list are important to think about," Janelle said. "Will some of them make a huge difference in whether or not we can sell the house? Probably not. But you never know."

She'd been through this a hundred times before. Sellers wanted to get the most money out of their house, and the "you have to spend money to make it" argument didn't always fly.

Her uncle sighed heavily. "Let me talk to Deb about it. And I'll give Marty and Bobby and John a call, too. I'll get back to you on the dishwasher. Have someone look at the hot water heater, see if you can get it fixed instead of buying new. Listen, I have to get back to work. Give my love to Mom, okay? I'll shoot you an email with what we've decided."

"Uncle Joey," she said tightly. "Listen. I need a working hot water heater that can handle three people living in this house. There are dishes, showers, baths. The laundry alone is..." Janelle sighed and put a hand over her eyes for a moment. "Nan's incontinent, okay? There are accidents. I need to be able to wash her things in water hot enough to get them really clean."

"When we asked you to come out here and take care of

her, it was with the understanding that you'd do that. That includes doing her laundry."

For a moment, Janelle couldn't think of how to reply. He'd totally missed the point. "I'm not complaining about doing the laundry. I'm just saying that I had to run a few loads of sheets and towels and other things today, and the hot water heater isn't—"

"You know, we could've hired a nurse to come and stay with her, Janelle."

"A nurse would've cost you more than a new hot water heater and a new dishwasher," Janelle snapped. "You've given me power of attorney for your mother's medical needs. Which means that if she goes to the hospital, I can sign her in. I can sign her out. I can determine if they give her lifesaving care. Or not. If she needs to be taken off of life support, I can do that, too, without consent from any of you. But I can't spend more than a hundred dollars at a time at the store, and I can't change any of the utilities or make repairs to this house without your permission."

She paused to draw a breath, forcing herself to keep her voice calm and steady, not to give in to her emotions. "How does any of that make sense?"

Silence.

"What are you so worried about?" she asked finally, when he wouldn't say anything.

"We're not worried…it's just that…look, the house is all she has," Joey said. "The house and that little bit of money in the bank. It has to last. That's all."

Janelle thought of Nan, sleeping when she ought to be awake, and wakeful when everyone else slept. Of how frail she'd become. "It's not like I'm asking to remodel the entire house. I don't understand what the big deal is. If you don't want me to tear up the carpet or make decorating improvements, that's fine, but…but…" Janelle let out another low sigh, hating that it had come to this. "I need to be able to do these other things. Necessary things. Without being hobbled."

"Your dad," he said. And that was all.

Janelle's stomach twisted. "What about my dad?"

"You don't know, I guess. You wouldn't."

Across the alley, Gabe's light went on. His curtain twitched, but he didn't pull it all the way open. Janelle stood at the window, not even pretending otherwise, though her attention was taken up more by the phone pressed to her ear than any sort of strip show going on across the way.

Janelle could easily believe the worst of her father, but this sounded bad. "What did he do?"

"He was always a big talker, your dad." Joey's laugh sounded harsh. "A storyteller. He could sell ice to the Eskimo, you know what I mean?"

Janelle remembered her father's stories. Promises made and broken. She'd learned not to count on him to show up on time for birthdays, but to expect something grandiose as a surprise when he did. "What did he do?"

"He talked Mom into giving him money. A lot of money. He talked her into taking out a second mortgage on the house to start some record producing business. He took things, too. From the house. To sell them." Her uncle paused as though to give her time to reply, but her stomach was too sour for her to speak. "He stole from Mom, Janelle. Right out from under her."

She hadn't known, but she wasn't surprised. "I'm not my dad. And you all asked me to come here, did you forget that? Because apparently none of the rest of you want this responsibility. Did you forget that, too?"

"Let me talk with everyone else about the repairs. About seeing you get a little more of a budget…."

Janelle shook her head, though of course, he couldn't see her. "No. No budget. When you asked me to come out here, it wasn't just to take care of Nan, it was to take care of the house. While she's still here, and after. You told me that you wanted someone who'd make sure it was in the best condition to be sold, someone you could trust with it. Either you trust me…or you don't."

"I can't just give you free rein! It's not up to me!"

Janelle didn't want to argue about it anymore. "Fine. Talk to them. Get back to me. But I need to be able to do things around this house, and I can't if my hands are tied. If you're really worried that I'm going to run off with something, or…I don't even know what, then maybe you'd be better off hiring a nurse."

"You'd leave Mom?" He sounded astonished.

"I don't have to leave St. Marys," Janelle told him. "Even if I don't live in this house. I can still love my grandmother even if I'm not the one changing her sheets. After all…you all do."

With that, it seemed obvious he had nothing more to say, so she disconnected.

Nan called her name from the bedroom. Tapping her phone against her palm, Janelle went to the door. "Hi. Can I get you something?"

"I'm going to get up, honey." Nan yawned and set her book aside. "Who were you talking to? Is Benny home from school?"

"No. He will be soon, though. I was talking to Uncle Joey."

"About the house." Nan sighed. "He doesn't want you to change things."

"How'd you know?"

Nan laughed. "Because I know my son. Getting him to come around here to do anything has been a trial for years. You'd think this place was a national monument or something. I'm the one who had to live here all these years, it was my house, but Joey…oh, Joey, he likes to hold on to things tight. Your dad, now, if he were here and in charge of things, he'd never have argued. Your dad…he was never one to hang on to things."

As a victim of her dad's lack of sentimentality, Janelle understood that very well. "I don't really want to change anything, either, Nan. I like your house the way it is."

Nan smiled. "Me, too, honey. I've lived in this house for most of my life. I had five children in this house. And I'll die in it, too."

"Oh, Nan." Janelle shook her head. "Don't say that."

"Don't you start," Nan scolded. "Nobody wants to talk about it, but that's the truth. It won't be long now. I've been hearing them calling."

Janelle didn't understand. "Who? The phone hasn't—"

"No, no, not the phone." Nan paused. "I hear them calling my name."

"Who, Nan?"

She shrugged slightly. "I'm not sure, but I think it must be…angels."

Janelle didn't laugh. She didn't even bite the inside of her cheek. Somehow the idea of angels calling out to her Nan seemed…right. "What do they say?"

"The first time it happened was just before I fell down the stairs. I'd taken a little nap, and I heard someone calling my name. 'Maureen,' they said. 'Maureen!'" Nan lifted one finger. "Well, I thought it must be Helen, maybe coming by to pick me up for card club, but it was too early."

Intent, Janelle leaned forward. "Who was it?"

"Well, that's the thing. I got up out of bed and went to the living room. I thought for sure someone had come in."

Nan leaned forward a little bit, too, to whisper, "But there was nobody."

"Maybe you...dreamed it?"

She sagged back onto the pillows and tossed her hands up. "Maybe I did! But it happened more than once."

"Have you heard them lately?" This story intrigued Janelle. She didn't discount it. She had never believed in ghosts, exactly, but she'd never *not* believed. It was a cliché to say that she'd met her share of New Age spiritualists while living in California, but it was true.

"Oh, yes," Nan said quietly. "I still hear them. They say my name."

"And that's all?"

Nan hesitated. "Yes. Just my name."

Janelle had experienced that sudden jerking feeling before falling asleep before. She tried to think if she'd ever heard someone calling her name. She thought of waking, heart pounding, sweating, ears straining for whatever it was that had torn her from sleep—Bennett's cry, the snick of a locked door opening, an alarm. "Does it scare you?"

"Oh, no," Nan said. "Why would it?"

"It would scare me," Janelle admitted.

"It wouldn't, if you knew it was someone who loved you."

Janelle laughed lightly. "But...how would I know if it was someone who loved me?"

"You'd know." Nan patted the bedspread again, then made motions of getting up. "Now help me up, Janelle, it's time for my program."

TWENTY

Then

GABE HAS A NEW BLAZE-ORANGE HUNTING VEST, an early Christmas present, his dad says. That means there won't be anything else under the tree, but that's okay. The new rifle that he can use now makes up for not having any presents on Christmas Day.

This is the first time he's been invited along to camp. Four days and three nights, a half-dozen guys in the cabin, all of them his dad's friends and none with sons of their own. Gabe's known these guys his entire life. Not one has a second's hesitation in cuffing him upside the head when he gets a smart mouth on him, but all of them make sure he's fully equipped and prepared for the hunt.

Archie Miller gives him a bottle of deer pee to rub all over himself. Eddie Smith offers advice on packing toilet paper in his backpack, "just in case." These men are like brothers, his dad included. And he's different at camp, Gabe's dad.

Gabe's never seen his dad smile so freely, much less burst out
in knee-slapping laughter. The jokes are dirty, some of them
going over Gabe's head, and he knows better than to laugh
or else face good-natured ridicule from the men asking him
if he knows what he's laughing at. Good-natured maybe even
from his dad, who's nothing like he is at home with his sour
face and ready fists, but Gabe's not taking a chance. He keeps
quiet, drawing no attention to himself.

For dinner they eat pork 'n' beans with franks cooked right
in the pan. Hamburgers. Deer sausage, the last from the previ-
ous year's hunting, and supposedly a good omen for bagging
a buck this time around. Gabe's never seen his dad so much
as brown a piece of toast, but here he puts on a silly chef's cap
and a fake French accent as he whips up a meat loaf that rivals
anything Mrs. Moser has ever left for them. After dinner, Gabe
does the dishes in the sink, which doesn't have running water,
just buckets drawn from the pump outside and heated on the
wood stove. The men play cards and drink beer and smoke
cigars until the smoke's so thick it turns them into ghosts.
They lift their legs and fart. More dirty jokes, more stories
that get louder and more graphic as the night wears on, until
Archie, who Gabe's dad has always said is half a moron, says,
"Talking about whores, I seen your old lady over in Dubois
last week. Damn, the titties on her...."

The sudden silence is thicker than the cigar smoke fog.

Then Gabe's dad says quietly, significantly, "Little pitchers,
Archie. Little fucking pitchers."

Gabe acts as if he didn't hear what Archie said, or at least
didn't understand it, and in another half a minute the men are
back to their laughter and jokes. Money's tossed on the table
along with a watch, a pocketknife, a slip of paper scrawled
with an IOU. It's become serious business, and Gabe's not invited to play.

He sneaks away upstairs, where the gables are so steep you can stand upright only in the center of the room, and if you're on top of one of the six sets of bunk beds you'd better watch your head if you sit up too fast. He has a top bunk, of course, away from the rest of them. The room's cold enough to show his breath, but he's warm in his sleeping bag. His eyes droop. He sleeps.

He's woken by the sound of shouting from outside. Blinking, Gabe sits, forgetting the slope of the ceiling. Stars explode in his vision when his forehead connects with the slatted wood. Something that might be a spider, please Jesus, not a spider, skitters across his lips and he swipes at it frantically. The pain's so fierce, so bright, he thinks it has made him blind.

Of course, it's just the darkness. Gabe twists in his sleeping bag to look out the window. The glass is rimed around the edges, but the center's clear. Everything's so cold in the room, even his breath, it hardly frosts the rest of the glass.

Outside is a lot brighter than in, because of the fire in the pit and the single spotlight. The snow around the pit has melted, the dirt beneath churned to mud. Benches made from split logs ring the fire, and one of them's been knocked over. Mud streaks the snow, which even farther from the pit has been gouged down to bare ground in places. That's because of the men who are fighting, Gabe thinks, his brain still a little blurry from the whack he gave his bean on the ceiling.

It's his dad; he knows that at once. Ralph Tierney fights when he drinks. His friends know it, though it never stops them from offering that next beer.

"You stupid bastard!" Ralph shouts, fists raised. Fluid that must be blood, but looks black, leaks from his nose. His thinning hair stands on end. His red-and-black-checked flannel shirt flaps open to reveal the stained white T-shirt beneath it. Gabe's dad is muscular and lean most everywhere but his belly, which sticks out now. "You stupid, loud-mouthed, lousy son of a bitch!"

"Jesus, Ralph, simmer down!" That's Archie, whose friends all know he does have a loud mouth, the way they know Ralph gets fisty after his sixth or seventh Straub's greenie. "How was I supposed to know?"

"You should've thought about it, you stupid..." Ralph seems to lose steam at that. He staggers.

Gabe turns away, feeling sick. The floorboards creak. It's Eddie with a palm-size flashlight, hand cupped over the light to keep it from blinding anyone.

"Go back to sleep, kid."

"I am." Gabe scoots down into the sleeping bag, though he's pretty sure it will be a long time before he can sleep.

Eddie moves closer. He's the youngest of Ralph's friends, part of the group because his older brother, Frank, went to school with them all, plus Eddie married Archie's younger sister, Denita. Eddie wears wire-rimmed glasses that always slip down his nose, and he pushes them up now as he looks out the window.

"It's just Archie," he says supercasually. "Running off his mouth. He should know better than to piss off your dad."

Gabe says nothing. Archie ran his mouth about a lot of things; that wasn't new. But what he ran his mouth about... *that* had been different.

"He doesn't know when to shut up, that's all."

Gabe doesn't look at Eddie. "He was talking about my dad's...girlfriend."

The word tastes funny. Men Ralph's age oughtn't to have girlfriends. They should have wives, or old-maid sisters who did for them. Or housekeepers like Mrs. Moser, who'd been with them since Gabe was little. But *girlfriend* is a nicer word than *whore,* which is what Archie had called her.

Eddie snorts softly. The light from outside flashes on his glasses when he turns. "Your dad has a girlfriend?"

"I thought that's what Archie meant."

"No. It was shitty of him to say it like that, but he meant your dad's old lady. His wife. Your mom."

Gabe's throat closes. His body goes stiff, like stone. He can't move anything but his mouth, and he wishes he couldn't move that because then he couldn't answer. "I guess Archie's an idiot then, because it couldn't have been my mom. My mom's dead."

A slow, awkward hiss of air slips from Eddie's mouth. He moves closer. "Jesus, kid. I'm sorry.... I think it's rotten your dad has been lying to you. But it's gonna come out sometime or other."

Gabe manages to turn his head on the pillow and prop himself up to look at the man. "My mom's dead."

Eddie shakes his head slowly. He smells like wood smoke and beer, and he's clearly drunker than Gabe thought he was, because he wobbles a little when he bends to unlace his boot. He pushes it off with the toe of the other, then takes a break with a sigh. Eddie scratches at his face, then his hair. His face is nothing but shadow except for the twin bright disks of his glasses, reflecting the firelight coming in the window. It makes his eyes look as if they're on fire.

"I'm sorry to tell you, kid. But she's not."

TWENTY-ONE

GETTING BENNETT TO TAKE A SHOWER WAS NOT yet monumentally difficult, but it was a whole lot harder than it had been even a year ago.

"It's cold!" he complained, hopping from foot to foot, already in his pajamas.

Compared to California, it *was* cold. Still, that was no excuse. "You can't go to school looking like a hobo. I'm sure your friends' mothers don't let them go to school in ripped clothes with knots in their hair, either."

"Who cares?" he cried, suddenly vehement. "Who cares what anyone there thinks about anything, anyway?"

"I care," she said.

"It's my hair! My clothes! I should be able to decide what I want."

Without thinking, Janelle ran her fingers through her own hair, which was sleek and without tangles. How many times had she fought the hairbrush? How often had she been allowed to face the world with a dirty face and clothes because her dad had been more concerned about being fun than firm?

"It's my job as your mother to make sure you are taken care of and that you learn to take care of yourself," Janelle told him. "No arguments. This is not a negotiation. Get in there and shower. Wash and comb your hair."

He stared at her, fists clenched, brow furrowed. Scowling. For a minute, Janelle thought he wasn't going to go, but then he turned, muttering things under his breath she didn't have the strength to ask him to repeat. She remembered the day she'd figured out her mother couldn't actually force her to do anything she didn't want to do. She'd never thought about the day when Bennett would figure out the same thing.

"It's my job," she said softly.

Then

On the TV is some weird program showing how to make a telephone out of some string and two soup cans. It looks like fun. Daddy and Uncle Marty and Uncle Bobby and Uncle Joey are all sitting around the table with their beers and pizza, playing cards. Nan's at work. Janelle's eyes are droopy, but she wants to stay up until Nan gets home so it will be easier to sleep late tomorrow. If she gets up too early, she'll make too much noise, and Daddy will yell.

Nan comes home in her white nurse's uniform. She hollers at all the guys to clean up their stuff and go home, but not like she's mad. She even eats a piece of pizza with them before noticing Janelle still on the couch.

"What's that girl doing up?" Nan shakes her head. "No rules. You're raising her like a wild animal, Ricky."

Daddy looks over at Janelle and gestures for her to come to him. She does, her eyes heavy with sleep, stifling a yawn she doesn't want Nan to see, because that's proof she's too tired to be up.

"Janny's okay, aren't you, hon?"

"Of course she's okay, she's doing whatever she wants." Nan shakes her head again. "Did they feed you, honey?"

"Yes, Nan."

To Daddy, Nan says, "A child needs boundaries and rules. And a bedtime. When's the last time she had a shower, for heaven's sake?"

"C'mon, Mom, who cares? It's summer. Let the kid have a little freedom."

At home with her mother, Janelle showers every other day whether she wants to or not. Bedtime is always too early, and they have pizza only once in a while, for a treat. When Daddy's got his own place, the routine is much the same as it's been at Nan's, only without any showers at all, and sometimes not even pizza. One time they ate saltines and peanut butter every day for a whole week until Daddy got a paycheck. Then he took her out for a steak dinner and bought her a new doll. It was great.

"There's freedom," Nan says, "and there's just lack of responsibility. You know her mother wouldn't approve of this at all."

"Her mother doesn't need to know anything, and who cares what she thinks?" Daddy's chair scrapes along the carpet. "It's my turn to have my kid. She's not in danger. She's got food, clothes. So what if she hasn't had a shower?"

"Or brushed her teeth, I'll bet. Definitely not shampooed her hair—there's a knot in it the size of my fist. Have you fed her a vegetable at all this week?"

"Mom," Daddy says, but that's all.

"More importantly, Ricky, have you spent any time with her?"

"She's with me every day."

Nan sighs. "She's here every day. You're here. That's not the same thing. You keep her up too late, then she's sleeping half the day away. Or she's up a the crack of dawn and neither of us are with her. She spends too much time alone."

"She plays with those kids next door, doesn't she?"

"The Tierney boys?" Nan laughs. "Sometimes."

"So? She's not alone."

Nan knocks her knuckles on the table. "It's her summer vacation. Take her to the pool once in a while. To the park. We could take a day trip down to Parker Dam, take a picnic...."

"I can't be doing all that stuff, Mom. I have to work. You know that."

Silence.

"Work is something that you get paid for doing."

"Oh, here we go."

"Just hear me out," Nan says, and even if Daddy's mad, he listens. "I know you're trying hard to make a go of this music thing, and believe me, honey, I want you to make it more than anyone. But how long are you going to go from job to job, never putting in more than a few hours here and there, just enough to get you through?"

"It's hard to have a full-time job and get gigs. I have to be able to travel. Why do we even have to go over this again?"

"Because you're living in my house and you have a child to raise," Nan says. "So at least for this summer, Richard, you need to pull your head out of your behind and find some steady work. Or send her home to her mother so you can run off all around the country playing in bars. You can't have it both ways."

Daddy flicks his lighter on, off. On, off. It's a big one, heavy and silver, with a picture of an eagle engraved on it. Some-

times he lets Janelle light it for him. She loves the smell of the
gas just before the flame appears.

"You don't think I can make it."

"I think you can do anything you set your mind to," Nan
answers in a tired voice. "But my God, Richard. Set your
mind to something. That's all."

"Janelle! Get your butt to bed! And in the morning, you
take a shower." Daddy snaps his fingers, waking her all the
way.

Janelle sits up, rubbing her eyes. "Huh?"

"You heard me. Get upstairs."

Nan reaches for her as she passes, kisses her cheek. "Tomorrow we'll do something fun, okay? I have the day off."

"Okay, Nan."

Upstairs, Janelle takes an extra-long time brushing her
teeth, even though she knows if Daddy comes up and finds
her not in bed he'll be mad. She has to take extra time because Nan's right, she hasn't brushed them in...well, she can't
remember the last time. She thinks of the tiny cavity monsters in her mouth, biting away at her teeth, making holes.
She scrubs and spits, scrubs and spits.

This visit, Janelle's in the big room with Daddy, because
the little room is full of his equipment and stuff in boxes he
brought from his last apartment. The window in the big room
looks across the alley into the window next door. There's a
light on over there, not in the bedroom, but the hall, so it
shines into the bedroom.

That's Gabe's room. Janelle goes to the window, meaning to see if she can wave at him. She thinks of the telephone
idea, those tin cans and the string. They could make one of
those, she's sure of it.

Because it's dark in her room, she can see into his, but nobody over there can see into hers. She pulls aside the curtain

only partway before seeing it's not Gabe moving around his room. It's Mr. Tierney. He's pacing next to Gabe's bed, and because of the way the light falls into the room from the open door, sometimes he's in shadow, sometimes he's in light. Dark, light, back and forth.

Then he stops.

He bends over Gabe's bed. He must be tucking him in. Janelle's mom does that, tucks her in so tight she can't move at all. Janelle likes that. It makes her feel as if she'll never fall out of bed.

Gabe must not like it, though, because all of a sudden he's sitting up. Hands are waving. Mr. Tierney stumbles back. The shadows move, making it hard to see what's going on, but whatever it is, it doesn't look good. In the light, Mr. Tierney's face is twisted, his mouth open as if he's shouting. He reaches for Gabe to shake him by the shoulders. Gabe pushes him back again. There's a muffled sound of yelling.

Daddy's feet thump on the stairs, and Janelle lets the curtain fall. She runs across the room to dive into the bouncy bed—it's not a real bed, it's a rollaway that folds up when nobody's using it. It bounces when she jumps into it, and she goes very still to keep the springs from creaking as Daddy comes into the room.

She closes her eyes. She slows her breath. Downstairs she was way more tired than she is now, but watching Mr. Tierney and Gabe fighting and knowing that she'll get in trouble if Daddy knows she's not asleep yet have both made her heart pound a little too hard. She snuggles deep under the covers, faking sleep.

Daddy runs the water in the bathroom. He turns off the light in the hall and moves through the bedroom in the dark, bumping into something and muttering about it. She expects to hear the creak and groan of his mattress in the big bed along the wall, but the darkness by her bed gets a little darker even through her closed eyes.

She thinks of Mr. Tierney shaking Gabe and tenses. What does Daddy want? Does he know she's not asleep? Is he going to be mad?

Her father touches his fingertips to her forehead, brushing away her hair. Then comes the soft press of his lips in that same spot. A murmured, "Love you, kiddo," and a few seconds later, the creak of his mattress as he gets into bed. Snoring, after that.

And after that, before she knows it, it's morning.

Her door creaked. "Mom?"

Janelle turned. "Yeah, buddy."

"Are we going to leave Nan's house?"

Janelle let herself sink onto her bed and gestured to him. He came to her willingly enough. He hadn't combed his hair the way she'd told him to, but she didn't have the strength to argue with him. It hadn't been so long ago that he'd have snuggled up close to her, but now he sat with some distance between them.

"No, buddy, we're not going to leave Nan's house. At least, I hope not."

"Will we go back to California?"

She couldn't resist stroking her hand over the damp tangle of his hair. "No. Do you want to go back?"

Bennett shrugged without looking at her. "I don't know. Maybe."

She knew he'd left friends behind, that they kept in touch through Connex and their online games. She'd expected him to make new friends here without much effort, because that was her sweet boy. But she did not know if her son was happy here.

"How's everything at school?"

Bennett shrugged. "It's okay."

"Any more trouble with those boys?"

"No."

"Don't you like it here?" Janelle asked.

He leaned against her, just a little. "It's okay. It's cold here, though. Does it get warm, ever? Is there summer here?"

She laughed. "You act like it's the North Pole."

"Feels like it," he said.

Janelle laughed again. "Yeah. I promise you, it'll get warm. And summer here's nice. We'll go swimming. We can go hiking, too. Out in the woods. We'll go to the elk preserve. How about that?"

Bennett looked up at her. "Who will stay with Nan?"

Summer was a few months away. Another few months of being chained to this house as caretaker, barely able to get away to the store by herself. An entire summer of it seemed intolerable, and when summer came, Bennett was right. Who would stay with Nan?

Probably, nobody would have to.

"Maybe," she said, pushing his hair away from his eyes, "she'll come with us. Wouldn't that be fun?"

TWENTY-TWO

APRIL SHOWERS BROUGHT MAY FLOWERS, BUT an overcast sky on Easter morning brought worried looks and anxious parents. With everyone dressed in their finery, frilly dresses and bonnets and white gloves for the girls, adorable little pastel suits with vests for the boys, Janelle didn't blame any of them. Her own son, of course, wore black cargo pants and a long-sleeved T-shirt with a picture of a tuxedo on the front. He had consented to tying back his hair, though it looked suspiciously uncombed.

"I think the rain will hold off," Janelle said to Karen Jones. Karen was a couple years older than her and had lived across the street from Nan her whole life, until she went away to college and moved to Pittsburgh. Now she only came back to St. Marys for holidays, to visit her parents so they could dote on their only grandchild, Emma. Janelle had heard the whole story already. Twice. "Look how much fun they're having."

"It was really nice of you and your grandma to add to the Easter egg hunt. Emma looks forward to this so much every year." Karen smiled, but her gaze never left her daughter, who was bobbing and weaving through the crowd of twenty or so kids aged three to twelve who were systematically foraging for the plastic and hard-boiled eggs planted everywhere. "Every year, she begs to come."

"That's great. I'm glad to hear it. I guess it's Mr. Tierney's thing, really."

Mr. Tierney held court in an ancient, sagging lawn chair that looked as if it might collapse at any moment under his bulk. Karen smiled. "Oh, yes. He really gets into it. I guess because he doesn't have any grandkids of his own."

Janelle didn't miss the assessing look Karen gave Gabe, who stood overlooking the festivities from his familiar place on the porch. He wasn't smoking, maybe out of respect for the children. Maybe a cigarette would've made him less grouchy, Janelle thought, then laughed silently. Probably not.

Karen gave her a curious look. "What?"

"Oh. Nothing. Just enjoying this hint of warmer weather. Even if it does look like rain." Janelle stretched her hands up toward the glimpse of yellow sunshine peeping through the gray clouds. "I'm glad winter's over."

"You wait. We've had snow in early May before," Karen warned, then must've seen her daughter heading for danger, because she took off sprinting, leaving Janelle behind.

Janelle didn't even have to turn around to know Gabe was looking at her. She zipped her hoodie a little higher on her throat and shoved her hands in her pockets. "It's a good thing the snow melted, huh?"

"We just wouldn't have colored the eggs, that's all. Would've made it wicked hard to find them."

"This is a nice thing you do. You know that, right?"

He looked at her. "It's my dad's thing. And Andy's. I'm just the muscle."

She thought of the hour or so they'd spent stuffing the plastic eggs with candy and pennies. "Uh-huh."

He looked at her again. "What's that supposed to mean?"

She shook her head with a smile and looked out to the yard, where all the kids were running and shouting. "You like it. Admit it. You like seeing them find all those eggs."

Gabe made a low, disgruntled noise. Janelle didn't poke him further. She left him there on the porch as she went out into the yard to help some of the smaller kids find the well-hidden eggs, both hard-boiled and treat-filled, that the older kids had missed. The grass was cool and soft on her bare feet, and when the sun finally managed to burst out from its prison of clouds, she stood in the center of the yard with her head tipped back and arms out, enjoying the warmth and promise of spring.

There'd been a few squabbles so far when more than one kid found the same egg at the same time, but this raised voice was adult. Janelle's eyes snapped open at the shout. Mr. Tierney was yelling, shaking his fist at Gabe, who had a hand on the old man's shoulder as though holding him back.

Most of the kids weren't paying attention, though of course, their parents were. Bennett, on the other hand, stood on the Tierneys' porch, a bag bulging with treats in one hand. His eyes were wide, his gaze going back and forth between Mr. Tierney and Gabe, who was now muttering something into the old man's ear.

Janelle moved carefully through the grass to avoid stepping on any eggs. "What's going on?"

Mr. Tierney was now fighting to shove Gabe's hand from his shoulder, but Gabe wasn't letting go. It had the look of something that could turn ugly...and with an audience, too. She stepped up.

"Hey!" She kept her voice light. "Is it time for the Easter Bunny yet?"

"Screw the Easter Bunny!" Mr. Tierney cried.

Gabe's fingers dug deeper into his shoulder. "Be quiet. There are kids here, old man."

Mr. Tierney's eyes had gone red-rimmed and watery. Gabe smoked but never smelled more than faintly of tobacco; Mr. Tierney stank of it. Also body odor and a mixed perfume of fainter, awful smells Janelle couldn't identify and didn't really want to.

"Where's Andy?" she asked.

"In the house," Gabe said without looking at her. "He'll be out soon."

Mr. Tierney muttered something and jerked away from his son's grasp, hard enough to send Gabe's hand knocking against the porch railing. With a venomous look, the old man spat to the side, pushed past his son and went inside. Janelle watched him for a second.

"Bennett, go play," she said. He did at once, but she waited another half a minute before turning to Gabe. "What was that all about?"

"He wanted to get in the costume."

Janelle frowned. "Okay?"

"Not okay." Gabe shook his head but kept his voice down, his gaze darting back and forth over her shoulder and not meeting hers. "Andy's the Easter Bunny, that's the way it is. That's the way it always is."

"Did Andy not want to do it, or...?"

"No. He's inside dressing right now. The old man just got it in his head that this year he was going to do it. And he can't. Jesus." Gabe's mouth twisted before he rubbed a hand over it. "Jesus Christ."

Janelle turned to look at their yards, where all the kids were finding the last few eggs and the parents had clumped into groups, gossiping or sorting through the baskets of candy to pick out a few treats for themselves. Something was going on here that she didn't understand, but she did know Gabe well enough not to push him for an answer. She watched her son bend to help a smaller child pick up an egg from the base of the apple tree at the back of Nan's yard.

Behind her, the back door opened and Andy came out in the white Easter Bunny suit. The head was so big he had to turn sideways to fit through the door, and one ear had been fixed in the back with a wooden spoon and duct tape to keep it from flopping. The suit had clearly seen better days, but none of the kids seemed to care. Some squealed and ran toward the chair they'd set up earlier for him. Some hung back, reluctant until their parents encouraged them to go and get the small paper bags of candy Janelle, Andy, Nan and Gabe had spent hours stuffing.

Andy nodded his giant, ponderous head slowly. Carefully. He held the smaller kids on his lap or posed with the bigger ones at his side for pictures. He hugged them all, never speaking to ruin the illusion, but using gestures to communicate.

"He's good with them," she said.

Gabe sighed. "Yeah. He is."

"Didn't see you at church this morning." She kept the words light, not quite teasing. More curious than anything else.

Gabe looked at her, one brow raised. "You don't see me at church any morning."

"Well. True. But Easter Sunday. I'd think you'd go to church on Easter, if you don't go any other time."

"I'll get my sermon when my brother comes next week."

Janelle grinned. "How is he?"

Gabe shrugged. "He's fine, I guess."

"He didn't want to come for Easter dinner?" They'd been invited to Joey and Deb's house for Easter dinner, a relief to

Janelle, since Nan had said she wanted to cook a full meal, and Janelle hadn't felt up to it.

Gabe snorted. "He's a priest. He was working today. We never see him for Christmas or Easter."

She felt dumb then. Of course. "Oh. So, he has a congregation?"

"Yeah. Down near Pittsburgh."

"Do you see him…often? I mean, other times that aren't priests' working days."

"No. He doesn't come home very often. He's busy."

"Pittsburgh's not so far away." Janelle looked out to the yard, where the children were still lining up for a chance to sit on the Easter Bunny's lap. "Surely he could just come home for a visit. Or you could go down there. Priests are allowed to see their families, have a social life. Aren't they?"

"I don't really know what priests are allowed to do, Janelle. I'm not a priest."

She'd pissed him off. It didn't matter how. Even if she knew the reason, it was likely she'd have found some other way to make him mad. She seemed to have that knack.

"I was just asking," she said sharply. "I haven't seen Michael in a long time. Thought it would be nice to see him again, that's all."

Gabe gazed at her for a few silent moments before he gave a derisive snort. "You think so?"

Janelle put her hands on her hips, but kept her voice low, not wanting to attract attention. "Yeah. I do. What's wrong with that? I always liked your brother. And he's a priest. That's interesting. So, yeah, Gabe, I guess I wouldn't mind seeing him again. What's your problem?"

He held up his hands and shrugged.

She'd stepped closer so she could make sure he heard her every word without having to raise her voice. It was too close.

Now she could smell him. Smell smoke and something like cedar, something like soap.

He backed up a step, but the porch railing was behind him. He was trapped. He looked down at her for only a second or two before his eyes darted away. He pulled a cigarette from his breast pocket and tucked it between his lips. He took a lighter from his pocket—a familiar Zippo lighter. One she hadn't seen in years.

Without thinking, Janelle took it from him. "Oh. Wow. You kept it? All this time?"

She looked at him, searching his eyes for something, anything that would give her a clue about what he was thinking. There was nothing. Without taking the lighter from her hand, Gabe flicked the top open and lit it. He brought her hand to his mouth to light the cigarette, his fingers warm and callused against hers. He looked into her eyes as he sucked in that first draw of smoke. He let it out slowly, slowly, so that it drifted across her face.

Then he moved back a little more, finding room despite the railing. He made a space between them, small in size but enormous in meaning. He touched the charm nestled in the hollow of her throat, but said nothing. When he withdrew his hand, Janelle touched the same place, also without a word.

Together in silence, both of them stood and stared at each other. She wanted to speak. She wanted, maybe, to do a lot of things. But in the end, she didn't.

TWENTY-THREE

MICHAEL AND ANDY WEREN'T IDENTICAL TWINS, but they'd always looked a lot alike. Time had painted lines on Mikey's face and streaked his hair with silver. Michael looked more like Gabe now, and when Gabe looked in the mirror, sometimes he was disgusted to see the old man. Out of the three of them, Andy had always been the one who looked like their mother, and time had been the kindest to him.

Seeing Michael and Andy sitting next to each other, Gabe found the differences even more pronounced. The black suit and white collar didn't help. Neither did the holier-than-thou attitude, though to be fair, Gabe thought, Mikey really was holier than any of them.

He'd already regaled them with stories about his parish and his hobbies and just about everything else he could talk about without giving any of them room to speak. The old man ate it all up, hanging on every word. So did Andy.

Gabe, on the other hand, couldn't help thinking how much of a smug sort of prick his younger brother had become, priest's collar or no. It didn't matter that Michael had brought the ham and all the trimmings and set out a feast to rival any gourmet restaurant, or that he'd given Andy an envelope full of scratch-off lottery tickets, or that he'd listened to the old man's confession in the back room, both of them in there for what seemed like an hour. Michael had always been thoughtful and considerate. Concerned and deliberate. But now those traits seemed somehow less genuine, more like he was faking them.

"You could stay longer," Gabe told his brother in the kitchen when the old man had settled himself in front of the TV and Andy was in the shower. "Andy could use a few more days with you."

"Can't," Michael said matter-of-factly as he packaged up leftovers into neat portions and labeled them in his sloppy, sloping hand before putting them in the freezer. "Now look, these will be good for Dad's dinner when you're not here. Make sure he knows where they are. Just tell him to reheat for five to seven minutes."

"He's not starving," Gabe said.

Michael didn't even look up. "It won't be good for him every day—there's too much salt in the ham. But once a week or so, that will be fine. Those frozen dinners I brought are better. Low sodium, low fat."

Gabe snagged his brother's sleeve. "Mike, what the hell are you doing?"

Michael paused, still not looking at him. "Just...trying to help."

"I told you, he's not starving. The old man can make himself a sandwich. He's not crippled."

"You should take better care of him!" The shout seemed to surprise Michael as much as it did Gabe, maybe more.

Gabe took a step back to lean against the kitchen counter. "You have a problem with how I run things around here?"

Michael's eyes narrowed. He frowned. "The place could be cleaner. You should get him out more, get him out of the chair and outside. Get him interested in something other than television. And Andy spends too much time playing video games."

Gabe stayed stoic, giving his brother plenty of rope and waiting for him to hang himself with it.

"Dad needs a better diet. For that matter, all of you do." Michael ticked off his grievances on his fingertips, really getting going now. "The bathroom down here is disgusting. That stack of newspapers by the front door is a fire hazard. How can you live like this, Gabe?"

"Could you do a better job?"

Michael hesitated, but finally looked at him. "You know I can't move home. C'mon. Don't be a..."

"A what?" Gabe's brows rose.

"Don't be ridiculous," his brother said quietly. "My life is with my parish."

"Andy could move down there, close to you. He could go to school. Get a better job. And the old man—"

"I wish you wouldn't call him that," Michael interrupted. "He's our father."

"And you live three hours away and see him a few times a year," Gabe replied pretty calmly, all things considered. "You bring presents and food and swan in here like you own the place, giving advice. Listening to confessions. Let me ask you something, Mikey, what exactly does the old man tell you in that back room?"

Michael's expression went stony. "You know I can't tell you."

"You don't have to. I'm sure I can imagine." Gabe went to the fridge to pull out a beer he didn't want, but would drink, anyway, just to wash the taste of bitterness away. "Whatever. If you can do a better job, you're welcome to it."

"I don't want to fight with you."

"Yeah?" Gabe gave him a look. "It sure seems like you do."

"You've always been the one who likes to fight," his brother said.

That was enough for Gabe. He pulled his cigarettes from his breast pocket and went out onto the back porch. His brother followed, letting the door close behind him. He held out a hand silently, waiting until Gabe handed him the pack. He shook out a smoke, tucked it between his lips and waited for Gabe to offer a light.

They smoked in silence for a minute or so.

"You know…I'd be happy to listen to your confession," Michael said. "When's the last time you went?"

"I don't have anything to confess."

Michael shook his head, drawing deep on the cigarette and letting the smoke seep out through his nostrils. He'd never smoked as a kid. Hardly drank. Funny how the collar had changed him in ways nobody would ever have guessed.

"Everyone has something to confess," Michael said.

"Even you?"

Michael paused. "Even me. Maybe especially me."

"So, who listens to yours?" Gabe let the cigarette burn, watched it become a tube of ash.

"God. Or another priest."

Gabe shrugged. "What good would it do me to confess? What do I get from it, Mikey, can you tell me that?"

"You can get God's forgiveness, Gabe." His brother put out a hand to touch Gabe's shoulder.

He didn't shrug away, just looked at Michael's hand until he dropped it. Then Gabe finished his cigarette and crushed it out in the coffee can full of sand on the porch railing. He opened the back door and waited for his brother to go through first, but Michael hesitated, clearly waiting for him to respond.

"It's not God's forgiveness I care about," Gabe said, and went inside.

TWENTY-FOUR

THE ONE THING JANELLE HAD EVER ASKED HER son to give her for Mother's Day was to be allowed to sleep in, but Nan would be up and about in a few minutes, anyway. For now Janelle relished the warm weight of her blankets in the chill spring air. Later today, they had planned a picnic with the aunts and uncles.

Her phone rang after another minute or so, and she rolled to snag it from its place on her nightstand. "Mom. Hi. Happy Mother's Day. You're up early."

"Wanted to catch you before you got your day started." Janelle's mom laughed softly. "Happy Mother's Day, honey. How's your grandma?"

"She has her good days and her bad days."

"She's a tough one," Mom said. "How's my Bennett?"

They talked for a while about Bennett's schoolwork, Nan's health, the gossip about family and friends. Janelle got out of bed as she spoke, dressed with the phone to her ear, even managed to brush her teeth. She went downstairs still talking, meaning to give the phone to Bennett so he could talk to his granny.

She went all the way through the kitchen, but stopped short at the sight of the dining room table, fully laid out with Nan's good china and a cloth. Even cloth napkins. A vase of flowers picked from outside decorated the center, and Bennett, grinning, sat next to Nan, both of them obviously waiting for her.

Janelle cried out, earning a startled query from her mother, who was concerned that something had gone wrong. "They've made me breakfast, Mom. That's all."

"Oh, how nice. I'll let you get to it, then. Have Bennett call me later. I miss him."

"We made eggs," Bennett said when she'd disconnected. "And toast, and Nan helped me make cinnamon buns."

"He did most everything but the icing." Nan wore a colorful dressing gown and had tied a kerchief over her hair. She beamed.

"Happy Mother's Day, Mama." Bennett came around the table to hug her, and she squeezed him tight. He'd grown, she noticed. His head came up past her shoulders now.

"Sit down, Janelle. Let Bennett bring you some eggs. Bacon, too." Nan waved for her to come to the table.

Janelle sat, suddenly emotional and overwhelmed with it. "This all looks so great."

"He wanted to do it," Nan said. "Come on, before it gets cold."

The eggs were delicious, light and fluffy, with a sprinkling of cheese. The cinnamon buns were, of course, amazing. Even the coffee was great. Janelle ate until she was stuffed, then sat back with a sigh to rub her stomach.

Nan hadn't eaten much, but she had eaten. Now she plucked apart a cinnamon roll and licked at the frosting. "What time is everyone supposed to come over today?"

"About noon." Janelle looked at the clock. They had a few hours until then, and everyone was supposed to be bringing a dish, so that she didn't have much to prepare.

"Time for a nap, then." Nan yawned and pushed away from the table. She staggered a little, though, and Bennett caught her arm.

Janelle was next to her in a another moment, both of them holding Nan so she didn't fall. "Got you."

Nan sighed, then managed to straighten her shoulders. "Just got a little woozy, that's all. I'm okay. I'd like to nap in my bed though, honey, not the couch. That way if I'm still sleeping when people get here, they can sit and visit."

"Do you need help, Nan?" Bennett asked.

Janelle was so proud of him she wanted to cry. Together, they helped Nan to her bedroom. It all went fine until just before they reached the bed, when Nan stumbled again. Bennett did his best, but as she twisted to keep her grandmother from falling, pain ripped through Janelle's neck, shoulder and back. She gasped aloud, barely keeping the worst sort of curse from flying out by biting her tongue, hard. That pain was nothing compared to her neck and shoulder.

Nan didn't seem to notice, though Bennett looked concerned as Janelle tucked the covers around her grandma as best she could with only one arm that felt as if it worked. In the hall, he asked, "Are you okay?"

"Yeah. Just wrenched my neck." She gave him as broad a smile as she could muster, which seemed to satisfy him. "Can you do me a huge favor and clean up the dishes from the table? And do your best in the kitchen. I'm going to need to put some ice on this."

She'd originally injured her neck and shoulder in a relatively minor fender-bender before Bennett was born. Riding in the passenger seat of her friend Heather's car, neither of them wearing seat belts, both more concerned with the music on the radio than watching for slowing traffic. Heather had rear-ended the car in front of them. She'd cracked the windshield with her forehead, while Janelle had managed to hit the dashboard with her neck and shoulder. It didn't bother her all the time, except when she slept wrong, or bent and twisted a certain way. Then the pain was excruciating. It had effectively ended her short-lived career as a dancer in Vegas—not that she'd expected it to last forever, and it had turned out to be a blessing, since it had forced her to get her real estate license.

People coming to the house would just have to deal with a mess. Janelle took a soft ice pack from the freezer and shaped it to her neck with a wince. She watched Bennett clear the table, thinking she could help at least a little bit, but knowing as soon as she lifted her arm that was going to be impossible. She'd be lucky if she could move tomorrow at all, and then only if she took care of this right now. Ice, anti-inflammatories and, in about an hour, a steaming hot shower.

"Thanks, honey, I appreciate it," she told her son.

Bennett looked up with a stack of plates in his hand. He might've been in the habit lately of arguing with her, but not today. "I'm sorry your neck hurts you."

She wanted to hug and squeeze him, but fortunately for him, could not. "How did I get so lucky to have such a great kid?"

Bennett shrugged. "I guess I have a great mom."

"Good one." With her non-aching arm, Janelle mimed punching a clock. "Cha-ching, that goes in your bonus account."

"Mom, is it okay if Andy comes over today for the picnic? I said he could. And Mr. Tierney, too."

Janelle shifted the ice on her neck. "I guess so. Why not?"

Bennett moved past her to put the plates in the dishwasher.

"Well, Andy doesn't have a mother to spend the day with, so I figured he could come over. But I thought maybe you wouldn't like it if Mr. Tierney came."

She would not, in fact, be sad if Mr. Tierney did not come, but that wasn't the same thing as not liking it if he did. "It was very nice of you to ask them." She paused, biting back her next question until it managed to wriggle free, anyway. "What about Gabe?"

Bennett, concentrating on slotting dishes into the rack, didn't even look up. "I don't know. I guess he might come, too."

Upstairs, she dosed herself with ibuprofen. Did she want Gabe to come to the picnic? Did she care?

Janelle had seen him a few nights ago, coming in late. She'd been up reading, half watching for the light in his bedroom to turn on, though she'd never have admitted it. When it did, she'd clicked off her reading lamp and pulled the blankets to her chin to keep herself from peeking at him through the window. Temptation had won.

He'd been out drinking. She could tell by the way he leaned a little too heavily on his dresser when he lifted one foot and then the other to untie his boot laces. Not drunk enough to be impaired, just enough to be a little loose. His hair had been rumpled, the tails of his shirt untucked. He looked like a man who'd been tussling, or who'd gotten dressed in a hurry.

He'd stripped down to his shorts and stood in front of the window as if he were putting on a show just for her. Not that he ever looked her way, even once, because he didn't. He moved from the dresser to the laundry basket to the bed without even glancing toward the window. She knew he slept in pajama bottoms or boxers, sometimes with a T-shirt when it was cool, so when he hooked his thumbs into the waistband of his briefs, pulled them off those long, lean thighs and kicked them aside, she expected him to put on something else.

She hadn't expected him to climb into bed naked and finish off for himself what the night had so obviously started.

Watching from her own bed, her line of sight obscured by the angle and the halfhearted attempt she'd made at closing the curtains when she went to bed, Janelle knew she shouldn't watch him. She should close her eyes and turn away from what was meant to be private. It was licentious and yes, creepy, to spy on him no matter what he was doing, but especially when he did...that. It didn't matter that back in those before times, the open curtains had been an invitation to whatever show Gabe felt like putting on. Time had passed, things had changed. They were adults, and he probably didn't even remember those days. She should've felt ashamed about the way her breath caught and held as she watched his back arch, when the pace of his stroking hand quickened. She should've felt guilty, and she would have, if only Gabe hadn't gone to the window when he was finished and stared right through it into the darkness of her bedroom before firmly and deliberately closing his blinds.

"Jerk," she muttered, but without heat.

Shaking her head at the memory, Janelle arranged her pillows to cradle her as she opened her laptop and typed in her Interflix password. She'd been working her way through a series of British comedies Bennett had no use for—he tolerated *Monty Python* and laughed sometimes at Benny Hill, but that was the limit of his patience for foreign funnies. She queued up the next in the series and settled back with her ice and her damp cloth, and in moments, was asleep.

She woke with a start, as if someone had touched her. Or said her name, she thought, looking automatically for Bennett. The room was empty, her door still closed most of the her barbecue tools by the grill. And it wasn't that she minded, not exactly, the way they all came in and helped themselves to everything in the house. Janelle knew how to be a gracious hostess, which to her included allowing guests to make themselves feel comfortable. And these weren't guests, they were her family...but they felt like guests. It felt as if they were moving in on her turf.

Stupid, she told herself as she showed her aunt Kathy where to find the platters. Nobody here was trying to take anything away from her, and it was good to have visitors. Nan would love it. She needed it.

Outside, Joey was firing up the grill. He and Deb had brought the burgers. Bobby and his wife, Donna, had supplied the buns, someone else the drinks, another the paper products. Janelle had made a gigantic bowl of potato salad from Nan's recipe—Nan overseeing, of course—along with an equally huge bowl of her mom's macaroni salad. She'd also bought plenty of chips, pretzels and dips, all stored on the shelving unit on the back porch.

"Oh, my God, Janelle!" Betsy hugged her hard enough to crack her spine—which would've been fine if she hadn't wrenched it earlier.

Janelle winced, but hugged her cousin back. "Wow. It's been so long. You're...blond!"

Betsy twirled a strand of her hair around one finger while she laughed. "Yeah. Turned forty. It was this or get a tattoo and a boob job."

Her mother snorted as she pulled out an oval ceramic platter from the cupboard. "Oh, good Lord, Betsy. Didn't these used to be in the cabinet over the stove?"

"I moved some things around," Janelle explained. "To make it easier for Nan. She can't reach up that high anymore."

way. From his room she heard the buzz and clang of one of his games. Maybe that was what had woken her.

Wincing, Janelle pushed herself up from the pillows. The ice pack had gone warm, the cloth on her forehead dry. She glanced at the clock, wincing again as she twisted, but the pain had backed off quite a bit. Everyone was due in about forty minutes, though of course, could show up earlier or later than that. She had enough time for a hot, hot shower to work out the rest of the kink, and as long as she kept herself from too much activity, she'd be fine. It could've been a lot worse.

She spent more time in the shower than she'd meant to, but for once the hot water didn't seem to be in any danger of running out, and it felt so good, just so good, to lean against the shower wall and let the heat pound into her. By the time she forced herself out, she had barely enough time to swipe a comb through her wet hair and slip into a pretty sundress and sandals before she heard a car in the driveway, the back door opening a few minutes after that.

"Bennett," she said. "Come on down. They're here."

"Couple of minutes, Mom, I'm almost to the save spot!"

Betsy had sons just a little older than Bennett. When they got here, Janelle would send them up to get him. For now, she needed to get downstairs herself and greet everyone. It was chaos, of course, the quiet disrupted in the best way by laughter and talk. Janelle hugged and kissed cousins, aunts and uncles she hadn't seen in ages.

It was a little disconcerting, how they all came in and made themselves at home. Of course they did—this was Nan's house. Her uncles had been raised in this house. Her cousins had spent more time in it than Janelle ever had, though she was the only grandchild ever to actually live here.

But she lived here now. Those were her throw blankets on the back of the couch, her Crock-Pot on the kitchen counter,

Kathy blinked for a moment, then smiled. "Oh, right. Sure, of course. Where is Mom?"

"She's napping." At least she had been napping. Janelle had a sudden, horrifying vision of walking in to check on her grand-mother and finding her passed away. "I could go check…."

"Oh, let her sleep. We'll get everything set up. She'll just want to get involved, and you know how she has to oversee things." Kathy said it like an aside, like a secret.

Kind of, Janelle thought, a little mean.

"So what've you been up to?" Betsy settled a few plastic grocery bags of food on the counter and started unpacking them, handing some off to her mom in a perfectly coordi-nated mother–daughter display that left Janelle standing awk-wardly in the corner, trying to stay out of the way. "I mean, I follow you on Connex and everything, but wow, it's been a long time. You look good."

Janelle touched her hair, tied back with a scarf and falling over one shoulder. "Um…thanks."

Betsy laughed and moved around her mother, who was fussing with the platters. She fell into a stream of chatter Janelle found herself caught up in as they moved around the kitchen, sharing gossip and comparing the bits and pieces of their lives—kids, jobs, favorite movies, books. The conver-sation was easy enough and flowed with laughter, making Janelle realize how long it had been since she'd simply…hung out. Relaxed. Laughed.

"We should get together," Betsy announced as she poured a bag of chips into a bowl. "Girls' night out, how's that sound?"

It sounded surprisingly good to Janelle, even if she wasn't quite sure how she'd manage it. "Great!"

"Janelle? What's all this?" Kathy had opened the cupboard under the sink, looking for the waste bin. "All this food?"

"Oh, I cleaned out the fridge earlier to make room for the

salads. They're in those huge pottery bowls of Nan's—they wouldn't fit otherwise. But I thought I told Bennett to take out the trash—"

She turned to see Deb, who'd come in the back door, and Kathy staring in confusion at the garbage pail. It overflowed with a thick and gloppy mess of potato and macaroni salads. Janelle gaped.

Deb shook her head. "Oh, gosh."

"But I don't…" Janelle shook her head, not sure what to say. Hours of work, ruined. All that food, wasted.

"Did you leave her alone?" Kathy's expression said she was trying to be understanding. Her tone, however, was more than a little judgmental.

"I took a nap."

"She does this. I told you," Deb said to Kathy in an undertone.

"You left her alone," Kathy stated with a frown. "I thought you were here to be making sure this sort of thing didn't happen—"

Janelle didn't stay to hear more. Nan's door was closed tight, though Janelle had left it cracked open. She knocked twice and opened it before Nan could tell her to come in. Her grandmother sat on the edge of her bed, the front of her nightgown thickly stained, the trash can at her feet filled with crumpled tissues. She pulled a few more from the box while Janelle watched, and used them to scrub at her hands. She looked up.

Nan looked so sad; her expression broke Janelle's heart. "I wanted to help for the picnic. I don't know what I thought, honey. I got confused. I didn't remember making that bowl of potato salad. I thought it had been in there for a long time."

"So you threw it away."

Nan nodded. "I threw it all away. I didn't want anyone getting sick from it. Then I came in here and thought I'd just lie down again until everyone came. And then I realized what a mess I'd made."

"You know we just made that potato salad yesterday, right?" Janelle took the tissue box away and set it on Nan's shelf. "Let me help you. That's not going to do it."

"Is everyone here?" Nan's voice shook.

Janelle forced a smile, forced herself to look Nan in the eyes. "Yes. So we're going to get you cleaned up. Put on something nice for your company. And then we're going to go out and have a picnic, okay?"

"But the potato salad..."

"Someone can run to the store and get some more. Or I'll just make up a quick pasta salad. We have plenty of elbow macaroni in the pantry, and with some Italian dressing, a few olives, cherry tomatoes, it'll be great. No problem." Janelle put her hands over Nan's, ignoring the slick goo of mayo and mustard. "Come on, Nan. It's fine."

"It's not fine!" she cried. "I ruined it!"

Bennett had gone through a tough period when he was in third grade, just after Janelle and Ryan had called it quits. He'd blamed himself for everything from the mail not being delivered on time to the teacher yelling at his class and making them miss recess, to his favorite TV program getting canceled. He'd cried out "I ruined it" more than once, just this way, and Janelle had done the same for him that she did for Nan now.

"You didn't." She squeezed her hands gently. "There's plenty of food."

"Who's out there? Deb? Joey?"

"Yes. And the cousins. Everyone we invited."

Nan sniffed. "Kathy will say something about it, you know she will. She can't keep her opinions to herself, never could."

"We'll tell her there were spiders in it."

Nan looked surprised. Then slightly gleeful. "No!"

"Sure." Janelle grinned. "I'll tell her you put the bowls out on the counter while I was napping, and spiders crawled in there and you had to throw them away."

"She'll never believe it." Nan laughed, then again.

"Doesn't matter. That's what we'll tell her, anyway." Janelle got up and went to the plastic stacking storage bins she'd tucked into a corner of the bedroom. When Bennett was a baby she'd kept them next to his diaper changing area to store supplies, and she'd found a similar use for them here. Wipes, lotions, medical supplies. She took a package of wipes and held it up. "Let's get you cleaned up."

As she wiped away the mess from Nan's hands, careful not to scrub too hard at the thin and fragile skin, her grandma sat quietly. When she was done, Janelle meant to move away, but Nan took her hands and held them. She turned hers over to show the brown spots on the backs, the swollen knuckles. She still wore her wedding band, plain gold, along with the broader band that had been her husband's.

"Sometimes I dream I'm young again," she said. "I dream I'm a girl. And then I look at my hands, and I know I'm really an old, old woman."

Janelle didn't know what to say to that, but when Nan squeezed her fingers and smiled, she realized that sometimes nothing needed to be said.

TWENTY-FIVE

"I SAW YOUR BROTHER AT MASS LAST WEEKEND."
Marlena Tierney's red hair had gone gray long ago, but in the
past few years she'd started dying it again.

The color was garish, unnatural. Clown-red. It matched
the bright lipstick she still insisted on wearing. The nail polish. She wasn't an old woman, but time hadn't been particularly kind to her, and she knew it.

"He sends his love," Gabe's mother continued. "Said to tell
you to make sure Andrew gets to church. You, too."

Mike probably included their dad in that, but Marlena
would've stuck her hand in a jar of angry wasps before she
mentioned Ralph's name. Gabe leaned forward to light the
cigarette she held up. She gave him a coy smile, the way
she always did, but refrained from cupping his hand the way
she would've if he'd been another man and not her son. He
knew her ways, all right.

"You should tell him we need to see him more often," Gabe
said, knowing it made no difference. "Andy misses him."

"He's very busy. He's got an active congregation, you know that. His parishioners need him to be there for them. It's not," she said, "like he can just go on vacation or something any time he wants to."

Since Gabe knew for a fact that his brother had indeed gone on a vacation, a cruise to Mexico and the Bahamas, no less, this argument held little weight with him. Gabe hadn't taken a vacation in years, not unless you counted the hunting trips to camp, which he did not. "We live less than three hours from him. He could make a day trip more than once every six months."

Marlena shrugged and drew in the smoke, holding it for a few seconds before letting it stream out the side of her mouth. She looked at him through squinted eyes. "You could go see him, too, you know. He'd love to see you. It wouldn't kill you to go to church, either."

"It might." He smiled.

After half a minute, she smiled back. That was the mother he remembered best, or at least wanted to. The one who smiled and laughed and got down on the floor with him to play with Matchbox cars and LEGO. Not the one who sat and wept at the kitchen table or locked herself in the bathroom for hours. Not the one who'd left them. And not this present-day crone who'd asked Jesus for forgiveness plenty of times, but never her own sons.

"How *is* your brother?" Marlena asked after the clock's second hand ticked in silence one time too many. "Andrew."

"You could come see him yourself. Find out."

Marlena stubbed out her cigarette only half smoked. "You know that's not a good idea. What with the…problems."

They'd been over this before, a dozen times over the years. Gabe guessed he'd go over it a dozen more without any expectation her decision would change. Marlena had come to the hospital to see Andy after the accident, when he was still unconscious. She'd stared at his bruised and bloodied face for a long time without a word, then turned on her heel. Gabe had followed her to the parking lot, where she'd fumbled with a cigarette and leaned onto the hood of her car as if she might be sick or faint.

"I never wanted it to be like this," she'd said without looking up at him. "I thought I was doing the right thing."

Gabe, who hadn't eaten or slept more than a few minutes at a time in the four days since the accident, had pulled his lighter from his pocket. It was the first time he'd lit her cigarette, and that time she *had* cupped his hand to hold the flame steady. Her fingers had been cold, the flirtatious smile she gave him warm before it slid from her face and left her expression blank.

"Nice lighter," she'd said.

"It was a present."

Marlena had nodded as if that made sense. He remembered how greedily she'd sucked at the cigarette, as if the smoke was oxygen. The sun had turned her hair to fire.

"Don't you understand? I thought I was doing the best thing," she'd told him.

Gabe knew the smell of bullshit. Whatever his mother had thought when she decided to leave her husband and three sons behind without so much as a forwarding address, he didn't believe it really had anything to do with anyone but herself.

"We all thought you were dead," he'd told her, just to see if she looked surprised.

She hadn't. "That was your father's idea. Not mine."

"But you let him do it."

That was the first time he'd seen her smile. "Don't you get it? Nobody *lets* Ralph Tierney do anything. He does what he wants, how he wants it, and you'd better do it, too, or else…."

"Or else you end up almost dead or wishing you were," Gabe had said.

That was when she got in her car and left him there.

Years had passed, but nothing changed. Andy woke up, forgetting most everything in his life. They never told him his mother was alive. Mike had sided with her on that one, and Gabe hadn't had the heart to fight them. Mike knew Andy better, after all. As for their father, when he heard his wife had gone to see her son in the hospital, all he'd done was spit to the side.

"It's not his problems that are the issue," Gabe said now. "It's yours."

Marlena scowled. "If you're going to talk to me that way, Gabriel, you can march yourself right out of here. I don't need a lecture from you on how to live my life."

"Surely the blessed Father Mike would tell you the same thing." Though he couldn't have, because if the hallowed priest-son had told their mother to visit with Andy, she'd have done it. With bells on.

"Michael agrees with me that it would be too much for Andrew at this point. It would be too confusing, too hurtful. It's better this way," Marlena said stubbornly, but without looking Gabe in the eyes, as if he might use some secret laser power to force her to agree.

Gabe sat back in the chair. "Right."

She gave him a narrow-eyed glare. "You're so much like your father."

It was the easiest way to get him to leave, comparing him to the old man, and she knew it. Gabe didn't give her the satisfaction. He crossed his ankle over his knee and leaned back with a small smile.

"You even look like him," she said. "I'm sure the ladies just eat you alive, don't they, Gabriel? I bet you have them lined up for blocks just waiting to get a piece of you. And yet here you are, almost forty years old and not married. Not even a girlfriend. I'll never have any grandchildren, at this rate."

"You'll never have any grandchildren, period."

She looked sad; he even believed she was. "I guess it's just as well, since if you had any kids I'm sure you wouldn't even allow me to see them."

"*I* see you," he pointed out.

"Once every few months, and then you come and sit for a while and berate or insult me." Marlena sniffed and delicately pulled another cigarette from the pack. It hung from her bottom lip as she spoke, gesturing toward him. "Light me up."

He did.

"I see you're still using that old lighter."

She'd given him a new one for his birthday a few years ago. Shiny, silver, engraved with his initials. He had it in a drawer at home. He flipped the lid closed on this one and tucked it back into his pocket.

"Michael tells me she's back in town. Living with her grandmother again. She has a son...."

Gabe got up from the table. "Don't. Even."

Marlena fluttered her hands, doing her best to look innocent. "What? What?"

She knew what. Gabe grabbed his coat from the back of the chair, already reaching for his keys. "Tell my brother he should come and visit his other brother more often. Andy misses him."

"I just want to see you have a family, Gabriel. A wife." Her words caught him at the back door. "I just want to see you happy."

Gabe paused with his hand on the knob. "Because that whole marriage and kids thing worked out so well for you, right?"

From behind him, Marlena gave a heavy sigh. "Don't judge everything by the mistakes your father and I made."

He laughed at that. Shook his head. "That's kind of all I have to go by, isn't it?"

She called out to him from the doorway as he was getting in his truck. "I just want to see you stop being so angry all the time!"

Gabe revved the engine in response and drove away. He looked in the rearview mirror and watched her wave. He didn't wave back.

TWENTY-SIX

Then

WHEN JANELLE WAS SMALL SHE COULD LEAN OUT and grab Gabe's hand across the alley. Surely now that she's bigger, her legs longer, she can actually step across to the window, so long as his is open on the other side. Trouble is, Gabe's window is closed, and he has his headphones on. And why would she want to try and get from her window into Gabe's?

The answer is simple. She's been watching him, on and off, for the past couple weeks. If she can see him, she knows he can see her. At first she made sure to keep her curtains closed. But one night after she'd turned off her light and lay in bed, September still hot enough to feel like summer, she'd watched him come out of the shower and into his room. She'd watched him take off his towel and lie down on his bed and do that thing boys do. The thing girls do, too.

Did he know she watched him? Janelle didn't think so. He'd acted too unselfconscious for that. Not like he was putting on a show. Not like she did the next night, when she came out of the bathroom with her hair slicked back and wet, her body still so damp her thin T-shirt clung to her. She'd put on some music and danced and danced, never once looking at the window or giving him any idea she knew he saw her... but she hoped he did.

It's been about a month of that, now. Back and forth, sometimes her light stays on and his goes off. Sometimes she sits in the dark and watches him. And now, tonight, she measures the distance between their windows with her eyes.

Gabe's not paying attention. He's on his bed, eyes closed, hands behind his head, headphones plugged into his stereo. He's wearing sweatpants and a T-shirt because it's finally getting chilly.

Janelle has a handful of beads left over from some craft project Nan packed away in the closet up here. Blue, red, green, yellow. Shaped like stars, with holes in the center to string them. Nan won't miss them, and since they're made of plastic, they won't break the glass. They will, however, catch Gabe's attention when Janelle starts tossing them, one by one, at his window.

She has to toss out ten beads before he looks up. Another two before he gets out of bed to peer out the window. And finally, after she throws the rest of her handful and the beads *plink-plink-plink* rapidly against the glass, he opens his window.

"Janelle?"

"Hey." She leans out, shivering a little in the chill, and with excitement. "What's up?"

Gabe hesitates before answering. She wonders if he's thinking about all the times he's jacked off over there, if he knows she's seen him. "Nothing. What's up with you?"

They were friends when they were little kids, but it's not as if they kept in touch when she was away from Nan's house.

She's been living here since August, and though they walk to the same bus stop, ride the same bus, even share some of the same classes, she wouldn't say they're friends now. Girls at school giggle about Gabe Tierney, and they don't even know what he looks like naked...but she does.

"Bored." Janelle leans a little farther, looking down. "What are you listening to?"

"The radio."

"Oh." That tin can telephone from so long ago had never worked that great, but she remembers stringing it between their houses. The distance had seemed a lot greater then; now it's next to nothing. "Can I come over?"

Gabe twitches back from the window and actually looks around, as though someone might've overheard. "Now?"

"Sure." She grins; he doesn't grin back.

"My dad's home."

"So? Doesn't your door have a lock?"

Gabe's mouth opens. Shuts. He looks at her suspiciously. "Yeah. It has a lock."

"So then he won't even know, right?"

Gabe looks around again. "How would you even—"

Janelle swings her leg over the windowsill. The night air that seemed cold a few minutes ago is now deliciously cool against her suddenly heated face. The wood presses between her legs. She's wearing an oversize T-shirt nightgown and a pair of cotton panties, and that's it. She wiggles her toes, swinging her foot.

"What the hell are you doing?"

"I'm coming over." Carefully but quickly, so she doesn't have time to think about it, Janelle grabs the windowsill and stands. With one hand gripping the ledge and one foot on it, toes curled around the edge, she stretches her other leg out, out. Her foot easily finds Gabe's windowsill. "Grab me!"

He does, his big hands gripping her around the calf and just below her elbow. Janelle pushes off with her other foot. For a few heady, giddy seconds she's hovering in the space over the alley, before her momentum launches her the rest of the way onto Gabe's windowsill with both feet. In seconds he pulls her down and through his window, but he yanks too hard and she ends up falling.

"Shit," Gabe whispers at the thump. "Shit, shit."

She'll have a bruise tomorrow, but Janelle doesn't care. "That was awesome!"

Gabe looks as if he's sweating. He pulls her to her feet before backing off. He goes to his door and double-checks the lock before looking at her. "You're crazy."

She laughs and bends to peek out at her window. "Hey, you have a good view here. As good as mine."

"What's that supposed to mean?"

She wants to tease him, not make him angry or shame him into keeping his curtains closed from now on. "Nothing. Just saying."

Gabe still looks nervous. At school he never says much. He stalks through the halls a head taller than most of the other guys in their grade, his shoulders broader. His clothes are never trendy. He favors torn jeans and T-shirts, mostly black, with band names on the front. Despite this, he's not a rebel. He gets good grades. He's not stupid and doesn't play at it, either. He's been in class his whole life with the kids in that school. They should all know him better than Janelle does, even though she's known him since childhood, too. But something tells her he's less a stranger to her than anyone else…or at least he could be, if he let her.

If there's anyone in this town who *does* know her, aside from Nan, anyway, it would be Gabe. She's not the little girl blowing bubbles or making a phone out of soup cans. She's changed, and out of everyone, he's the one she wants to know it.

"What did you think of the history test?" She doesn't care, but needs something to talk about.

"It was okay."

Janelle sits on Gabe's bed. He stares at her. He pulls up a chair from his desk and turns it backward to sit on it.

From the hallway comes a muffled thumping. Footsteps. Gabe puts a finger to his lips.

"Your dad?" Janelle whispers.

Gabe nods.

"Will he come in?"

Gabe shakes his head.

This time, when Janelle smiles, he smiles back.

TWENTY-SEVEN

THIS TIME, JANELLE KNEW ENOUGH TO GO around to the back door. The front was for visitors and salesmen, not neighbors who'd known each other for something like thirty years. The front door wasn't for friends, and if she was going to make this work she had to act as if that's what they were.

Even so, she knocked hesitantly, softly, thinking that even though she saw lights on, saw Gabe's truck parked out front, maybe nobody would be home to answer. Andy did, though, after a minute or so, just as she was starting to leave. Janelle turned back.

"Andy, hi!"

"Hi, Janelle." He peered around her. "Where's Bennett? Was I supposed to come help him study tonight? I didn't think so."

"He's at home. And no, you weren't. I came over to talk to Gabe."

One brow lifted. "Huh?"

"I'm here." Gabe looked around his brother to stare at her. He didn't seem surprised. "Don't be a turd, Andy, let her in."

Andy muttered and stepped aside to let her pass. "Right. Sure. I'm not a turd," he added under his breath.

Janelle tried to think if she'd ever been in the Tierneys' kitchen before, and couldn't. It was bigger than Nan's, with room for a table. "Sorry, was I interrupting dinner?"

"No. We already ate," Andy said. "I was just having a snack."

Janelle eyed the litter of dishes on the table, the crumpled wrappers. "Some snack."

Andy shrugged. "I got hungry."

"Andy, man. Beat it," Gabe said.

"He doesn't have to go," Janelle told him. "What I came to ask isn't...private, or anything."

Gabe smiled, just a little. "I didn't think it was."

Same old Gabe...though, not exactly. Time seemed to have given him a better sense of humor than she remembered. Or maybe she was imagining it.

"I really, really need you to come over and do some work for me."

Gabe's brows lifted and he pointed at himself. "Me? What?"

"Yes. You." She pointed, too.

Gabe's smile had faded. He gave her a narrow-eyed look. "I already told you about the dishwasher...."

"I've got some carpentry, some plumbing, some electrical. I know you can do all those things." She ticked them off on her fingertips.

Gabe glanced at his brother, who was busy digging into what looked like a plate of nachos. "Yeah. I can. But why should I?"

"You know, your job? Your business, what you do for a living? You fix things, right? I can pay you." Her chin lifted.

She didn't mention anything about favors this time. That had been a cheap shot.

"You could pay someone else," Gabe said.

She'd thought of that, and it was true. Yet here she was, like a beggar with her hand out. And why? "My uncle Joey's the executor of the estate or something like that, and he won't approve any major repairs without a lot of legwork on my part. Any legitimate service or person wants a deposit, wants to charge an arm and a leg, and they can't give me any reasonable estimate of when they'll be finished."

Gabe frowned. "What do you mean, he won't approve them?"

"I have a budget," she told him. "It's embarrassing. It's ridiculous. They want me to get the house in order, so they say, for when Nan...when it comes time to sell the house, it'll be ready to go on the market. That's what they told me, anyway, when they asked me to come and stay with her, until..."

"She dies," Andy interjected.

"Jesus, Andrew. Way to be sensitive." Gabe reached over casually to knock the back of his brother's head.

From the living room came a shout. "Watch your language!"

Janelle burst into giggles. It was so much like it had been back then, when they were young. Gabe didn't laugh, but he did lean against the kitchen counter with his arms crossed.

"So you think I'll just fix a bunch of stuff for you on the down-low? For cheap?"

"I think," Janelle said honestly, "that you'd do a good job and let me pay you how I can, and if you say you'll do it, I can count on you to finish."

Gabe's expression didn't change. His gaze didn't flicker. His lips didn't twitch. "What do you need done?"

Janelle pulled her list from her pocket. It had gone soft from being folded and refolded over and over again. "I listed every-thing I think needs to be fixed or changed, but I prioritized. Major repairs at the top."

"What's his problem? Your uncle?"

"I don't know." She wished she had a better answer than that. "He doesn't want to face his mother dying? He wants to pretend it's not inevitable? I wish I could tell you. All I know is, I'm tired of running out of hot water and washing dishes by hand."

On impulse, she crossed the kitchen toward him. She reached, but didn't quite touch him. "Gabe. Please? I know I could hire someone else, but...I want you."

From his place at the table, Andy let out a snort. Gabe and Janelle both looked at him. He held up the empty plate of nachos.

"Maybe you can get him to buy a dishwasher for this place, while you're at it," Andy said. "I'm tired of washing dishes by hand, too."

TWENTY-EIGHT

"I DON'T UNDERSTAND." IT WAS ALL JANELLE could think of to say. The school had called, told her to come get Bennett because once again he'd been in a fight. The same boys, Bennett the victim, yet Mrs. Adams's frown of disapproval had said he was also somehow to blame. "What is going on with you?"

"Nothing." Bennett looked out the truck's window.

Janelle had pulled into the parking lot of a fast-food place, not wanting to wait until they got home to talk about this. At the house he could escape into his room. Lock her out. She supposed he could get out of the truck now and run down the road away from her, if he wanted, but so far he seemed willing to stay put.

"Bennett, I had to have Andy come over and sit with Nan so I could pick you up today. I can't be doing that all the time. We're just lucky he wasn't at work. So I need you to look at me, and I need you to tell me what's going on with those boys."

He shook his head, arms crossed tight over his chest. His lower lip trembled. He still wouldn't look at her.

"Mrs. Adams seems to think you're friends with those boys."

"They're not my friends. I don't have any friends here," he muttered.

Bennett had always made friends so easily, Janelle couldn't believe that he'd had trouble here. "If they're not your friends, are they bullying you?"

He hesitated, then shook his head. Janelle tried to keep herself calm, but it wasn't working. She wanted to shake him. What had happened to her get-along kid, her smiley-faced boy? When had he become this grim-mouthed gremlin? This changeling?

"So why were they pushing you down in the hall?"

His shoulders rose and fell as he heaved a sigh. Bennett leaned closer to the truck door, pressing his forehead to the glass. "They were mad at me."

One piece at a time, that was how she'd solve this puzzle. "Why?"

"Because they said I owed them...something."

"What? What do you owe them?" Janelle cried, frustrated and afraid. "Why would they push you down in the hall or give you a swirly?"

Bennett reached to his feet to pull up his backpack. He dug inside it, still without looking at her, and drew out a plastic Baggie. He handed it to her without a word.

"Oh, my God." Janelle stared at the Baggie, the plastic slick and cool in her fingers. She thought she might drop it, but her hand closed convulsively around it.

Harsh smoke filters into her lungs and she coughs. Gabe laughs and take the joint from her, holding it over her head so she has to jump to get it. They're both high, and she loves being high with him because sometimes—not all the time, but sometimes—it makes him giddy and silly, and he laughs like he never does when he's sober.

Basically, Janelle just loves being high.

She hadn't smoked a joint or had more than a couple drinks in years. She'd talked often with Bennett about the dangers of drugs. She never told him about her past habits.

"Why do you have this? Where did it come from?"

"I brought it from California," Bennett said in a low, shaking voice. "I got it a long time ago, from Ryan's house. I had it with my stuff."

Ryan. It figured. Dull and aching fury filled her, drying her mouth so speech was nearly impossible until she forced herself to swallow hard, several times. "Did you smoke any of this?"

He looked at her then, eyes wide, mouth turned down. "No, Mom."

"Bennett, don't you lie to me. Did you smoke any of this pot?" She tucked the plastic Baggie with its load of four or five joints against her thigh, out of sight in case anyone happened to look into the truck.

"No! I didn't. But those boys at school, they wanted it. They offered to pay me a lot of money for it, so I said I would."

"How did they even know you had it?" Visions of child protective services being called rose up. Of being arrested. Worse, of Bennett being arrested, tossed out of school.

"I told them."

She sagged. "Bennett. Why? Why would you do something like that? Didn't we talk about how drugs are bad for you? Even pot?"

"They were all bragging about how they could get drugs. I thought maybe everyone did it here." He gave her a bleak look. "I didn't want to do it, but they said they'd give me money. I wanted to buy the new Crazytown game, and you said you wouldn't get it for me. They promised to pay me, but only after I gave them the stuff, and I said I wouldn't do it until they gave me the money up front."

She'd raised a dealer. Janelle clapped a hand over her mouth to keep herself from bursting into hysterical laughter. Some strangled chuckles leaked out, anyway.

Bennett looked alarmed. "I'm sorry, Mom!"

The school couldn't know, or else Bennett wouldn't just be sent home. He'd have been suspended. The other boys, too. "Mrs. Adams has no idea?"

Bennett shook his head. "I don't think so. They told her we were just fooling around, and I said the same thing. She never said anything about the money or anything."

Janelle pushed the Baggie deep into her pocket and took a long, slow breath. "You're done with this, you hear me?"

"But the guys—"

"Done," she said sharply. "Do you understand? You go to school and tell them your mom found your stash and took it away. Tell them you can't get more. And you pay them back any money you took from them."

"They didn't give me any money," he said sullenly. "That's why we were fighting."

Janelle rubbed at the spot between her eyes. "Do you understand me, Bennett?"

"Yes. Mom, I'm sorry."

"Your grades, homework, all of it better improve. You'd better put your focus on school. I want to see an improvement, immediately. No comics, no video games, no TV, no computer. No iPad," she added, "until I see that your grades are better."

A moment ago he'd looked grateful; now Bennett's expression darkened. "You don't ever let me do anything. You don't trust me to do anything!"

"You think I should trust you to do anything when this is

the sort of thing you do?" she cried. "My God, Bennett, how could you be so stupid?"

"It's not fair!"

"No!" Janelle shouted, startling them both. "What isn't fair, Bennett, is that you took drugs to school and offered to sell them to other students! Do you even know what that could do to you? To me? Do you have any idea what sort of trouble you could get into? They could take you away from me!"

"Maybe I want to be away from you!"

She couldn't speak. Couldn't breathe. They stared at each other. The joints in her pocket seemed to have taken on weight, to be on fire; she could feel them burning her.

"You don't mean that."

Bennett didn't answer.

"Why would you say that to me?"

"Because," he told her, "you're never any fun. Nan says when you were a kid, you were fun. But you're not now."

"I'm your mom. I'm not supposed to be fun," Janelle said through numb lips. "I'm supposed to raise you with good morals and values, and make sure you're taken care of. I'm supposed to make sure you're disciplined and that you do well in school so you can be a success in life."

The words exploded out of her in short, sharp jabs, stabbing the air between them.

"I'm supposed to be your parent. Not your friend," Janelle said.

She put the truck in gear and drove them home in silence.

TWENTY-NINE

RYAN HAD ALWAYS CALLED AT NIGHT. LATE. THIS time, Janelle was the one waking him.

"How's Bennett?" he always asked.

"He's been selling pot he says he got from you."

Ryan coughed. "The hell? No. I never gave the kid any weed."

"He got it from your house," Janelle said. "The last time he was at your place, he was eight years old."

"Wow."

"Yeah. Wow. Do you know what kind of trouble he could've gotten into? Or me?"

"Wait, wait, wait," Ryan said. She imagined his familiar hand gestures, telling her to chill.

"He's doing shit in school. He's not making friends. And now this." Her throat closed, and Janelle forced herself to take a breath. Then another. "And your damned weed!"

"I didn't know," Ryan told her. "I'm sorry. Believe me. You want me to talk to him?"

She found a small laugh. "You haven't seen or spoken to my son in four years, Ryan. What are you going to do, tell him drugs are bad?"

"They are bad, for little guys."

"Somehow I don't think you're going to convince him. No, thanks. I'll just keep making a mess of my kid all on my own," Janelle said bitterly.

Ryan was silent for a few seconds. "That kid is anything but a mess."

"It all feels like a mess."

"You want to talk about it?"

"No," she said shortly. "Thanks."

Ryan sighed. "How's your grandma?"

"She has her good days and her bad days. That's to be expected. She's probably awake now. I should go check on her."

"Tough business, taking care of someone like that. Just want to make sure you're okay. That's all. You don't tell me anything, Janelle."

That's because you're not my boyfriend anymore and haven't been in years, she thought, but didn't say. "I'm fine. Tired."

Normally, Ryan was light as air. The fiddling grasshopper instead of the toiling ant. Now he sounded so serious it disturbed her. "You should be careful, Janny. You're in a weird place."

He was the only one besides her dad who'd ever called her that. She hadn't liked it, had only tolerated it while dating him because she'd imagined herself in love with him. Thick and cloying nostalgia swept over her at the sound of it, surprising her as much as his question had.

"Careful of what, exactly?"

"Trying to do everything yourself."

"There's nobody else to do it for me," Janelle said.

"I know you, Janny. That's what I'm trying to say."

"I'm sure you think you do." Across the alley, Gabe's light came on. Janelle turned her face from it, though his curtains were drawn. From the baby monitor came the first noises of Nan waking. She hadn't yet called out for Janelle to help her, but she didn't always. Janelle swung her legs over the bed, feet finding her slippers. Gabe's curtains twitched, then opened, and she twisted her body to shield the light from her phone that would alert him that she was awake.

"You can say you know me, Ryan, but the truth is, you didn't know everything about me, and you don't now."

"I didn't say I know everything about you. Just that I know you."

"What did you do, a tea-leaf reading? Chant over a prayer bowl?" It was mean, and she wished she hadn't said it.

Ryan didn't sound as if he'd taken offense. "You might not believe it, but I loved you. Always will."

"I know that." It was true, but Ryan "loved" a lot of things. Weed, rainbows, surfing, spirit quests. "But I'm fine."

"Is there a guy?"

"What? No!" She sounded as if she was protesting too much.

"Just asking. You know you could tell me."

"I don't want to tell you anything about my love life, Ryan. God."

"Is he the one from that newspaper article? The one who shot his brother."

The world spun, making her dizzy. "What?"

"You have a newspaper article about it," Ryan said blithely, as if he hadn't just punched her in the gut with his words. "You keep it in your yearbook."

"You…" She couldn't accuse him of snooping. The memento from her senior year had always been on her bookshelf, next to her commemorative coffee table book about the movie *Titanic* and one on polar bears. It had never been a secret.

"I asked your grandma about it once when she called and you weren't home. She said they were your neighbors."

Janelle's mouth and throat had dried; she swallowed hard to moisten them. "His name's Gabe. It was an accident."

"You never talked about him to me."

"I didn't talk about a lot of things with you, Ryan." The words were hard, but true.

"Is it him? He still lives in town?"

The lights on the monitor went from green to orange, then briefly, red. It sounded as if Nan was opening drawers. Maybe opening and closing the closet door. "I have to go."

"How do you feel about your grandma dying?"

The question came out of the blue, yet somehow smacked Janelle hard. "How do you think I feel about it? Terrible!"

"But it's going to happen, anyway, right? She's old and sick. You can't do anything about it. Anyway, everyone dies, am I right?"

"Yes. Everyone dies. She is old and sick, and I can't do anything about it. What would you like me to do, Ryan? Mourn for months and months? Spend the last bit of time I have with her wondering how much I'll miss her when she's gone?"

Ryan huffed. "How can you be so practical about something so emotional?"

"Why," Janelle said through gritted teeth, "are you being such an asshole?"

"And this guy, the one you like. There's no point in getting close to him or anything, right? Because it won't work out. It never works out, really. One way or another, everything ends. Right?"

They were her words, she realized. Said to him long, long ago, one night after they'd spent a few hours wining and dining, smoking up a little. It had been the first and last time she'd smoked since finding out she was pregnant. Bennett had been safely asleep. She and Ryan had talked about a lot of things that night. They'd been dating for nearly a year, with only two more left before the relationship ended. If you'd asked her then if she thought they'd be together longer than that…well, Ryan had asked, hadn't he? And what had she said?

"Nothing lasts forever," Janelle whispered now through numb lips. "You are the last person in the world I'd have thought would throw that back in my face. What are you trying to say? What are you trying to do?"

"I just wanted to make sure you were okay. I know you loved your grandma a lot. I know she was important to you. You never really talked much about when you lived with her, but I know she was."

Janelle swallowed the bitter flavor of tears. "She still is. Jesus, Ryan. She's not dead yet."

"You're right. I'm sorry. I'm being a major douche canoe."

That made her smile a little. "You are. God. Why?"

"I don't know. Maybe I got a little jealous."

She laughed out loud at that. "Sure you did. After all this time, suddenly, you're jealous? You want another go?"

Ryan laughed, too, sounding embarrassed. "Nah. We were a train wreck."

It was true, but hearing him say it wasn't very flattering. "So, what?"

"So, someone's in your life, and he's going to be able to hang out with you and your awesome kid… Oh, shit. Shit, Janny, I forgot. I'm sorry."

Most of the time, Janelle was able to follow Ryan's ramblings, but not this time. "Huh?"

"It's just this guy showed up here a couple weeks ago. Said

he knew you, he'd tracked you down, I guess. From our old place."

"What guy?" It had been a long time since she'd lived with Ryan.

"This old guy. Shit, I can't believe I didn't tell you. I meant to, the next day, you know, but I got into something and then I forgot...."

"Ryan. Just tell me. Who was it? What did he want?"

"He said he wanted me to tell him where you were. So I said you'd gone home to Pennsylvania."

Frustrated, Janelle spit out a sigh. "You told some stranger how to find me?"

"Oh, no," Ryan said with another laugh. "He wasn't a stranger. He said he was your dad."

THIRTY

Then

THE LAST TIME JANELLE ACTUALLY SAW HER DAD, he'd promised to take her on vacation to the beach. Not the normal beach, either, but one of those all-inclusive resorts with all-you-can-eat food and swimming and snorkeling and meeting dolphins and stuff. She knows better than to believe him. Her dad likes to promise lots of things and then not deliver.

But this is different than a pony or a new stereo or even the car she knows she will never get, no matter how many times he tells her that when she turns sixteen she'll have one sitting in the driveway. This is a trip, and she knows for a fact her dad is going because he booked a gig. He'll play guitar for the drunk people by the pool during the day and drunker people in the bars at night. This is a good job for him, because he gets to play music for money, and also have a place to live and food to eat. And, he tells her, he gets to bring his family down to enjoy it.

Dad left for the Caribbean still promising to send for her. Maybe over Christmas break, he says, but the weeks pass and Christmas comes and goes. Maybe spring break, he tells her on a postcard that arrives crumpled and stained sometime in February. But spring break also comes and goes without word, without an airplane ticket. And after that...she doesn't hear anything again for a long time.

He isn't dead, she knows that much for sure, because she hears her mom hollering at him on the phone one night when Janelle's supposed to be in bed. Randall knows she's listening at the top of the stairs, because he passed her in the hallway on the way to his bedroom. He squeezed her shoulder as he did, but he didn't say anything, which was the perfect thing to say.

After that, sometimes postcards arrive from exotic locations, usually with nothing more than a scrawled signature. Envelopes with cash arrive even more infrequently, though those often also include photos. Janelle throws away the pictures but keeps the cash. She uses it to buy a VW Rabbit pickup truck.

Still, when it comes time to send out the graduation announcements, Janelle has only a short list. Her mom and Randall, of course. Relatives from her mom's side who won't make the trip to St. Marys but will probably send her gifts. Her uncles and aunts from her dad's side already know, of course, but they get their own announcements stuffed into the pretty envelopes and carefully addressed in Janelle's best handwriting. Most of them will come to the barbecue at Nan's, and hopefully they'll all bring presents, too.

Janelle has to ask Nan for her dad's address, though. She's not even sure Nan has it, but she asks. And Nan gives it to her.

Janelle sends her dad an announcement, along with an invitation to the graduation party. A week later, he sends her a long letter telling her all about what he's been up to, where he's been. She doesn't care much about that, but the part about how proud he is of her…that does matter. Even after every-thing else that's happened, that matters.

At least until the day before she's set to graduate, and the phone rings. Nan calls her down from upstairs, holding out the phone with a small, sad smile. Janelle already knows who's on the other line, and what he'll say.

So it's no surprise, but it's still a disappointment. Just one more. But the last one, she tells him.

"Forget it, Dad," Janelle says, thinking she might cry, and proud when she doesn't. "It doesn't matter."

"I'll come get you in a week or so. Take you traveling with me this summer—"

"No."

He sounds surprised. "What? What do you mean, no?"

"I mean, no, Dad. I'm not going anywhere with you. Ever. Don't bother calling me anymore, either."

"Aww, Janny, don't—"

"Don't call me that."

That's when he launches into a long, exaggerated explana-tion of why, exactly, why she shouldn't be mad at him, why she ought to just "get over it." And that's when Janelle hangs up on him. She does it softly, gently, the handset practically kissing the cradle.

And she never speaks to him again.

"Yes. He called here, can you believe it?" Janelle's mom snorted derision into the phone. "I told him he was an idiot."

"But he asked you where I was?" Janelle kept her voice low, mindful that Nan was knitting slowly on her afghan, and Ben-nett and Andy were at the kitchen table, working on math. With her luck, at any minute Gabe would show up with his tool bag and his sleeves rolled up. They could make it a party.

Her mom hesitated. "Yes. I told him."

"Mom!"

"He has the right to know his mom is dying, Janelle. He has the right to know his grandson."

"Yes to the first, no to the second. And frankly, if he doesn't know about his own mother, maybe he doesn't deserve to know."

Janelle's mom was quiet for a moment. "I know you're angry at your dad...."

"Yeah, see, that's the thing. I'm not angry. Not anymore. I got over that a long time ago." It tasted like a lie she told herself so many times she no longer noticed how bitter the flavor.

"Believe me, I'm not telling you to just greet him with open arms. But maybe you could find some way to forgive him. He's your dad, for better or for worse. Mostly for worse."

"Did he say when he was coming?"

"He didn't say if he was going there at all," her mom said. "He seemed pretty shaken up about your grandma."

"Yeah, and it wouldn't be the first time he didn't come through for someone, would it?"

Janelle's mom sighed. "No. It wouldn't."

"I'm sure he does want to make his peace with Nan. But not for her sake. It would only be for his. And he doesn't get a chance to mess up my son." The words came out in a hiss. They hurt her tongue.

Janelle peeked around the living room archway through the kitchen. At the dining room table, Andy laughed as he bent over Bennett's work. Bennett laughed, too, and ducked away when Andy ruffled his hair.

"He cannot," she said, "mess up my kid."

THIRTY-ONE

JANELLE HAD OFFERED HIM COFFEE AND HOME-
made cinnamon rolls when he finished fixing the molding
around the front screen door, but instead of lingering over caffeine and sweets, Gabe lingered over the task. It hadn't been
complicated—just cutting out the wooden trim that had gone
soft with rot, and replacing it. She'd told him he didn't need
to paint it to match, that she could handle it, but Gabe had
cracked open the small can of paint and dipped the brush in.
He'd started the job; he meant to finish it.

That, and the longer it took him in here, the longer he
could stay listening to all of them laughing and chatting without having to actually join them.

He was such an idiot. He should finish up here the way
he'd planned, then go home. Or out. It was Friday night. He
didn't have to work tomorrow. He hadn't gone out in weeks.
So why was he over here, making repairs and thinking about
all the other things on the list she'd given him? She hadn't
even paid him for most of the stuff he'd already done.

And there she was, leaning in the doorway, holding out a fresh mug of coffee.

"Hey." Janelle smiled.

Gabe straightened. "Hi."

"Brought you some more coffee. I could get you a beer, if you'd rather have that."

"No. Coffee's fine." He didn't move forward to take it. "I'm just about finished with this."

"Oh, looks great!" She moved forward to check out his work. "I said you didn't have to paint it."

"It's okay. I don't mind."

"Did you bring me a receipt?"

She'd always had a great smile; she'd always been able to use it to get him to do what she wanted. He'd always liked it better when she smiled.

"No, sorry. I forgot." Gabe said it as if he regretted it. Truth was, he didn't care. He could afford the twenty bucks here or there that he'd spent so far.

The inside of her cheek tucked inward, another old habit he remembered. "Oh. Well…okay. Can you tell me how much I owe you, then? It's just I need the receipts for record keeping…."

"Don't worry about it."

"I do worry about it," Janelle told him. "I told you I'd pay you for the work. It's not charity, Gabe. I don't expect you to work for free, much less buy all the supplies and stuff."

"I'll get them to you." He reached for the mug. "Maybe you can pay me in coffee and cinnamon rolls."

She laughed. "What a bargain. C'mon, then. Andy and Bennett are helping me and Nan sort through old pictures. You can help."

"Oh, I—"

She snared him with that smile. "C'mon, Gabe. There are some of you in there you might like to see."

He followed her into the family room. "Pictures...of me?"

"Gabe hates having his picture taken," Andy said. "Hey, Gabe."

Bennett gave him a grin so much like Janelle's it felt sort of like a stab. "Gabe, look at all these old pictures we found!"

"They're embarrassing," Janelle warned.

Mrs. Decker pushed the plate of cinnamon rolls across the table. "Sit down, grab a bite. You've been working hard."

"Not that hard, Mrs. Decker." He sat, though.

In front of him on the table were several piles of pictures, some with sticky notes beneath them, scribbled with people's names. Andy had a small pile in front him. Bennett was sorting through another set from an old shoe box. Janelle took the seat next to Gabe and filled her empty mug with coffee.

"Anyone want a top-up?"

Andy offered his mug. "Me, thanks."

"How many have you had?" Gabe gave his brother a suspicious look.

Andy grinned. "Just one."

"You'll be up all night," Gabe warned.

Andy and Bennett high-fived. Janelle shook her head.

"They're planning an all-night Crazytown marathon. I told them they could...if it's okay with you?"

He'd never known her to be a second-guesser, but she gave him a hesitant smile as though asking his permission.

"What's it to him?" Andy said.

Gabe frowned. "Maybe she doesn't want you hanging out here all night, did you think of that?"

"What's Crazytown, anyway?" asked Mrs. Decker.

"It's a video game, Nan. Andy just got it. And it's so fun!" Bennett thumped the table.

Mrs. Decker shook her head. "What's this 'so fun' you always say? So fun. When I was young, we'd say something was 'so much fun' or 'so very fun.' Somewhere along the way, you started dropping out words."

Bennett leaned over to put his arm around her, rocking a little bit as they both laughed. "It's what young people do."

"It won't bother me," Janelle stated. She waited until Gabe looked at her, then smiled. "Andy's welcome over here anytime. Just like…old times."

"Look, Gabe. Here's you." Andy held up a faded snapshot. "When you were little."

"Let me see that." Gabe took the picture. He tipped it back and forth, studying it.

Janelle leaned over his shoulder to look, too. "Nice pants."

Red corduroy. Wide belt loops. Flared legs. "I loved those pants."

"Haha, eww, you didn't!" Janelle punched him lightly on the arm.

"I wouldn't laugh so much, if I were you." Gabe pulled another picture from Andy's pile. He flipped it up to show her. In it, a small girl with red hair pulled up into pigtails gave a gap-toothed grin to the camera as she held up a fish in one hand, a rod in the other. She wore a pair of white tube socks with red stripes, and matching short shorts, red with white piping.

"Oh, God. Give me that!" Janelle grabbed it out of his hand. "*Eww!* Oh, my God. I remember those shorts. I remember that day."

Her smile faded. "I was fishing with my dad."

Bennett took the picture from her. "That's a big fish, Mom."

"Yeah. It was." Janelle cleared her throat and cupped her hands around her coffee mug.

"What did you do with it?" Bennett tilted his head to study

the photo. Again, he looked so much like Janelle it gave Gabe a pang.

"Well. First we cleaned it. Then we put it in a frying pan and cooked it up and ate it."

It was Bennett's turn to scream out *"Eww!"* which made Andy guffaw loudly. Mrs. Decker shook her head, but fondly. Janelle didn't laugh. Her fingers twitched on the mug. When her eyes met Gabe's, they shimmered.

"I've never been fishing," Bennett announced. "Do you always have to eat the fish you cook?"

Andy let out a loud laugh. "What? Never been fishing? That's crazier than Crazytown!"

"Maybe we can go this summer. When we go to Parker Dam. That's what it's called, right, Mom?" Bennett looked at his mother with wide, expectant eyes.

"Yes. Maybe." Janelle took the picture back from him and turned it over and over in her fingers.

"Andy can come too, right, Andy? Do you like to fish?"

"Yep." He nodded. "I sure do."

"How about you, Gabe?" Janelle asked. "Do you like to fish?"

He did, but hadn't gone in years. "Sure."

That earned him a smile. "Good. You can come with us."

"Oh, look," Mrs. Decker said suddenly, peering over the edge of her glasses. "Here's a picture for you."

She passed it to Andy first, who looked at it with a small frown. He passed it to Gabe. "Who's that?"

Gabe took the picture. He recognized himself, younger even than in the other one Andy had shown him. He recognized the woman in the photo, too, the one holding an infant in one arm. "It's you."

"Me?" Andy took the picture back. "Where's Mikey?"

"He was taking a nap or something." It would've been useless to point out that Andy and Mike hadn't done every single thing together their entire lives, even if it had seemed that way.

"Who's that holding me?"

"Oh, honey," Mrs. Decker said with a laugh. "That's your mother."

Andy looked harder at the picture without any sign of grief. "Oh. Before she died."

"Oh…she died?" Mrs. Decker gave Gabe a questioning look.

"I was some kind of cute baby." Andy put the picture on his pile. "Can I keep that one?"

"Of course." Mrs. Decker stifled a yawn. "What time is it? It's late. Oh, I believe I'd like to think about getting to bed."

"I'll help you, Nan." Janelle stood and glanced at Gabe. "Are you going to stick around a little longer?"

He shook his head. "Gotta run to the store, pick up a few things."

"Hey, I need to head to the store, too. Can I hitch a ride?"

She asked so casually, so nonchalantly, there was no good way for him to say no without sounding like a giant bag of dicks. While she helped Mrs. Decker get ready for bed, Gabe finished up a few little things he'd left undone in the living room. Andy and Bennett passed him, heading for the stairs, but Gabe snagged his brother's arm.

"You're not really going to stay all night?"

Andy paused. "Sure. Why not? I don't have to work tomorrow, and Benny doesn't have school. It's the new Crazytown, Gabe. C'mon."

The kid was already halfway up the stairs, but he stopped to look back. "My mom said it was okay, really. She doesn't care."

The question was, why did Gabe care? "Do you have your medicine?"

Andy sighed. "Yes. Of course."

"What about, like…a toothbrush and stuff?"

"What do I need a toothbrush for?" Andy asked with a frown. "I'm not going to be brushing my teeth. Jeeze."

"We have an extra one he can use, if he really needs one," Bennett offered helpfully.

Gabe stepped back, thinking of a hundred reasons why his brother shouldn't stay over here, and unable to express a single one. He watched Andy follow the kid up the stairs and into the room on the left. He was still looking when Janelle came back, shrugging into a hoodie and looking at him expectantly.

"Ready?"

"You sure you want Andy staying over all night?"

Her mouth pursed. "I don't care, so long as they're quiet. Besides, you really think they'll stay up all night? They'll play until one or two in the morning and then pass out."

"Yeah…but he should just come home then. Not sleep over."

Janelle looked at him curiously. "It's not a big deal to me, really. And…it will be fun. For them."

Gabe thought of the times his brother woke screaming in the night, bathed in sweat, fighting nightmares he claimed to never remember. Or worse, the times when the meds failed him and he had a seizure. It had been a while, the last one so mild nobody would've noticed if they didn't know what to look for, but even so…

"He hasn't spent the night away from home before, that's all. Not unless he was in the hospital."

Both her brows went up, her mouth parting. "Oh. Wow."

"I mean since…you know. Not that he never did in his whole life." Gabe swallowed more words, an explanation, anything that would make him sound like some kind of freak.

She nodded. "I understand. The first time Bennett slept

over at a friend's house, I was so anxious I burned a meat loaf and the fire department had to come."

But Bennett was her kid. Andy was his brother, and an adult. Gabe frowned. "I just don't want him to be a pain, that's all."

"He's not. Believe me, if he were, I'd tell him so and send his butt home." Janelle grinned.

Her smile didn't make Gabe feel much better, but he nodded stiffly and gathered up the last bits of garbage from the painting project. "You ready?"

"Yep." She followed him through the kitchen, where he tossed the trash, and out the back door. Then to his truck, parked in his driveway. Silent the whole time. Until he pulled into the street, anyway. Then she cleared her throat and half turned toward him. "You take good care of him, Gabe."

He didn't look at her. "Don't."

"Don't what? It's true."

"I don't need you to pat my head. He's my brother. That's all."

More silence. He leaned to switch on the radio, punching the button to play the CD he had loaded. Old-school, Violent Femmes, the song order set to shuffle. Too late, he remembered she'd been the one to turn him onto the Femmes.

"Is this my CD?" Janelle asked after the first two songs had played through and they were nearing the edge of town, almost to the twenty-four-hour department store.

Gabe didn't answer her.

"Gabe Tierney," Janelle said with a laugh. "I know this is mine. You borrowed it and I never got it back before I left."

"Well," he said tightly, because what she said was true, "you left in such a hurry I didn't have time to give it back."

They pulled into the parking lot, but he didn't turn off the ignition. The music kept playing. Janelle tapped her fingers

to the beat, then her feet. Twisting to face him, she started
to sing along.

"Listen to this song," she says. "It's a great song."

*Janelle dances, hair swinging, hips swaying. Eyes closed. She twirls.
She's magic when she moves, and all he can do is watch her.*

"This is a great song," she said now, dancing in the passenger seat even with the seat belt restraining her.

"I know," Gabe said, and turned off the truck to make the
music die.

"Hey," Janelle protested. She got out when he did and came
around the front to follow him toward the store. "I was listening to that."

"I have stuff to do. Need to get home. You do, too," he
added. "You shouldn't leave them there alone for too long."

She had to take a couple running steps to catch up to him.
"They're fine."

"I don't want to be out here all night. I have stuff to do,"
he said again.

"What sort of *stuff?*" she demanded from behind him. "Big
date? What?"

That didn't slow him, but he did glance over his shoulder.
"Do you really want to be out at Wal-Mart all night? Is that
your idea of a good time?"

"I'm just happy to be out of that house," Janelle said crisply.
She stopped walking. "God. Wow. I'm just glad to be away
from there for a little while."

Gabe turned, walking backward, watching her get farther
and farther away. He waited for her to move, to catch up to
him, but she didn't. She stayed right where she was, right in
the middle of the dark parking lot.

Gabe stopped.

They stared at each other across the asphalt, the glare of the
parking lot lights making shadows on her face.

"Let's go somewhere," she said.

"We are somewhere."

Janelle smiled. "Somewhere else. Just for a little while, Gabe."

Gabe said nothing as she took a step closer, then another and another until she was right up next to him, her face tipped to look into his. He didn't move when she brushed her hand down the front of his shirt, or when she tugged at the hem of it. He couldn't move.

"God help me," she whispered, "I just want to get away for a little while. Is that wrong? Am I a terrible person?"

"No."

"Take me somewhere, Gabe," Janelle said.

He let out a long, slow breath. "Where do you want to go?"

"I don't know. Somewhere…somewhere away. Like the song says, somewhere only we know."

If nothing else had happened just then, he might've said yes. He might've taken her into his truck and played the Violent Femmes at top volume as they drove and drove and drove, someplace in the dark, someplace away. But a horn blared at them as a car passed, someone shouted at them to get out of the way. Janelle let go of the hem of his shirt and stepped back. The moment was lost.

She didn't say another word to him before they split up and did their shopping. They didn't talk when they met up again at the register, or when they paid, or even when they got back into his truck. But when he slipped something from one of the plastic bags and handed it to her, she let out a small, breathy sigh. She turned the square plastic container over and over in her hands, then ran her fingertips over the title of the CD.

Violent Femmes.

Then she said, "Thanks."

THIRTY-TWO

JANELLE JUST WANTED TO DANCE. THAT WAS ALL. Drink a couple beers, listen to some music, get her hips swaying and her feet shifting. She didn't even need a partner, though it would be a miracle if she got out of here tonight without at least a few offers, she thought as she tipped her first greenie to her mouth and sipped the crisp, yeasty flavor.

"I haven't had a Straub's in… God. Years. Decades."

"You can't get it out in Cali?" Betsy asked. She had a green bottle of her own. "You probably just spent all your time drinking mimosas or whatever, anyway, huh?"

Janelle wanted to assume her cousin was joking, but couldn't be sure. "Oh, sure. Me, Brad and Angie totally hung out in the hot tub all the time just quaffing Cristal and OJ."

"You're kidding, right?"

Janelle laughed. "Um. Yes. I'm kidding. The closest I ever got to a celebrity offering me a drink was when I helped Justin Ross originate a mortgage."

"Who's that?" Betsy twisted in her chair to survey the rest

of the bar. "It's pretty lame in here tonight. It should get a little better soon. I hope."

Justin Ross was the star of Janelle's favorite TV show of all time, *Runner*. It was in its last season, and she hadn't been able to keep up with it. She mourned the loss in a totally embarrassing way she wouldn't have shared with her best friend, much less a cousin she'd barely seen in the past twenty or so years. "It's okay if it doesn't," Janelle said when Betsy turned to her with a look both expectant and apologetic. "I'm happy to just get out for a little while."

"I hear that." Betsy sighed. After a pause, she added, "How's Nan been since the picnic?"

"She has her good days and her bad days. You should bring the kids over to see her more often."

Betsy looked guilty. "Oh. I didn't want to tire her out."

Janelle hadn't meant to make her cousin feel guilty or anything...but. "She'd love to see you."

"The kids are maniacs," Betsy said in the sort of voice all mothers who think their kids are perfect use when they're trying to pretend otherwise. "But I'll come over. I will. And hey, Bennett could come over sometime, what do you think?"

"Sure. Of course." Janelle wasn't going to argue. It would be good for Bennett to get to know his cousins better. "They seemed to get along fine at the picnic."

Betsy nodded with a grin. "Sure, sure. He can come over, spend the night some weekend. We always have tons of kids over playing video games and watching movies. I bet he'd have a blast. And it would give you a bit of a break, huh? Where is he tonight, hanging out with Nan and my mom?"

"He's at a sleepover."

"Oh...so he's making friends in school? That's good." Betsy nodded again and lifted her beer bottle.

Janelle clinked her bottle to her cousin's, wondering if she could tell Betsy about everything that had happened, or if she should just count her blessings that he'd finally made a friend. It was a boy in his math class, a quiet kid named Rodney. She decided on simplicity. "Yes. He's made some friends."

"Thank God, right? When we moved from Dubois to Kersey and my kids had to change schools, I thought they were going to die. Well, they said they were going to die."

"He's been having a rough time," Janelle blurted.

Betsy nodded as though she was expecting it. "Big changes?"

"Yes. He's always been such a good kid. I never had to worry. Never had to get on him about his work. Never had to worry about him making friends. And here…" Janelle shook her head. "It's so different."

"And what about you?"

Janelle sipped her beer. "What do you mean?"

"Well, what's it been like for you? You lived in California for a long time. Coming back here to St. Marys has to be sort of tough on you. Different, at least."

"Yeah. Different. Really different."

Betsy lifted her bottle again. "Here's to new beginnings, right?"

It was the right thing to say. Janelle waved at the bartender to bring them another two beers, and ordered a platter of mozzarella sticks, because what difference would a few more lumps and bumps in places she didn't want them make? Just like Dorothy after she stepped out of the house that had crunched the Wicked Witch of the West, Janelle was in a whole new world. One where the fashions were far more forgiving than in California.

"I'm so glad you came out with me tonight," Betsy said. "I bet you don't get much time to go out. Being a single mother and all that. And taking care of Nan."

"I get out. To the store," Janelle said with a laugh. "That's

about it. But it's okay. Mostly, I'm fine to stay home with a
book or a movie. Nan gets up so early...."

Scanning Betsy's face, watching her cousin's expression
change from interested to slightly blank, Janelle let her words
trail off. The first one of her circle of California friends to
get pregnant and then have a baby, she'd quickly learned most
people tuned out overly long descriptions of Bennett's sleeping, eating and pooping schedules. It was going to be the same
regarding Nan, she saw.

"Thank God for my mom, I guess."

Janelle took another drink before answering, to keep herself from sounding snarky. "Yes."

After what Janelle's quirky brain insisted on calling the
Great Potato Salad Incident, Kathy had been a little more
overbearing than usual. It was one thing for her to call to
check in on Nan, see how she was doing. To actually talk to
her mother-in-law as if she were having a normal conversation. It was another thing altogether for her to call to check up
on Janelle. When she'd offered to come and "sit with Mom"
for an evening so Janelle could go out, it had been a welcome
offer, but not necessarily a generous one.

"Say no more." Betsy held up a hand. "She's my mom, but
I totally get it. Personally, I think she has too much free time."

Janelle laughed and lifted her bottle to clink it. "Amen."

The conversation turned to other topics after that. Janelle
was happy to find out that she and Betsy had more in common than she'd thought. Betsy knew a number of the girls
Janelle had hung out with the year of high school she'd spent
here, since many of them had sisters in her grade. Janelle hadn't
heard from any of them in years, but Betsy was happy enough
to fill her in on the gossip.

They had something else in common, too, Janelle discovered when Betsy let out a low hum of appreciation as they

took a break from dancing to grab another couple of drinks. "Ooh, Gabe Tierney," her cousin murmured, glancing across the room.

Janelle couldn't help laughing. The beer had helped her mood immensely, the dancing even more so. "What about him? You think he's hot?"

"Don't you?" Betsy's eyes went wide. "I used to have such a crush."

More laughter snorted out of her at that. Liquor lubricated Janelle, made her loose; beer made her warm and fuzzy. "He's an asshole."

"Whatever." Betsy waved a hand. "It's not like I'd be able to take a shot with him. But you could."

That sobered Janelle a little bit. She eyed Gabe, watched him lean against the bar with his beer tipped to his lips. Watched him scope the room like...like what? A wolf stalking a deer. "Oh, please."

"He still lives next to Nan, right?"

"Yes. Him and his brother Andy. And their dad." Janelle shrugged as though it didn't matter. As though if she pretended hard enough, that could be true.

"So...?" Betsy grinned expectantly.

Janelle looked at him again. Some young blonde in a tight denim skirt had snared him with the hair toss, the hip sway. "So, nothing."

"Too bad," Betsy said. "He's really, really cute."

"I told you—"

"How is his brother, anyway?"

Janelle paused. "Who, Andy?"

"The one that lives with him. Yeah."

"He's fine." Janelle shrugged again. Gossip didn't seem quite as much fun when it was about people she knew.

"He works at the grocery store, right? Has that funny hand."

Janelle thought of the curled, hard-to-use fingers. "Yes."

"He's cute, too," Betsy said with another grin as the music changed. She let out a whoop and got off her bar stool to grab Janelle by the wrist. "I love this song! Let's go!"

And since that was what she'd come to do, that's what Janelle did. They danced hard, too. Heads bopping, hips popping, hair flying. Janelle had a couple beers in her, enough to blame for her abandoned footwork, but the truth was, she hadn't danced like this in way too long, and she needed to get it out. In California she'd managed to go out dancing at least a couple times a month. Sometimes looking to hook up, sure. But most times just to have fun.

Her dancing did attract a bit of attention. She saw that easily enough. A woman knows when a man's eyeing her, especially one she wants to be sure is noticing the way she moves.

She'd danced for Gabe a few times, back in the day, though never *with* him. He wasn't a dancer, he'd always said, and that didn't seem to have changed. He stood along the wall, beer in hand, watching. Despite the blonde's aggressive attentions, he was watching Janelle.

So...she danced.

The song changed again to something a little more old-school, a remix of The Cure's "Friday I'm in Love" mashed up with some new pop song she didn't know. With her eyes closed, she could almost imagine she was seventeen again, her hair dark and spiked, her eyes lined with black, her fingernails painted to match. Back when she'd thought dancing might actually be her life, her living, not just a hobby. She wore flats that could easily have been the ballet slippers she'd favored back then, and she had the same moves, even if a few of them were a little more...painful...to do.

Breathless, sweating, laughing, Janelle shimmied. She shaked. She looked across the room and she met Gabe's gaze, and she smiled, dancing now not just for herself, but also for him. And when the music changed suddenly, becoming slow and dreamy, she took a couple steps toward him, waiting for him to meet her halfway.

Some other guy got to her first. He stepped between her and Gabe, his smile open and friendly and gap-toothed. He wore a flannel shirt unbuttoned over a T-shirt with a sports team logo on it. No baseball cap, but the line in his hair showed he wore one more often than not.

"Wanna dance?"

The blonde was wriggling in front of Gabe. They weren't slow dancing, not quite, but she did take his hand and put it on her waist as Janelle watched. The other hand still held a beer he tipped to his lips, his gaze on Janelle.

"Okay," she said. "Sure."

How bad could it be? She discovered that a few minutes later as Jay, her partner, kept pulling her closer and closer. Where was that ruler the nuns had brought out at school dances? Janelle wondered, uncomfortable as Jay insisted on pulling her so close that she couldn't even look at his face without it blurring. She turned her head, refusing to put it on his shoulder or, God forbid, go cheek-to-cheek with him. But God help him if he put his hands on her ass.

He didn't. Jay talked, though. Asked her where she was from, said he knew she couldn't be from around here just by the way she looked. He told her about his job working at the Sylvania plant, and his ex-wife who spent too much money and thought it grew on trees, and how his parents had named him Jay because his mom had dreamed about jaybirds when she was pregnant with him. All this in the span of one song, which seemed to last forever instead of approximately three minutes, and which, to Janelle's horror, blended immediately into another slow number.

All around her, couples were snuggling. Betsy had gone back to the bar, her head bent close to a woman telling a story that involved a lot of hand gestures. Janelle tried to catch her attention, to call for backup, but couldn't. As if that wasn't bad enough, she caught sight of Gabe locked deep in a tongue-wrestling match with the blonde. It shouldn't have made her jealous or anything; it had been years since she and Gabe had been a thing…not that they'd ever been a "thing…."

"You know that guy?" Jay had caught her staring.

"Oh. He's my neighbor."

Jay's frown eased. "Oh, okay."

Janelle put another inch or so between them, but it was almost impossible to fight Jay's rubber-band hands. She'd inch back, he'd ease her forward again. It was a dance within a dance, and it made her laugh.

"What's funny?" Jay asked, but all she could do was shake her head and giggle.

That's when Jay leaned in and took a long, deep breath of her hair. She'd worn it in loose curls around her shoulders tonight, but now it hung limp and tangled from all the dancing. She startled when he took an exaggerated sniff.

"I'm getting a buzz off your hair," he said.

The giggles got worse. She tried to bite them back, but short of clapping a hand over her mouth, couldn't totally contain them. They'd been spinning slowly as they danced, and this last shuffle brought her facing Gabe again. His mouth was no longer fused with the blonde's, though she'd turned around to wiggle her butt against him.

Their eyes met.

Gabe smiled.

"So, you wanna maybe see about doing something sometime?" Jay asked, dragging Janelle's attention away from Gabe's face, and the moment was lost while she stammered out an excuse about why she couldn't. She wasn't sure exactly what she said, just that it seemed to satisfy Jay without offending him, because the song ended and he backed off with a smile and a nod.

But by that time, Gabe and the blonde were already gone.

THIRTY-THREE

SHE'D TOLD HIM HER NAME, BUT TYPICALLY, Gabe didn't bother to remember it. He thought she was a Hoffman, one of the younger ones. Much younger ones. Probably not a daughter of one of the Hoffmans Gabe had gone to school with…he didn't think he was old enough for that, though she sure as hell might've been.

"Shh…" She put a finger to her lips, so drunk she tripped over her own feet and stumbled forward into his bedroom. "We don't want to wake up your dad."

His old man slept like a corpse, so Gabe wasn't worried about that. Andy, on the other hand, was still downstairs in the kitchen and would be coming up to bed at any moment. Gabe kicked the door shut behind him. The woman's eyes went wide.

"Privacy," Gabe explained as he moved toward her. "Then you can make all the noise you want."

"Oh…I'm not a screamer." She managed to sound coy even through the thickness of booze in her voice. She tipped him

a smile he thought she might practice in the mirror—it was that good. She kicked off her shoes and toyed with the top button of her shirt.

"Is that a challenge?"

She fit nicely enough in his arms. His hands found her hips, jarringly bony through the sleek material of her shirt and above her denim skirt. She was light enough that he could easily lift her.

She squealed, clutching at but not fighting him. Her mouth found his. She tasted like sweet liquory drinks and lip balm. Her fingers dug into his shoulders. She wrapped her legs around his waist.

It turned out she'd been lying about being a screamer.

After, Gabe pulled the sheet up over his hips and dozed, too lazy to get up and get a cigarette. Not interested in standing outside in the cold for once. The woman beside him had already started snoring lightly, and he was also too lazy to shift her awake, make her get dressed and kick her out.

He drifted into dreams.

Then

Underneath all that pale makeup, Janelle Decker still has freckles. Gabe's sure of it. She thinks she needs all that eye liner and hair spray to make herself prettier, but he likes her best this way, with her hair wet and slicked back from her face, wearing nothing but a T-shirt and pajama bottoms. Bare feet.

"Stop bogarting." She holds out her small hand, the nails clipped short but painted black.

Gabe draws in smoke, long and deep. It burns, but he doesn't care. This is decent weed; he got it from his friend Steve, who lives outside of town and grows it in his parents' greenhouse. But it's not great weed. Gabe passes the joint.

Janelle's eyes squint shut as she takes a drag. She holds it

longer than he did before letting it stream out slowly as she
tips her head back to look up at the ceiling. She tucks her bare
feet underneath her as she hands him back the joint, then lets
herself fall onto his pillows.

They'll smell like her, later.

"What do you want to be when you grow up, Gabe?"

"Grown-up."

She snorts softly, on her back, pointing her toes at the ceiling. "I want to be a dancer."

She's a good dancer, but if he tells her that, he'll have to
admit he watches her dance. She knows he does, but he's not
going to say it, because then maybe she'll stop. "Don't you
have to go to school for that?"

"Yeah. Well, I guess so. I don't want to be a ballet dancer.
I just think it would be great to dance in shows."

"You want to be a stripper." He laughs.

Janelle flips him the finger. They smoke a little more. He
hasn't answered her question, but he's thinking about the answer. What does he want to be when he grows up, other than
away from this house and this town?

"I should go home." She curls on her side, one hand beneath her cheek, to look at him.

He won't ask her to stay, though he thinks she wants him
to. Instead, Gabe smokes. He offers her the last drag, but she
waves it away. He stubs it out in an old coffee can he seals
with a plastic lid, then shoves under his bed. He lies down
next to her.

It's a double bed, but not really big enough for both of
them. Not when she's got her ass stuck out like that, right up
against his hip. So when he rolls onto his side, he tells himself it's because of the bed. But it's not. And there's no keeping room for the Holy Spirit between them; maybe at school
at one of the lame dances he doesn't ever go to, but not here.

Janelle's butt fits neatly into the hollow of his crotch—which rapidly becomes a bulge.

His mouth finds the back of her neck. Her shoulder blade, exposed by the low neckline of her T-shirt. She moves against him when his hand slides over her hip, her belly. Between her legs.

They don't speak. They never say a word. Sometimes she's the one with her hand on him. Sometimes, her mouth. But tonight he moves against her, his fingertips sliding beneath the waistband of her pajamas to find her heat.

Girls have been after Gabe since the seventh grade, and the truth is, he's gone with one or two. But he's never made one shiver and shudder and moan this way. Janelle's hair, soft without all the product she insists on putting in it for school, brushes his face. Gabe closes his eyes and gets lost in it. His hand moves in slow, slow circles. He pushes his crotch against her, just a little faster. When she stiffens and gasps and puts her hand over his, he knows she means him to stop moving, but he can't. Not yet. Not until…just…a minute…more…

He becomes aware of her soft breathing just as the door slams downstairs. "My dad's home."

Janelle sits up, shifting his hand from under her pajamas with a casual effort. "My cue to leave."

She looks at him over her shoulder at the window. "Remember when we used to have those tin-can phones?"

"Yeah." Gabe props himself up on his elbow. His heartbeat's slowing, but the heat low in his belly is taking longer to go away. He won't get up to go to the bathroom until she's gone.

"We were stupid little kids, weren't we?"

"Yeah. Total assholes."

She smiles at him, almost as if she means to say more. Gabe hopes she does, though he's not sure what, exactly, he hopes she'll say. Instead, Janelle pushes aside his curtains and slides the window up. With one leg over the sill, she makes a show of looking down.

"If I ever break my neck doing this…"

He sits up straighter, thinking there's something important she means to say. He's a little too high for it, whatever it is. He should be more serious, he thinks. Though she isn't.

If she ever broke her neck doing that, if she ever fell when she tried to jump…what would he do? Would he jump after her? Would he pretend he didn't know what she was doing? Would he lie and say he pushed her, just to keep everyone from knowing the truth?

The next morning, not high, in fact, so deathly sober it's like someone put a stack of encyclopedias on his head, Gabe is late for the bus and has to run. Everyone's laughing at him when he gets on the bus, even Janelle. She sits in the middle, her mask of makeup turning her into a stranger. She doesn't look at him until he pauses at her seat, thinking this once he'll ask if he can sit with her. Wondering what she'd do if he leaned down right this minute and kissed her for the first time in front of everyone.

"Sit down back there!" hollers the bus driver, and Gabe moves to the back, his usual seat.

From there he can watch Janelle's head and see her profile when she turns, as she always does, to look out the window. So he watches. She never looks back.

Gabe woke to morning light so pale it might've been the moon. He blinked against it for a few seconds before remembering he wasn't alone in his bed. The blonde beside him sprawled out, her mouth slack. Her makeup had smeared. He nudged her.

"Get up."

She smacked her lips together and snuggled deeper into the

pillows. He pushed her again, harder this time. Then again, until she looked at him.

"The hell?" she said. "What time is it?"

"Time for you to leave. It's early. Get your shit and go before my brother gets up."

She stared at him, uncomprehending. "What difference does that make?"

"I don't want him seeing you, that's all." Gabe swung his legs over the edge of the bed. The floor was cold. His stomach was sour; the craving for a cigarette had become a physical burn. He wanted to light up more than he wanted anything else, even to pee. Even the "breakfast BJ" this chick-without-a-clue offered.

"Jesus…" she muttered.

"Hey. I didn't promise you eggs and toast in the morning." Gabe shrugged and got up to pad across the cold bare floor to find a pair of pants and a pullover shirt. He looked over his shoulder at her, still tangled in his sheets. He remembered her name now. Gina Hoffman. Definitely related to the Hoffmans he went to school with, and definitely a younger sibling, not a kid. The light of morning showed off the crow's-feet and lines around her mouth that proved she wasn't as young as he'd thought last night.

"No, I guess you didn't." She ran a hand through her hair and got out of bed. She found her clothes, moving slowly but steadily enough. "I didn't know you were going to kick me out before the sun was barely even up, though. I'd have left last night."

Gabe shrugged again, showing her it wouldn't have made a difference to him, one way or another. Gina frowned. She pulled her shirt on without her bra, which she shoved in her purse. She hooked her fingers into the impractical stiletto heels and carried them with her out the door, where she paused.

"Should I bother giving you my number?"

Gabe looked up from the dresser, where he'd been sorting through his top drawer, searching for cigarettes and finding none. "I'll probably just see you around."

She sucked in her lower lip. Then nodded. "Yeah. I guess so. See you around."

Gabe let one hand lift, but didn't look in her direction again until he heard the creaking of her footsteps on the steps. When he heard the front door open and close, he went downstairs. The living room smelled faintly of body odor, a little like urine, a little like onions and grease. He looked at the litter of fast-food wrappers and empty cola bottles on the dining room table and muttered a curse.

"Watch your mouth."

Gabe should've known the old man would already be awake. He hardly left the recliner anymore and probably had even slept there last night. "You're not supposed to eat this crap. You know that."

His father shrugged and looked at him with bleary eyes. "Your brother brought it home for me last night, since you couldn't be bothered to leave anything for me."

"You're not a cripple. You can make yourself a sandwich." Gabe gathered the trash, crumpling it in his fists, mindful of the way the sloppy leftover mayo squished through the paper and onto his hands. "This stuff'll kill you. On second thought, let me run out and get you an egg, cheese and heart-attack biscuit."

His father laughed, the sound like rusted gears no longer capable of turning, but trying hard. "You're a son of a bitch. You know that?"

"So you've told me my whole damned life, old man." Gabe paused before grabbing the last bit of trash. "You should get out of that chair. Do some exercise or something."

"What's it to you?" the old man asked with a weak shake of his fist. "Don't act like you wouldn't be tickled spitless if you came down one morning and found me in this here recliner, already cold."

Gabe's lips skinned back from his teeth in something more grimace than grin. Sometimes even liars told the truth. Sometimes they just lied. "Naw. That would break my heart."

His father snorted, yanked his hanky from his pocket and hawked into it. He folded the cloth over the mess and raised a crooked finger at his son. "Go make me some eggs and potatoes. That crap your brother fed me last night went right through me. I'm empty."

Cigarettes were still foremost on his mind, food a close second and a long, hot shower as soon as possible after that. Without answering, Gabe found a pack of smokes in the pocket of one of his jackets hanging in the hall closet. Leaving his dad muttering behind him, Gabe stalked through the kitchen to the back door. The first cigarette he pulled from the pack was broken, precious tobacco spilling from the white tube, but he had the second tucked between his lips in seconds. His lighter flared. He drew in the smoke, slow and deep. Let it out.

"It's a little early to be lighting up, isn't it?"

Startled, he almost dropped the lighter, but caught it with fingers already tingling with cold. Janelle, bundled in a hoodie with the hood pulled up, perched on the concrete steps of her grandmother's back porch. She'd sounded teasing, but didn't smile.

Silently, Gabe held out the pack to her. He didn't expect her to take one—not from him, anyway, even if she still smoked, which he doubted. She heaved herself upright and crossed the two squares of pavement to stand below him. She held out her hand.

Gabe pulled the pack back. "No way."

"Don't be a jerk, Gabe. You offered. Gimme."

He shook his head. "You don't really want one."

"Don't you tell me what I want!" Her gaze went hard and flat. Glittery.

Shit. Gabe tucked another cigarette in his mouth, lit it. Handed it down to her. He tucked his bare hand under his armpit and shifted to keep warm. Janelle puffed, coughed and puffed again.

"Gross," she complained, but didn't stub it out. Her second drag seemed to go down easier. She gave him a slight smile. "Rough night? Or just long?"

"Not really that rough. You?" He wondered if she'd gone home with that loser from the night before. He didn't think so. He hoped not. He wondered if she'd been sitting out here when Gina left the house, and if she'd seen her leaving. He hoped no to that, too.

She hesitated. She had circles under her eyes, he noticed now. And the hollows of her cheeks were too deep. She looked away with a shrug.

"Nan had a rough night. Yeah."

"Which means you did."

Janelle nodded silently. She let the cigarette burn between her fingers for another few seconds before putting it to her lips again. "I hate smoking. It tastes like shit, it stinks, it costs too much money. It gives you yellow teeth. And cancer."

"So don't smoke."

She looked back up at him with a frown, tossed the cigarette to the pavement and ground it out with the toe of her boot. "Okay, Mr. Chimney. How about you don't tell me what to do?"

He took the last drag off his own smoke and stuck it into the coffee can on the porch railing. He held up both hands. "Peace."

Without another word, Janelle turned and went inside her house with a slam of the door. Gabe stared after her for a minute. He considered another cigarette, but his rumbling stomach convinced him breakfast would be a better order. Inside, the sound of laughter drew him to the living room, where he waited in the doorway, watching.

The old man watched raptly as Andy told him some story about what had happened at work the day before. Andy could tell the hell out of a story. Probably because he forgot so many of the words he wanted to use and had to rely on gestures or phrases he made up to get his point across. He'd always been a clown, but he'd become a talented mimic. He stuttered on some of the phrases, but that just made their dad laugh harder.

Andy looked up. "Gabe! Did your friend go home?"

Gabe stifled a groan. He knew it had been a mistake to bring that girl back here. Usually he went to their houses so he could make a quick escape, no witnesses. Now he was sure Janelle knew—of course she did, because she'd been at the bar last night and seen him with the other woman. And not that she should care, or that he should care if she knew. But now Andy knew, too, and Gabe did mind about that.

"She's not...yeah." He scrubbed at his hair with his hand and rubbed his eyes. "She did."

"Should've asked her to stay for breakfast. I'm going to be make toad-in-the-hole. Or frog-on-a-raft. Your choice." Andy grinned. "Dad, what do you want?"

"Jesus, just eggs and toast," their dad said with a shake of his head. "You and your fancy schmancy stuff."

Andy dropped Gabe a wink. "How about you?"

"Eggs. Toast." Gabe yawned, thinking how nice it would be to crawl back into bed with a full stomach and nothing to do all day but sleep. No work, no chores, no errands. Nobody breathing in his ear. A shower first, though, because he wanted to rinse off the stink of skank. "I'm going to shower. I'll be down by the time you're done. Eggs over easy. Toast not burned."

By the time he finished in the hot water, though, his eyes stung, and not from the shampoo, as he'd thought. It was the burn of smoke, and as he stepped out of the shower, the smoke alarm went off. Cursing, Gabe wrapped himself in a towel and hopped down the stairs and into the kitchen, where he found Andy running his hand under water at the sink while the old man limply waved a tea towel under that alarm.

"Open the back door, for God's sake," Gabe cried, and did. Then he turned on the fan over the stove, and the ceiling fan, too. He waved his hand in front of his face, coughing. "What happened?"

Andy turned from the sink with a frown. "Nothing. I just let the toast go a little too long, and we didn't have butter so I used some oil for the eggs, but that made them too slippy, so when I was turning them, I almost dropped the pan." He lifted his bad hand, frown deepening. "It was my damned fingers. They just gave out."

"Language," their father said, and Andy looked chastened.

"You burned yourself? Let me see." Ignoring the old man, Gabe took his brother's wrist. Carefully, he uncurled the fingers. A blister was rising on Andy's palm, but it didn't look bad enough to need a trip to the emergency room. They'd had their share of those visits over the past few years. "Be more careful."

"I was being careful," Andy said stonily. "It was my hand. My goddamned hand, it just doesn't work right...."

This time, their dad said nothing about the cursing. Gabe found some bandages in the kitchen drawer and wrapped Andy's hand after applying ointment. Then he cleaned out the burned pan, emptied the crumb drawer, pitched the burned toast and eggs, and made them all breakfast.

Andy ate in silence, carefully picking at his food. The old man shoveled down two helpings of everything, then pushed away from the table without so much as a thank-you, to disappear into the living room and watch television. Andy got up to put his plate in the sink, and nearly dropped it; Gabe bit out a command to just freaking leave it. Andy put the plate down but didn't leave the kitchen.

"What?" Gabe barked.

"I was thinking about later, umm…I was going to see if maybe Janelle wanted to go see a movie with me. Think she would?"

"The hell if I know," Gabe said. "Why are you asking me?"

"Did she…like me, before? Ever?"

"I'd be more worried about if she likes you now," Gabe said, treading carefully, not sure what to say. The thought of Andy asking Janelle out was enough to stun him. "What difference does it make about before?"

Andy rubbed at the stripe in his hair, frowning. His gaze went a little blank, his mouth slack. It passed in seconds, with him blinking rapidly before focusing on Gabe again.

"Get out of here," Gabe said quietly. "I'll clean up."

Andy did, without another word about Janelle. Gabe looked around the mess of the kitchen, still stinking of smoke. Forget about napping all day, forget about sleeping for a few hours. He wanted to run away. But this was his life, he thought as he got up from the table to start cleaning up. He'd made his choice, and he was stuck with it.

Stuck.

THIRTY-FOUR

Then

EIGHTEEN'S SUPPOSED TO FEEL DIFFERENT, BUT so far it's only been more of the same. Nan's making lasagna and homemade garlic bread for dinner, Janelle's favorite. The aunts and uncles and cousins will all come over and sing to her, maybe slip her a five dollar bill in a card or something. Her mom already called this morning to sing the birthday song she's sung to Janelle every year of her life that she can remember. This year it should feel different, if only because she's living with Nan, because she's almost an adult, because the last time she saw her mom it was through the back window of a car and her mom had turned away without waving. Because, because.

Eighteen doesn't feel any different at all.

"Are you going to invite any of your friends?" Nan asks. "I have plenty of food, I just need to know."

Janelle does invite some friends. Mandy, Dawn, Kendra,

Barbie. Not Gabe. It would raise questions, maybe earn some good-natured teasing that might hit too close to home. She doesn't want anyone getting even an inkling that there might be something more to her and Gabe than being neighbors.

Her friends and family sing "Happy Birthday" to her and there's cake. Chocolate, Nan's homemade. Ice cream, too. Her friends, who've lived in St. Marys their entire lives, know Janelle's cousins better than she does. It's not the first time she's reminded that she doesn't really fit in here. Not all the way. Not the way she would've if she'd lived here with her dad as a kid instead of visiting every once in a while.

Then again, Gabe has lived in St. Marys his entire life and he doesn't exactly fit in, either. It's because he doesn't try. People would like him better if he just tried. That's what Janelle tells him later that night when she opens her window to crawl into his.

"You're going to kill yourself one of these days." He ignores what else she said.

Janelle doesn't. "It's not that you weren't invited because they don't like you, Gabe. Or even because I don't like you."

She likes him too much, as a matter of fact, but she won't say so.

He frowns and closes the window behind her. "Who says I even care?"

She holds up the note he taped to the outside of her window and starts to read aloud. "'If your done,' it's spelled *y-o-u,* apostrophe *r-e,* by the way. 'If your done with your fancy party and want to hang out—'"

Gabe tries to snatch the note from her, but Janelle dances out of reach. Laughing, she ducks his much-longer arms. She can't escape him entirely, though, she discovers when he grabs her by the hip and spins her. He backs her up to his bed, and she falls down on it, looking up at him. Daring him to get on it with her.

Gabe takes the note away, crumples it up. Shoves it in the trash. "Fine. There."

Janelle scoots back on the bed to prop herself up on his pillows. "I didn't think you'd want to come over. It was all family. And Mandy and them. You don't even like them."

Gabe frowns. Then scowls. Shrugs. "I don't care."

All at once, Janelle wishes he did. "I thought we agreed, that's all. About anyone knowing anything."

"We did. It's cool."

It's really not, but she's not going to push it. She rolls over to reach for the tin box beneath his bed. Gabe watches without expression when she pulls out a joint he already rolled. She holds it up, then digs in her pocket for the Zippo lighter her dad left behind in the closet. He's never come back for it, so finder's keepers. She flicks it open, then closed. Open again. Gabe loves this lighter, and she knows it.

"Happy birthday?" she says.

"You already helped yourself, might as well go ahead." After a minute or so, he sits beside her. He takes the joint from her and takes the first toke.

Janelle waits for her turn. She watches him. When he hands her the joint, she takes a drag from it without taking it from his hand. When she looks up at him, she smiles.

Gabe smiles back.

Some time later, flat on their backs on the bed with Janelle's feet propped on the slanted ceiling, she says, "I should've brought you some cake."

"I don't like cake."

She'd sit up if it didn't feel so good to keep still. "What do you mean, you don't like cake? That's…that's like saying you don't like blow jobs."

"No, I like blow jobs. I just don't like cake." Gabe sounds drowsy and warm.

She turns her head to look at him. "Why?"

"Because blow jobs are awesome."

His grin makes her want to rub herself all over his face. "I'm sure they are. But why not cake?"

"I dunno. I just don't like it. I like pie. I like cherry pie. I like apple pie. I like blow job pie."

"You're an idiot," she tells him.

"That would be the best kind of pie, ever."

"I think I'd rather have cake."

"You wouldn't think that if you'd ever had a blow job."

Janelle can hear how slow and syrupy they both sound. How silly. She laughs, then some more. "Girls can't get blow jobs."

"Sure they can. It's called something else. Something complicated. But it's the same thing."

"Well. Duh." She knew that, of course she did. Oral sex. "Going down. It's called going down. And I'll take your word for it."

"You never...did it?"

She's blown him dozens of times by now, so she knows that's not what he means. "Nope."

"Why not?"

"Nobody ever offered," Janelle says, for the first time realizing how annoyed she'd been by that.

"I'll do it," Gabe says.

They've never, no matter how high or drunk they've been, ever talked about the things they do together that make them not just friends. They somehow just...do it.

Now everything inside her tightens and tenses. "No."

"Why not? It'll make you feel so good. And it's your birthday. And soon you're leaving. You're going to go away."

"You're going away, too," she says. "Aren't you?"

Gabe snorts soft laughter. "Hell, yes. As far away as I can go. Never coming back."

"We'll never see each other again," Janelle says.

"That's why I'm going to do this for you now."

"No," she repeats, not sure why she's so adamant about it.

Somehow, he's moved her on the bed, he's leaning over her. His mouth moves along her throat. Lower.

Lower.

It's not her first orgasm—Janelle's known that pleasure since she discovered the joys of the detachable shower head at age thirteen. It's not her first with a boy, or even her first with Gabe. But this...this is...too much. His mouth on her, kissing her down there when he has yet to kiss her mouth. Everything spirals up and up and then down so hard she can't breathe.

She can't breathe.

She can't look at him when it's over. This is also different from the other times, when they finished what they'd been doing and she went home. Now she can't move, can't sit up. Something's changed, and she doesn't know exactly what.

Janelle manages to force herself upright. Off the bed. She finds her clothes. Gabe's eyes are closed; he's breathing low and slow. Sleeping? She hopes to sneak away, if her legs will even hold her, if she can get through the window and across the alley into her own room without falling.

She finds her clothes. She opens the window. His voice stops her.

"Hey, wait."

The high's worn off, leaving her wide-eyed but no longer hungry for cake. She turns to face him. Gabe's sitting, hair tousled. He pulls something from beneath his pillow and stands.

"I got you something for your birthday. I mean...a real something."

The box is the size of her palm, inexpertly wrapped in plain brown paper without a ribbon. She pulls the tape free, takes off the paper. She lifts the lid. Inside, on a bed of flat cotton, is a small Blessed Virgin charm on a silver chain.

It's beautiful.

She lifts it from the package, the silver chain threading through her fingers. She looks at him. "It's the one from the thrift store."

"You liked it," Gabe says.

He listened to her. More than that, he heard her. She hands him the necklace and turns, lifting her hair. "Put it on me."

He does. For a guy with such big hands, he's surprisingly delicate. He smooths the chain against the back of her neck, and Janelle tenses, eyes closing, waiting for him to kiss her there, too. But he doesn't.

She doesn't tell him she likes it, though she does. He doesn't ask. When she turns to face him, he's already backing away, his expression hard to read.

"Gabe," she says, thinking of all the things she could say, but doesn't or won't or can't. She settles for the simplest, though it's also the most important. "I love it."

THIRTY-FIVE

IT WASN'T THE FIRST TIME THE CHAIN ON THIS
necklace had broken. This time, it snagged on a button as
Janelle pulled her shirt over her head. The medallion slid over
her skin and got stuck in her bra, but the chain slithered farther while she fumbled to grab it. She missed and let out a
soft curse as the chain hit the floor in a long silver coil. The
clasp was fine, she saw when she bent to pick it up, but a few
links had broken.

It was senseless to cry over something she'd broken before,
so easily fixed, but somehow the tears rose, anyway, and Janelle
found herself on her hands and knees with her palm clapped
over her mouth to press back the sobs. She'd worn this necklace for years, thinking every day of the boy who'd given it
to her, but she'd worn it for more years not thinking of him
at all. It had become habit.

She touched the place at the base of her throat where the
medallion always rested. It felt naked. Her fingertips pressed,
pressed against the hollow, then to the left along the curve

of her collarbone, and to the right. Somehow she'd stopped crying and hadn't noticed, though her face still felt hot and her eyes swollen.

Janelle took the chain and medallion and put them carefully in her jewelry box. She'd never been one for expensive jewelry. The Virgin Mary nestled between a set of silver bangle bracelets and a few pairs of novelty earrings Bennett had bought for her from the school's Christmas bazaars over the years. Santa, Rudolph, Frosty. They made her ears sore, but she could never throw them away. She closed the lid of the box, letting her fingers rest there for a moment or two, thinking about the night Gabe had given her the necklace.

What it had meant then.

It should mean nothing now.

Janelle washed her face and finished changing her clothes— it was past seven, time for lounging pants and an oversize sweatshirt. Comfy clothes. She had nobody to impress.

Downstairs, she found Bennett at the dining table with Andy, both bent over math homework. Nan was in the recliner with her feet up, switching channels at random and pausing no more than a few seconds on each program. She looked up when Janelle came in.

"Ready?"

"Yep. Let me go grab a few boxes."

Nan smiled and twisted a little in the chair. "Benny, are you finished with your homework?"

"Almost, Nan."

"He's doing really great." Andy smiled at Janelle. "What are you doing?"

"Sorting more of Nan's pictures. Hey, Andy, I could use a hand with some of the boxes. Could you—" He was up and out of his chair before she could finish the sentence.

"Sure, yeah. Finish that work, man. I'll check it when I

come back." Andy rubbed his hands together, straightening the curled fingers of his right hand. To Janelle, he said, "Anything you need."

The back room had a set of floor-to-ceiling shelves against one wall. A couple dozen shoe boxes without lids, each stuffed to bulging with packs of photos, lined a few of the shelves. Nan had albums, too, the kind with magnetic pages, each labeled with the year and with hand-scribbled notes of who, what, where and when in the margins. They were all shoved haphazardly into the cabinet in the living room. They'd be easier to sort, so Janelle had started with the years' worth of snapshots that had been shoved away without any rhyme or reason, while Nan was still here to help her decipher the faces in each picture.

"Can you help me get those down?" She pointed to the top corner, the one she'd be able to reach only if she stood on something.

Andy was a good five or six inches taller and could easily reach the boxes, but could use only one hand to grab. "Sorry," he said as he handed her one at a time.

"For what?" Janelle stacked the boxes in her arms as he passed them to her.

"For being slow."

She laughed. "It's fine. I appreciate the help."

Andy gave her one of those brilliant grins, not paying close enough attention to what he was doing. The box he grabbed tore as he pulled it, the cardboard rotten with age. Half of it came away in his hand. An avalanche of paper envelopes filled with pictures cascaded off the shelf, onto Andy's head, his shoulders, onto Janelle's stacked boxes. Onto the floor.

"Look out!" he cried, too late.

Janelle managed not to juggle the boxes in her hands into another waterfall of photos. "Oops."

"Sorry, sorry!" Andy shook his head and went to his knees. "God, I'm so stupid. What a freaking idiot. I'm sorry."

Janelle set the three boxes in her arms carefully on the floor next to the pile that had fallen. "Hey."

He didn't appear to hear her. Andy scooped up the pictures on the floor, the ones in his good hand piling neatly while the ones in his bad hand fluttered and skittered out of his grasp. Janelle put her hand over his to stop the frantic fumbling. Andy quieted.

"Hey," she repeated. "Chill out, dude."

He smiled tentatively. "I don't want to ruin your grandma's pictures."

"They're fine." Janelle patted his hand. "The boxes are old. Don't worry about it."

She was holding his hand, she realized. The bad one. She didn't let go, not right away—that would've been more awkward than this. She turned it over in hers and ran her thumb along his fingers, one by one, feeling the resistance that wanted to keep them curled against his palm.

"Does it hurt?" Gently, Janelle let go of his hand.

Andy pulled it close. "No. Not really. Nothing hurts except sometimes my head. I get headaches. Bad ones. They used to mean I was probably going to have a fit, but the pills I take helped that a lot."

"A… Oh. A seizure? You had seizures." Without thinking, Janelle pushed the hair away from his eyes. Dark hair, except for that white section.

Andy looked at her seriously. Too seriously. "Yeah."

"I'm sorry." Janelle bit the inside of her cheek, her old habit, to keep from saying more. There weren't words for what had happened back then, or her part in it. Nothing could change it, especially not regret.

"Hey, look," Andy said. "It's you."

There were sure to be a bunch of pictures of her in these boxes, but the one he showed her was from her senior year. "Oh. God. The hair."

Every time she saw it, she wanted to cringe and laugh at the same time. The clothes, the hair, the makeup. Who had she been? Who had she been trying to be?

"I think you looked pretty." Andy tapped the picture, taken in Nan's backyard sometime in the fall. Janelle was posed under the apple tree, staring at the camera as if she meant to bite it, not smile for it. He pointed off to the side. "There's me. And Mikey."

They were a blur, running through their yard, caught by the camera. They weren't identical twins, but Janelle couldn't have told them apart in the photo. She didn't have to, because Andy ran his finger along one of the figures.

"I wonder what we were doing."

She remembered that day, Nan insisting on the picture. The stickiness of sweat trickling down Janelle's back because she'd been stupid and dressed as if it were fifty degrees outside, not in the Indian Summer seventies. She'd spent an hour on her hair and makeup, all for a silly snapshot.

"You were playing football." Janelle took the picture and studied it. There in the corner, another blur, just the tiniest sliver. "With Gabe."

"Did I… Did we know you then?"

She smiled. "Yes. A little. You got to know me better later."

Much better.

Much later.

"I wish I remembered."

"Me, too, honey." She patted his arm and tucked the picture back among the others, gathering them into a pile. There was no box to put them in, so she grabbed an empty laundry basket from the closet and dumped them inside. The other boxes went on top.

"I could get more down," Andy offered. "There's room in the basket."

"I don't think we'll even get through these tonight. This is enough. Thanks."

He was still staring at her. Awkwardly, she hefted the laundry basket and waited for him to move out of the way. He didn't at first, not until she made a shooing motion with the basket. She felt his gaze on her the entire way down the hall toward the family room.

Bennett had already put away his math homework by the time they got there, and set out a bowl of cookies and glasses for milk. Nan looked up from the recliner, blinking sleepily. She settled the remote into the knitted holder attached to the chair's arm and started to her feet.

"Hold on, hold on, Mrs. Decker." Andy pushed past Janelle to help Nan up. He did it easily, despite his own disability. He steadied her gently with his good hand and helped her to the table, where he pulled out her chair. "There you go."

"Thanks, honey," Nan said. "Ooh, cookies. Bennett, did you do this?"

"I like cookies," Bennett said with a grin. "With milk."

"Pour me a glass, honey, and let's get started. Janelle, grab my glasses." Nan tapped the table as Andy moved toward the back door. "Where are you going, Andy?"

"Oh…I thought I'd better go home."

Nan shook her head. "You can stay, help us sort these pictures. I wouldn't be surprised if we found a few more of you and your brothers in here. I'd like you to have them, if we do."

Janelle already knew there was at least one, of course, but was a little surprised to think there could be more. Andy looked surprised, too. He put a hesitant hand on the back of a chair.

"Really?"

"Of course. Absolutely." Nan nodded. "Sit down."

People didn't argue with Nan when she spoke in that voice, and Andy was no exception. He sat. Janelle got out the archival safe marker she'd ordered online, and brought in a bunch of sandwich bags and rubber bands from the kitchen. They all helped themselves to cookies and milk and got started.

It went far slower than Janelle had thought it would. She could easily and quickly sort the pictures into piles if she knew for sure who was in them—piles for uncles, cousins, family friends. Photos of landscapes and buildings, and any that were out of focus, she set aside. But there were many pictures of people Janelle didn't know, and those she gave to Nan, who studied each one for several minutes apiece.

Most of them had a story. This person had said this or done that, just before the camera clicked. Nan remembered most of their names and the places, and Janelle wrote the information carefully on the backs of the pictures with the pen that wouldn't ruin them, and put them into their piles according to how Nan categorized them.

"Mom, you look hilarious," Bennett said over and over, having a laughing fit each time he pulled another picture of her out of the pile. It didn't matter if it was one of her in the height of eighties fashion as a kid, or in her goth phase. He laughed and laughed.

The more he laughed, the more she laughed. Andy laughed, and Nan laughed, too. Janelle lifted a photo of herself decked out in full fashion.

"Look at this one."

"Mom, you look like a rooster was sitting on your head!"

"I think she looks beautiful," Andy said suddenly. "She always did. Look beautiful, I mean."

Nan's giggles faded and she gave Janelle a knowing glance. Bennett wrinkled his nose in distaste. Heat rose in Janelle's face, not quite a blush.

"Thanks, Andy."

"I mean…I don't remember, exactly. I look at the pictures. I look at you now." He smiled at her. "I'm sure I'd have thought you were beautiful back then."

With the three of them staring at her, all Janelle could do was clear her throat awkwardly. "Well…thank you, Andy. That's really nice of you to say."

They spent the next hour or so sorting through pictures before Nan began to get tired. She didn't say anything, but Janelle could tell. Nan protested a little when she suggested it was time for bed, though.

"I believe I'll stay up a bit," her grandmother said. "I'd like to finish with this box. You help Bennett get ready for bed."

Bennett didn't need any help, but when he opened his mouth to say so, Janelle stopped him with a look. To Nan, she said gently, "It's getting late. Let me help you with your pills and stuff, okay?"

"I don't need any help!" Nan shouted, and struck a trembling hand against the final box of photos they hadn't yet sorted.

Pictures scattered, fluttering to the floor. Andy reacted with a startled cry, backing up in his chair until it hit the wall behind him, and Bennett looked as if he might cry. Janelle carefully kept herself from reacting.

"Nan. It's late, and you're tired."

"Don't talk to me like I'm a child," Nan cried. "I want to finish this, and I'm not tired! You go to bed if you want to, Janelle, but don't you tell me what to do. I want to finish this."

"Bennett, go on upstairs. Andy," Janelle said, "thanks for your help. You should probably head home."

He nodded. "Should I come tomorrow?"

"Call me," Janelle told him, and stood to walk him to the back door as Bennett eased past her toward the kitchen. On the back porch, she said, "Thanks for your help."

"You want me to stay? I could. If she needs something, if you need something, I mean." Andy looked so sincere it made Janelle's throat close.

She put her hand on his shoulder. "No, it's fine. She's old and sick.... I'd be cranky, too. Wouldn't you?"

Andy nodded after a second, brow furrowed. "Yeah. I guess so. But if you're sure you don't need any help..."

"I'm okay. We'll be fine. Thanks, Andy." Impulsively, Janelle hugged him. She meant for it to be a simple embrace, a quick hug, but the moment his arms went around her, it felt so damned good to have someone holding her that she melted into the touch like a cat beneath a stroking hand.

He put both arms around her, the good hand flat against her back and the other resting lightly at her hip. She fit just beneath his chin, her cheek against his chest, on his soft T-shirt. She didn't mean to cry. It just happened. A few tears, nothing major, most of which she sniffled back because she didn't want to totally break down. Andy stroked his hand over her back, his fingers tugging on her hair just enough to return her back to reality.

"Sorry," she said as she stepped away. "God. Sorry, Andy. I just..."

He shook his head. "No, it's okay. I'm sorry this is hard for you."

Janelle glanced over her shoulder, but though the back porch door was open, she couldn't see Nan from this angle. Which meant Nan hadn't seen them. "I'm fine."

Andy's brow furrowed again. He rubbed at the white line of his hair as his mouth worked, before he said finally, "I feel like there should be something I can say, but it's not coming out right. I can taste the words, but they're stuck."

"It must be frustrating." Janelle wiped discreetly at her eyes.

"I hate it," Andy told her. "I hate being stupid."

She took both his hands in hers. "You are not stupid. You never were."

"You remember me from before."

"Yes." Janelle paused, but didn't want to lie to him. "Of course I do, Andy. And you weren't stupid back then, I promise you."

He took his hand from hers to touch the white stripe in his hair again. "I must've been a little stupid."

"Careless, maybe. All of you. But it was an accident."

Andy didn't say anything for a few seconds before he nodded. "Yeah. I know."

Janelle hugged him again, this time not for herself but for him. "Thanks for coming over tonight. We'll see you, okay?"

He looked as if he might say something else, but didn't, just nodded and let himself out the back door. Janelle took a deep breath and squared her shoulders before going inside, to find Nan still sitting at the table, looking through the pictures. Her grandma looked up when she came in.

"I just want to finish this," she said stubbornly. "All these pictures need to be sorted, Janelle. I don't want to leave it undone."

"We can do more tomorrow, Nan. It's really late, and honestly, I'm tired, too."

Nan frowned and waved a dismissive hand. "So go to bed."

"You know I can't until you're all settled." Janelle eased herself into the seat across from her. She'd need to check on

Bennett in a minute or so, too. Her head was starting to hurt, her eyes itchy with sleep.

Nan said nothing, a photo held tight in her fingers. She stared at it in silence while Janelle waited, until at last she looked up with a frown. "I don't need you!"

"Fine." Janelle tossed up her hands and pushed her chair back. "I'm going to bed. You stay here all night, Nan, if you want to. I'm not going to argue with you."

With that, she left her grandmother sitting at the table, and went upstairs to make sure Bennett had brushed his teeth and put on clean pajamas. Of course he hadn't, but Janelle didn't feel like arguing with him, either. Instead, she went into her room and dropped down onto the bed, where she lay unmoving until her phone vibrated from the nightstand. She rolled to check the number, which was unfamiliar, though the name underneath it wasn't.

"Shit," she muttered, and didn't answer.

After a minute, her phone chimed to alert her to the new voice mail. The cherry on top of the shit sundae the evening had become. She thumbed the screen to look at it, but didn't listen.

A message from her dad.

THIRTY-SIX

Then

"WHERE ARE WE GOING? IT'S A SECRET? WHY are you taking me someplace secret?" Janelle dances back and forth in front of him instead of getting into his truck, dances so much he almost has to wrestle with her just to get her to the passenger-side door.

"It's not… I just don't want to say anything to you ahead of time." In fact, Gabe's not sure why he's even taking her, except that he doesn't want to go by himself.

Janelle stops dancing, but bounces lightly on her toes, up and down. "Give me a hint. Just a little hint."

He knows she thinks that maybe he's taking her someplace…not romantic, because that's not what they do. Private, though. Special. The cabin, maybe. He's taken her there a few times already, the only girl he ever has. Both of them act as if it's not a big deal, but he thinks she knows it is. He should tell her up front that's not where they're going, but he says nothing as they drive out of town in the opposite direction.

Janelle pushes a CD into the slot and turns up the volume. The familiar guitar riff starts, then the drums. She claps her hands in time. When the lyrics begin, she sings along without self-consciousness about walking, strutting her stuff, blister in the sun. It's not his favorite song on the CD—that would be "Gone Daddy Gone"—but he likes hearing her sing along.

They drive while the music plays, three or four songs, until she turns down the volume. "When will you tell me where we're going?"

"When we get there."

Other girls would wheedle and beg, but Janelle only shrugs and looks out the window again. Gabe could never be sure if he likes that about her or not. Sometimes it's good to have someone force something out of you, he thinks as he takes the last few turns toward their destination. He pulls into the driveway of the small house with overgrown grass, and turns off the engine.

In the silence left behind, without the Violent Femmes begging someone to please, please not go, the sound of Janelle's surprised half laugh is very loud. "Where are we?"

"My mother's house."

Her mouth opens. Then shuts. She looks again out the window at the house. He figures she'd say something, but instead she turns toward him and reaches for his hand. She links their fingers tight, squeezing.

Janelle's never asked him about his mother, and he's never talked about her. He's not sure if Janelle heard she was dead—that's what everyone thinks, so if she ever did ask someone what was up, that's what they'd have told her. Even his brothers still think their mother's dead.

Sometimes, Gabe wishes he thought so, too.

"She's expecting me," he says. "I didn't tell her you were coming with me, though. I didn't tell her anything about you."

Janelle's fingers squeeze again, and then she lets him go. "So...what's the plan?"

He hadn't thought about a plan when he asked her, and the thought makes him laugh, just a little. It makes this better, and he finally figures out that's why he asked her to come with him. Because she makes things better.

"You want me to be your girlfriend?" she asks, and for a moment Gabe feels his heart thump too fast, thinking she means for real. "Like, you want to impress your mom or something? 'Cuz maybe you picked the wrong girl for that."

Janelle laughs and tips her face up, runs a hand over her hair and along her brows, gesturing. "I mean, I'm not really any mother's wet dream."

No, but she's *his* wet dream, which, of course, he doesn't say.

"Oh...never mind." Janelle laughs again before he can speak. "I get it. It's the opposite, huh? You want to freak her out."

He doesn't realize that as truth until she says it, but once the words are out there's no denying it. "Yeah. I guess I do."

She laughs again and bounces on her toes. "So. Let's go freak Mama out."

The house is small and poorly kept, the grass in the yard too long. The door knocker looks like a face, but Gabe doesn't use it. He just goes right in. The whole place smells of cigarettes, so much he expects to see a haze in the air.

His mother's in the kitchen, hovering over the stove. She turns when they come in, her smile fading at the sight of Janelle before returning even brighter than before. She lifts the spatula in greeting.

"You brought a guest? You should've told me. I'd have gussied up a little more."

She's already painted up like a clown, her hair and mouth too bright. She lifts a cigarette from an ashtray on the countertop and watches the two of them through a veil of smoke.

"This is Janelle."

"Hi," Janelle says.

"Hello, Janelle. Why don't you two have a seat?" His mother points to the table, set for two. "Let me get another plate. I'm making sausage. Gabe, honey, grab those rolls from the bread box. Janelle, you like hot sausage?"

"Oh, yeah," Janelle says. "I love sausage. Can't get enough of it."

The way she says it, all wide eyes and innuendo, makes Gabe want to laugh even as a flush of heat creeps up his throat to his face. His mother pauses, as though thinking of an answer. Janelle takes her place at the table and folds her hands, staring at them both.

"So…how did you two meet?" his mother asks when she slides the frying pan full of hot sausage onto a trivet on the table, along with a bottle of ketchup and a bowl of macaroni and cheese from a box.

"Key party." Janelle helps herself to a nice portion of mac and cheese, then adds a swirl of ketchup onto the bright yellow noodles.

"Key party…?" Marlena stares at the mush Janelle's making of the pasta. She doesn't eat. She hardly ever does, which is why the food she serves when he visits is usually such shit. "I'm not sure I've ever been to one of those."

Gabe's never heard of a key party, either, so when Janelle starts to explain, he's as surprised as his mother.

"Oh, it's simple, really. It's kind of like an orgy," Janelle says as she loads a hoagie roll with a sausage and takes a huge bite. "Oh, God. Wow, this is awesome."

Marlena coughs. "An orgy."

"Yeah. You all throw your keys in a bowl, then everyone picks one out. Whoever's key you pick, well, that's who you end up with for the night. It's tricky business," Janelle says with a wink. "But I made sure to pick Gabe's key."

Gabe focuses on his plate, because if he doesn't he's sure he'll burst into horrified laughter. It's exactly the sort of thing he didn't know he wanted Janelle to say. It's terrible. It's perfect.

"And so...how long have you been...umm, dating?" Marlena lights another cigarette.

"Oh, we're not really dating. But I didn't get knocked up yet or anything, so it's all cool. Stellar sausage, by the way." Janelle makes a show of taking another bite, giving Gabe a wink as she practically deep throats the sandwich.

He almost chokes on his food. Marlena stubs out her cigarette and gets up from the table. When her back's turned, Janelle mouths, "Too much?"

Gabe shakes his head. He's not sure why he wants his mother to be made uncomfortable, just that watching her squirm gives him some sort of sick satisfaction that should make him ashamed but doesn't. Janelle plays it just right, too. Not too over the top. Believable. Enough to make Marlena's eyes go wide and her face go white beneath the harsh bright circles of rouge.

At the end of the visit, she hugs her son, but doesn't even offer Janelle her hand. "Gabriel, you come back soon, you hear me?"

He won't. This will be the last time he sees her for a long, long time, and he knew that before he came. She watches them from the doorway as they drive away, but though she raises her hand in a wave, Gabe doesn't wave back.

He doesn't head for home right away. He goes into town, parks on a side street in front of a small hospital thrift store. The mannequins in the window don't have heads, and one's

missing an arm. There's a shelf of sad stuffed toys at their feet. He needs to sit for a few minutes before he can drive home and face his brothers, knowing this secret they don't.

Janelle doesn't ask him if he's okay. She sits with him in silence for a minute or so. Then she punches him in the arm.

"Let's go in there." She points at the thrift shop. "I love places like that."

Because she did something for him without question, Gabe gets out of the truck and follows her into the dusty smelling shop, where she flips through old record albums and sorts through countless paperback novels. She passes up the housewares section, but stops in front of the large glass jewelry case to stare down at the velvet-covered boards glittering with costume pins. On top of the case are several spinning racks, and Janelle turns them slowly.

Her fingers push at the dangling chains and beads, the rosaries. She lifts a pendant engraved with the face of the Virgin Mary, and studies it longer than she has any of the others. Her fingertips cradle it before she lets it go, swinging on the peg.

"You think Jesus ever got mad that his real dad was never around?" Janelle looks at Gabe, totally serious. "I mean... he knew Joseph wasn't his real dad, right? But his real father wasn't around, and then he ended up dying for him."

Gabe goes to church because his dad makes him, but he hasn't prayed in a long time. He has no opinion on Jesus or his mother. "I'm never having kids."

"Me, neither." She twirls the rack again slowly, stopping once more at the dangling Virgin pendant. "If you ask me, she ought to have dumped Joseph and never told Jesus where he came from. Having no dad is better than having a shitty one. I guess having no mom is better than having a shitty mom, too."

Janelle looks at him. "C'mon, Gabe. Let's go home and get a little high."

At home in his bed, her back pressed to his front and his chin tucked into her neck, both of them pleasantly buzzed, she curls her fingers in his again and holds them tight against her.

"How come you asked me to go with you?" she asks.

He thinks for a minute before he answers. "Because I knew you'd say yes."

"How'd you know?"

"I just...knew," Gabe says. "I knew you'd do something for me if I needed it."

She shakes a little. He wants to ask her if she's crying, but is afraid she'll say yes, and after a while she stops. She turns to face him, her eyes dry. She slides her hand against him, inside his jeans, and then that's all he can think about.

THIRTY-SEVEN

WHEN THE PHONE RANG, JANGLING, JANELLE picked it up automatically without looking at the caller ID. Nan was napping after having been awake on and off for another night, calling for Janelle to help her, which should not have been, but was, worse than if she'd tried to rearrange the fridge by herself, or any of the other useless tasks that took hold of her in the wee hours. She got argumentative when Janelle told her she needed to go back to sleep. Nan had been sick, too, dry heaving. Not since Bennett was a baby had Janelle been operating on such constantly interrupted sleep, and it was taking its toll.

She snapped up the phone with a curt "Hello." Silence greeted her, going on for so long she was just about to hang up when a rough male voice said her name. She froze, twisting the cord of Nan's old-fashioned landline in one hand.

"Dad."

"Hey. Yeah." He sounded pleased she recognized him.

She cut that sentiment off at the knees. "What do you want?"

"You never answered the messages I left on your cell. I thought I'd call directly."

"What do you want," she repeated, keeping her voice down so that not only wouldn't it wake Nan, but she couldn't possibly overhear if she was awake.

"I want to see my mother. And you. And my grandson." He must've known she'd protest, because he added quickly, before she could speak, "You have every right to be pissed off at me, Janelle. But just listen…"

"There's no money for you."

He paused. When he spoke again, he sounded angry, not contrite. Typical. "Don't you think I care more about saying goodbye to my dying mother than money?"

"I have no idea what sort of things you care about, but being there for your family has never seemed to be one of them." Janelle twisted the cord harder, tighter around her fingers, until it hurt. She didn't unwind it, either.

"You can't keep me from coming to see her." Another pause, then his voice was softer. "Look. I understand if you don't want to have anything to do with me. But I want to see her before it's too late. And it's not your decision, Janny. It's hers."

"She won't want to see you." Even as she said it, Janelle knew it wasn't true. Her uncles would want their brother to stay far away, but Nan… Well, Janelle had a son. She was pretty sure Nan would want to see her oldest boy, no matter what he'd done.

"Ask her."

"She's sleeping now."

He sighed. "Fine. So ask her when she wakes up. I can come next Wednesday. Around noon."

"No," Janelle said automatically, then recanted. At noon Bennett would still be in school, assuming there was no more trouble. She hadn't had a call since the last one. "Fine. Noon. But you can't stay more than an hour. She tires easily, and I don't want you here when my son gets home from school."

"You sound like your mother when you talk that way, you know it?" He sounded begrudgingly admiring, not mad. "Fine. I'll be there at noon. I'll stay an hour. We'll work from there. Okay?"

"Fine." She hung up without saying goodbye, her stomach sour and her mouth dry.

Nan called out from the bedroom, crying Janelle's name over and over again in a voice that rose in pitch until it was nearly a scream. Janelle got there as fast as she could and found her grandmother fighting at the sheets tangled around her. She clawed at them, kicking feebly.

"Nan, calm down. You're fine. Did you have a bad dream or something?"

"Get me out of here," Nan cried.

Janelle tried to ease her out of the blankets, but Nan kept fighting. Her hand came up and smacked Janelle in the face, hard enough to make her see stars. She staggered back, her hand on her nose.

Nan quieted at once. "Oh, oh, honey, I'm so sorry!"

"It's okay." Eyes watering, nose starting to run, Janelle grabbed a tissue. "It was an accident. I'm okay."

Really, her nose hurt like hell and she wanted to scream, but she pasted on a smile and sat on the edge of the bed to let Nan take her hand. They sat that way for a few seconds, Nan patting her over and over. When her grandma had quieted, Janelle extracted her from the sheets and helped her sit up.

"Are you okay, Nan? Were you dreaming?"

She shook her head. "They were calling my name again,

that's all. I heard them, clear as a bell. And I thought they were leaving without me." She smiled sadly. "I'm a silly old lady."

Janelle squeezed her hand. "You're not. Let's get you up and changed. We can have a snack, watch some TV until Bennett gets home, how's that?"

Nan nodded and allowed Janelle to help her swing her legs over the edge of the bed. "Did I hear the phone ring?"

Janelle paused, focusing on making sure both of Nan's feet, clad in thick slipper socks, were firmly settled on the floor before she helped her stand. "Oh. Yeah."

"Was it Helen? I told her I'd let her know about that recipe I was telling her about." Nan struggled to get up, but couldn't quite manage to push herself off the bed until Janelle pulled her.

The pain in Janelle's eye and nose intensified, as did the almost constant ache that had cropped up in her neck and shoulder and refused to be put aside no matter how many hot showers she took. "No. It was someone trying to sell me something."

"I hope you told them to buzz off," Nan said fiercely, eyes twinkling.

Janelle smiled. "Yep, Nan. I sure did."

THIRTY-EIGHT

JANELLE HAD HAD DATES FOR WHICH SHE'D spent way less time getting ready. She'd spent an hour on her hair. With her makeup. Finding the perfect shirt to go with just the right pair of jeans that wouldn't make it look as if she'd tried very hard at all.

It wasn't Nan's best day. She'd woken later than normal, allowing Janelle to get Bennett off to school, but when she did finally get up she'd made a mess in the kitchen while trying to pour herself some cereal. She'd resisted Janelle's help in the bath, insisting she was fine without washing her hair—but Janelle couldn't let her grandmother see her oldest son after so long without making sure she looked her best.

Janelle also didn't tell her why she was so insistent about everything.

She had experienced firsthand the disappointment of waiting for her dad over and over, only to have him be a no-show. There was no way she was going to put her grandma through that. So she insisted on a bath, a blouse and comfortable skirt instead of Nan's usual nightgown and housecoat. Even a little lip gloss, all while Nan grumbled and protested about being "tarted up" and became more and more suspicious.

By 11:00 a.m., when it was time for Nan's midmorning medicine, Janelle was running on caffeine and anxiety. She'd lost her patience for watching her grandmother fumble with the bottles. She opened them all and laid out the pills, poured the liquid iron supplement and set everything up before calling Nan to the table.

Her grandma paused, leaning on the back of her chair, when she saw it. Then she looked at Janelle. "Why did you do this?"

"I was trying to help. You need to take your meds and then have some lunch. I'm making grilled cheese and tomato soup." And there needed to be enough time for both the medicine and the food to go down, as well as time for Nan to deal with cleanup or post-meds upset, which was happening more and more frequently.

"I can get my own medicine."

Janelle sighed. "I know, Nan. I was trying to help."

Her grandmother sniffed but said nothing else. She took the pills and drank the liquid, then settled everything back into place. When Janelle slid a bowl of soup and a sandwich in front of her, though, she shook her head. "I don't want it."

"You have to eat." Janelle's own stomach was jumping up and down. "Especially after taking your medicine. You know your stomach will get upset if you don't."

"My stomach gets upset if I don't eat or if I do." Nan pushed away the soup, turning her head. "I don't want it."

"Well...what do you want?"

"Chicken salad."

There wasn't any chicken salad. "I could make you tuna salad."

"It's not the same," Nan said.

No. It wasn't. Janelle went to the kitchen, anyway, to make some, adding mayonnaise and a little mustard. By the time she'd finished, it was close to noon. With an eye on the clock, she slid the plate in front of Nan, who didn't reach for the sandwich.

"It's not the same," she repeated. "Anyway, I'm not hungry."

Janelle had eaten only a dry piece of toast earlier, but now her stomach rumbled and gurgled. "Fine. I'll eat it."

She sat across from her grandmother and pulled the plate toward her. The soup, too, now cold. She spooned a bite, then broke up the cold grilled cheese and dipped it into the bowl before eating that, too. Nan frowned, watching her. Janelle ate with an eye on the clock as it ticked just past noon. Another minute passed while she ate Nan's lunch and Nan ate nothing.

At quarter past twelve, still early enough that her dad could still be coming, but late enough she was convinced he wasn't going to, Janelle finished all the food she'd put out on the table. Now her stomach groaned, and she clapped a hand over her mouth to stifle a belch. Nan had watched it all in silence, but now spoke up.

"You're going to get fat if you keep eating like that, Janelle."

Janelle laughed, regretting the gluttony for many reasons, including the way her jeans now cut into her gut. "Yeah. I guess I am."

Nan wagged a finger. "You know who makes a delicious chicken salad. The Pit Stop."

"Is that place still around?" The diner had been a popular hangout when Janelle was in high school. She'd never had the chicken salad.

"Oh, yes. The Pit Stop's been there for years. I used to go there when I was a girl." Nan gave Janelle a significant look. "They have a very good apple pie, too. By the time we get there, you might even have room for a piece."

Janelle looked again at the clock. Twelve-thirty. If her dad was coming, he'd better get there in the next ten minutes. "You want me to take you to The Pit Stop?"

Nan dimpled, and in that grin was the schoolgirl Janelle had seen in so many of the old snapshots. "Oh, that would be lovely. You did have me get all gussied up. It would be a shame to waste it."

That was that.

At The Pit Stop, Nan held court in a way Janelle had missed seeing. Old friends, neighbors, acquaintances, all stopped by their booth to greet them and spend a few minutes chatting. She looked better than she had in weeks, her cheeks pink and her eyes sparkling. Nan was tired by the time they got back to the house, but in great spirits.

"I needed that," she told Janelle as she let her settle her into her bed for a late-afternoon nap. She patted Janelle's hand. "It was good to get out."

"We should do it more often," Janelle said. "I wish you'd said something earlier, if you wanted to get out. There are a lot of things we could be doing, if you wanted."

Nan sighed, eyelids drooping. "I did tell you, honey. And we went."

Janelle held her grandmother's hand, watching her drift into sleep. "Nan…if there's anything you want to do that… Is there anything you want to do? That you haven't?"

Nan made an effort at staying awake. "You mean something foolish, like skydiving? Or what do they call it, that cord jumping. They do it off bridges."

"Bungee jumping."

"No bungee jumping." Nan smiled.

"But is there?" Janelle persisted. "Anything you want to do that you haven't? Something you feel you missed?"

Her grandma yawned. "No. Oh, do I have my regrets, here

and there? Sure. I suppose we all do. But is there anything I ever did that I really wanted to do, that I wish I'd done? That I could do now, you mean. Before I die."

"Yes." Janelle swallowed, the sweet taste of pie still lingering. "Before you die."

She shook her head. "No. But is that a question you're really asking me, honey? Or maybe are you thinking about yourself?"

"There are a lot of things I haven't done, Nan."

Nan patted her hand and sank back against the pillows, her eyes closing all the way. "Still have time…."

Janelle sat there for a few minutes, watching, then left her grandmother to sleep. She was cleaning up in the kitchen when her phone vibrated in her pocket. She pulled it out, saw the number and pressed the button to send it automatically to voice mail. A few seconds later, when the phone buzzed again, this time with a message, she deleted it without listening. Then she opened up an app she'd downloaded some time before to deal with a blind date who'd become a little too stalkerish for her tastes. She entered her dad's number.

Blocked.

THIRTY-NINE

SHE FOUND THE REPORT CARD IN THE TRASH can. The grades weren't terrible—mostly A's with a B in science, but math was still a big D. Janelle looked at it carefully, then took it upstairs.

Bennett was hastily tucking a comic under his pillow when she opened the door. "What?"

She ignored the comic. Held up the report card. His face fell.

"You know I need to see this, right? I have to sign it and send it back to school. Did you think I wouldn't find out?"

Bennett frowned. "Figured you'd be mad."

"Well. I am mad, but I'm also concerned." She sat on the edge of his bed. "I haven't had any calls lately, so that's good. But you have to tell me if there's something going on. More stuff like there was before."

He rolled his eyes. "No. I don't have any more stuff. You took it."

"That's not the right answer, Bennett!" Janelle said. "The

right answer is that you wouldn't do anything like that again, even if you did have more stuff!"

"Sorry," he muttered.

She took a few breaths to keep her temper steady. "I'm so disappointed. You got a D? I thought Andy was helping you. I thought you were making an effort. I thought you were really going to try."

"I did try. I worked hard."

"You can't have worked that hard," she pointed out.

"Sorry, I guess I'm not perfect the way you want me to be."

This stopped her. "I don't expect you to be perfect. I just want you to try your best."

"I did try my best."

"Getting a D is not your best," she told him, and stood, holding up the report card. "It's unacceptable. You can do better. I expect better from you."

The words spilling from her were an echo of the ones her mother had said to her all those years ago, and this stopped her. Janelle pressed her lips together. Oh, God. She'd been in high school, a teenager, when she'd gone out of control. Bennett was only in the sixth grade.

"I've tried so hard," she said. "To make sure… I just wanted to make sure you grew up right, that you didn't turn out like…"

He watched her, silent, eyes wide. Janelle swiped at her tears, embarrassed and angry. She focused on the report card, folding it in half, then again, making creases.

"I didn't want you to turn out like me," she said. "I want you to be better than that, Bennett."

"I can only be what I am," he said with an edge in his voice that made him sound much older than twelve, though the way his lip trembled and his eyes welled with tears kept him a little boy. "And it's not perfect."

"Is that really what you think I expect?"

He nodded.

"Well, it's not. Nobody's perfect. Especially not me."

She thought of the years of lectures, restrictions, guidelines and rules, the private school and lessons she'd put herself into debt to provide. She thought of her mother, telling her she'd done everything she could to make Janelle perfect so she could prove to the world she hadn't messed up. Her mom had done it by trying to force her into a small box, and Janelle had done the same thing by trying to expand Bennett's horizons.

"I don't expect you to be perfect," she told him. "I just want you to be you."

"I am me, Mom!"

"Is 'you' a boy who sells drugs, Bennett? Gets into fights? Fails in school? Is that who you want to be?" Janelle's mom had never asked that. Neither had her dad, for that matter.

He looked at her. "No. I don't hang around those kids anymore. I told them they had to leave me alone."

"Good. Then let's figure out a way to get you through this, okay?" She drew in a deep breath. "We'll have Andy come over to help you a little more often. And you're going to try to bring up your grades in math, for sure. And I'll…I'll try to remember you're twelve now and give you a little more credit for being responsible, okay? But you have to earn it," she warned. "There will be consequences if you don't."

Bennett smiled slowly. "Okay. It's a deal."

"Deal." She held out her hand for him to shake, then pulled him close for a hug instead, holding him tight, wishing she never had to let go, and knowing she had no choice.

FORTY

"CALL ME WHEN THE MOVIE'S OVER." JANELLE twisted to look into the backseat at Bennett, then handed him a ten-dollar bill. She handed Andy one, too.

"What's this for?"

"Popcorn, duh." She grinned at him and retreated against the driver's-side door when he tried to hand it back to her. "No. You keep it."

"I have money!"

Janelle shook her head. "This is my treat. Don't argue."

Bennett was already getting out of the car. "Yeah, Andy. Don't argue with her. You can't win."

Andy frowned and turned the bill over and over in his hands as he stared at it. He looked up at her, his brow furrowed. "You don't have to."

"I don't have to. I want to." Janelle shrugged. "You're doing me a real favor. I want to treat you."

He hesitated, still frowning. "You want to come with us?"

The movie was a shoot-em-up sci-fi flick with lots of what

she was sure would be gratuitous violence and probably a good share of women in skimpy outfits. It was the sort of movie she'd have forbidden without a second thought even a few weeks ago. It was the kind of movie she'd have loved when she was Bennett's age. "Nah. It's okay. I can always catch it on DVD if it's that good." And besides, Bennett would rather see something like that with Andy than his mom.

Andy tucked the ten into his front pocket and nodded. "Okay. Thanks, Janelle."

"You're welcome."

He didn't get out of the car.

"Andy?" Janelle asked gently. "You okay?"

Bennett rapped on the window before Andy could reply. "Hey, c'mon! They're letting people in already! I want to get a good seat!"

Andy jumped at the thud of Bennett's knuckles on the glass, but gave Janelle a smile. "We'll see you later."

"Call me," she told him. "I'll come get you."

"You don't have to. We can walk."

She wasn't ready to be that lenient with her kid. "Don't be silly. I can pick you up. It'll be late."

"C'mon, Andy!"

With another small smile, Andy got out of the car. He bent to look through the window for a second, giving her a thumbs-up she returned, then backing away to give her room to pull out of the parking spot. She watched them for a few seconds in the rearview mirror, but though Andy stayed put as she drove away, Bennett danced with impatience until his much taller and older friend finally turned toward the movie theater.

It took her only five minutes to drive home, and even that felt like too long. Janelle hadn't had the house to herself since they'd moved here, but tonight with Nan at her card club and Bennett at the movies, she intended to take advantage of every single second. She was already imagining the orgy of corn chips and cheese dip in front of a deliciously soft-core porn flick—*Lake Consequence,* maybe, with pre-bald-headed Billy Zane. Or *Red Shoe Diaries* with that other Billy, Billy Wirth. Huh, maybe she had a thing for guys named Billy....

"What the—!" The words shot out of her as she tripped through the back door and into the family room, courtesy of a pair of giant work boots that someone had left right in the middle of the doormat. She kicked one out of the way, already knowing what she'd find as she gripped the door frame and looked into the kitchen.

Gabe.

"What are you doing here?"

Kneeling in front of the sink, Gabe gazed up at her. His dark hair was rumpled, sticking straight up. His white T-shirt showcased a pair of truly lovely biceps, which flexed as he held up a wrench in one hand and a length of plastic pipe in the other.

"I'm fixing that leak in the sink. You wanted me to, right? It was on the list."

"Oh." It was the only thing she could think of to say. "I didn't know you'd be here."

Gabe got up slowly, wincing and creaking. He rolled his shoulders, popping his back. "Same here. I thought you were going out to the movies."

"I just took Bennett and Andy. I never planned to stay."

"Oh."

It pleased her to hear him sound just as dumb as she had. For a moment they stared at each other without saying anything. It used to be they didn't have to speak, that silence was fine and possibly preferred. Now it just felt awkward.

"How's it going?" Janelle asked. Lame.

He'd spent so much time being grouchy with her that the

slowly spreading smile surprised her. It tipped the corners of his mouth first, then crinkled the corners of his eyes. It lit up his face in a way she hadn't seen for a really, really long time.

There was no thinking about it; Janelle kissed him. She moved into his arms, hers going around his neck, her thigh between his and his butt pressed up against the counter so he had no room to back away from her. She kissed him as if it were the most natural and expected thing in the world for her to do, as if she had no fears that Gabe would turn her aside.

He didn't. He made a muffled, startled noise against her mouth, but his arms went around her without hesitation. His lips parted. The stroke of his tongue was not familiar, not after all this time, but it was delicious and delightful. The kiss got harder. She pressed against him, and the kiss went on and on until she had to break it to breathe.

She looked up at him, thinking there ought to be something to say about this, but the words wouldn't come. Gabe touched a fingertip to her forehead to push her hair away from her eyes, and Janelle no longer cared about trying to speak. There was no time for it, anyway. They'd wasted too much of it already.

She kissed him again. She took him by the belt loops and pulled him, her mouth still on his, backward through the kitchen. The living room. She stood on the first stair and took his face in her hands. She could've ended it then and there, or he might've backed away. She didn't. He didn't.

In her bedroom, Janelle pulled her shirt over her head and tossed it to the floor. Gabe's came next. When they embraced again, belly to belly, his skin was so warm she shouldn't have shivered in the chilly air, but she did. His hands splayed against her shoulder blades as he kissed her.

As he kissed her.

The first time he'd ever touched her, his fingers had fumbled on her skin. They'd found their way to pleasure through trial and error, not skill. Times had changed, she thought a little incoherently as Gabe's teeth pressed on her throat, when his hand slid between her legs. Everything about this all felt new. Not familiar, but not uneasy.

The clock on her wall ticked and tocked, reminding her that every minute passing was one more lost. She urged him with her hands and mouth to move faster. Then a little harder. A little deeper. She cried his name at the end and wondered if she should've bit it back, but was too replete and sated to worry too much.

Gabe rolled off her and onto his back, his head on her pillow. Their shoulders touched. So did their hips. His breathing slowed as he turned his head to look at her. "Sorry."

Janelle got up on one elbow. "For what?"

"For being so...fast."

She laughed. "Mmm. We had to hurry. Next time we'll make sure to take our time."

"Next time?" Gabe got up on his elbow, too.

"Next time," Janelle said, like a promise, and kissed him.

This time was different. This time, he let her kiss him instead of kissing her back. The difference was marked. She pulled away with a frown.

"No next time?" She watched him sigh and sit up, swinging his legs over the edge of the bed. His broad shoulders tapered to a lean waist, begging her to touch him, but she didn't.

"I need to finish that sink."

"And I'll need to go pick up my kid and your brother in a few minutes," she said with a glance at the clock. "And Nan will be home shortly after that. You're not just going to run off, Gabe. Tell me you're not."

He didn't look at her, but he didn't get off the bed, either. "You...shouldn't."

"Shouldn't what?" She scooted closer to him, but still didn't touch. "Want you?"

"Yes." He got up then. Started hunting for his jeans, his shirt. He didn't look at her.

"Gabe," Janelle said quietly. "Look at me."

He did.

"I always wanted you," she said.

He smiled, slowly. He kissed her again. Then he left her in the crumpled tangle of sheets still smelling of him, and went downstairs.

FORTY-ONE

YOU GOT TO KNOW WHEN TO HOLD 'EM AND
when to fold 'em, as the song goes, and in this case, Janelle
knew it was time to fold. She'd been sure Gabe wouldn't consent to shooting lessons for Bennett, and that would've been
fine. Janelle wasn't sure how it had happened, just that one
minute Gabe had been tinkering with Nan's hot water heater
while Bennett handed him tools, and the next Bennett had
been upstairs telling her the when and the where.

That was how they ended up here in the woods in the same
clearing, in front of what looked to be the same wooden railing. Hell, by the state of some of those cans and bottles, they
might've been the same, too. This time, thank God, instead
of knee-deep snow, they walked on wet leaves and squishy
mud; instead of being bundled in heavy winter clothes they
could get away with sweatshirts. They also had safety goggles
and hearing protection, courtesy of Gabe, who'd insisted on
as much protective gear as possible.

She'd insisted on coming along, of course. Gabe hadn't

looked too happy about it, but too bad. She wasn't going to send her boy off into the woods with him and a gun without her supervision. She'd made that clear.

Gabe had smiled without much humor. "What do you think might happen, Janelle?"

She hadn't answered. It had stung him, she thought, watching him now as he went through a series of instructions with a serious-faced Bennett. She'd taken a seat off to the side and couldn't hear everything they were saying, but when Bennett moved to pick up the gun from the weather-battered card table on which Gabe had set everything up, and Gabe put his hand firmly on the boy's to stop him, everything inside her relaxed.

Then

Janelle's never shot a gun. She's never wanted to shoot a gun. She thinks she could probably go her entire life without shooting a gun.

But Gabe wants to show her how.

So here she is, out in snow up to her shins, freezing her ass off while he sets up a series of cans along a railing made of two-by-fours. It's not from a set of stairs or even part of a fence; Gabe and his brothers and a bunch of other guys built it out here specifically so they could line up cans and jars and bottles from the garbage and take turns blasting them to bits. They shoot at paper targets, too, tacked up against trees or bales of hay. It's apparently quite the hangout.

Last night brought nearly a foot of thick, white snow that normally wouldn't have caused a bus delay in a school district so well-accustomed to such weather, but the storm had ended with a long spell of freezing rain that coated everything in ice. School had been canceled, a rare holiday. Most of the other kids are out sledding or ice skating, or at home making out under blankets. Gabe convinced her this would be more fun.

His brothers are here, too, tromping through the snow. Janelle's little brother, Kenny, used to drive her insane, but Mike and Andy make her miss him. They toss snowballs back and forth and at Gabe, and she likes the way he lets them get away with it. Earlier he was angry with them, mad enough to punch them. But now they're making him laugh, and she likes watching him be happy.

"My hands are going to freeze if I take my mittens off," she says.

Gabe has waded through the snow, busting the icy crust with his big boots, to set up the cans. Every step he takes leaves a distinct hole. He's dressed better for the weather than she is. He looks up at the sky when she complains, then shrugs.

"It's not that cold, Janelle. C'mon."

"For you, maybe. I'm not from around here, remember?"

Gabe's not a jokester like his brother Andy, and he's not a Goody Two-shoes like Mike. Still, his smiles are rare as rainbows and usually make her feel sort of the same way. He gives her one now, and suddenly he's right—it's not so cold.

"You'll be fine," he assures her. "And it'll be fun."

Andy and Mike have their own guns, and they take turns shooting at the targets. When Gabe shows her how to load the gun, Janelle knows enough to be impressed with how accurately and swiftly he handles it, but also how carefully. He's no cowboy, no sharpshooter. Everything Gabe does with the gun is precise and deliberate. No flash. She doesn't really care about how a revolver works, but she listens and watches his face, because obviously, Gabe cares.

He won't let her even aim the gun until she can demonstrate to him she understands how to empty the cylinder and how to check if the weapon's loaded or unloaded. He's a patient teacher, and this surprises and impresses her because the Gabe she's always known has a short attention span and shorter temper.

"Now," he says, and presses the gun into her hand. "Shoot the shit out of something."

She can't, of course, not at first. His hands on her hips, tilting her body, distract her. He straightens her shoulders. He aligns his body with hers, one arm stretched out along hers to help her level the gun.

"Squeeze the trigger," he says into her ear. "Don't jerk it. Don't pull it. Squeeze it."

The shot rings out into the snow-covered trees. A Straub's greenie bottle explodes. Janelle, stunned with success, hoots and hollers, but Gabe's hand on her arm keeps the gun pointed away from them both.

"You did it," he said. "I knew you could."

The kid was eager to get shooting. Gabe understood that. But first he made Bennett go through all the paces his own dad had taught him. How to make sure the cylinder was empty. If the kid got bored before the end and didn't want to pay attention, Gabe was prepared to call off the lesson right then.

"My mom says guns aren't toys," the boy said as Gabe walked him through everything one more time.

Gabe glanced at Janelle, sitting on a fallen log with her fingers linked around her knees. She was watching them pretty intensely. He guessed he couldn't blame her, considering what he was sure she believed to be true. "She's right."

"She doesn't even really like me playing shooting games that much, unless it's zombies or monsters. No real people." The kid sighed. "No soldier games or anything like that."

Gabe had never understood the appeal of those sort of games, anyway. He like pinball or old-school, arcade-style Pac-Man, Donkey Kong, things like that. "Why do you want a play to game where you blow someone's head open, anyway? Pick up the gun. Stand here, in front of me. You never point the gun at anyone, you got it? You keep it pointed away from people. And your own feet."

The kid nodded and picked up the gun, too gingerly. Gabe put his hand over the boy's to curl his fingers into place. He leveled the kid's arm. Steadied it. He almost said, "Hold it like you'd hold your dick," but that seemed a little too mature. With another glance at Janelle, Gabe murmured a few more instructions, then stepped back.

The kid's first shot went wild, but he didn't get upset. He planted his feet a little wider, fixed his stance and aimed again. Gabe's revolver was heavy enough for a grown man, but Bennett did pretty good with it. His next two shots blew off a pair of soup cans. The fourth nicked the wooden railing. The final shot shattered a bottle.

Carefully, the kid let his arm drop to his side, keeping the gun carefully pointed away from anyone else and his own feet, just as Gabe had instructed. "That was cool! Can I go again?"

"Sure." Gabe pointed at the table. "Show me everything you learned."

He had to help a little, but the kid quickly got the hang of things. As he set his stance and aimed again, Gabe stepped back. This time, Janelle got up and walked over to him.

"You're a good teacher," she said.

"Thanks."

They watched in silence as Bennett managed to shoot a few more of the cans. He turned to both of them with a look of pure glee that made Gabe smile. "Can I do it again?"

Gabe looked at Janelle, who hesitated, but nodded. "Okay. But we can't be out here all day, Bennett. I'm sure Gabe has other things to do."

He did not, as a matter of fact, unless you counted clean-

ing up after the old man and arguing with him over what to
watch on the television. Andy was working until closing, and
Gabe had promised to pick him up, but that was hours away.
He wasn't going to tell her that, though.

"I need to set up the cans again, right?" The kid looked at
Gabe. Without being told, Bennett made sure the gun was
both unloaded and had the safety on before setting it on the
card table and running across the clearing toward the railing.

When he was out of earshot, Janelle turned. "I mean it,
Gabe. You're a good teacher. You're patient, and you know
what you're doing." She paused, tilting her head to look him
over. He hadn't seen that expression in a long, long time, but
he recalled it all too well. "Remember the day you took me
out here?"

Gabe busied himself with arranging the ammunition on
the table. "Yeah."

Janelle stepped around the table and pressed her fingertips
on the edge of it. "You showed me all those things that you
just showed Bennett. It was a long time ago, but I remember
a lot of it."

He looked up at her. "You want to take a crack at it?"

Her slight smile didn't fool him. She was still looking at
him as if she could see right through him. "No, that's okay."

The kid was certainly taking his time setting up the next
round of cans and bottles, pulling them from the box where
everyone dumped their empties, and inspecting each thor-
oughly before setting it on the railing.

"C'mon, kid, you're not decorating out there. Set 'em up
so you can knock 'em down!"

"Gabe," Janelle said quietly. "I was thinking about that
time when you showed me how to shoot. I've been thinking
about a lot of things...."

He didn't want to hear it. He didn't want to talk about it. Most of all, he didn't want her to think about it.

"C'mon, kid! I've got stuff to do!"

Bennett turned from his careful arrangements. With a grin, he ran back toward them, slipping in the mud onto one knee. Janelle let out a low groan.

"Bennett. Your clothes…"

"Boys get dirty," Gabe said. "That's what they do."

Janelle looked at him again. This time, she didn't smile. "Yes. I guess they do."

FORTY-TWO

Then

MOST OF THE TIME, GABE MOVES LIKE A CAT—
sleek and silent and sort of ripply. As if he's full of coiled energy
that could burst out at any time. Janelle's seen him running,
fists and feet pumping, and that was what she thinks it might
be like if Gabe ever lets himself really go. But not quite.

Mostly, he moves smoothly, but not today. He jitters and
paces and jiggles his foot restlessly when he does finally manage to sit on the couch next to her. He shakes it so much the
couch's wooden feet squeak on the floor. At last, she can't
stand it anymore and puts a hand on his knee, pressing his
foot down.

"Enough."

He goes still. Silent and motionless, his gaze fixed on the
crappy TV's snowy picture. She'd only been pretending to
watch while she waited for him to push her back against the
cushions. Janelle lets her hand travel a little higher on his thigh,

her fingers squeezing muscle. She watches his profile, his un-blinking stare and the curved-down corner of his mouth. She takes her hand away.

"What the hell's going on with you, Gabe?"

There'd been that small graduation party at her house. Nothing for Gabe; his dad was such an asshole she'd bet he didn't even care. She knew what that was like—no matter how much you thought you'd get used to it, you never really could. And even though Nan had made sure Gabe had his own cake, with his name on it, Janelle knew it wasn't the same.

In a softer, gentler voice, she says, "Are you okay?"

He kisses her.

All the times they've fooled around, he's never kissed her. Janelle's imagined his mouth on hers a thousand times, maybe more than that. Soft, sweet, slow, hard, fierce, fumbling…a thousand different ways he would kiss her for the first time, and this is nothing like any of them. Gabe takes her face in his hands, holding her still. His lips slide against hers, parting them with his tongue—or maybe she'd gasped with surprise and her mouth was already open. She can't tell. All she can do is kiss him back.

She's on his lap before she knows it, straddling him. Her fingers dig into his shoulders. He hasn't let go of her face. She can't move away, but doesn't care, not even when his kiss be-comes bruising. She rocks against him, wanting to feel him get hard, and that's when he breaks the kiss.

Breathing hard, Gabe looks into her eyes. His mouth is wet and open. When he slides his tongue across his lower lip, she imagines him tasting her. The thought is huge and sud-den and powerful. They've been fooling around for months. He's made her come, and she's done the same for him. But this feeling is somehow adult and terrifying.

Janelle pushes back from him a little, but Gabe lets go of

her face to grab her upper arms instead, holding her in place. "Hey!"

"Janelle." His fingers tighten.

Something is so wrong about all of this…and yet it's Gabe. Gabe, who Janelle thinks loves her, though they've never even gone on a date. He has to love her—why else would he look at her the way he does when he thinks she doesn't see? The way he looks now? She could lose herself in those blue eyes and never find her way out, because Gabe Tierney is nothing if not made of secrets.

She stops struggling. She puts her hands on his face, mirroring him, though her touch is more of a caress. Her thumbs stroke along the edge of his cheekbones. She leans in to kiss him, and at the last second, he turns his face just enough that she'd end up kissing the corner of his mouth if she kept on. She stops. His breath fans over her lips. She doesn't move away, and when she speaks, her mouth brushes his. It's nothing like a kiss.

"Tell me what's wrong."

He pushes her away, too hard. He goes to the dresser, pulls out a pack of cigarettes. Fumbles with his lighter. Watching him, Janelle thinks she should get up and get out of this room, because whatever's going on is bad.

Really bad.

His lighter sputters but won't flame. Gabe mutters a curse. He throws it, just a cheap plastic thing, onto the floor, so hard it cracks and breaks. He grips the dresser, his head down.

Janelle crosses to him, but stands out of his reach. She's cold, suddenly, in front of the open window, despite a warm spring breeze. Her arms hump with goose pimples, and she rubs them. She says nothing.

Eventually, he turns, still gripping the dresser, to look at her. "Go away."

"No. Not until you tell me what's going on."

Gabe shakes his head. He lets go of the dresser and stalks toward her, but he's aiming for the bed, not her. He tosses back the pillows and covers, searching. Muttering a curse, he yanks open the nightstand drawer so hard it flies off its rails and the contents scatter on the floor. Coins, miscellaneous junk. No lighter. Gabe curses louder and pounds his fist against the nightstand hard enough to rock the lamp.

She's seen him angry before. When he and his dad go at it, it's like watching two bears in a ring, circling, ready to attack. To the jerks at school Gabe always shows a different face, colder and somehow scarier because of that. He doesn't even have to throw a punch to make people run away. And of course, with his brothers he's mocking, snide and sneering. A condescending big brother who grabs them in headlocks and rubs their hair to make it stand on end.

Janelle's never seen him cry, and she thinks that's what he's doing when he sinks onto the bed and puts his head in his hands. All she can do is shift from foot to foot and rub at her bare, cold arms. If she takes a step away, will he look up at her? She doesn't want to see tears. She's not sure what to think or do or say, or how to feel about the fact that Gabe might really... need her.

So when she sits beside him, puts her arm around his shoulders, and he turns to press his face into the curve of her neck, Janelle doesn't think about what to say. Or what to think. She just holds him, and she strokes his hair. When he shudders against her, his face wet and hot, she lets him push her back onto the pillows and climb on top of her.

She lets him kiss her. She lets him touch her. She lets him scrape his teeth along her throat, and that makes her arch up against him in response.

When his mouth finds hers again, the kissing is still so new it shocks her. Kissing, kissing, she pulls his shirt off over his head. Her hands move over his body, exploring the ridges and curves of all the places she's always admired but never given herself permission to learn. His hand slides over her belly, into her jeans. She undoes the button and the zipper and tips her hips to urge him to move beneath her panties. She unbuckles his belt.

They are naked, arms and legs tangled. All of it feels so good she wants to cry with it, even the pain when he pushes inside her for the first time. When she makes a noise, half startled yelp and half groan, Gabe stops. His hair hangs in front of his face. His arms are corded with muscle as he pushes himself up.

They're connected. He's inside her. This is it, this is sex, unexpected and uncomfortable and perfect, because it's with him. She pulls him closer, makes him kiss her. She hooks her heels over the backs of his thighs and makes him move. It's nothing like she thought it would be. She thought she wouldn't like it as much as she does.

He's still kissing her when he shudders again, though this time not with grief. Her name sighs out against her mouth. She never imagined she might have an orgasm the first time, but that pleasure explodes through her at the sound of him saying her name, because that means something. It means he's with *her,* not some random girl. He's with her. She let him start this, but they finish it together.

Breathing hard, not sure what to say, Janelle stares at the ceiling when Gabe rolls off to lie beside her. Their heads are very close on the pillow. He's not twitching or jittering anymore. Gabe's gone smooth and silent again.

Janelle links their fingers. She's not cold anymore. She fits next to him just right, the hollow of her hip matched perfectly to the jut of his. She doesn't look at him, but studies the ceiling. "Are you going to tell me what's wrong?"

"No."

"Okay."

After another minute, he sits and bends to fumble with the mess on the floor, cursing again when he finds no lighter. Janelle gets up, finds her inside-out jeans. She pulls her father's Zippo from her pocket and hands it to Gabe. He lights his cigarette and offers her one, but she shakes her head. When he tries to hand her back the lighter, Janelle curls his fingers around it. She cups both her hands over his. Giving it to him.

They sit that way for a minute, before Gabe says, "I can't ask you. I was going to, I thought it would work, it would be the right thing. But I can't—"

She stops his words with a kiss. "Ask me."

He shakes his head. She kisses him again, longer this time. When she breaks it, she looks into his eyes.

"Ask me, Gabe."

"I can't."

"What is it? A favor?"

"Yes." It's not, it's so much more than that, but she won't know that until later.

Janelle rests her head on his shoulder. "Whatever it is, are you afraid I'll say no?"

Gabe shakes his head. "I'm afraid you'll say yes."

Which of course, she does.

FORTY-THREE

NAN FOUGHT SLEEP THE WAY BENNETT HAD AS a toddler. First, she called out for a new book, complaining she didn't like the one she had. Then she wanted a drink of water. Next, the toilet, which was better than if she'd been unable to make it, but meant Janelle had to haul her up and out of bed, and walk her to the bathroom, then wait while she finished. Then Nan wanted to see if the mail had arrived, and if there were any bills that needed to be paid. If the newspaper had been delivered. She insisted on heading for the living room to check the front door.

Janelle said, exasperated, "Nan, if you don't want to take a nap, nobody says you have to."

Her grandmother turned, shuffling, her shoulders hunched. "No?"

"No." Janelle shook her head and shrugged. "If you're tired, you should sleep. If you're not tired…don't sleep."

Nan blinked rapidly, her lower lip trembling. "But I am tired, honey. I'm so tired."

That made sense, since she'd been up several times last night. Janelle was tired, too. She sighed and gestured toward the hall. "So…sleep."

"But I—" Nan broke off and gave an embarrassed laugh. "I'm being a cranky old fool. That's all."

Janelle found a smile beyond her own need for a nap and the ache in her back and shoulder, beyond the creeping edge of anxiety about the three loads of laundry she needed to get to, and the fact that Bennett hadn't brought home his last math test. Beyond even the unpaid bills she hadn't shown Nan because they would only get her worked up about the cost of electricity.

The soft thump of the newspaper being delivered at the front door caught Nan's attention. "Ricky?"

Janelle froze. "What?"

Nan shook her head and pressed a hand to her eyes. "Oh. No, never mind, honey. I was thinking about something else, that's all. About your dad."

"What about him?" Janelle went to her grandmother to hook a hand beneath her elbow. "C'mon. If you don't want to go to bed, at least come sit on the couch."

In the family room, settled not on the couch but in the recliner, with her feet up and the remote close by, her legs covered with an afghan, Nan shook her head again. "He just came into my mind, that's all."

Janelle had faced her grandmother while high on pot and more than a little drunk, after sneaking out of a boy's room where she'd spent hours using her hands and mouth to give him pleasure. Thinking about how she'd blocked her dad's number, she felt guiltier now than she ever had any of those times. But he deserved it, she thought fiercely. Just as Nan did not deserve to be disappointed once again by her prodigal son.

"He was a terrible father," Nan said.

Janelle coughed into her fist. "Nan."

"It's true. No matter what I did, no matter how I raised him, he never quite got the hang of it. That's all. I think he wanted to," Nan said thoughtfully. "I'm sure he did. But he never really managed."

"No. He didn't." Janelle took a shallow breath, old anger sweeping over her though she tried to push it aside.

"I'm going to watch a program now."

"Okay, Nan." Janelle made sure the volume was set to the right level, and went into the kitchen to pour herself a mug of coffee. She needed the caffeine.

Then

"Nectar of the gods, Janny." Her father's voice is gruff, his eyes smeary with sleep, his hair a mess. He stinks like smoke and BO. He holds up the mug, sloshing the black liquid, and shows her how to add a lot of sugar and some cream. "Here."

He pours a little into her mug, and Janelle sips it cautiously. The smell is good. The taste, not so much. She'd have preferred a soda, but when the waitress came, her dad ordered her a coffee. Eggs, toast, pancakes, bacon. Orange juice. You don't drink soda for breakfast, anyway. Janelle sips again, letting the flavor flow over her tongue.

"You don't like it now, but you will." Her dad holds up his mug for her to clink against in a toast.

The fourth or fifth sip goes down much nicer. By the time the eggs and toast come, Janelle holds out her mug for a refill, and her dad laughs, shaking his head, but he gives her one. He winks and smiles at the waitress, who doesn't seem to like him very much. Janelle understands. Dad thinks he's being charming and funny, but he looks kind of like a bum.

"Coffee ain't good for kids," the waitress says in a flat voice, her eyes skimming over Janelle's mismatched clothes, all she had left that was clean. Over her bushy, uncombed hair. The waitress puts the check on the table, facedown, close to Daddy, then goes away.

"You drink up, Janny," her dad says.

Later, when she feels every color is too bright, all the noises too loud, when everything is sharp and clear and there's a ringing in her head and her stomach's sort of sick, her dad laughs and watches her jump from the couch to the chair to the couch again. He laughs and laughs until she underestimates the distance and leaps, arms and legs spread, mouth wide open in a victory yell, but misses. Goes down. Her leg is cut open, blood everywhere, requiring a trip to the emergency room for stitches.

Her dad takes her, leg all bandaged, to a local carnival, where he gives her dime after dime to try and win a goldfish, a glass plate, a mug in the ring toss. He buys her the wristband so she can ride the rides, although after the first spinny one her head hurts too bad and she can't ride anymore. Then her dad gets mad because he wasted the money, and he takes her back to her mom two days early.

That was the price she'd paid for her dad being her friend instead of her parent. She still had the scar, though it had faded over time. Not all of them had.

She moved through the house, clearing clutter. Tidying. She found Bennett's backpack, still overflowing with miscellaneous garbage and papers, though most of them were corralled inside an accordion folder. She found a handful of test papers, emblazoned with red, and pulled them out, already gritting her teeth. Ready to bring the hammer down.

They were math tests, yes, but each had been given a B, with extra credit problems on the back applied to his overall grade. He wasn't going to finish the year with a math grade higher than a C, even with these tests, but at least he was improving. The question was, why hadn't he shown her the work, the way they'd both agreed?

She peeked in on Nan, who was finally dozing. From upstairs she heard the faint noise of Bennett's video game. Lots of shooting and screaming. She'd checked it out ahead of time, of course, so either she was the best mom ever for letting him get it, or the worst. She climbed the stairs, pausing in the doorway to watch him. Her golden-haired son. Though getting him to do his homework was still a struggle, the tests in her hand proved he was at least making more of an effort. He'd been invited to a birthday party and had invited that same friend over to work on a school project, two occasions Janelle had let pass without more than the briefest comment, aware of how he might react if she made too much of it. Too aware of how he'd accused her of not wanting him to grow up, of never trusting him. Of being too strict.

Of being no fun.

"Hey, buddy." Janelle crossed the room to sit down next to him. "How's it going?"

"Good." Eyes on the game, Bennett manipulated the controller back and forth. "Just leveled up, killed the big boss, now I'm almost out of health and I need to get to the next save point."

"Can you pause for a second?"

With a hefty sigh, he did, not giving her his full attention until she held up the tests. "Want to tell me how come you didn't show me these? I thought we agreed you'd show me every test you got, and the homework, too."

As soon as the words came out of her mouth, she regretted them, but there they were. She couldn't take them back. Instead, she settled papers on top of the dresser and sat on the edge of his bed.

"I was afraid you'd be mad," he admitted. "Because I didn't get A's."

"Oh, Bennett. Did you do your best?"

He nodded.

Janelle sighed, wondering if there was ever any easy way to be a parent. "When we talked about your grades, I never said I expected you to only get A's. B's are great, so long as you did your best. That's a good grade."

Bennett shrugged, still looking at the screen, though the game was paused and his eyes glittered suspiciously. "Okay."

Janelle opened her mouth to say more, but she could still taste the regret from her words of moments before. Sure, she could talk this to death. She could be stern or lecture. She could make certain he understood the consequences of not showing her the tests, the consequences she'd promised for the next time he hid something from her.

Or she could let it go.

In her day, Super Mario had been a big deal. This game system had cost as much as her car payment, and featured graphics and stories as complicated and impressive as movies shown on the big screen. Janelle had never had any desire to do more than watch for a few minutes, but now she gestured at the monitor.

"Can I play?"

Bennett looked up. "What?"

"The game. Can I play?"

He laughed. "Oh, Mom."

"I'm serious! What, you think your mom can't shoot a zombie?"

Bennett shook his head, still chuckling, then saw she was serious. He handed her the controller. "Okay. Go ahead."

She had no idea what she was doing, which made him laugh all the harder. When she got killed, the screen filled with dripping, gory blood. Bennett didn't take the controller from her. He put his hand over hers and showed her how to manipulate the buttons and levers. Then he reset the game.

"Go," Bennett said.

She did her best, which was really all she could do.

FORTY-FOUR

Then

EVERYTHING'S GONE WRONG, AND IT'S ALL
Gabe's fault.

Probably everything has always been, ever since the beginning, when whatever he'd done as a kid had sent his mother
packing. It's something inside him, so deeply rooted he can't
pull it out. Not without killing himself in the process, anyway,
and yeah...he's thought about that. More than once.

He asked Janelle to do it—to fool around with his brothers—
because he wanted Andy to feel better. He wanted him not to
focus so much on what the old man had done, which wasn't
Andy's fault. It was Gabe's fault, just like everything else was.
So he'd tried to fix it, tried to get Andy to see that no matter
what the old man had done, Andy was fine. He was good.
He was okay. He wasn't any of those names the old man had
called him. And even if he was—the way Mikey might be,
shielded in his desire to become a priest, as if giving his life

to the church would make it easier to forget what he really wanted—well, even if Andy was a fag like the old man had said, Gabe wanted to show him that it didn't matter. It just didn't fucking matter.

But it did.

Now he can't even look at Janelle without thinking about her kissing his brothers. Touching them. Them touching her. He thought because he trusted her more than anyone else, that she was the right one to ask, and the fact she'd agreed told him he was right.... But that didn't help things now, when she was sitting on his bed with her face streaked with tears and her knees clamped tight. She'd chewed her lower lip so hard it bled, and he shouldn't be an ass, he should hand her a hanky or something, but he doesn't.

"So," she says. "That's it? It's over?"

"Nothing's over. For something to be over, you have to start it." Those words taste bitter and mean.

That's how they must sound, too, because Janelle flinches. She's not the sort to just take anything lying down, though. Her lips thin. Her eyes narrow. She raises her hand slowly, slowly, giving him the middle finger.

But when she gets up to push past him, something makes him put out a hand to stop her. His grip's too tight, he sees that immediately by the way she winces when he grabs her, but he can't make it softer. He needs her to leave, but he can't make himself let her go. He should tell her he's sorry. About this, about the other things. About everything. But the words don't come.

"You're hurting me." Janelle manages to sound dignified even though her voice shakes. She doesn't try to yank her arm from his grip. She just looks at him as if he's something she scraped off the bottom of her shoe.

It makes him mad. Furious, even. Because he already knows

he's being an asshole, that he's worthless, a piece of shit. She doesn't have to look at him like that. Like she's never made a mistake, never done anything wrong. He wants to shake that look right off her face.

He wants to kiss her.

He wants to maybe even hit her, and she juts her chin forward as if she's just waiting for him to do it. But Gabe won't give her the satisfaction. Instead, he lets her go. Janelle rubs her arm, the pale skin already going dark. He left his mark on her, and that seems fair enough, since she sure as hell left hers on him.

"You told me," she says in a stiff, rough voice, "that it would help make things better for them. I saw how Andy was acting in school. I know he's in trouble. I love your brothers."

She doesn't say she loves *him,* and though he deserves that slap, it still stings.

"You told me it would help them, but I did it for you! You asked me for a favor, and I did it!"

He knows that's true, but it doesn't make him feel better. "Yeah. You did it. Now you can get out."

"I didn't know it would change things...."

That's it; he can't stand it anymore. Everything is swirling and tipping and twisting all around him; the whole world has gone dark and he doesn't know what to do to make it stop. All he has is the power of his words, and knowing which ones, exactly, will hurt her the most.

"Change what? What could it change, Janelle? Us? What about us could this change?"

He's so angry he spits when he talks. She wipes the splash away with a knuckle. He thinks she shouldn't be able to look him in the face, but she does.

"Everything! Us! What we've been doing. What we are."

Her voice dips low. Becomes sad. "I thought we were friends, at least."

This forces a harsh laugh from him. Sharp like barbed wire. Like breaking glass. She flinches in the face of that laugh, which feels as if it cut him open from guts to throat.

"I was just convenient for you. That's all. Someone who could get you high and get you off." Even as he says it, Gabe knows it's too much. He's gone too far. She will never forgive him.

"What is the matter with you?" she cries. "Why are you doing this?"

Because he has to. Because he can't stand it. Because if she knew the truth about what's been going on in this house, she will hate him, and he'd rather have her hate him for this.

He'd rather hate her.

"I wish you'd never come here," he tells her. He doesn't mean it, but that's what pours out. "You fucked everything up, Janelle. I wish you'd never come into my life."

Janelle's mouth opens. She blinks, fast. She breathes fast, too. She straightens her back, squares her shoulders. "You don't mean it."

His lip curls.

She takes a step backward. Then another. At the doorway she turns to look over her shoulder, everything about her tense and angry, and worst of all, betrayed and sad. He did that to her. He did it.

"It's not how someone comes into your life that fucks it up," she says. "It's always how they go out of it. It's the leaving that makes the difference, Gabe, don't you get it? Is this how you want me to leave?"

He wants to tell her to come back. He wants to get on his

knees and beg her. He doesn't. *She's right,* he thinks, as he watches her go.

It's always the leaving that matters.

FORTY-FIVE

"WHAT ARE YOU THINKING ABOUT?" THAT SORT of question usually wasn't a good one, but it slipped out of her before she could stop it. Besides, she wanted to know. Janelle traced the line of Gabe's ribs and waited for him not to answer her.

He surprised her. "The day you left."

"Oh. That." She rolled onto her back and blew the hair out of her face. From outside she heard the faint and far-off noise of a lawn mower. It seemed impossible that summer was almost here. "That was a long time ago."

"I know. But…don't you?"

"Think about how you were such a jerk to me? Broke my heart?" She squinted at him. He frowned, and she felt bad for an instant. "Sorry. Guess I'm more bitter about it than I thought."

"You should be. I was an asshole."

"Some people would say you're still an asshole."

He laughed at that, without shame. "Well. Yeah."

She rolled onto her side again, her head propped on one elbow. She couldn't stop herself from running her fingertip over his belly and the jut of his hip bone. Gabe had always been tall and lean, but time had given him muscle and weight that suited him. Or maybe her tastes had changed. Grown up.

"What were you thinking about it?"

"That I was sure you'd never forgive me," he answered at once, with no pretense. He was being honest.

She liked that about him, how he said what had to be said even when it might be easier not to. "I didn't, not for a long, long time."

He tucked one arm under his head and stared up at the ceiling. "What did you think after you left, and you found out what happened?"

"I was horrified. Of course. I felt terrible. Like it was somehow my fault."

"It wasn't."

Janelle shrugged. "I still feel like at least part of it was."

Gabe looked at her, brows knitted and mouth thin. "It wasn't."

"You saying so doesn't just take that away," she answered, annoyed. They lay in silence for a few minutes. "Gabe. How come you never went away?"

She thought she knew the answer, but wanted to hear him say it.

"I couldn't."

"I know you felt like you couldn't," she said softly.

He looked at her. "Who would've taken care of Andy? The old man couldn't. Mike couldn't. My mother sure as hell couldn't. How about you, anyway? You didn't become a dancer. I thought you would."

She laughed, a little embarrassed. "Oh. Well, turns out you need to actually train and stuff if you want to be really good. I

was never great, just good enough. Did some dancing in different shows, always the chorus. I was in Vegas for a while."

"Really?"

She smiled. "Yes. I was a nudie dancer in a Vegas show.
That's what you really wanted to know, right?"

Gabe shook his head, then nodded. "Why'd you quit?"

"Got hurt in a car accident. Got pregnant. I thought being
a mom was more important than dancing."

He kissed her slowly. "You used to think nothing was more
important than dancing."

If that was how he remembered it, she wasn't going to
correct him. She looked at the clock. "Helen said she'd have
Nan back by nine. Andy and Bennett should be finished at
the movies about that time, too. I told them they could walk
home this time. We should get up."

Gabe nodded and started to dress as Janelle watched him
from the tangle of her sheets. She didn't want to move just yet.
Didn't want to pull on her clothes over skin that still smelled
of him. She admired the play of his muscles as he bent to grab
his shirt and pull it over his head. He caught her looking and
gave her a small smile.

"What?"

"You," she said. "So much has changed, and yet…so much
hasn't."

His expression clouded briefly. Then he surprised her by
sitting next to her. Taking her hand. He kissed the knuckles,
each one, then held her palm to his mouth. He said nothing.

Janelle stroked a hand over his hair and pulled him a little
closer. "What?"

He shook his head. His shoulders lifted and dropped as he
sighed. He pressed her hand to his lips as if he meant his kiss
to keep him from speaking.

Gently, Janelle took her hand away to cup his face. She searched his gaze. "Gabe. Talk to me."

"I'm shit with words."

"You're not."

He shook his head again. "You're the only person who ever made me feel like I could...just...talk. Like I could say anything to you, and it would be okay."

This honesty speared her. She let her thumbs stroke the line of his jaw. "You can."

Gabe said nothing for another few heartbeats, another few breaths. At last he blinked rapidly and put his hands over hers to take them away from his face. He held them tight. "What did you think when you heard what had happened?"

It wasn't what she'd figured he'd say. "I thought I'd pushed you to it, somehow. Because of the favor. I thought about how I left, how bad it was. I spent a long time thinking that if only I'd been better, Gabe, a better person, that if I hadn't ever started up with you like that... Well. I thought if I'd been better, none of that would've happened."

"When you heard...did you believe it?"

"I didn't want to." She searched his gaze again, trying to figure out what, exactly, he was getting at. She thought of that day in the woods when he'd taught her to shoot. Of how he'd taught her son. "Because...it wasn't true, was it? I mean, it wasn't an accident."

Gabe pushed her away, gently but firmly. He got up to look out the window. "It was not an accident. No."

Janelle got out of bed and dressed slowly, waiting for him to say more, and not surprised when he didn't. They had only another few minutes before Nan would be back, and Gabe needed to be out of her bedroom before then. "Let's go downstairs. We can have a drink. You can tell me about it."

They got downstairs mere seconds before Helen's car pulled

into the driveway. Nan was beaming, full of stories about the card club, but clearly exhausted. She didn't give Gabe more than a second glance as she went to her room.

"Be careful with him," she warned as Janelle tucked her into bed. "He's always been trouble for you."

"Oh, Nan."

Nan shook a gnarled finger, but gently. "You thought I didn't know, back then?"

Heat flushed Janelle's cheeks. "There was nothing to know, Nan. Gabe and I were friends. We are friends."

Her grandmother snorted softly. "He's got troubles."

"Don't we all?"

Nan softened at that and patted Janelle's hand as her eyes closed. She took up almost no space beneath the blankets; her head barely made a dent in the pillow. She looked younger in sleep. More peaceful, maybe. Janelle sat by her side for another minute or so, counting each rise and fall of Nan's chest as she breathed.

"When Bennett was a baby," she said to Gabe, who was waiting for her in the kitchen with two open beers, "I would creep into his room at night just to put a hand on his back and make sure he was still breathing. It's like that all over again. I feel like any moment she could be gone."

It seemed natural enough for him to take her in his arms then. Janelle closed her eyes to breathe in his scent—beer and cigarettes and sex, and something else that had always been there and would never change. She put her arms around him, her cheek on his chest. She breathed.

She breathed.

She moved too slow when the back door opened and Bennett burst through on a wave of excited chatter, Andy on his heels. Bennett paused at the sight of them, but didn't spare a beat before launching into a description about the explosions, the spaceships, the alien spores. Janelle let go of Gabe as he let go of her, not a big deal.

Andy stopped in the doorway. "What are you doing here?"

"Just leaving," Gabe said with a look at her.

Without another word, Andy turned on his heel and stalked out of the kitchen. The back door slammed behind him. Bennett, still chattering, didn't seem to notice. But Gabe did. He sighed and rubbed his eyes, then gave her a look she couldn't interpret.

"Go brush your teeth," she told her son. "It's late."

"But tomorrow's Saturday—"

"Yes," she said. "So you can watch TV in your room or whatever, but it's still late now. Go."

Bennett mumbled something that any other time would've earned him a reprimand, but this time Janelle let it go. She snagged Gabe's sleeve as he made for the back door. Her fingertips skidded on his shirt's soft flannel.

"Gabe. What's going on?"

"I need a smoke." He patted the breast pocket of his shirt.

With a sigh, Janelle followed him out to the back porch. When he offered her a cigarette, she waved him away. She found a place on the concrete retaining wall and drew her feet up, her arms pinning her knees to her chest as she watched him. In the flare from the lighter, he looked like a stranger, if only for a second.

Gabe drew on the cigarette, making the tip glow in the dark. She heard the hiss and whoosh of his exhalation, and smelled the smoke on the fresh night air. Above them, the stars were sharp and cold.

"He thinks you two used to be together."

"Who? Andy? And me?" At this, she had to stand. The sidewalk was rough under her bare feet, but she paced, anyway. She shivered suddenly. Held out her hand. "Okay, give me one. That's...ridiculous! Why?"

The light from the house illuminated only bits and pieces of Gabe, but she could see enough to watch him shrug. "I think you know why."

He lit the cigarette for her and handed it over. Only the first drag ever tasted any good, and she savored it for a few seconds in silence before taking another. Gabe shuffled his feet, kicking at the porch step.

Sickness roiled in her belly, and she pressed a hand to it. "I thought you said he didn't remember anything."

"I guess he remembers some stuff, maybe just a little. Or maybe just feelings."

Janelle frowned. "You have to tell him it wasn't...like that. It wasn't true. I mean, not like that."

"Do you think that will change how he feels about you now?"

"It might," she said. "And if it doesn't, you still have to tell him, Gabe. Jesus. And you have to tell him that we're... that we—"

Except, of course, what would Gabe tell his brother? What were they? Friends with benefits, or something more? They'd never talked about it.

"I'm not telling him anything!" Gabe tossed the cigarette to the concrete and ground it out. "Neither are you. You say nothing to him, you hear me?"

"Yeah. I hear you." Sullen, she threw her own cigarette to the ground, where it lay burning, until Gabe did her the favor of stepping on it. "I get it. You don't want to tell your brother that we're together because he has a crush on me. Because that would be so much worse than just letting him think he has a chance with me or something, right? Worse than letting him find out the hard way, like tonight, when it will only make him feel betrayed?"

Gabe said nothing.

"Oh, God," Janelle said, after a moment of staring as his dark form, unable to see his expression. "You don't want to tell him, you don't want to tell anyone. Right?"

"Janelle..."

She turned away from him, her arms crossed over her chest to help warm her against another wave of chill. "I'm such an idiot."

"You're not. I'm an asshole."

"You keep saying that," she snapped, "like it's a good excuse."

"It's not an excuse. It's true."

She bit at the inside of her cheek until she tasted blood, before she could trust herself to speak without her voice cracking. "Well. Fine. I'll tell him, then. I'll tell him the truth."

She moved to go inside the house, but Gabe grabbed her. It was an echo of that long-ago last night she'd seen him, though they'd been in his bedroom then. She'd carried the marks of his grip for almost two weeks, and sometimes had pressed the bruises, making them hurt, to remember how his hand had felt on her. The pain had been a sort of guilty pleasure.

She threw his hand off her now, no longer some messed-up eighteen-year-old girl who didn't know which end was up. "Don't!"

He put his hands up immediately, though he didn't move away. "I'm sorry." A pause, a breath. His voice, lower. "I'm so sorry."

He tried to hold her again, but Janelle pushed away from him. He caught her again on the top step, his fingers shackling her wrist loosely enough for her to pull away if she wanted to. She didn't. She turned.

"You can't tell him the truth," Gabe said. "Because Andy doesn't know."

"I know he doesn't remember, but if he's thinking that we were together, then he must have some idea—"

"No," Gabe said hoarsely. "You don't get it. It's not just that he doesn't remember. It's that…he doesn't know. The truth. And he can't know, okay? He can't ever know."

She thought of what Gabe had said upstairs, how he'd asked her what she thought about what had happened. If she'd believed it. That it had not been an accident, which meant it had been on purpose.

Gabe had shot his brother on purpose.

"So…what is the truth?"

But if he'd meant to tell her earlier, the moment had been lost. Gabe let go of her wrist and stepped away. He shook his head.

There was no way she could keep her voice from shaking this time, and she didn't even try. "That's it?"

"I'm sorry."

"Not sorry enough," she told him.

Then she went inside.

FORTY-SIX

Then

MICHAEL—HE DOESN'T LIKE BEING CALLED MIKEY anymore, not even Mike—sips at the beer and makes a face. "Bleah."

Andy, on the other hand, is already finished with one and halfway through another. He keeps tapping his fingers on the side of the bottle until Gabe wants to strangle him to get him to stop. He's nervous as hell himself, and the clink-clink of Andy's class ring on the glass is driving him nuts.

"Where is she? She's not coming." Michael looks as if he's ready to bolt.

"Shut up. She'll be here. She said she would." Gabe moves in front of his brother as if he means to stop him, and Michael steps back. "Stop being such a pussy."

"Maybe she lied to you." Andy tosses the bottle into the woods, where the glass shatters on a rock. He's bouncing on the balls of his feet now. Sweating.

"Jesus, Andy. Calm down. She's never going to get into this if you look like you're nuts." Saying it out loud, Gabe wishes he hadn't said it like that, but Andy doesn't seem to notice. He pulls another beer from the cooler and cracks the top. "And slow down. You're gonna be too wasted to do anything."

"She's not coming," Michael says again, then sits on one of the logs around the fire.

Gabe spits to the side. "She'll be here. She's a girl. They're always late. She's probably fixing her hair or something. Or she had to do something for her grandma."

"Maybe she got lost." Andy is up again, pacing, kicking at the dirt so small stones clang against the metal tire rim they use for a fire pit. "Maybe she got…she got abducted by aliens. Or Bigfoot."

Now he really sounds like a lunatic. Could be the beer talking. Could be that other stuff, those things that have led Andy to write all those letters and poems that have worried Gabe so much. Lots of shit has been going down, but Gabe would rather believe it's just the booze and not his brother's brain.

There's a crackling in the leaves, a snapping of branches, and a minute later, she's there.

She's taken the time to do her hair and makeup, that's evident even in the fire's shifting light. Her clothes, too. She's made a real effort for this, and though he doesn't want to let it, jealously shoots through him. She's never made an effort like that for him. He can tell himself he likes her better with her hair soft and her face clean, and it would be true. But this Janelle is scorching hot, and it's not for him.

But it's too late now.

"Hi, guys." Her voice is lilting, breathy. She points at the cooler. "Got one of those for me?"

If she's nervous, she doesn't show it. Her hair's grown long enough now for her to flip over her shoulder. It's such a girlie move, so flirty and not like her at all, that Gabe takes a step back. She's not looking toward him.

"Yeah. Here, you can have mine." Andy holds out the bottle to her.

Janelle puts her hand on his wrist instead of taking the beer. She pulls him a little closer and has him tip the bottle to her mouth. Her eyes never leave his as she takes a swallow. As she licks her mouth. "Mmm."

Gabe wants to punch something. Hard. He settles for curling his fingers tight into his palm, where his nails cut into his flesh. He did this, he reminds himself. He asked her to do him this favor, to help his brothers. He told her it's because Andy's depressed about their dad calling him gay, that anything she does for Andy she had to do for Michael, too, because they're like that. He told her he's worried Andy might do something to hurt himself if he can't prove to himself he's not what their dad called him. It's not a lie, not exactly, even if the story Gabe told her isn't the whole truth.

So, he can't be jealous and angry that Janelle looks so beautiful and that she's willing to mess around with his brothers, because he asked her to. She said yes. She's doing this for him, because he asked her.

But damn it, does she have to make it look as if she wants it so much herself?

She tugs Andy just a step closer. His eyes are wide, his mouth a little wet and open. He looks like a moron. Gabe doesn't want to watch his girlfriend kiss his brother, but he can't look away. And she's not really his girlfriend, is she? He's never taken her on a date, she won't even sit with him on the bus, in school they pass each other in the halls and barely say a word.

But he can't stop thinking about how she tastes and smells, and how her body clutched at his when they did it. Just last week, and they haven't fooled around or anything since. But he can't get out of his mind the feeling of how she moved under him, so even though his palms ache and burn and bleed, he keeps his fists clenched tight to keep himself from hitting anything.

Michael's watching with wide eyes, a mirror of his twin's. Janelle looks down at him. Holds out the hand not gripping Andy's wrist. Michael takes it, and stands when she pulls him. He doesn't move away when she leans close to kiss him, but he doesn't quite kiss her back. More like he just stands there and takes it.

Janelle looks at Gabe over her shoulder. He doesn't know if it would be better if she looked scared or nervous, but anything would have to be better than this settled, assessing gaze. It's like she's asking him if he's sure he wants her to go through with it, and though he isn't, not at all, Gabe nods at her. If something flickers in her gaze it's gone so fast he can't be sure he saw any hesitation in her at all, and then she turns back to both his brothers and he can't see her face.

She laughs low, saying something he can't catch. The fire shifts, sending up sparks. He can't really see them clearly. She's leaning in, first to one, then the other, urging them both to sit side by side on the log. She stands over them, blocking Gabe's view. She shakes her hair again. Her hips move from side to side.

He can't watch. He can't stand it. He asked her to do this because he thought it might be the only way to help his brothers, both of them, because even though it's Andy with the problems, anything Andy does, Michael does, too. It's been like that since they were babies—poke one, the other cried. Andy's the one their dad likes best, though. Andy's the one with the razor blades. Mikey's just along for the ride.

She kisses one and then the other. Back and forth. She

doesn't hesitate or fumble. The light trickle of her laughter floats toward Gabe over the crackling of the fire.

It's too much.

Away from the fire, the woods are so dark he stumbles and falls. Branches scratch him. His knee hits a rock and pain hurtles through him, so sharp it makes him want to vomit.

Gagging, on his hands and knees, Gabe heaves into the dirt. Sour beer puke, nothing worse than that. He hasn't eaten all day, his stomach too twisted to handle food. He heaves again and brings up only spit. He gets to his feet, kicks dirt over the mess, and blinks up at the small glimpses of night sky he can catch through the trees. He has a flashlight in his pocket, but he doesn't want to use it.

Instead, he sits with his back to a tree and listens to the faint sound of laughter become silence.

Not long after that, the bushes rustle. Andy barrels past, stumbling like Gabe did on the same jutting root, but catching himself before he can fall. Gabe shines the light, but Andy puts up a hand to shield his eyes, and barks a curse. He pushes past his brother and deeper into the woods, heading for the path home. Michael's behind him by only half a minute, his own flashlight gripped tight in one hand.

"Andy! Wait up!" Michael cries, his voice thick. "C'mon, Andy! It's okay!"

"What happened?"

"Fuck you, that's what happened." Michael never swears, so the curse coming from him is extra foul. "Just…fuck you, Gabe."

Then he's off, after Andy, leaving Gabe in the dark. He makes himself count to ten, then to twenty, before he starts back to the fire. He's afraid he'll find her naked, sprawled out, maybe even with a self-satisfied, cat's-got-the-cream grin. It will kill him.

But Janelle's not smiling. She's fully dressed, sitting with her arms wrapped around her legs, chin resting on her knees. Tears have streaked her black eyeliner. Her hair's a mess. She has a small, purpling bruise on one cheek.

Gabe goes to his knees in front of her. "Which one did that to you? I'll kill him—"

"Shut up."

He obeys.

Janelle draws a shuddering breath. Her eyes are bright with tears, but she's not crying now. She rubs at her face, pressing lightly on the bruise. Her pupils are wide and black, swallowing the blue of her eyes.

"He couldn't do it," she says.

He knows she means Andy. Gabe sits back on his heels. "Shit."

"Michael… He was… He could've. He didn't, but he could've. But Andy…he tried. But he couldn't do it. Any of it. I mean, I tried, but he was just… He couldn't…" Janelle shakes her head. Then she buries her face in her hands. Her shoulders tremble.

He should touch her. Put his arms around her. He should kiss her and tell her it's okay. He should tell her that he loves her.

But all Gabe can do is get up and walk away.

FORTY-SEVEN

"SO, HOW IS SHE?" BOBBY ASKED THIS QUIETLY,
so Nan wouldn't overhear. "She looks good."

Janelle wished he'd ask Nan herself how she felt. She wished
all of them would stop tiptoeing around the fact their mother,
mother-in-law, grandmother—whoever she was to them—had
cancer. It would kill her, sooner rather than later.

"She's been better these past few days. She's tired a lot, of
course." Janelle bent to pull out the pan of lasagna from the
oven and set it on the stove. She swiped her hair off her forehead, which was sweaty because the house had become an
oven itself with all the people in it. She pulled out the pan of
garlic bread, too.

Laughter rose from the living room. Deb came into the
kitchen to help with the food, followed by Betsy and Kathy,
and there wasn't any more talk about how Nan was doing.

Dinner was great. Family sitting around the table, the kids
at TV trays on the couch. Nan had her usual spot at the table,
and it was the most animated Janelle had seen her in a long

time. She had a plate piled high, though she wasn't eating much of it. Or any of it, really. Nobody else seemed to notice, or wanted to notice, but Janelle did.

After dinner, there were birthday presents. Books of number puzzles, new pairs of slippers. Nan oohed and aahed over everything, beaming. There was cake, ablaze with eighty-four candles Nan needed help to blow out.

"Bring me my pills, honey," Nan said when the plates had been cleared, hers scraped into the trash, and the aunts and cousins in the kitchen bringing out slices of cake and ice cream.

Janelle brought the pill bottles on the tray. "You didn't eat very much. Do you want some cake?"

"Oh, no, honey, bring me an English muffin with a little peanut butter, okay?"

"Mom, we just had dinner." Joey said, overhearing this. "You want a muffin now?"

"She needs to eat with her medicine," Janelle explained. "Or she'll get sick."

He nodded as if he understood, but really didn't. "I'll get it for her."

If anyone else noticed Nan picking halfheartedly at the muffin instead of digging into the gorgeous, homemade pineapple upside-down cake, they didn't say anything. But what was there to say? Nan tore the muffin into small pieces, tucked a bit of peanut butter onto each one and feigned eating it without even a hint of joy.

"Sure you don't want some cake, Nan?" Janelle sliced off a piece, thick with sugary syrup, and pushed it toward her grandmother. "It's good. You should have some."

"Should she?" asked Kathy, sounding a little shocked.

"Yes," Janelle said firmly. She pushed the cake even closer. "She should."

Nan smiled. "Thanks, honey."

But Nan only picked at the cake, too, tearing it apart with her fork without eating more than a bite or two. The room filled with laughter as someone brought out the cards. Nan moved to the couch, where she could watch and listen and enjoy the company of her family.

It was like old times, Janelle thought as she slapped a card out of her cousin's hand during a particularly heated round of Uno. Like the visits she'd made with her dad when she was a kid.

"This was wonderful," Donna said as they were leaving. She took the time to take both Janelle's hands in hers. "Thank you so much."

Janelle squeezed her aunt's fingers. "For what?"

Donna looked a little embarrassed. "For making us all get over here. But a birthday is a good reason, huh?"

They shouldn't need a reason, Janelle thought. "You all came tonight. That's what matters. It was fun."

Donna smiled sadly. "Yes. It was. I think she looked good, didn't she?"

Janelle thought of Nan dissecting her food, eating only because she had to and not because she wanted to. If she ever got to the point where not even eating brought her any sort of pleasure, Janelle thought she'd rather die, but there was no point in telling this to her aunt, who looked so sincerely hopeful. "She's been feeling pretty good, I think."

"When she decided not to go for chemo, we thought it would be over much sooner." Donna's eyes welled with tears. Her grip tightened on Janelle's, almost too hard. "Bobby's been beside himself. Well, we all have. Your Nan's such an amazing woman. What are we going to do?"

"We're going to love her as much as we can until it's time for her to go," Janelle said, her own throat closing. She untangled her fingers from Donna's, but gently. "That's all we can do."

Everyone had pitched in for the dinner cleanup, so Janelle didn't have that to deal with. Bennett sprawled in the recliner, ostensibly watching some adult cartoon program his older cousins had put on, but his eyes were at half-mast. Janelle nudged him.

"Go to bed."

Nan had begged off at the end of the visit, later than her normal bedtime, but still early. By now she'd been in bed for an hour or so. Janelle assumed she'd be asleep, but she peeked in the door, anyway.

"Who's that?"

"It's me, Nan. Janelle," she added, in case for some reason Nan didn't know or didn't remember.

"Oh, honey. Come in. Did everyone leave? Did you tell them I was sorry, but I just had to get to bed?"

"They understood. It's okay." Janelle sat on the edge of the bed. "You need anything?"

"No, I'm fine." Nan gave a long, deep sigh. Her fingers tangled together on top of her coverlet, beneath which she barely made a bump. "How are you?"

"Fine."

"You don't look fine," Nan said. "You look terrible. Where's that Gabe Tierney been? Does that have something to do with it?"

That did it. Janelle opened her mouth to brush off Nan's concerns, and let out a huge, braying sob instead. The tears gushed forth, hot as a geyser. There was no holding them back, restraint not within the realm of possibility. Janelle let it all go, up and out of her like squeezing a blister until it popped. There were words, a scramble of them, muffled and incoherent but mostly about Gabe and how stupid she'd been to think it might mean something, how she ought to have known better. How nothing ever turns out the way you think it will.

Through it all, Nan said nothing, just made soothing noises as she patted Janelle's back and handed her tissue after tissue until the box was mostly empty.

"I'm sorry," Janelle said. "I got carried away."

Nan laughed softly. "Don't worry about it. I'm here for you."

This made her want to cry all over again, and Nan must've seen it because she reached for her hand. "Don't start again. Not about that."

"I'm going to miss you so much, Nan."

"I'll still be with you, honey. I believe that. Don't you?"

Janelle wasn't sure what she believed about life after death, but knew at least the memories of Nan would be with her. The lessons she'd taught. The color of her eyes. "Yes. I believe it."

"Then there's no point in being sad." Nan's eyes glittered. "But I'm glad you told me."

Janelle reached for another tissue and wiped at her face. "What do you mean?"

"Oh. Everyone just tippy-toes around it, that's all. They don't want to talk about it. They don't want to hear about it. They wouldn't hear about it," Nan added. "That's why I made them get you to come here, honey. I needed someone who'd be able to handle things, you know."

"And you thought that would be me? Why?"

"Because you've always been a little like your dad. He could be a hard case, your dad."

Janelle frowned. "You think I'm...a hard case?"

"I think you know what needs to be done and you do it, even if it's hard, that's what I think. No," Nan amended. "I don't think it. I know it. Now, your dad, he was also stubborn as heck and a more than a little reckless. But he also knew how to do the right thing, even when it was hard, and he was an honest man when he had to be. You have that honesty in you, Janelle."

It was nice to hear Nan thought so, but it didn't make Janelle feel any better. She thought about her dad. "I have my share of secrets, Nan. Things I'm not proud of."

"We all do, honey. We all do." Her grandma's hands moved restlessly on the comforter. "That's not what I'm talking about. I mean that you don't tiptoe around things, even if it's hard for you. You know I'm going to die."

Janelle didn't protest this, and Nan smiled.

"Any of the rest of them would be telling me to hush, or poo-pooing. But you know it's true, honey. Don't you?"

"Yes." Janelle fought more tears. "I know."

"Well, I'm ready to go." Nan nodded firmly. "I've made my peace with things, I've taken care of everything that needs to be taken care of, or made sure someone else will be able to do it. I've had a long, good life, not without its share of sadness, but we all have that. I've had a lot of happy times, too. And so it's my time, and God willing, I'll go soon and not linger any longer than I have to."

"I hope so, too," Janelle said.

Nan smiled. "Good. That's good, honey. I appreciate you saying it. Are you going to bed now?"

Janelle looked at the clock. It wasn't late, not for a Saturday night, but it wasn't early, either. "I might read for a while. Maybe watch a movie. Why?"

"Because," Nan said, as she slowly pulled off the comforter and swung her legs over the edge of the bed, "I b'lieve I'd like a piece of that pineapple cake now."

Janelle grinned and helped her stand, then handed her her dressing gown. "You know what? Me, too."

FORTY-EIGHT

Then

THE OLD MAN IS AT IT AGAIN. DRINKING. CHAIN-smoking until the smoke hangs so thick in the kitchen it's like walking through fog. He stares nonstop at Andy all through the shitty dinner Mike managed to throw together from whatever he could find in the fridge and cupboards. He makes snide and sideways comments about the food and doesn't eat any. None of them do.

As always, Gabe lies in his bed with his hands tucked under his head and stares up at the ceiling. Counting sheep is shit, even when he tries to start from one hundred and go backward. He can't sleep. His stomach, empty, tries to eat itself. If he turns on his side, he'll be able to look out his window and into hers, but he already knows her blinds are drawn and her light's off. She's shut him out, and he can't blame her.

He lies in his bed listening to the creak of his old man pacing downstairs. The low mutters become profanity-laced shouts. Gabe waits for his father to climb the steep and narrow stairs. Across the hall, he knows his brothers are waiting, too.

A figure appears in the doorway, and Gabe pushes up onto his elbows. "What do you want?"

"Can I come in for a while?"

"Where's Andy?" Gabe says, not refusing his brother permission, but not giving it outright.

Michael sidles into the room, his hair slick from the shower he spent half an hour taking. Cold water, like a punishment. His fists clench at his sides before he notices and makes an obvious effort to relax them. "He's in our room."

Downstairs, the old man hollers something about whores. Michael flinches. Gabe sits up and swings his legs over the bed.

"Tell him to come in here."

Michael hesitates, then shakes his head. "You know that won't help."

Gabe stands as the first footstep creaks on the bottom stair. Michael doesn't wait for his brother to say it's okay; he steps inside the room and shuts the door behind him. Then he presses his back against it.

"Open the door, Mikey."

Michael shakes his head.

Gabe can't think. Doesn't want to think. Or feel. He wants to get back into his bed and pull the blankets up over his head so he can't see or hear anything, either. But this can't go on.

It just can't.

He moves to the door, expecting his brother to step out of the way. When he doesn't, Gabe grabs him by the upper arms to move him. He believes without even thinking about it that his brother will simply let himself be moved, but Michael has made his legs as strong as tree trunks, his arms like iron bars. He won't be pushed out of the way.

Gabe's bigger and stronger, but Michael's got a stupendous

left hook that comes out of nowhere. Gabe sees stars and the floor comes up to meet him. On his hands and knees, he looks up at his brother, who's never hit him before. Never hit anyone, as far as Gabe knows. With the taste of blood in his mouth, and his ears still ringing, Gabe gets to his feet.

He punches his brother first in the gut. When Michael doubles over, the face. And still his brother refuses to get out of the way.

Gabe hears the old man in the hallway. The thud of his boots. The door across the hall opens and shuts. There is silence.

"I don't understand you," Gabe says. "How can you just... let him? How can you just..."

The question has no good answer. Gabe should really ask it of himself, because he's just as guilty as Michael. Guiltier, isn't he? Because he, at least, could've changed some things long ago and made a difference. It was his job to do that, right? To stand up for his younger brothers. That's what the old man always told him to do, to stand up to bullies in school or strangers on the street who had nasty things to say about the Tierney boys. It should've applied to the old man, too.

He moves again, toward the door, and Michael shoves him back. His brother's eyes are wide and wild, and he's breathing hard. His breath is sour, his wet hair flops into his face and his fingers grip Gabe's shoulders when he pushes him back.

"You can't," Michael says in a hoarse and frantic voice. "You have to just leave it be."

But Gabe can't do that. Not anymore. Too much has happened. Too much hasn't. His fingers close around his brother's throat and squeeze until Michael chokes and gags.

"I have to." This time, Michael doesn't struggle against him as Gabe goes through the door.

It takes him only a few steps to get across the hall to his

brothers' bedroom. The knob turns, but the door won't open. It's locked. From inside comes a series of shouts and the sound of breaking glass. Gabe throws his shoulder into the door, but it doesn't budge.

He shouts his brother's name, but Andy doesn't answer. Gabe hears the old man cursing. The solid thud of flesh on flesh. More glass breaking. There's another sound he hasn't heard in a long time, years. The swick-swick of the old man's leather belt being pulled from the belt loops. A minute after that, the crack of it against skin.

And then…nothing.

The doorknob rattles. Gabe backs away, but not fast enough, because when the door opens to reveal the old man, nose bloody and shirt torn, he's still on the threshold. The old man lifts his fist, the belt still wrapped around it. At the sight of Gabe, his lips curl back. He has blood on his teeth.

"Get the hell outta my way." The old man's grin is meant to be hard and mocking, but the tremor in his voice and hands matches his shifty gaze.

Gabe steps to the side. His father pushes past him and goes down the stairs one slow, thudding step at a time. Gabe looks into the bedroom, where the mirror over the dressers has been smashed. One of the twin beds has been tossed, the mattress askew, the blankets on the floor. The window is cracked but not broken. The trophies that normally line the windowsill have been swept away.

Andy stands in the middle of the room. One eye is red and swelling. His lip is split. One of his fists is bloody.

The other holds a gun.

Andy's shaking so hard the gun rattles. When he swings toward the doorway, Gabe ducks, bracing himself for the crack of a shot. He murmurs his brother's name and risks a look around the door frame.

He knows the gun. The old man got them each a hunting rifle when they turned twelve. Gabe got a handgun when he turned sixteen. Andy and Mike got theirs last year. Their father made them take a hunter safety class, and has spent some time with them out in the woods, teaching them to hit paper targets as well as bottles and cans. It's one of the few things he's ever done with them that makes him smile.

"Is it loaded?" Gabe asks, knowing that's a stupid question, but needing to be sure.

Andy nods. He looks at the gun in his hand. He sets it down gently on the dresser. Then he sinks onto the bed that hasn't been upended. He puts his face in his hands and his shoulders heave, but if he weeps he does it in silence.

Gabe's not sure what to do or say. He wants to sit by his brother, maybe put an arm around his shoulders. Maybe even cry with him, a little. But he can't. Michael pushes past him to take that role. He hugs Andy, who buries his face against his twin's neck. Watching them like that, Gabe envies them, and not for the first time. They've always had something he's never been able to share.

His shoulder hurts from hitting the door with it. His face aches from the pounding Michael gave it. Everything else hurts, too. There's a pain in his chest as if someone ran him through with a spike, and when he staggers to the bathroom to run the shower—hot for him, not cold like his brother—all Gabe can think is that dying would feel better than this.

FORTY-NINE

A QUIET HOUSE WAS BLISS. JANELLE'S FINGERS moved over the keys of her laptop as she switched between her email and her accounting program, with a few stops here and there to check her Connex page or several of the funny blogs she followed. Upstairs, Bennett was supposed to be doing his homework, but was probably engrossed in the games on his iPad. So long as that's all it was, she thought. She wasn't ready for the end of her son's innocence, though she knew it had to happen sooner or later.

"Later," she murmured. "Please, God. Later."

A girl might've been easier. They could've talked about boys and periods and hairstyles and nail polish. Those were things Janelle could handle. Boy stuff seemed foreign and awkward and weird…not that she'd have any choice about it. Maybe she'd have to get him a book….

Nan had gone to bed an hour ago, complaining again of a headache and upset stomach. She'd refused to take her meds or even brush her teeth, and Janelle hadn't pushed. The woman was eighty-four years old and dying of cancer. If she didn't want to brush her teeth before she went to bed, did it really matter?

From someplace in the house came a low, restless thumping. Janelle's fingers paused on the keyboard as she listened, uncertain if the noise was coming from Bennett's room upstairs or from Nan's. The noise stopped. Then started again. She got up, went through the kitchen to the hall, still listening. As she passed the arched entrance to the living room, the noise got louder, steadier. Definitely coming from Nan's room.

By the time she got to the end of the hall, Janelle was running. She pushed open the door, prepared to find her grandmother knocking on the headboard for help, or possibly fallen out of bed. What greeted her instead was Nan writhing, her back arched and foam frothing at the corners of her mouth. Her eyes had rolled back. The covers had torn from their carefully tucked place at the foot of the bed.

"Nan!" Janelle ran to put her hands on her grandmother's shoulders. Frail as she'd become, Nan's bucking was strong enough to toss off Janelle's grip. Her arms flung out, hitting the side of the bed and the headboard, but it was the fierceness of the seizure causing the bed to thump on the floor.

No phone in Nan's room, her cell not in her pocket. Janelle screamed for Bennett, even as she searched for something, anything, to stop Nan from convulsing. Something to put between her teeth—wasn't that what they did when people had seizures? So she didn't bite or swallow her tongue? Janelle had nothing…no idea what to do.

Bennett had still not arrived when the seizure passed. Nan blinked. Her mouth hung lax and her body softened against the mattress. The acrid stink of urine made Janelle cough.

"Dick?"

"No, Nan. It's me. Janelle," she added in a shaky voice, when it was obvious her grandma didn't recognize her.

Nan blinked, struggling to sit, but couldn't. The foam at the corners of her mouth dripped over her chin and onto the front of her nightgown. Janelle didn't know if she should help her up or force her to lie back. She screamed for Bennett again, rewarded in a minute by the thump of his feet on the stairs and coming down the hall. He cried out in the doorway, and she turned, determined to keep calm.

"Bring my phone."

"What's the matter with Nan?"

"Now, Bennett!"

On the bed, Nan let out a shuddering sigh. Her shoulders tensed and she blinked rapidly. Her hands swam in the air as she fought against Janelle's grip.

"Shh, Nan. Shh." Janelle blinked away her own tears, trying to remember to breathe, though the smell in the room threatened to choke her. "It's going to be okay."

Nan quieted. "Janelle?"

"Yes, Nan." Bennett handed over the phone and Janelle turned to him as she dialed 911. "Nan's sick, honey. I'm calling an ambulance."

"I don't need an ambulance!"

Janelle ignored Nan, who started struggling again. "Bennett, I'm going to have to go with her to the hospital. Can you call Andy on your cell phone, see if he'll be able to come stay with you?"

She thought her son might argue that he was old enough to be here by himself, but he must've been scared, because he nodded and ran upstairs. As the dispatcher answered the call, Nan let out series of low, hooting groans and started to convulse again. Somehow, Janelle managed to keep her grandmother from writhing off the bed as she gave the dispatcher the information he needed. By the time she hung up, the seizure had started to ease and Bennett was back in the doorway.

"Is she going to be okay?" His eyes welled with tears and his face had gone pale beneath the freckles.

Janelle had spent her life trying to protect her son, but now she could only say, "I don't know, honey. I hope so."

"Janelle. Bring me my coat, I want to check the teapot. It's been crying."

"Andy's not home, he's at work. But he said I could go next door and wait for him. He'll be home as soon as he can get a ride." Bennett stared at his great-grandma, who'd fallen back, panting softly. "Nan, you'll be okay."

Nan's head turned toward him. Incredibly, she managed a smile. She held out her hand, and Bennett, God love him, took it. Janelle had never been prouder of her boy than at that moment, when he gently squeezed Nan's fingers despite the mess and smell. He stayed with her until the ambulance came ten minutes later.

"You stay at the Tierneys' until Gabe or Andy gets home, okay?" Janelle said from the back of the ambulance as the EMTs pushed Nan, strapped to the gurney, inside. "You call me when Andy gets there. No. Just text me, I'm not sure what I'll be doing. And I'll call or text you—"

"Ma'am, we have to go." The EMT said it respectfully, but without much patience.

"Go," Janelle said, and the ambulance doors closed off the sight of her son.

FIFTY

Then

AFTER THE SCUFFLE IN THE TWINS' ROOM, THE old man goes out and doesn't come back for two days. Andy locks himself in his room and doesn't go to work. Mike calls in for him, says he's sick. Gabe doesn't miss work—it's a shitty job but it's all he has until he can get out of this place. He knocks on the door the third morning and opens it even when Andy doesn't tell him to come in.

His brother sits at the window, still cracked but not broken, and stares outside. He doesn't even turn to look around when Gabe comes in. His shoulders rise and fall with every breath, but other than that, he might as well be a statue.

"You going to work today?"

Andy says nothing.

Gabe tries again, moving closer. He even puts a hand on his brother's shoulder, but it's like touching wood or stone or metal. Unmovable.

"C'mon, Andy. You have to...you should go to work."

Andy says nothing.

Gabe sighs and tries again. Mike got a job in the church office for the summer, but Andy's working at the plant, same as Gabe. Same as their dad. "They'll fire you."

His brother looks at him then, blue eyes shuttered, mouth closed tight against whatever words might be trying to make their escape. Andy's always been a jokester, the silly one, a cut-up. Class clown. Just now it looks as if he's never smiled in his life.

"I couldn't do it," Andy says. "I tried. I wanted to. But I just couldn't do it."

Gabe's fingers squeeze. He thinks of Janelle and what she was willing to do for him, and he wants to punch a hole in the wall. She's gone, and it's too late to make things better. "It's okay. Lots of guys have trouble the first time."

Andy blinks. Then again. And finally, brilliantly, he smiles.

"No," he says. "Not that. I wanted to kill the old man, and I couldn't do it. When it came right down to it, I just couldn't."

FIFTY-ONE

IT WAS CLOSE TO THE END, AND THERE WAS nothing to do but wait. It shouldn't even have come as a surprise, but apparently things like this always did. That was what the doctor said, anyway. A young guy, he looked tired. He told Janelle they'd done everything they could for her grandmother, but with the cancer and her age…

"I know," Janelle said. She felt somehow as though she needed to reassure him, instead of the other way around.

Nan had stabilized. They'd given her a cocktail of medications—some for the nausea and pain, some to prevent more seizures. Her blood pressure was completely out of control.

"They doped me up," Nan said in a wavery voice, her hand searching for Janelle's.

"I know, Nan. Just to keep you comfortable."

Nan nodded after a second or so, and closed her eyes. She kept them shut for so long that Janelle thought she'd fallen asleep; the rise and fall of her chest, however slight, told her

MEGAN HART

she was still alive. She opened them when Janelle started to pull her hand free.

"I expect you've made the phone calls."

Janelle nodded. Bobby and Donna were on the road, but wouldn't get here for another few hours. Same with John and Lisa. "Yes. Joey and Deb will be here pretty soon. Marty and Kathy, too."

"Oh, you don't have to tell them to come," Nan protested, but weakly. Then she changed her mind and gave Janelle a trembling smile. "Well. I guess they should come, shouldn't they? Will they let the children in, do you think?"

"I'm not sure." It was long past visiting hours, but this close to the end, and surely it was the end, wouldn't someone have compassion?

Nan closed her eyes again. "I b'lieve I'll sleep for a little while. Would you… Will you bring Bennett?"

"Yes. I think that would be a good idea." Janelle waited another minute, but Nan's soft, even breathing didn't catch or stop. She didn't open her eyes, either.

In the hall, Janelle scrubbed at her face and waited to dissolve into tears, but found herself dry-eyed. Her stomach churned, and the idea of even sipping at a mug of gross hospital coffee made her throat sting with bile. She took her phone into the lobby to call Bennett, who didn't answer. Nor did Andy when she tried his number.

Janelle tried Bennett again. Then Andy. Again, neither picked up. She rang Nan's house phone, thinking maybe they'd pick up, but there was no answer there, either. Worried now, she tapped her fingers against the phone and thought about what to do. She didn't want to leave the hospital, she wanted to get her son, but without a way to get in touch with him…

She dialed the only other number she could think of. When he answered, he sounded both so wary and so hopeful, it broke her heart. "Gabe," she said. "I need you."

FIFTY-TWO

Then

THE KITCHEN STINKS OF SOUR MILK. GARBAGE
overflows the pail. Gabe remembers the days when Mrs. Moser
would be there waiting with fresh cookies and milk when he
got home from school, but of course, it's been years since she
came to take care of them.

It's not time for him to be home yet, but he told the plant
nurse he'd puked. When she left him with the thermometer,
he pulled the old trick of holding it to the lamp to mimic a
fever. He's pretty sure she knows he was faking, but she sends
him home, anyway.

The kitchen is disgusting. If the old man comes home and
sees it this way, there will be hell to pay. Gabe doesn't care so
much about that, nor about the fact that his father hasn't been
back in three days. If they're really lucky, he thinks, maybe
the old man won't ever come home.

He knew, Gabe thinks. The old man knew how close he'd

come to pushing Andy over the edge. Maybe it scared him, just enough.

Gabe thinks about washing the dishes and taking out the trash, but first he wants to check on his brothers. He climbs the stairs and pushes open his brothers' bedroom door, prepared for a hundred different things except an empty room.

The beds are perfectly made. Their identical desks are both cleared off, which isn't strange for Mike's, but is definitely out of character for Andy. A piece of lined paper on the dresser flutters when Gabe passes it; the breeze picks it up and carries it under the bed, where he'll have to get on his hands and knees to pull it out.

He almost doesn't.

But something tells him this piece of paper is important, and that even though he doesn't want to know what it says, he'd better find out. He snags it with his fingertips and pulls it toward him. He knows Mike's handwriting, which slants slightly to the left and is sloppy, considering how neat and tidy Mike is about everything else. The writing is Mike's, but the words are Andy's.

If it can't end one way, it has to another.

Gabe crumples the note. Shoves it in his pocket. He looks in the closet for the guns, but already knows they aren't there.

And then he runs for his truck.

The drive takes too long and at the end of it, he runs along the curving path strewn so thick with pine needles the thud of his sneakers barely registers. He can't breathe. He chokes. He would spit if his mouth wasn't so dry. He would scream his brothers' names if he had any air. But he doesn't and he can't, so he runs until his legs burn, and the woods get thicker and trip him.

He hits the clearing with a clatter and crash of snapping twigs, which tear both his clothes and his skin. His heart pounds so fast he can't see anything but a blooming, shifting kaleidoscope of red and black and gray. He puts his hands on his knees and bends forward, thinking he might puke for real, but holds it back. He swallows again and again. Sweat stings in his eyes. He manages to say just one word.

"No!"

But it's too late. Andy has aimed his gun at Mike, who stands a few feet away from him, doing the same. Mike's hand shakes. Andy's does not.

It's Andy who turns and looks at Gabe in the last second as Mike fires, and that's probably what saves his life. Mikey's, too. Andy's head jerks back. His hand jerks, too. His shot goes wild, skidding off a tree and leaving a thick white mark.

There's blood. A lot of it. So much that at first Gabe can't see his brother's face. He thinks for sure that Andy's dead, until he opens his eyes, startlingly blue among the dark red blood. Mike is screaming and fighting Gabe to get to Andy, but even with blood-slick hands, Gabe manages to keep Mike from getting in the way.

"I'm sorry! I'm sorry!" Mike says, over and over, though Gabe can't tell if he's apologizing for hitting his twin…or for missing.

Gabe takes his shirt off to make a bandage for Andy's head. He knows there's something else he should be doing, probably a hundred other things, but all he can think of is to stop the bleeding. Andy's eyes are closed, but his heart's still beating. Gabe can feel it in Andy's chest, beneath his palm.

"We have to get him to the truck," he says to Mike.

Mike doesn't move at first. He sits on his heels, rocking. His face is pale. He might pass out, Gabe thinks, and reaches without hesitation to slap a bloody hand across his brother's face. Mike's head rocks, but his eyes clear.

"He's not going to die," Gabe says. "We'll get him to the hospital."

"What will we tell them? What will we say?" Mike's teeth chatter so hard he bites his tongue. Blood paints his lips and dribbles down his chin. "Oh, Jesus. Oh, God. Oh, holy Mary, mother of God, pray for us sinners…now and…now and at the hour of our death…."

Gabe presses the shirt to the wound in Andy's skull. He doesn't dare take it away to assess the damage, but he doesn't think there are any brains splattered anywhere. "I told you, he's not going to die!"

"He wanted to!" Mike cries out. "We were both supposed to!"

For Mike, this has to have been a serious decision. Suicide is a mortal sin, will send him straight to hell. No redemption. Gabe shakes his head.

Mike staggers to his feet. "I didn't want to, Gabe. But… he's my brother."

Then Mike takes off running through the woods, leaving Gabe and Andy behind. All Gabe can do is cradle Andy and keep the pressure on the wound. The shirt is soaked through. Andy's heartbeat flutters. He doesn't open his eyes again.

"He's my brother," Mike had said, as if that made every kind of sense, and Gabe supposes it does.

"I'm your brother, too," he says aloud, with only the trees to hear him. Maybe Andy does, too, in some far-off manner. It doesn't matter. "I'm your brother, too."

FIFTY-THREE

WHEN THE PHONE RANG, GABE ALMOST DIDN'T answer. Just before it would've gone to voice mail, he thumbed the screen to take the call. He should've known she wasn't calling just to chat.

The hospital was between him and his house, and he got there within minutes. Nobody could like hospitals, he thought as he signed in and was informed he wouldn't be allowed to go to Mrs. Decker's room. He felt bad for the people who worked there. He was able to get Janelle to come meet him in the lobby, though. She looked beautiful and terrible at the same time.

"How is she?"

She shrugged. "Sleeping. She had two seizures at the house. Her blood pressure's completely out of control. It's close to the end, Gabe."

He was certain she wouldn't allow him to hold her, but she did. "I'm sorry."

She tipped her face to his. "Thanks for coming. My uncle

Joey got here just a few minutes ago, but…I don't want to leave her. In case…you know. Can you get Bennett and bring him here?"

"Sure. Of course."

"He's at your house." Janelle hadn't moved out of his arms, had in fact snuggled close again, so her words were a little muffled.

"My house?"

"Yeah. Andy wasn't home when we had to leave, but he said he would get there as soon as he could get a ride from work. He thought maybe an hour or so. And I know Bennett would've been okay by himself, but I didn't want to leave him alone, worried."

"So you sent him to my house?" Gabe pushed back from her so he could look into her face. "Jesus, Janelle. Didn't I tell you, that kid's never supposed to go to my house?"

Her brow furrowed. She stepped out of his arms. "What is your problem, exactly?"

There was too much to say, too much to tell her, and this wasn't the time or place. So he did what he'd always done. He walked away.

He was already on the phone to his brother by the time he got to his car, but Andy wasn't picking up. Gabe didn't leave a message. He just disconnected and dialed again. Then again, when his brother didn't answer. He sent a text as he pulled out of the parking lot, then set the phone on the dashboard in case it rang.

Ten minutes to the house, twenty tops. He only slowed at stop signs, turned right on red in order to shave a few precious seconds off the trip. By the time he pulled into his driveway, his shirt clung to him with sweat. Gabe was out of the car and across the yard, up the front steps and through the front door in a flash. He didn't bother slamming the door behind him. His boots skidded on the hardwood floor of the front entry.

The old man wasn't in his recliner. The chair had tipped onto its side. It was too heavy for the old man to have pushed it, which meant that Andy had done it.

Gabe found his father at the kitchen table with his ever-present oxygen tank at his side. In front of him was a bottle of Old Knob and an empty glass. Also, a hammered-metal ashtray. A pack of cigarettes. The familiar Zippo lighter... Gabe's lighter.

"I hope you're not going to smoke those," Gabe said from the doorway.

His father looked up, eyes rheumy, mouth wet. His hair stood on end. He looked as if he ought to be covered in blood and bruises, but Gabe couldn't see any.

"I should," the old man said. "I should just light it up. Haven't had a cigarette in years, and goddamn, do I miss them."

Gabe could relate to that, maybe the only thing he ever could've related to with his father. He moved slowly into the kitchen, scanning for signs of a struggle or some other uproar, like he'd seen in the living room. Everything seemed to be in its place...except for his dad. "Where's Andy?"

"He's outside with that kid from next door." The old man shook his head slowly, then ran a trembling hand through the few strands of hair he still vainly combed over his bald spot. "Should just light one up. Go out with a bang."

"Do me a favor and wait until I get out of here first."

His father looked at him. "You'd love that, wouldn't you, you son of a bitch? Get rid of the old man for good. Don't know why you're in such a hurry. I don't have shit to leave you when I go."

He didn't have much to give him now, Gabe thought, but

didn't say. He looked through the back door, craning for a glimpse of Andy and Bennett. He saw something like a shadow and relaxed, just a little. He turned to his father.

"What happened?"

The old man shrugged and gave Gabe a defiant look that suddenly and alarmingly crumpled into despair. He slapped a hand over his eyes, bowed shoulders shaking. The sight was enough to set Gabe back a few steps. His stomach knotted. He tasted bile.

"What did you do, old man? What the hell did you do?"

His father let out a low, racking sob, the noise like someone had dropped a beer mug in a blender. "Nothing. I didn't do nothing."

Gabe didn't believe that. Andy must not have believed it, either. Gabe slapped the old man's hand away from his face and bent to get right up in it. "If I find out you did something to that kid...!"

"I didn't do nothing!" the old man shrieked.

Spittle flew. Disgusted, Gabe wiped his face and backed up. The old man shook and shuddered, his face crimson, his nostrils flaring as he struggled to suck enough oxygen into his withered lungs.

"I didn't do a goddamned thing!" Ralph Tierney shouted. "He wanted to see my trains. That's all. I just...I just thought I could show him the trains—"

He broke off, wheezing and choking until he twisted the knob on the tank. He sucked in the oxygen as greedily as he'd consumed everything his entire life. He pointed at Gabe, then wilted.

"Your brother came home. Came looking for us. And he just went...crazy," the old man muttered with a cough. He didn't look at Gabe again. "He said he was going to kill me."

Neither of them said a word about how it wasn't the first

time Andy had made such a threat, but Gabe could see the memory of it in his father's eyes. Gabe put a hand on the back of a kitchen chair to keep himself upright. All at once it was all he could do not to sink to his hands and knees.

"I should just light this goddamned cigarette," the old man whispered hoarsely. "Just end it all. Make everyone happy."

If his father was looking for sympathy, he wasn't going to find it here. Gabe grabbed his lighter and went out the back door to find Andy sitting on the porch steps. The gun was in his hand, lying loosely on his knee. Bennett wasn't there, but the lights on in the house next door left him pretty confident the kid was at home.

Gabe sat next to his brother, close enough that their knees touched. He could've taken the gun, but he didn't. He simply sat, shoulder to shoulder, hip to hip. Their feet, next to one another, were the same size, and he couldn't remember when the hell that had happened.

They sat in silence long enough for the night to fully arrive and the first few stars to come out. Gabe took a cigarette from his breast pocket, tucked it between his lips. The Zippo in his pocket was heavy, and heavier in his palm when he took it out to flip open the lid. He lit the flame, which was set too high. The afterimage of the flames stayed with him when he closed the lid and blinked against the sudden dark.

"I told Bennett he should go home, watch some TV," Andy said. "That I'd be there in a few minutes to hang out with him, we could maybe play some of that new Sky Shooter game."

He lifted the gun from his knee, letting it dangle from his finger. Then he opened the cylinder and emptied the bullets from inside. They clattered onto the concrete steps below his feet. He handed the gun to Gabe, who took it and set it to the side.

"I sent him home f-f-first," Andy said, and took a breath to stop the stutter. He looked at the sky. "I made sure he wasn't there. And that he was okay, I made sure he was okay, Gabe. And he was. When I came in and saw them, saw the old man putting his hand on his shoulder like that, that look on his face, that smile, I thought, *No. Not the kid. Not the kid, too.* Do you know why I thought that, Gabe?"

"Yeah, Andy. I do."

Andy shuddered. He rubbed his face with both hands. He bent forward to press his cheeks against his knees, but only for a moment before he sat up again. He looked at his brother. "Me, too. I remember. I remember...not everything. But enough, I think."

"I'm sorry, Andy."

Andy nodded, once. "I think I didn't want to remember, not for a long time. But when I saw him with Bennett, I couldn't afford to keep forgetting."

Gabe had no answer for this. So he did what he thought he should've done years and years ago, when he had the chance to make things different. He put his arm around his brother's shoulders and held him tight. Andy buried his face in Gabe's neck and clung to him, his skin hot. But only for a couple seconds. Then he took a long, deep breath, sat up straight and looked Gabe in the eyes.

"I could've done it," he said. "This time, I really could've. But I didn't."

Then they sat in silence again for a long time.

FIFTY-FOUR

NAN WAS GONE.

There was grief, but there was no denying there was also relief. Janelle had slept through the night without interruption every night for the past week, and that simple, human luxury had made all the difference. She woke now without an alarm.

The family would be descending on her in a few hours. There'd be food and laughter and no small amount of tears. She had envelopes of photos to distribute, along with a list Nan had left for specific items she wanted given to certain people. Janelle sat, stretched. Swung her legs over the edge of the bed, the bare floor cool under her toes, though the day would get much hotter.

She looked through the window next door, but the curtains were drawn, the way they'd been for the past week. She'd seen Andy at Nan's funeral. He'd been at the church and the meal in the social hall after. He'd hugged her hard, his eyes bright, and had ruffled Bennett's hair. She hadn't seen Gabe since the night Nan died and he'd told her everything.

Showered and dressed, she checked on Bennett, who was still sleeping. It was summer, and he'd been up late playing his video games the night before. He'd grown, she thought as her gaze traced the familiar lines and curves of his face. He would always keep growing.

Downstairs, Janelle made a pot of coffee and pulled a plastic bag of Nan's cinnamon rolls from the freezer. She defrosted one and tucked the rest back behind the frozen peas and broccoli, where nobody would find them. She had three dozen of Nan's rolls, and she intended to make them last as long as she could. Eyes closed, Janelle savored the sweet icing and let herself mourn.

She didn't open her eyes at the click of the back door opening, but she knew who it was. Not Andy. Not Gabe.

"Dad," she said quietly.

Time had been harsh. He still wore his hair long, but it had gone thin and mostly gray, the ponytail at the back of his neck straggly. Lines had carved themselves into his forehead, and bracketed his mouth and nose. His shoulders were a little hunched, though his clothes—a pair of faded jeans, cowboy boots and a faded black concert T-shirt—were the same as she remembered. His smile hadn't changed much, but it faded quickly when she didn't return it.

"Your uncle Bobby said you're all getting together today."

"He invited you?"

Her dad had the grace to look a little uncomfortable. "No."

"I didn't think so." Janelle gestured at the coffeepot. "You want some coffee before you leave?"

His mouth opened, eyebrows going up. "Janny. C'mon."

Janelle cupped the mug, warming her hands and sipping at the fragrant liquid. Steam bathed her face. She looked at him without smiling. Without blinking. Without much of anything.

"I can understand why you might hate me," her dad began, but stopped when she gave her head a minute shake.

"I don't hate you, Dad."

"I've let you down. I know it. But, Janny...I really want to—"

She held up a hand then. "You can stop. Just stop, okay? You're not going to change. You're not going to say anything to make up for all the years you let me down or broke your promises, all this time when you simply just didn't give enough of a damn to be around. You can't make it up. Ever."

Her dad took a step back, hands on his hips. "That's harsh."

She shrugged.

"I have a right to be here today," he said, his voice a little ragged. "Bobby said you've got a list Mom left, of things she wanted given out."

"You're not on it."

This seemed to hit him harder than anything else she'd said. He took another step back, this time to put a hand up in the doorway. His shoulders hunched farther. He hung his head.

"I don't believe you."

She shrugged again.

He looked up at her, mouth thin. "I grew up in this house, Janelle."

"From what I understand, you took what you wanted from it already." Her chin lifted, the coffee slopping a little when her hands shook. She gripped the mug harder to quell it, not wanting to give him the satisfaction of seeing her in any way distraught. "There's nothing here for you."

Her father shook his head. "That's not true."

"Oh, I think it is," she said. "You're not on Nan's list or in her will, and I'm pretty sure your brothers won't be in favor of giving you anything but a boot to the ass on the way out."

"I'm not talking about stuff," he said finally, running his

hand over his straggly hair. "I'm talking about…you. And my grandson. I'd really like a chance to get to know him, Janny. A chance to get to know you again, too. Can't you… Jesus. Can't you just find it in yourself to forgive me?"

She had, she realized, forgiven him a long time ago. But forgetting was something else. When she didn't reply, her father let out an exasperated sigh.

"I'm your father."

"Which doesn't mean very much, at the end of the day," she said calmly. "I wish you the best, Dad, but you don't get to waltz in and out whenever you feel like it. That's not how it works. Not for me, and certainly not for Bennett."

"You won't even give me a chance," he said sullenly.

Janelle gripped her mug hard enough to turn her knuckles white. "You've had your chances, plenty of them. You had your chance when I was a kid, and when you told me you were going to come visit Nan and you didn't show up. You don't get a chance to mess with my kid's life. Period. You don't deserve him."

"Something came up. I had every intention of visiting her," he started. The same old song and dance, the same shifty eyes, the same swipe of his hand over his mouth to show he was telling a truth only he believed.

"And now she's dead, and you'll never get a chance to make it up to her," Janelle cried, then bit her tongue to finish calmly. "It's too late, so spare me the excuses, okay?"

"But it's not too late for us," her dad said.

There had been times in her life when this tender scene would've ended differently, with the pair of them falling into each other's arms and sobbing happily as they reconciled. Other times when he'd have been lucky to get out of the kitchen without a steak knife hurtling after him. But now… now all she felt was…

"Nothing," Janelle said. "There is nothing you can give me or that I want or need from you. And there is nothing I want or need to give you. That includes my son."

Her father said nothing, maybe shocked into silence, or for once in his life admitting his faults.

"You should go," she told him. "You should go now."

He did.

FIFTY-FIVE

JANELLE HAD PACKED THE BASKET CAREFULLY. A few of Nan's cinnamon rolls, wrapped in foil. A bucket of fried chicken with all the side dishes, including biscuits. For dessert, an apple pie she'd picked up at The Pit Stop. A small cooler bag in her other hand clinked with icy bottles of beer.

It wasn't meant as a seduction, but she wasn't sure she'd turn it down if one came her way.

The drive to the cabin seemed shorter than it had before, maybe because at every curve she was sure she'd turn the car around. She didn't, though. She kept driving, and wasn't that the best metaphor for life she'd ever thought of? No matter how many curves in the road or how many times you wanted to turn around, you just kept driving?

By the time she pulled up the grassy lane, past the metal gate hanging open, and beyond the marshy spot that threatened to snag her tires, she'd already gone over the scene a thousand times in her mind. What she'd say. What he'd say. How she'd offer him a beer and take one for herself, tipping them together casually, as if nothing much mattered, just two old friends sharing a drink while they talked—or didn't talk—about the past.

Of course, that wasn't what happened. When she parked the car and took the rest of the trip on foot, carefully picking her way along the path, which was much clearer and easier to navigate than it had been before, all Janelle could think about was making sure she didn't drop anything. It was easier to focus on the weight of her physical burdens than the mental ones.

Gabe was outside when she came through the trees. A ladder leaned against the cabin, and he was on top of it, hammering up a line of shingled siding. He wore a pair of jeans and a T-shirt that clung to him with sweat, his mouth full of nails, a tool belt hanging low on his hips. He didn't turn when she came into the clearing, though he'd probably heard the car.

Janelle, mindful that she didn't want him falling off the ladder, stepped carefully across soft grass that looked as though it had been planted. A lot had changed. The fire pit was in the same place, but looked neater, the weeds around it pulled away and a set of low benches made from logs and split-rail fencing taking the place of the battered lawn chairs she remembered. The yard itself had also been cleared of debris, leaving what would never quite be a lawn, but a space that could easily accommodate a horseshoe pit and a volleyball net.

The cabin itself looked more like a house now than a ramshackle hut. Real windows, a real door, even a small front porch with an overhang and two concrete steps replacing the sagging wooden ones. The shingled siding, too, gave the building a more finished look. Through the open door she could glimpse the space she remembered as an open living room and kitchen, now furnished with real furniture.

"What do you think?" Gabe asked without turning around,

his voice muffled. He paused to take the last nail from his mouth, and hammered it into place. "Looks good, huh?"

"It looks great." Janelle set down her basket and the cooler, but didn't move closer.

Gabe came down the ladder and grabbed up a bottle of water from the ground, twisting the top and taking a long pull on it as he stood beside her to stare at his handiwork. "Thanks."

"I brought beer," she offered. "Food, too."

"Bring it inside," Gabe said. "I have a table."

He did. And chairs. And a couch, a love seat, a chair, a rug. A woodstove. In the kitchen, a fridge and oven, a sink.

"Propane and solar panels," he explained as Janelle set out the food. "And a water tank. I collect rainwater, but also can have the fire department come out with the pumper truck and get a fill-up that will last me for the summer. I'll dig a well at some point. But for now, I can take showers and brush my teeth. That's what counts."

Janelle cracked open a beer and handed it to him, then took one for herself. "You've done an amazing job. I'm so impressed."

"Thanks." He hesitated, sipping his beer, then sounded almost shy when he said, "I'm being interviewed for *Sufficiency* magazine. You won't have heard of it. They feature articles on homes people build off the grid. And...I have a job offer to go out to Oregon and help some rich old guy build what's essentially a glorified tree house."

Janelle didn't know what to say. "Wow."

He grinned. "Yeah. I know, right? Crazy. But he's got the money. He thinks I have the skills. So, I'm going for it. If it works out, I'll probably be able to do more work like that."

"I'm...just, wow. Wow, Gabe." She shook her head, sipped more beer. "I'm really happy for you. Proud of you."

"Thanks." He stared at her for a long moment. "You know Andy moved down to Pittsburgh. He's going to school there. Just community college, but if his grades are good enough, he's going to keep going. He wants to teach math."

"He'll be good at it." Janelle pulled out a carton of coleslaw and a package of paper plates, making her hands busy so she could focus on that rather than looking at his face. "He's close to Michael?"

"Yes."

"That's good," she said.

Gabe said nothing.

Janelle looked up. He stared. She put down the plates, the food. She wanted to open her arms and hug him, but all she could do was stand there.

"How's Bennett?"

"He's fine." She shook her head a little. "Enjoying the summer. He's visiting my mom for a couple weeks."

Gabe laughed a little. "Just like you used to do with your grandma."

"Yes." She smiled. "She's glad to have him."

Another heartbeat or two of silence. Gabe finished his beer and set the empty bottle on the counter, then leaned against it with one leg crossed over the other at the ankle. Janelle put her hand on the back of the chair, shifting her weight from foot to foot.

"I should've said something. Back then," she said. "I think I always knew."

Gabe cleared his throat. "It wasn't your fault, Janelle."

"No. It wasn't. But I might've been able to help somehow."

"You did," he told her. "Don't you get that? You did help."

She ran her fingertip along the carved wooden chair, having so much to say and not sure where to begin. "You know my dad came around after Nan died. He wanted to make amends, though I'm sure he just wanted to feel better about himself. And I could've just pushed aside everything that had happened and let him pretend he really wanted to become part of my life, of Bennett's life. I could've put the past in the past and let him back in. But I didn't, because even though he's my dad, there's no place in my life for him. I can forgive him for all the times he let me down, but I don't have to keep letting him do it. Sometimes, things get broken and you don't fix them, you know?"

"I know."

"But...you..." She shook her head, not sure how to say everything she'd been mulling over for the past few weeks as she went to bed every night, hoping for a glimpse beyond the closed curtains of the room next door and never getting one. The lights were on, but she never saw inside. "You're still living there. With him."

"He doesn't have anyone else, and he can't take care of himself."

"Still," Janelle said softly. "How can you?"

"Because he doesn't have anyone else," Gabe said. "Because whatever I could do or say to him is not nearly as bad as what he does to himself every single day. That man hates himself."

"Maybe he should," Janelle whispered.

Gabe laughed, low. "Yeah. He should. And he does."

"Do you forgive him?"

"No," Gabe said.

Janelle paused. "Does Andy? Does Michael?"

"Michael has to, that's his job. But no, not Andy. When he remembered... Well, it really set him back for a while. But he's getting better," Gabe said. "That's all anyone can really do, right?"

"And you? Are you getting better?"

He didn't answer right away. Outside, a bird chirped. The wind soughed through the trees, rustling the leaves.

"Yeah," Gabe said finally. "I am."

This time, she held out her hand to him, and Gabe took it. They moved together across the bare wooden floor. She pulled him to her, or he pulled her; it didn't matter. All that counted was that they met each other someplace in the middle.

"Me, too," Janelle said. "Me, too."

★ ★ ★ ★ ★

1. Like Janelle, many young people feel the desire to move away from their hometowns and never come back. Why do you think this is such a common feeling?

2. Janelle decides to live with her grandmother for many reasons, not all of them noble. Did it make a difference as to how you felt about her character that she's a little selfish in her desire to come back "home" after so long?

3. As kids, Janelle and Gabe made sure to keep their relationship, especially the romantic aspect of it, a secret. How would things have been different if they'd "come out" as a couple, both in the past and present?

4. Gabe's relationship with his dad is complicated. Should Gabe have left home the way he wanted to,

the way his brother Mike did? Did he make the right choice in staying to take care of Andy?

5. Andy and Mike have a closer relationship than Gabe does with either of them, but it's Gabe who ends up taking care of things at home while Mike goes away. Should Mike have stayed closer? Should he have made more of an effort to return? Why didn't he?

6. Gabe's mother allows the deception about her existence to continue, with no solid explanation about why (other than perhaps her own selfishness). Was any part of her rationale reasonable? Why or why not?

7. *The Favor* presents an underlying theme of selfishness versus selflessness. Which characters do you think best exemplify those traits, and why?

8. Janelle is so determined to avoid making the same mistakes her dad did that she goes a little overboard with her son. Was she wrong in trying to make sure history didn't repeat itself?

9. Janelle's dad doesn't seem to grow much throughout the story. Did her decision at the end come as a surprise, or was her choice not to allow him to be part of her life justified? Is forgiveness always the right choice?

10. Compare Janelle's decision about her relationship with her father to the one Gabe has with his dad at the end of the book.